THE
ALCHEMISTS

BY CRAIG DILOUIE

Cover design by Eloise Knapp Design.

Published by ZING Communications, Inc.

www.CraigDiLouie.com

For Chris Marrs, who fills my world with adventure,
and my children, who infuse it with magic.

Notes

Taddeo's chess games depict those played by Gilles Andruet and Boris Spassky in 1988 and Pierre Charles Fournier de Saint Amant and W. Fraser in 1836.

All foreign language translations are courtesy of various online translation tools such as Google Translate and Translate. com. They were vetted to the best of the author's ability.

Great care was taken to reconstruct daily life during the Renaissance and the major events of 1529; however, dramatic license was claimed to produce an exciting and cohesive story. Any historical errors are solely the author's and are likely intentional.

1529

Spain

~ Chapter I ~
The Magus

The lancers advanced at the gallop, commanding Myrddin Wyllt to stop in the name of the Emperor. The Magus kept walking, his tread shortcutting time and space. With each step, the steel-clad riders fell further behind in a cloud of dust and curses and shrieking horses. After an hour, they had become mere dots on the horizon. By nightfall, they would be leagues behind.

The Magus had lived hundreds of years, or so he said. Even he wasn't sure. As with all things with the wizard, one couldn't easily separate truth and illusion. Standing over six feet, he towered above the men of his time. In all seasons, as befitting what people expected of a wizard, he wore a long dark wool cloak embroidered with faded patches of stars and moons and astrological signs. A tall conical hat perched on his head over a leather skullcap. His nose was long and pointed, his eyebrows arched, his black eyes sharp. His long gray beard spilled down his chest; he was an old man in a harsh world where few lived to grow old. The overall look lent him a natural grandeur, that thing the Italians called *terribilità*.

A few paces behind, Marie Dubois pulled the two-wheeled cart in which they stored their provisions, her mangy greyhound panting at her heels. Knee-length breeches and hose and a black doublet with brass buttons covered her slim, athletic body; on her head, she wore a wide-brimmed hat adorned with a single ostrich plume. Marie dressed this way for comfort, not disguise. She was rarely mistaken for a man even so attired. Her prominent cheekbones, fair skin, and red hair, kept pulled back in a tight ponytail, marked her as a beautiful young woman.

Marie forgot about their pursuers and focused on the road that snaked across the rugged foothills and into the mountains. It was a good old road, a Roman road. Her piercing gray eyes swept the rocky landscape ahead for outlaws. There wasn't much to see here. Workers toiled in a vineyard in the north; a flock of sheep grazed in the south. A few buzzards circled the sky. Myrddin believed the world was deeply alive, and everything in it—trees and rocks and water and even thunder—had a soul. Marie saw the world as vast, harsh, and empty. Life was hard. The strong ruled the weak. The weak died like flies.

Famine swept Normandy when she was nine years old. The endless starvation broke body and spirit. The peasants stripped the woods of game. Cats and dogs and even rats disappeared. People boiled tea from weeds and roots and tree bark. They ate the leather from their shoes. As winter wore on, things got even worse. Thieves arrested for stealing food died twitching in the gallows and then were torn down and devoured raw by ravenous crowds.

Marie's father and brothers went out one morning and never returned. Her mother told her to go to the convent near Alençon— six leagues through dense frozen forest—and throw herself at the mercy of the nuns. The journey was a virtual death sentence, but it was her only hope. On her way out of the village, she saw a crowd gather around an old giant and his two-wheeled cart.

The stranger raised a deck of cards splayed like a fan. One by one, the villagers stepped forward to take a card and have their fortune read. Marguerite, he declared in a strident voice, would have three more sons. Etienne would find a purse filled with gold buried under a tree on his farm. Mellin's wife would come home. They liked what they heard; some smiled for the first time in months. The old man put the cards away and opened a box filled with tiny bottles. He cured Jennine's itching rashes with a smelly ointment, Philippe's pox with a bitter elixir. The villagers pooled what was left of their money and bought him a scrawny chicken as payment, and then he was on his way, a stooped vagrant leading his rattling cart back into the forest.

The old man awoke the next morning to the sound of a child singing and the smell of wood smoke. Opening one eye, he saw a small girl boiling his chicken in a pot, mixing in a little handful of wild onions and mushrooms she'd scrounged from the forest floor. The savory smell pleased him; he had the appetite of a bishop but had always been a terrible cook. Marie watched him, sniffling and hugging her dolly. The Magus invited her to join him for the meal; she devoured her bowl and emitted a tiny belch, smacking her lips.

The man eyed her. "I was hoping for a strapping young lad for the job, but you'll do."

Marie wiped her nose. "What job is that, Mister?"

"I need a bodyguard."

"Go to!" she chided. "I'm too little to be a bodyguard."

"You won't always be so little." He tapped his wrinkled forehead. "I know these things."

"Can you really divine the future?"

"Would you like me to tell you your fortune?"

"Aye, please!"

He squinted at her. "You will be a great warrior."

"That's impossible."

"It's going to happen."

"But how do you know this?"

"Because I'm going to make you a great warrior. The greatest fighter of the age, in fact."

Marie remembered the first years traveling with Myrddin Wyllt as truly magical. Service to the Magus proved hard work, but her days had always been filled with labor, and now she did it for a cause that transcended mundane survival. The wizard brought light into people's dark lives. He called himself a servant of light. He derived his powers from the evocation of angels, which made her feel closer to God. Over time, she came to love him as a father, though she doubted he loved her back. The hunger born during the famine—a fierce desire to feel loved, safe, full, parented—was never satisfied. She speculated he simply wasn't capable of love. At times, watching him snore or blow his nose or scratch his arse, he seemed so ordinary, yet Marie wondered if this were just another illusion. Part of the show. She doubted he was human at all.

Myrddin had loved once, or so he said. The staff he carried provided a constant reminder of such folly. He'd whittled it from the tree where he'd been imprisoned by the witch with whom he'd fallen in love. He'd slumbered in its warm trunk for centuries among beetles and worms and fungus, dreaming his melancholy dreams. Four gnomish faces, smiling in sleep, adorned the staff, fellow prisoners of the tree. He carried them with him in the hopes he would remember who they were and how to release them. He sensed they were fellow suitors like himself, damned to eternal sleep in the oak. And if he could wake them, perhaps they could tell him why he'd been reborn into the world of men.

All this she learned from knowing him a short while. It took her a little longer to discover that the man she idolized was a fraud. The Magus wrought genuine miracles—of that there was no doubt—but most of the time they lacked substance, being mere illusion. He showed people what they wanted to see, and it became real in their heads. Sometimes, it became truly real, as in the case of his cures, which sometimes had a lasting effect. Myrddin liked to say reality and illusion often blended in the mind. Wasn't that what human love was about? Seeing what you wanted to see, something no one else could, and making it real? It was as Jesus taught, the Magus said. Belief is everything. Belief can move mountains. But as belief made it real, Marie knew, so did doubt reveal it as illusion. A single doubt, and it all came undone.

Instead of using his powers to change the world for the better, Myrddin sold men's hopes and desires back to them for money. In Athens, he posed as an alchemist and converted a chest of lead-rich ore into gold at the request of the local merchant guild. When he opened the chest, the merchants saw what they wanted to see:

gleaming gold nuggets. That time, Marie believed they deserved what they got. Why would an alchemist accept a little gold as pay to turn lead into a lot of gold? Why wouldn't he simply buy the lead himself and turn it into a fortune? Only fools would believe such a ruse. Fools and extremely greedy men.

In Poland, Marie killed sheep grazing outside a village, took the best cuts, and left a mess for the villagers to find. When they did, an ogre roared in the woods, putting them to flight. Myrddin entered the village and conjured a dragon that ate the ogre that had eaten the sheep. Except the dragon wasn't real, the ogre wasn't real, and the sheep had been eaten by the wizard and his servant, who now expected to be paid for their effort.

"We are here to do good," Marie reminded him when all things were done.

"As you wish," Myrddin answered.

"Terrifying people with ogres isn't good."

"We need to eat."

Marie said nothing for a moment. That was another thing. The villagers had stiffed them on payment. In the end, the ruse had been for nothing. Her stomach growled.

"Fie on them, they saw you conjure a dragon," she said. "They should fear you. Why didn't they pay up? It's like they knew it was all fake."

The Magus nodded. "It's time for you to begin your training."

"What kind of training?"

He didn't answer.

That night, before falling asleep, she realized she'd served the wizard for five years. She wondered why she stayed with him, day after day struggling to make a living. They'd gone everywhere but always ended up nowhere, which was precisely where they started. She wanted something more but owed him her life, at least the life she led. She hoped he would use his power to make the world a better place. While she waited for this to happen, she prayed she would learn her own true purpose, just as Myrddin roamed the earth trying to remember his.

If she left him, she had to have somewhere to go. She'd traveled the whole of the continent, but everywhere it was the same. She had few choices and most of the good ones involved marrying the right man, which likely would never happen. Most of the men she met were ignorant, greedy, and violent. Myrddin avoided the masters who ruled the lands, so her chances of meeting a handsome lord were slim, and besides, she was of lowly birth.

No, she couldn't leave him. Right now, Myrddin Wyllt was all she had. Remaining in his service was the closest thing she had to real freedom. It was better to stay hungry than fill up on weeds. He was the closest thing she had to family.

Marie woke in an open air courtyard over which an exotic castle loomed in the mist. This place is a *dojo*, she understood. Specifically, the *renshujo*, or training area. Weapons adorned the walls.

The great gates groaned open, and a stocky man strutted into the place, holding a sword in each hand. He gave her a quick once-over and frowned at what he saw.

"My name is Hiroshi Shibata, your *sensei*," the man said in his strange language, which she somehow understood. "Here, I will teach you *kenjutsu*. You are going to learn to fight."

"I'm a woman, *sensei*."

He eyed her heels to head again. His frown deepened. "Yes."

"I'm not strong enough to fight men."

"The art of the sword does not require you to be strong. It requires you to be precise."

"But I don't know anything about fighting."

"The longest trip is started by putting one foot in front of the other. Enough talk!"

He tossed her one of the swords. It clattered to the ground at her feet, which provoked a gasp from the *sensei*.

"How long will it take to learn?" she said. "By the morning, I have to wake up from this dream."

Hiroshi Shibata shrugged. "A few moments to learn. A lifetime to master. Pick up your sword. Good. At least you can do that. Treat it with the utmost respect. Now observe." He raised his weapon. "*Chudan-no-kamae!*"

All night, the blades flashed. She woke up singing.

"Why are you teaching me to fight?" she asked Myrddin over their meager breakfast.

"I swore an oath renouncing violence," the Magus replied. "I cannot directly hurt a man."

"But I can."

"The next time someone doesn't pay our bill, you are free to hurt them until they do."

"What if I don't want to hurt them?"

"I trust your discretion."

"It just doesn't seem like something a servant of light would do."

He shrugged. "We need to eat."

It was a line of logic she could never refuse. Survival trumped everything.

Each night after that, for the next three years, she attended the schools of war in her dreams. Different techniques, different masters, different nations. *Kampfringen, bataireacht, krabi krabong,* she studied it all. She learned knife fighting from an Iroquois war chief in an ancient grove, *wushu* from a Shaolin warrior-monk in a temple carved from a mountaintop, assegai fighting from a Zulu general in a dust-filled kraal. At seventeen, she'd mastered the art of every weapon.

And with her learning, the fierce hunger that ruled her life began to fade. She still had no purpose but enjoyed her growing powers, which she hoped would give her choices. Marie started to develop chivalrous ideas. She often pictured herself using her skills to protect the weak. She wanted to meet a great lord and pledge her sword to his service. Aye, she was a woman, but some women became knights. It was not unheard of.

The air grew colder as they entered the small, tree-covered mountains of the Sierra de la Demanda range, which unfolded

11

before them like a giant's wrinkled blanket. The sun moved across the sky as they came out the other side, trudging through a light snowfall. The Spanish cavaliers had fallen far behind. At Marie's feet, Leo whined, constantly hungry, though he never ate. The road led to a hilltop village built high above the range of mosquitoes.

"We'll stop here for the night," the Magus said.

Marie squinted at the sky. "Plenty of light left. We could make Valladolid by nightfall."

"We have to give the men chasing us a chance to catch up."

"Why would we do that?"

"I thought you wanted to meet the Holy Roman Emperor."

"I'd like that very much."

"Then we need them to introduce us."

They got ready. One couldn't show up at someone's door covered in dust like a beggar. If one presented himself as a person of means, one was more likely to get supper fed to him. Erect stance, healthy complexion, smooth hands, and polite speech distinguished the high born from the riffraff. Myrddin raised his cloak, exposing his hairy calves, and dropped it. The dust exploded outward in a cloud, leaving him clean. Marie did not have the benefit of magic. She slapped her hat, brushed her jacket, and washed her face from the water barrel mounted on the cart's sideboard. Then she buckled her sword Artemis, forged of good Toledo steel and her most prized possession, onto her hip.

A red-faced, balding peasant burst from the door as they approached. He gripped a flagon of beer in one hand and slapped his howling wife with the other while their five daughters marched single file into the house carrying firewood. All of them stopped and gaped at the two strangers.

The wife sized up Myrddin. "Oh my," she shrilled. "This one's a bloody giant."

The lout leered at Marie. "Oh my, indeed."

Leo growled and pawed the dirt.

"Pardon our intrusion, dear sir," Marie said, trying to sound rich. "My master and me are bound for court at Valladolid on the morrow and seek safe lodgings with ye."

"Aye, we'd be happy to lodge you, if you've got coin," grinned the peasant. He took a final swallow of his beer and flung the dregs onto the family dung heap.

"If the price be fair, we shall stay with ye," Marie said.

"How much are you offering?"

"How much are you charging?"

"Next year, this woman shall give birth to a son," Myrddin's voice boomed.

The peasants gathered around, waiting for more. The Magus stood as if in a trance. Slowly, he raised his arm and pointed at the woman, who sighed and leaned against her husband.

"And his name shall be Jerónimo," he intoned.

The ruse, simple as it was, worked; it often did for a meal and a roof over their heads for the night. What peasant with five daughters didn't want to hear he'd soon have a son? The man practically demanded they stay the night in his house. It was a typical peasant hut. Built of wood, thatch, mud, and wattle, it held living quarters, cattle shed, pigpen, hen house, corncrib, and space filled with straw and hay. The Magus had to stoop and was thankful when invited to sit at the table. He surveyed the room and sighed with contentment. A fire in the hearth warmed the living room and kept iron pots of soup and stew boiling. A bed of piled straw pallets, large enough for the whole family and teeming with vermin, dominated the space.

The man was Antonio, his wife Damita. While Myrddin plied his trade—describing their fictitious future son, telling their glowing fortunes, casting their flattering horoscopes, and performing minor magic tricks to confirm his bona fides—Damita stacked the table with food. Pork sausages, rolls of black bread, cheese soup, local wine, and a trencher consisting of a loaf of bread with the top cut off, filled with rich stew. The peasants asked him about their son. What would he look like? Would he be strong and healthy? Would he have his own sons and carry on the family name? Myrddin told them what they wanted to hear. They knew he was half fraud but didn't care. They had little entertainment in their lives. To sweeten the pot, Marie sang bittersweet French songs, songs about being away from home, her voice melodic and haunting.

The wine, warmth, and long day's march had tired her. As was custom, Antonio invited his guests to sleep in the family bed, leering again at Marie. Myrddin climbed in, his stockinged feet sticking out from under the blankets, and promptly began snoring. Marie decided to sleep with Leo in the small space packed with straw.

Lying on her back staring at the dark ceiling, she thought about her mother and wondered whether she survived the famine so many years ago. Was Mama lying in bed in their home right now, thinking about her? Marie rolled onto her side, her chest aching with the old hunger. Leo whined in his sleep. She switched her thoughts from her past to the life she lived now. Her mind swirled with magic, memories of their arrest by the Spanish lancers, and excitement at the prospect of entering Valladolid to meet Charles V, the man who ruled one-third of Europe.

She awoke in a *dojang*, where a shaman taught her *hapkido*.

❧ Chapter II ❧
The Scientist

Prospero di Lodovico Buonarroti Simoni did not enjoy being robbed, particularly by powerful lords like Don Pedro. He was Italian, a Florentine to be precise, the brother of the great Michelangelo, though he enjoyed none of his elder sibling's awe-inspiring reputation. At nearly fifty years of age, he had a stocky build, beard trimmed to a meticulous goatee to slim his round face, black eyes glittering with superior intellect under bushy eyebrows, and a mass of curls on his head dyed a youthful black with a boiled mixture of quicklime, lead oxide, and silver. Michelangelo's Isaiah in his grand painting of the Sistine Chapel reveals the spitting image of Prospero as a young man before his disgrace and exile. He wore a red jacket with bulging sleeves, tight-fitting trousers, and a codpiece one might have considered a tad ambitious for a man his size. He modeled himself on Castiglione's book, *Cortegiano*, or *The Book of the Courtier*, which had been published the year before in Venice. The ideal courtier served his lord with modest grace as a sage adviser and diplomat. The most important quality a courtier could possess was *sprezzatura*, or the ability to be awesome without appearing to work at it. Prospero played the courtier as well as he could until his natural personality as a brilliant overgrown child asserted itself and grated on everyone's nerves.

Taddeo, son of the great merchant Gregorio di Cellini of Venice and heir to the family's Mediterranean trading empire, watched his mentor strut like a peacock in front of the Spanish lord and blushed furiously at the attention of Don Pedro's wife, Doña Fermina, who made eyes at him. Seventeen years old and already an accomplished engineer, he'd served the scientist faithfully for three years. When he was a boy, his father had presented him with his reflection in a clear glass mirror as encouragement to pay more attention to his disheveled appearance, but Taddeo only wanted to know who had invented such a wonderful thing. Prospero had, some years earlier— to better see his own disgrace and wallow in the misery of exile from his beloved Florence.

Impressed with the doctor's inventions, Taddeo had asked his father if he could study under him but had been given a flat no. The problem wasn't lack of recognition of Prospero as one of the greatest minds of the age. The problem was the eccentric man's toxic effect on reputations, as trouble seemed to follow him everywhere. Gregorio relented after Taddeo made the persuasive argument that Prospero's friendship might lead to an introduction and opportunity to work with Michelangelo, the great artist, architect, poet, and engineer.

Such an opportunity never materialized, and the relationship proved less than the earthshaking brainstorm he'd fantasized. Prospero often invented things that either could not be built, cost a fortune to build, or lacked skilled labor to maintain them. A steam-powered mechanical calculator. An automatic flour mill. A threshing machine. Refrigeration, for God's sake. Taddeo tried to steer his mentor toward more practical inventions, but once Prospero had an idea, he poured everything he had into it, months of labor and all their earnings, until he either succeeded or got bored and abandoned it half finished. Now they were back on the road to raise capital. They'd dodged warring armies in Lombardy and reached Spain, where Prospero foretold they would be showered in contracts.

It was a good idea; the Spanish, after all, had more silver than sense. After they conquered Grenada and completed *La Reconquista*, they grew paranoid and kicked the Muslims and Jews who refused to convert out of the country, losing many of their best artisans. But instead of finding this honest work that Taddeo knew how to do and could do well, Prospero spent most of their time peddling pornographic books to aristocrats. Powerful men like Don Pedro had daughters and wed them to other powerful men in the hopes of expanded influence and commerce, and their girls were expected to please their husbands and hence produce robust heirs. Prospero had plagiarized choice bits from the *Karma Sutra*—which he'd obtained from an Egyptian in Venice—and translated it into multiple languages, adding his own corrections and improvements based on his modest belief that Italian men were the world's greatest lovers.

Now Don Pedro didn't want to pay for Prospero's love manual.

"Prospero told me you wrote the book," Don Pedro's wife whispered near Taddeo's ear. "Is that true?"

The boy turned bright scarlet and emitted a choking sound.

"But we are friends," Prospero cried as the deal went sour. What could he do? He stood on the top floor of the tallest tower in Don Pedro's castle, surrounded by homicidal knights ready to hack irritating people like him to pieces at their lord's command. Not that Don Pedro needed these things to be intimidating, being large as a bear. With his fur cloak, he even looked like one. No, if the Don wanted to rip him off, Prospero would have to live with it. But not without a fight. No, first, he would put up a fight.

Unfortunately, pouting was his only weapon.

"We entered our bargain in good faith. You would leave me destitute."

"I could pay you, doctor," boomed Don Pedro. He enveloped Prospero's shoulder with his massive paw to stop him from pacing. "Do not worry yourself! But I was hoping you could help me with something. It would double your money."

"I am your servant, Don Pedro," Prospero said gravely, playing the courtier again with visible effort. "And how may I be of service to you?"

The Don stroked his massive beard, his thick fingers twinkling with rings. "I brought you here because this is a very special part of my keep. You are privileged to be here, understand? I keep all my special things in this tower."

Prospero looked around the cold bare room with its stone walls and weak sunlight entering through a single pane of cloudy glass. "I assure you, it is lovely."

"I will tell you plain: I have come into a great deal of raw silk. Here is the tale. A long time ago, the Count of Oliveto seized Tripoli for Spain, which we gave to the Knights of St. John after the Turks kicked them out of Rhodes. They have done wonders helping to keep the Barbary pirates out of the Mediterranean, but it is expensive work. I made them a sizable loan, but they could not afford the interest, so they sent me this shipment of silk to clear their debt. Good, huh? I tell you: It is the last time I will ever play the banker like some Medici. What am I going to do with a bunch of silk? Am I a trader? If the Knights could not turn it into cash, how am I supposed to do it? But you—you are from Venice! You know traders. Your city has the greatest shipyards in the world! Your merchants trade as far north as London! Broker a deal for me with one of these merchants, and I will double your fee as a commission."

Prospero wiggled a pinky in his ear. Don Pedro could be deafening when he got excited. "What you are saying is feasible. But it entails significant time and effort."

"It is a harmless little introduction. No trouble for you at all, a man of your stature."

"For them to buy trust in you, I would have to sell their trust in me, which I hold dear."

"Then speak your terms plainly," Don Pedro said. "You are the genius, and I am a simple man."

Prospero inspected his nails. "I believe a straight percentage would be worthwhile should I be able to make this happen for you. Shall we agree on three percent? And of course, you'll pay us for the book now at triple the initial price, which will cover our expenses for the project."

Taddeo suppressed a sigh. It was all a bluff. By agreeing to the Don's scheme, Prospero would get paid handsomely for the book, walk out of here safe and sound, and then forget all about their deal.

The low commission was the bait as well as the giveaway. Don Pedro, being greedy, fell for it.

"Bring us wine!" roared the Spaniard, clapping Prospero on the back. The servants scattered like mice. "The good wine! Doctor, I accept. Now come see my stuff. I want you to be able to give your friends a full accounting of its quality."

"*Così sia*," Prospero said. *So be it.* He winked at Taddeo. "My young protégé, you stay here and entertain our gracious hostess."

"Your man appears to be choking," Don Pedro observed. "A cup of wine will brace him."

"My protégé does not drink alcohol," Prospero told him.

"He does not drink?" The Don glared at Taddeo as if he'd been tricked into letting a Muslim into his castle. "What is this fresh nonsense?"

"It dulls the senses, my lord," Taddeo explained.

"*Sì!* Good! So?"

"I'm always working on my projects, my lord."

Don Pedro shook his massive head. "Doctor, you must teach this young man to play."

Prospero shrugged. "What can I do? I try, but he is a very serious young man."

"He reminds me of my son. Always at the books and dreaming about God." The Spaniard snorted. "He wants to be a monk."

The Don unlocked a door with an iron key and ushered Prospero inside. Taddeo could see rolls of silk carefully bound and tied in bundles. Then the door groaned shut.

"Alone at last," said Doña Fermina. "Now we can talk."

Taddeo gulped and stared out the window. The green plain glowed green in the light of spring. The smoke of cooking fires rose above the distant village. A large crowd of filthy peasants marched toward the castle along one of the muddy, potholed tracks the Spanish called roads. He pretended they were interesting.

Doña Fermina was a beautiful woman. She reminded Taddeo of Tiziano Vecelli's painting of a Junoesque Venus—big, bouncy, and full of raw sex appeal. A scarlet velvet bodice and long skirt, trimmed with mink fur, covered her ample figure. Her slim waist and the remarkable elevation of the massive breasts bulging out of the bodice suggested she used a wore a well-designed corset, which she'd tightened to near asphyxiation with a key to accentuate her hourglass figure. A heavy gold necklace hung from her neck, its pendant lost in flaunted cleavage.

Everything in Taddeo's world had a scientific explanation that could be discerned through empirical study, but his chronic shyness around beautiful women remained a perpetual mystery to him. The moment he felt attracted to the opposite sex, he flushed, stumbled, and stammered. He'd tried everything, but nothing dulled the terror. If it weren't for his father's expectations that he carry on the family name and business, he might have gone for the priesthood.

"Taddeo, I read your book, and I find some of it rather confusing," she said. "For example, this wheelbarrow business."

He blinked. "Wheelbarrow, my lady?"

"Indeed. If I am to help my daughter learn your techniques so she will please her Portuguese husband, I must understand them myself and appear properly experienced in her eyes. Otherwise, I should lose respect, and we would not receive the full value of your wisdom."

"You mean sexual techniques," he stammered and gaped out the window. The peasants waved rakes and scythes. He could hear them shouting.

"Of course, young man. So this wheelbarrow is like the game children play, yes? But with fervent copulation?"

Taddeo emitted a strangled cry. "Yes, my lady."

"I just don't see how it would be very pleasant."

"The techniques are not for all tastes. That is why a palette is offered."

"Nonsense. I am here to learn. Where does the man actually hold the woman?"

"The ankles, ma'am. The woman's legs are bent for this purpose.

Alternately, the thighs."

"Is the woman expected to hold herself up by her hands then?"

Her tone signaled a purely academic interest. Maybe he'd read things all wrong. Maybe she did just want to learn. He began to breathe easier. "The lady may rest on her forearms if she tires. The man just need bend his knees a little to compensate."

"Perhaps you'd better show me."

He felt his legs weaken. "My lady?"

"Taddeo, I am your patroness, am I not?"

"You are, my lady."

"So you must obey my commands until I am completely satisfied. Is that not true?"

"It is," he croaked.

"Then chop, chop."

Doña Fermina stood in front of him, her back turned, and got down on all fours with her generous rump in the air. "Now pick up my legs."

Taddeo gripped her thighs. He heaved.

"Oh my," she said. "The blood has rushed to my head."

"I believe you've mastered it, my lady."

"Don't be shy with me, young man. Let me have it."

She pushed her rump against him. His brain swam with pleasure and horror. He stared out the window and tried to think of something, anything, as she wiggled her hips. Ptolemy's model of the universe as a system of nested spheres, with Earth at its center. His own refutation of the geocentric model in favor of a heliocentric model. The theories flew out of his head as soon as he thought them. Not even picturing the internal workings of Gutenberg's wondrous machine that printed with movable type, which usually calmed him, worked. He needed to focus on something tangible. The peasants. Yes, the peasants had entered the gate and were down in the courtyard.

"Oh, young Taddeo! Is that your codpiece, or have you risen to the occasion?"

The peasants murdered the guards, who fell in fountains of blood.

"We're under attack!" he howled.

"WHAT?"

The door burst open and Don Pedro stormed into the room. Taddeo dropped Doña Fermina and then toppled onto her in a pile of flailing limbs. The Spaniard gaped at them, his face turning six shades of purple. Prospero stood behind him wearing an impressed smile. No one said anything for several moments.

"CHRIST ON A CROSS! WHAT IS GOING ON IN HERE?"

Taddeo leaped to his feet. "I was demonstrating one of the techniques from the book, my lord."

"I can see that, you coxcomb!"

"It wasn't him, you beast!" she howled from the floor. "It was me. I seduced him. I seduced him because I love him!"

"My Lord—"

Don Pedro's eyes grew bright with rage. "You," he hissed at Taddeo. "It is not enough for you to conquer her vagina. You must conquer her heart as well!"

"Nothing happened!" Taddeo cried.

"*Nothing?*" said Doña Fermina. "Don Pedro, are you going to let him speak to me like that?"

"Silence, you flap-mouthed tart! I will settle with you later!"

"You will settle nothing! My father will have your head on a spike!"

A stout man-at-arms entered the room in dented blood-splattered armor. "My lord, the peasants are revolting."

"*Si?* They are peasants!"

"I mean to say they are attacking the castle."

Don Pedro stomped to the window and looked down at his men being chopped to bits. "God's Wounds, it is the *Comuneros* all over again!" *Comuneros*, peasants who'd staged a bloody nationwide revolt demanding social justice and reform before being slaughtered.

The man pointed at Prospero. "It's our guests, Don Pedro. They're after him."

"What do they want him for?"

"They said he gave them smallpox. Half the village has it."

"I was inoculating them against the disease," Prospero explained. "To give them immunity."

Don Pedro wheeled sputtering. "Are you mad? You mean you gave my workers smallpox to keep them from getting smallpox?"

Prospero stroked his goatee. "I had it in principle."

Don Pedro held out his large hand. "Tomás, give me your sword."

"As you command, Don Pedro." The man-at-arms handed over his weapon.

"Now go rouse the men and squash those rebellious pignuts outside. I have business to settle here first."

"I—I—at once," said Tomás, staring longingly at his sword.

As he left, a smiling servant entered with a tray of cups. "Your wine, my lord!"

"Get out!" Don Pedro roared at him, sending the tray crashing to the floor and the servant fleeing with an anguished cry. He flung the sword to clatter at Taddeo's feet. "Taddeo, the great lover. I will not reclaim my honor by slaughtering an unarmed man. I will slaughter you while you are holding a weapon. Pick it up."

"Oh my, you don't have to fight over me," said Doña Fermina, her bosom heaving.

Don Pedro snarled at Prospero. "And when I am done with him, I will hand you to the serfs."

"I assure you, I am as sad as you are," Prospero said in defense of his dignity. "But that is science. The greater the progress, the greater the risk. Surely, a great man like you knows—"

"Silence!" Don Pedro unsheathed his heavy blade. "The man does not drink. Now let us see if he can fight."

Taddeo picked up the sword and felt its unfamiliar weight in his hand. He'd always considered it ridiculous that people made such things so they could hit each other with them. He knew something about swordplay; his father had forced him to learn the martial arts as befitting a gentleman of Venice. People fought in the street all the time over things like the weather. If you bit your thumb, some psychopath was apt to challenge you to a duel. The problem was that he wasn't any good at it. Now he wished he'd paid more attention to his lessons.

"Prepare to die, little man."

Taddeo raised the sword as he'd been taught by his fencing teachers, wondering why he bothered. He couldn't beat a born fighter like Don Pedro. He thought about the Spaniard's statement: *Prepare to die*. What an intriguing instruction. How did one prepare to die? By evacuating one's bowels in shrieking terror?

He needed a last thought, something to comfort him into oblivion. *My dad will be really disappointed*, was all that came to mind.

"Doctor," he said, putting on a brave front, "you must tell my father I—"

Prospero cried, "*Basta!*" (*Enough!*) and kicked Don Pedro in the testicles from behind with a resounding crunch. The Spaniard flinched and went pale. He gurgled. His great body shook. Then he dropped his sword and fell to his knees with a groan, cupping his gonads.

"Come, Taddeo! There is no time to waste!"

Taddeo raced past Don Pedro, sparing a last longing glance at the heaving bosom of Doña Fermina, who sat on the floor quaking with laughter. Prospero led him into the room where the silk was stored. The scientist barred the door with a thick wood slab.

"There is no way he is getting through that door. We are safe here, my amorous friend."

Taddeo looked around. "There's no other exit, Doctor."

Prospero winced and slapped his forehead. "Ah! I will think of something." He put on a pair of glasses made of layers of glass discs laid on top of each other. After a few adjustments to provide binocular magnification, he peered out the window. "Yes, it is a long way down."

They were trapped.

The door shook on its hinges. Don Pedro was hacking at it with his sword. "You kicked me in the balls, you half-faced varlot!"

"Think, think, *think*," Prospero muttered as he put the glasses away.

The door thudded again. "I am going to chop you into little pieces!"

Taddeo sagged. "We could always jump to a mercifully swift death—"

Prospero snapped his fingers. "Eureka!"

He took the sword from his apprentice's trembling hand and cut the nearest parcels open. Piles of silk spilled onto the floor. "Some of my colleagues call the age *La Rinascita*, the Rebirth of Europe, *renaissance* in French. They want to go back in time and rediscover the intellectual glories of Greece and Rome. *Idioti!* We must look forward, not back! But sometimes one can learn from the past. Yes, that is where progress begins." He paused. "I am mentoring you, Taddeo. You may want to write this down."

Taddeo gaped at the splintering door. "What are you talking about?"

"Hundreds of years ago, in Cordoba, an Arab jumped from a tower wearing a billowing cape to break his fall. We shall use this silk to similar effect."

"Did it work? The Arab's experiment?

"Not so much, but he had it in principle. Air offers resistance to falling things. If you drop a stone, it falls faster than a feather, *capisce*? The stone pushes the air aside, the feather not as well. We shall be a stone under a feather. You are my engineer. Will it work?"

"How the hell should I know?"

"Then what good are you—"

"Yes!" Taddeo said to make his mentor stop talking. "It will work! Do something!"

"*Buono!* Because we really have no choice!"

"What can I do to help?"

"Keep Don Pedro out of the room," Prospero muttered, hacking at the silk.

Taddeo looked at the door and yelped in terror. The point of the Don's sword emerged and withdrew. An eye, burning with rage, appeared in the hole.

"I see you, you little maggot-pie!"

"We're going to burn your silk," Taddeo shouted back. "If you keep trying to get in, we'll burn it all up."

"You would not dare!"

He heard Don Pedro arguing with his wife. Apparently, the silk, once converted to cash, would serve as their daughter's dowry for her wedding.

Prospero tossed him a spool of string that had been used to tie the parcels. "Unwind it and feed it to me, Taddeo."

"I don't have time for this," Don Pedro shouted. "I have to slaughter my peasants!"

"Now tie this off," Prospered ordered. "And there, see? Thread it through and knot it."

"I will make you a deal! You spare the silk, and I will let you go. *Por favor*?"

Prospero and Taddeo paused in their work and exchanged a glance.

"Bluffing," they said together.

Prospero stuffed as much silk as he could fit inside his jacket and pants.

"What are you doing now, Doctor?"

"Do you know how much this stuff is worth? Plus the padding will help break my fall in case we have it in principle but not quite in reality."

Taddeo frantically stuffed silk into his own clothing until he bloated.

"I see you there!" Don Pedro said. "What are you doing to my silk?"

The scientists hoisted the parachute and stretched it out. Taddeo tied loops of string around each of the scientist's shoulders and knotted them tight.

Prospero climbed onto the windowsill and kicked out the window. "You will ride on my back." The window blew at their faces. "We will jump on three!"

"This isn't going to work," Taddeo moaned as he imagined his body smashing against the hard ground far below the tower. Elementary physics. "We're going to die. Maybe we could—"

Prospero laughed. "One, two—"

Don Pedro tore a chunk out of the door. His large bearded face appeared in the hole. "Ah, ha! I am going to—"

"Three!"

Taddeo hugged his mentor for dear life as they stepped off the ledge.

And plummeted screaming to the earth.

Taddeo's stomach lunged into his throat and cut off his scream. Then a strong wind from the west struck their billowing sail and gave them buoyancy with a jerk. They sailed over the courtyard, where Don Pedro's men-at-arms busily cut down the fleeing peasants. They all stopped and stared at the bizarre sight of the flying men.

"Wonderful!" Prospero cried.

The wind carried them over the wall and into a distant field of wildflowers, where they came down hard in a tangle of limbs.

Darkness. Then light.

Taddeo moaned. A sheet covered his face. A funeral shroud?

He pawed at it. "Don't bury me! I'm not dead!"

Prospero pulled back the silk sheet and helped the boy to his feet. He began to roll up the material. "My young friend, you are an Italian man, so I do not blame you. You are my disciple, after all, and I am a disciple of Epicurus. While we survived our fall, it is not enough to live; one must enjoy life. But next time you want to teach a lady the wheelbarrow, you must employ greater discretion. *Bene?*"

Taddeo sighed. "Yes, Doctor."

"You may want to write that down. Now let our flight be swift. We have a decent head start on those *bastardi*. The steam wagon is in yonder trees. We will load the cannon just in case. If the Don gives chase, we shall pepper him with grapeshot!"

They limped toward the forest, where they'd hidden the steam wagon under canvas. Prospero had an Italian sensibility about wealth—that it was the source of virtue (which was why, he said, he himself was amoral, being penniless most of the time)—but trusted no one with his favorite toys.

Lord, please let me out of this, and I'll go home and do everything my father says, Taddeo prayed to his Deist God he knew would ignore him. *I'll marry a nice girl, be ruthless in pursuit of gold and power, make a reputation fighting duels, serve in city government, and expand the family trading empire as far as Russia.*

"Did you see how purple the Don's face was?" asked Prospero as he huffed through the grass. "If only I could recreate that color on canvas. It was like a sunrise yet better than a sunrise, was it not?"

A line of armored horsemen emerged from the trees.

"Halt, in the name of His Majesty, Charles V!"

"*Merda,*" Prospero said. *Crap.* "We surrender." Next to him, Taddeo put his hands in the air.

The riders approached, led by a knight wearing a helmet topped by a mass of red plumes.

"*Saludos*, gentlemen. I am Don Rodrigo of His Majesty's Royal Guard. Would you be Prospero Buonarroti, the renowned scholar and alchemist?"

Prospero puffed out his chest. "I am indeed." He added with a flourish, "At your service!"

"I have been ordered to deliver you to Valladolid to stand before the Emperor."

"And what are the charges?" Prospero demanded.

Don Rodrigo shook his head. "There are no charges."

"Then I place myself and my protégé under your protection, noble sir!"

They led the horsemen into the woods to retrieve the steam wagon.

"We're going to meet the Holy Roman Emperor," Taddeo said in wonder. "I can't believe it."

The Holy Roman Empire, founded by Charlemagne the Great seven hundred years ago, was a disunited mass of fiercely independent principalities, duchies, and other states sprawling across central Europe. It was an idea more than a country, with strong princes, a weak central government, and a barbaric soul. But it was the descendant of the Western Roman Empire, and as such, it inspired awe, as did all things Roman.

Currently, the King of Spain, Charles V, held the office of Emperor.

"I shall call my invention, 'Prospero's *Para Cadere*,'" the scientist said. "*Para*, Latin for 'against,' and *cadere*, meaning 'fall.' Yes, it has a ring to it." He passed a loud kiss to his fingertips and flung it into the wind. "*Buono*. Rather than rest on my laurels, I should like to explore the principle even further. A shirt drying over a fire will sometimes billow in an upward direction. Fire contains gases that rise in the air. I shall burn a gas to produce hot air and throttle it, which will cause the parachute to lift to whatever height I desire."

"You'd need a lot of gas," Taddeo said to remind Prospero that he was the engineer.

"As you say. Construction is your concern. I have a working design in my head already. We just need fresh capital. Don Pedro never paid me. We are back where we started, unless the Emperor wants to give us a contract."

"Not exactly, Doctor. Look." He opened his fist and showed Prospero Doña Fermina's gold necklace. He'd accidentally grabbed it when he'd fallen on top of her and had been so terrified that he'd never let go of it. Prospero put on his glasses, adjusted the discs for microscopic inspection, and studied its length. He whistled.

"Ha! I am teaching you well, it seems. See how fast you learn? Soon, I predict, your cunning shall surpass even your mentor's!"

Taddeo found this an altogether depressing prospect.

Chapter III
TRIAL BY COMBAT

The Spanish cavalrymen arrived during the night, sagging on blown horses and covered with dust. Don Jorge and his men kicked open the door and charged inside with swords and maces. Myrddin woke to a view of the Don's blade angled toward his throat.

"Now who is the smart one?" demanded Don Jorge.

"You are?" guessed Myrddin.

"That's right. You did not expect to see me again, eh?"

"Actually, we were waiting for you."

"Do I have your surrender?"

The Magus didn't answer. He'd already gone back to sleep.

Don Jorge stared down at him, dumbfounded. After riding hard all day chasing his quarry on a mission from the Emperor, Myrddin's loud snoring was anticlimactic.

One of his men yawned. Don Jorge grabbed him by the collar. "You—and you. Take first watch. Never let this man out of your sight. The pages will feed and groom the horses. The rest of you, shut up and sleep."

The troop sprawled on the floor while the men who'd drawn watch sat by the hearth, took out a deck of cards, and played Tarocco.

Marie, who'd been watching from the shadows the whole time, returned to her bed of straw.

She and Myrddin had been passing through the villages around Zaragoza, spreading the tidings of strange events in Christendom. A two-headed goat had been born in Navarre, he said, the heads fighting as soon they emerged from the womb. While the peasants watched this wondrous thing, a wolf came along and gobbled it up. Myrddin prophesied that the goat's heads were Charles V of Spain and the Holy Roman Empire and Francis I of France, fighting over Italy, while the wolf was the Turk, preparing to devour them all.

Slightly seditious, but it played well, particularly the lurid fear mongering about the savage Turk, who terrified everyone as a creature of legend. Then Don Jorge and his men appeared and demanded Myrddin come and stand before the Emperor. Marie already knew Don Jorge by reputation as one of the toughest fighters in the realm, a member of the vaunted Old Guard of Castile. He'd earned the ugly scar running diagonally across his face from fighting in Italy. Too bad he turned out to be kind of a jerk in person.

Marie stirred just before dawn. Damita wrapped some roast lamb and pork-scratching bread for her dinner on the road. As Marie prepared the cart for travel, two men, one tall and one short, limped out of the house wincing over cuts and bruises.

"What happened to you idiots?" Don Jorge demanded.

They glanced at Marie, who wagged her finger.

"Nothing," the short one said and rubbed his jaw. "We got into a fight."

"A fight? What were you fighting about?"

"A woman," the tall one answered as he rubbed his arm. He glanced at Marie again.

Don Jorge turned and looked at her. "Save yourselves the trouble. Take her next time."

Marie laughed. The knight frowned.

"In fact, why not have a go at her now? Just take her into the hay."

The lancers' eyes widened as Marie crossed her arms and smiled at them. They wagged their heads and assured Don Jorge they needn't harrass the poor girl, and shouldn't they be getting on their way? Mustn't keep His Majesty waiting, ha ha. Don Jorge shook his head in fresh puzzlement. He squinted at the sky. The sun was up, the horses saddled. It was time to marshal his troop and get back on the road. They'd be in Valladolid by the sunset.

Marie watched Myrddin approach. "We're ready."

"But our friends are not, it seems."

"We still don't know why they arrested us. What if we're in trouble with the Emperor?"

"What if we are?"

"Well, what would we do about it?"

The old wizard set his conical cap on his head. "I suppose I'll simply disappear in a puff of smoke or something. You may have to fight your way out."

"It'll be worth whatever happens just to meet the Holy Roman Emperor, though."

"Kings are overrated. I have no use for them. I learned that lesson the hard way. We'd do well to stay clear of that character."

Marie frowned. "Listen, Myrddin, I've pulled this cart for you for over a thousand miles." A thousand miles of shaky bridges, mud up to her knees, hostile idiots, freezing winds, bandits, and inns crowded with bugs and rats and whores. "Eight years of my life. I want to see how a king lives. I want to eat good food and sit on a soft couch like a rich woman. Just once. Let me have this, okay?"

Myrddin shrugged. "As you wish."

She watched the Spanish mount their horses and collect their backup mounts. They were a band of twelve. Don Jorge wore plate of polished steel and a helmet decorated with red plumes. The rest were lancers—light cavalry in blue cassock-covered armor and open helmets, carrying twelve-foot lances with colorful streamers—and Don Jorge's pages and valets. She wished she could be one of them, riding into battle led by men she believed in for a cause that was just. She particularly liked the red plumes sprouting from Don Jorge's helmet; the man had style, even if he was a jerk. All she had was her old cuirass that had a bullet hole in the back and squashed her boobs. Then again, she wore Artemis, expertly forged from the world's finest steel by the blacksmiths of Toledo, on her hip, and there was no finer weapon in Spain, of that she was sure. Myrddin claimed it was unbreakable. He'd spent every coin they'd put away over three years to buy it.

This realization made her smile. He didn't have to get her the best. Maybe it was his way of saying he cared. Maybe he did feel something for her, something like paternal love.

Don Jorge caught her smiling. "You're a saucy wench, aren't you? Sorry, lass, there's no time. You're a fetching piece, but no one wants you this morning."

His men laughed. Marie laughed too, which silenced them.

The knight shook his head. "Witch," he muttered.

"Pig," she said, making him blink.

"Your emperor is waiting," Myrddin said, stabbing his finger at the rising sun.

"Then we shall not tarry." He glared at Marie, his scar livid on his reddening face. "I'll break you of that sauciness later."

Myrddin set out on the road. Marie followed with the rattling cart. Don Jorge and his lancers cantered after them.

"This time, we stay together," the knight said. "No sorcery, Magus. Do I have your word of honor on that?"

"Absolutely not," Myrddin said.

Don Jorge cursed and urged his men on, but they quickly fell behind as the Magus shortcut time and space. In the knight's eyes, his charges appeared to be walking and slowly zooming away at the same time, a disorienting effect. Soon, his troop had to gallop to keep up until falling away in a cloud of dust.

"I command you to stop in the name of the Emperor!"

"We'll just have to wait for them when we get there," Marie said.

"I know," Myrddin said. He was actually smiling. A tiny little half smile, but it was there.

"I swear on this ring I will find you!" Don Jorge called across the hills.

Marie walked with a spring in her step, feeling strong today. The two lancers had found her sleeping in the hay last night and thought they'd have their way with her. Little did they know she'd mastered kung fu.

Women were the same as men, Marie believed, and men were the same everywhere. They copulated like goats with anyone who'd have them. But not her. She discriminated. Yes, she'd kissed many a boy during her travels, blacksmiths' sons and stable hands, but she'd never known a man in the Biblical way. When the time came, she wanted it to be special. She didn't care that many women her age and even younger were already getting married; she wanted her mate to be meant for her. She believed she'd simply know he was the one. Unfortunately, every man she met proved to be an idiot and a pig, obsessed with himself and his own immediate needs. No one challenged her mind, stimulated her heart, and stirred her passion. Everywhere, she found a soul-crushing, predictable sameness. Some proved worse than others, however, like these overprivileged cavalrymen, who'd thought they could take her by force because she was a woman of low station and hence of no real importance.

The great walled city of Valladolid loomed over a flat and rocky plain half covered with sprawling vineyards. Originally built by the Romans at the convergence of two small rivers, it had become the most important city in Spain. Though Charles V had no fixed capital, with his nomadic court constantly on the move visiting the provinces of his far-flung empire, he preferred Valladolid. It was here, after all, that King Ferdinand of Aragon and Queen Isabella I of Castile married to found a new Christian nation, Spain, which went on to drive the Moors out of Iberia during the *Reconquista*.

A squad of bored soldiers with halberds guarded the gate, which stood open to travelers coming and going. Marie and Myrddin paused to scan the countryside behind them. Don Jorge and his merry band appeared as ants on the distant plain. Myrddin raised his cloak and lowered it, shedding every particle of dust, while Marie brushed her jacket and washed up at their water barrel. Leo paced and whined, his eyes shining with excitement.

"So what do you want to do now?" Marie said.

"I think we should go sightseeing."

She clapped her hands. "Oh, thank you!" They hadn't visited

a city in years, Myrddin preferring the company of simpler, more gullible country folk.

Soldiers and common people thronged the streets. With the Emperor in town, a high level of energy pulsed through the crowds. It was more than just the desire to look busy with superiors around; when the Emperor was here, the very air crackled with power, and everyone felt it. More importantly, the presence of the Imperial court created a temporary boom to the local economy.

The street vendors called out to her. Marie bought some cheese made with fresh cream and sprinkled with sugar. She and Myrddin took in university buildings, the Chancery where the people received justice, and the Casa de Moneda where coins were minted for distribution. It was a beautiful place, but the overall effect, like other cities she'd seen, felt a bit depressing to the soul. Her generation was one of a long succession accustomed to living in another civilization's ruins. With the exception of castles, walls, and a few cathedrals, no one built anything anymore that lasted; most of the buildings were Roman as was the road that had brought them here. She lived in a post-apocalyptic age, in the long shadow of mighty Rome, constantly reminded of its superior culture and technology. The Rebirth of Europe intended to rediscover that intellectual greatness. Marie refused to believe the zenith of mankind's glory lay in the past. She was young and thought her generation could make a difference. That just she, herself, could.

Don Jorge found them taking in a jousting tournament at the vast central plaza. Myrddin had placed a bet on Don Sebastian to unseat Don Alfonso. Marie knew Myrddin considered such bets a sure thing, as he could make a horse rear from up to a furlong away. The lancers rode through the crowd to arrest them again at sword point.

"Ha! Found you again! I told you I would!"

"*Saludos*, Don Jorge. We were waiting for you."

"If you attempt to escape again, I will cut you down where you stand."

Myrddin shrugged. "If you like. I thought we might get here a lot faster my way, and I was right. Now we have enough time to get this over with before the day ends."

"Look, being called before the Emperor is considered an immense honor."

"If you say so," frowned the Magus, who considered the whole thing an irritating chore.

The knights formed a tight cordon of horseflesh around him and Marie and escorted them to the old Roman basilica where Charles V held court. She told Leo to guard their belongings and followed the others into the colonnaded great hall, her stomach twittering with excitement.

The multitude of courtiers in their bright clothes overwhelmed her. Charles V sat surrounded by priests, notaries, agents, and the august Queen. Next to him, Mercurino Gattinara, the Grand Chancellor, leaned on his cane, his sharp eyes noticing everything. A massive tapestry bearing the Emperor's personal coat of arms, the fierce two-headed eagle of the Holy Roman Empire, hung behind the throne.

Muscular brown men, naked but for loincloths and feathered headdresses, juggled logs with their feet for the pleasure of the Emperor. Charles V looked on wearing the expression of a man forced to endure an elaborate prank.

"*Indios* from New Spain," Don Jorge whispered when Myrddin asked about them. "Entertainers. They once performed for their emperor, now they perform for ours. Some move a ball only with their hips. Some play a game called *patolli*, which uses beans as dice and counters. The savages get so obsessed with this game they gamble themselves into slavery. They did, anyway, until the priests banned it. Now they can only play it here to entertain our nobles."

"Why did the priests ban it?" Myrddin asked. "I'm curious, was it because of the gambling or the slavery?"

"Neither. The savages get so obsessed with the game, they invoke their pagan gods for aid. The priests punish those who play by burning their hands."

"Savages, yes," agreed Myrddin, though it was unclear about whom he was referring.

Charles V—the Duke of Burgundy, Count of Flanders, Archduke of Austria, King of the Romans, Emperor, the Defender of Christendom—was one of the most powerful men in the world. He'd been crowned King of Spain at the age of sixteen, though he was Austrian and raised in the Netherlands. At nineteen, upon the death of his grandfather Maximilian, the reigning Holy Roman Emperor, he became Archduke of Austria and bought his own election as emperor with the help of a massive loan from the Fuggers. Now, at twenty-nine, he was master of a third of Europe and vast lands in the New World, an empire on which the sun never set.

The first thing Marie noticed about the man was his oversized bearded jaw and large meaty lips set in a dull face. He nursed a flagon on his lap, which she learned was beer flavored with honey and bay leaves, a favorite drink. He dressed conservatively compared to his nobles, wearing a black and gold doublet with puffed sleeves. Isabella of Portugal, the Holy Roman Empress, sat next to him in a heavy satin dress, her neck adorned with pearls and her hair expertly braided. Marie found her quite beautiful. Occasionally, the Empress glanced at her husband to gauge his current mood, though how she might detect his true feelings was beyond Marie. He appeared cold, expressionless, and politic as a rule.

So this is what a king looks like, she thought. She'd never met anyone so important before and felt quite star struck. He looked so regal and grave. She sensed the weight of the world he must have felt on his shoulders. The huge obligations placed on him. The hard work involved in keeping such a large and diverse empire working together for the common good. The responsibility of protecting millions of Christians from the Turk. *No wonder kings claim divine right*, she thought, for only special men could do what they did. Surely, they were chosen by God to rule.

So rapt was she that she barely noticed the *Indios* leaving the room, which quieted as official business resumed. Apparently happy to return to his natural element of conducting business of the realm, Charles V welcomed the *conquistador* Don Francisco Pizarro, who'd recently returned from New Spain. One of the men who, after expelling the Moors from the Iberian peninsula in 1492, set out to explore and conquer distant lands.

Don Francisco boasted of discovering the Pacific Ocean and trying but failing twice to conquer an *Indio* kingdom he believed held even greater wealth than the Aztecs—the legendary El Dorado, kingdom of gold, ruled by nobles called *Incas*. After the Governor of Panama refused to furbish men and supplies for a third expedition, he'd sailed home to request the Crown directly finance it.

He presented Charles with many wonderful gifts, from gold vessels to a strange animal called a llama, but the most impressive of all was a chocolate drink from Mexico, which Charles had never enjoyed before and particularly liked, being a bit of a glutton.

"Don Francisco's a bastard," Don Jorge gossiped. "His father was a colonel who knocked up a girl between campaigns."

"How badly do you want to stay here?" Myrddin whispered to Marie. "In this city, among these fools?"

The imploring look in her eyes answered his question.

The wizard sighed. "All right, I'll see what I can do."

Charles V embraced Don Francisco and told him he would have the Crown's support for a new expedition. While the Imperial court applauded, the herald called Myrddin to come forward. The court quieted at the sight of the strange magician.

Mercurino Gattinara began the questioning while Charles, wearing the tiny pleased smile of a child on his normally inscrutable face, finished his chocolate drink.

"Are you Myrddin Wyllt, the man called the Magus?" the Chancellor said.

"I am he," conceded Myrddin.

"You are able to perform feats of magic?"

"That is correct."

"From whence do you derive these powers? Are they white arts or dark?"

"My power is derived from the evocation of angels," he answered truthfully. "I practice hermeticism."

"Do you practice demonology or any of the other *artes magicae* prohibited by Church law? Divination through earth, air, water, fire, palm reading, or the throwing of bones?"

"Absolutely not," he lied.

"Good. Now, is it true that you are a learned alchemist able to transmute base metals into gold?"

"Of sorts. I am an alchemist in that I transform base reality into treasured illusions."

Charles V stiffened. Gattinara frowned and said, "The man is playing coy with me."

"As far as the observer is concerned, the miracle occurs," Myrddin explained.

"I'm getting tired of this game, Magus."

"The human heart sees what it desires. True alchemy occurs in the beholder's mind."

The Emperor cut off Gattinara's next question with a dismissive gesture. The Chancellor called out, "Don Jorge, your sovereign calls upon you as a constable of the Crown."

"If it is within my power, I will do anything you ask," the knight said.

"Good. We wish you to take this petty charlatan where you found him and dump him there." To Myrddin, he added, "*Eodem cubito, eadem trutina, pari libra.*" In other words, *what you give, you get.*

Don Jorge grinned and patted the Magus on the back. "With pleasure, Your Excellency."

"*In omnia paratus,*" Myrddin said. *Ready for anything.*

Acting without thought, Marie drew her sword and flung herself onto bended knee, leaning on the pommel with her head bowed.

"Your Majesty, I have been seeking a monarch to whom I would offer a life of service, if he would so value it. I believe you to be that august king. I would swear an oath of fealty—"

Blood pounded in her ears. The entire court was *laughing*.

"Forsooth, I will prove my case by fighting any man here," she cried.

Charles massaged his chin as the crowd roared again. He raised his hand for quiet.

Gattinara slammed the tip of his cane against the floor. "Where are the guards? Throw these vagrants out!"

"Not quite yet, Grand Chancellor," the Emperor said.

"As you wish, Majesty."

"Come forward, *jonge dame*. Do not be afraid. Let us have a look at you."

She bowed. "Your Majesty."

"You're French, not Burgundian."

"Your Majesty is observant."

"We shall not hold it against you. If all the French swore fealty to the Crown so enthusiastically, the world would be a much more peaceful place."

"Thank you, Your Majesty."

"We are pleased to let you have your trial by combat."

Charles lived for his office. He had to test her. Otherwise, he had to take her breathless oath of fealty as a joke.

He snapped his fingers. "You, there. Constable. Don Jorge."

The knight bent his knee. "Your Majesty."

"The girl wants to fight to defend the honor of her declaration of fealty. Fight the girl."

"My code forbids murder of women and children, Your Majesty."

"Your liege commands it," warned Gattinara.

"Then I obey, Excellency."

Marie refused an offer of armor. She'd left her cuirass in the cart, and while it squashed her boobs, it was as familiar to her as a second skin. Anything else would slow her down and make her vulnerable. She also turned down the offer of a large, heavy heater shield. She chose instead a small round Moorish buckler mounted on the wall as a trophy of the *Reconquista*.

She'd have to be fast. Don Jorge didn't seem like the kind of man who pulled his swings. A single slice could cut a girl like her almost in half. Even if he struck her only with the flat of his sword, it could snap her bones.

"Fie on you, girl," Don Jorge said. "You're making us both fools."

"If I best you, you'll give me one of those plumes from your helmet for my hat."

"If you last more than two swings, you may take your pick."

He cracked his knuckles and assumed a fighting stance with shield, sword, and plate armor, the very portrait of the modern professional fighting man.

"Art thou ready?" he asked.

Marie nodded and focused on her breathing. The crowd backed away to give the fighters space. They saluted each other and waited.

Charles nodded. Gattinara announced, "You may begin."

She came in fast. He lashed out with a flash of steel. She raised her buckler just in time. The blow sent her reeling.

She looked down at her shield, which now bore a deep groove down the middle. Her arm still vibrated from the shock.

The knight backed away in disgust, giving her time to take measure. She'd hoped his hubris would be his undoing. He was overconfident, and she'd intended to use this as a weapon against him. But no matter how cocky he was in the fight, he'd never let his guard down. He'd been born and bred for war; he'd earned his scars. His training was too strong.

"I'm waiting," he said.

She considered her options, worried now. Where should she hit him?

He took the initiative. His blow flung her gasping into the arms of a richly attired nobleman. "Give up this folly before you get yourself killed!" he hissed in her ear before tossing her back in the ring. Marie saw the disapproving faces of the nobles and courtiers, the judgmental frowns of the ladies. Her eyes blurred with tears of shame, which she blinked away. She never should have issued a public challenge to fight in front of these people. Most of her instructors would not have approved, though the *Okichitawak* Cree war chief would have applauded her foolhardy, headlong rush into danger.

Marie shook her head to clear it. *Don't think*, she told herself. *The hawk doesn't plan its attack any more than it does its next breath.* When she'd thrashed the two cavalrymen in the straw, they were drunk, it was dark, and she had the element of surprise, yes; but she also did it without thinking. *Let your training fight his training*, she heard her *sensei* in her head, *and keep your honor, alive or dead, no matter what the result.*

Don Jorge was used to matching men in a contest of strength, brute force meeting brute force. Her *sensei* whispered: *Hit him where he is not.*

Marie was singing now. She watched for her opening.

She lunged high into the air to bring the bottom of the buckler against the top of his shield with a loud *crack*, pulling it down as she returned to the earth. She used the top of her shield to aim her blade's precise thrust into a seam in his armor. She struck quick as a snake.

Don Jorge roared, already swinging his sword in a gleaming arc. Marie ducked and rolled away to spring back to her feet. She felt confident now. Like Artemis, she'd been expertly forged but had never been truly tested in deadly combat against a skilled opponent. That was exactly how she felt as she circled Don Jorge like a wolf and struck again. Like a precise and exquisite instrument built by a master craftsman.

He charged, raising his sword in a defensive posture while lashing out with his shield. Marie sidestepped and pricked his calf.

The court had fallen into stunned silence. A single face emerged into focus. Myrddin was watching her with a slight sly smile.

She beamed back at him. *Are you seeing this? Are you proud?*

Don Jorge's backhand caught her by surprise. His shield flashed before her eyes and smashed into her body.

Marie woke on the floor fighting to breathe. The knight stood over her.

"I yield," she gasped.

Don Jorge raised his sword with a primal roar, his scar etched across his enraged face like a jagged bolt of lightning.

"Enough!" Charles said. "The girl has conceded the match. It is finished."

The knight restrained himself from the killing blow with a visible effort. He backed away.

The Emperor began a slow clap, which the court imitated as it emerged from its shock. "*Groot!*" he said. "So very *groot*. Well fought, Don Jorge. *Jonge dame*, you may approach."

Marie rolled groaning onto her side and struggled to her knees. "Your Majesty."

"You gave a good account of yourself—what is your name again?"

"Marie. Marie Dubois."

"You have fought one of the strongest knights in the realm, if not Christendom, and nearly bested him. If we had not seen it with our own eyes, we would not have believed it."

Gattinara glared down at her. "Your Majesty, this was obviously witchcraft at work."

"Nonsense. We saw speed, agility, and above all precision account for her success."

"What about the singing? Did you not hear the singing?"

"*Jonge dame*, what was the singing? We found it quite rousing to our ear."

"It was my death song, Your Majesty."

"Ha!" said Gattinara. "See? A spell!"

"No, Excellency. Forsooth, it is no magic." She winced again at the pain in her ribs. "A true warrior must take life lightly, living every minute as his last. It's the warrior's dilemma—to survive and win, he must first accept that he has lost and died. To sing the death song is to say you are ready to die. That you would welcome it. I find that it also helps you control your breathing. In a fight, measured breath is everything."

Charles rubbed his large chin. "Do you have ears to hear, Grand Chancellor? That is a warrior speaking, not a witch. Let not the pretty face and devilish red hair fool you. You must look past appearances, as we did." The Emperor gave him a smug look.

"Your Majesty is an astute judge of character," the Chancellor noted with a bow.

Charles smiled again. "We accept your oath of fealty, Marie Dubois. You are welcome in our court. But next time, be sure your opponent is defeated before seeking accolades from your master." He winked with delight. "*Ja, jonge dame?*"

"*Ja, Uwe Majesteit,*" she stammered. She turned and smiled at Myrddin. She'd had her moment of fame. A dream had come true. She was satisfied.

"I can turn base metals into gold," Myrddin announced.

The court roared at this fresh excitement.

Marie gasped. What was he thinking? He couldn't do real alchemy. If he could, would they be in such obvious poverty? Wasn't this obvious to everyone?

"We are pleased with your answer," said Charles V. "However reluctantly given and however trying to our patience you happen to be. We would welcome you, Magus."

"Thank you, Majesty," Myrddin replied and quoted Hannibal of Carthage, "*Aut viam inveniam aut faciam.*" That is, *I shall either find a way of make one.*

Marie stared at him. Did he agree only because she wanted to stay?

He handed her his staff for support. She followed him limping out of the Imperial court. Outside, a haughty squire tapped her shoulder and handed her an object wrapped in a handful of cloth.

A red plume.

Chapter IV

A Lesson In Fulmen

The steam wagon *Prometheus* lumbered north on the old Roman road linking Toledo and Valladolid, clanking and hissing and belching smoke from the long black pipe jutting from its roof. After a few hours, it slowed to a rasping halt, breathing hard at the bellows and ramping up enough power for another go. Taddeo stepped down into the carriage and shoveled coal into the firebox inside the boiler. Satisfied the engine was in working order, he resumed his place on the driving bench at the front of the vehicle, where Prospero steered using a tiller attached to the single front wheel. Don Rodrigo and his men-at-arms kept their distance. They hated the machine almost as much as their horses did. After a wait so long it grew embarrassing, the piston turned the crankshaft, which drove the axle of the driving wheel. The giant wheels gripped the road as they began to turn. *The Prometheus* was Prospero's pride and joy; he often remarked it had solved his midlife crisis.

Don Rodrigo watched the machine's asthmatic progress for a while longer before making an expansive gesture across the length of the vehicle and asking: "Why?"

Prospero cupped his hand to his ear. "What?"

The knight repeated the gesture and shouted, "Why?"

The scientist laughed. "Why go to the moon?"

The knight looked up at the sky in bewilderment.

Prospero said, "To go from point A to point B. That is your answer."

"It doesn't go very fast."

"My precious can travel up to four, five leagues per hour on the flat in the highest gear."

"My horse can beat that at the gallop. All she needs is a saddle and a bag of hay."

"Yes, well," grumbled Prospero. "I prefer to travel in style."

The knight guffawed and cantered away with a salute.

The scientist turned to Taddeo, who sat with one hand resting on the barrel of the *peterero*, the three-foot swivel gun they kept loaded with grapeshot to keep bandits at bay. "And you, my thoughtful friend, I see you daydreaming about your latest conquest. It is only natural for a young man to love, but let your thoughts not tarry on that amorous Juno. As your mentor, I consider it my duty to help you navigate these treacherous waters." He paused to take a puff from the hookah between his feet. "There are many fish in the sea, yes, but you may only keep one. The rest you must throw back. Do not confuse practice with the real thing."

Taddeo, his ears still dulled from firing the engine, became aware his mentor was speaking to him. "What?"

Prospero toked from the hookah tube. "One does not order the main course after seeing only one item on the menu. Especially considering you will have to eat the same thing every night the rest of your life. And what a menu! Valladolid is filled with beautiful women eager for sensual instruction by the virile Italian lover. Ah, to be a young man again! I remember when I was a bright-eyed boy at the University of Bologna, arguing natural philosophy and getting into fights with the townies at the taverns. Everyone wanted to be the *homo universale*—the universal man, a man who could do anything he put his mind to do, like the great Leonardo and my thrice-blessed brother. Me, I would read the Songs of Solomon to pious young women. Very efficacious. Within every pious woman rages the lust of a bawd, hey? I share this trade secret with you free of charge."

"Actually, I was thinking about those poor peasants, Doctor. We gave them smallpox."

"Do not worry about them. If we had not infected them, the wretches would have died off from something else next year, I assure you. Instead of continuing their miserable existence, they are now safely tucked in the warm bosom of Abraham in Paradise, and that is a happy outcome for all concerned, no? On the other hand, imagine if it had worked. We could have saved all of Europe from a terrible disease. Was this not worth the risk?"

"Perhaps, but it still doesn't seem quite ethical."

"*Mama mia*. Ethics, he says. Who decides these things? Are you not the one who is always telling me the needs of the many outweigh the needs of the few? That all decisions should be made in favor of the course offering the most good for the most people?"

"Well, yes, but—"

"But nothing. Trust me on this one. It was my decision in any case; your conscience is clear. Surely, if Don Pedro had not slaughtered all of them, we could have found out if the other half of the village had been rendered immune." He patted his protégé on the back. "Be happy. We have a meeting with the Emperor! Our luck is looking up."

"That's bothering me too. Why did you tell Don Rodrigo you're an alchemist? As you know, we can't do alchemy."

"Yet," Prospero said. "Science always finds a way. Nothing is impossible, only unlikely. In any event, I did not say I am an alchemist. Don Rodrigo did. I simply did not correct him."

"I'm worried we're going to get into trouble." The prospect terrified Taddeo, in fact. His father would not be pleased. Gregorio would call his son home, ending Taddeo's career as an engineer and beginning another as an accountant.

"Trouble, eh? On the contrary, we will find our fortune with the good Emperor Charles as our patron, you will see. They may know me as an alchemist, but Charles has no use for me producing gold. He has entire fleets of treasure ships delivering the plunder of the Aztecs. The Habsburg family is bankrolled by the Fuggers, who have more money than God. Now these are people from whom you can learn about love. The Habsburg House of Austria now directly rules Spain, Bohemia, the Netherlands, and what is left of Hungary after the Turks wrecked it—all through dynastic marriage. Marriage is mightier than the sword. And money is mightier than marriage."

"We have the benefit of neither," Taddeo remarked, though he liked what he'd heard. A prestigious contract with the Habsburg monarch might impress his taciturn father, even if the Empire was currently at war with Venice.

"We are free men," Prospero grinned. "*Homo universale*. Might, marriage, and money do not apply to us. Our might comes from the mind. We are married to progress. Knowledge is our currency."

Taddeo smiled. He liked the sound of that too. It sounded a lot better than they'd gone broke inventing things no one could use.

"Do not worry yourself about getting into trouble. Look at me. Am I worried?"

"You never worry."

"Exactly," Prospero said. "Never worry. Write that down."

Taddeo chewed his lip pensively. "Doctor..."

The scientist puffed on the tube. "You are still worrying. Tell me what else is on your mind."

"About women. How will I know which one I will marry?"

"You will just know. You will know her the moment you see her."

"Really," Taddeo said, mystified by the whole thing.

"Just make sure she is young, beautiful, and rich as King Midas."

The citizens of Valladolid heard *The Prometheus* before they saw it. By the time it rolled through the gates led by Don Rodrigo's lancers, a large crowd had peeled away from the jousting tournament to take in this fresh spectacle.

"Look, it's the scientist!"

"The great one is here!"

"My young protégé, you may steer our chariot," Prospero said, handing over the tiller. He stood and acknowledged the acclamation with a flourish. The crowd responded with a wild cheer. He called out to Don Rodrigo, "Now you know why, *Signore*.

To make an entrance!"

The knight laughed.

The crowd roared as it followed the steam wagon's slow but steady progress through the streets. Everywhere, people pointed and waved at Prospero.

"*Dios mio!* It's him! The scientist!"

"The great architect is here!"

"The artist!"

"Do you hear them, Taddeo?" Prospero struck a pose, hand on his hip and nose in the air, as he soaked up their adoration. "My reputation precedes me!"

"*El Divino,*" someone shouted, and others took up the chant. "*El Divino! El Divino!*"

Taddeo wiggled his pinky in his ear and listened again. They were calling Prospero the Divine One. He looked up at his mentor as if seeing him for the first time.

Prospero laughed and waved. "I like this town!" People reached up to try to touch his feet. Fathers held their children high so they could see the great man.

A beautiful woman blew him a kiss. "We love you, Michelangelo!"

Prospero's grin faded to a scowl. He sat and took the tiller from Taddeo. His face turned the color of a bruise.

"I'm sure they'd still be cheering if they knew you were his brother," Taddeo said.

"That is a great comfort," Prospero said. "You think you are the only one with pressure to live up to the family name? Try my shoes on for size."

Don Rodrigo halted his troop in front of the columns of the cracked old Roman basilica where the Emperor Charles V held court. Taddeo cranked a lever to apply the brake to the flywheel, bringing the steam wagon to a slow panting halt in the adjacent forum. The machine shivered and exhaled a final wave of steam as it powered down.

"Say something smart!" someone called out.

Prospero and Taddeo followed Don Rodrigo into the building past royal guards in blue and yellow livery who stood leaning on halberds. The knight brought them through an empty gallery and into the colonnaded hall in which the Emperor held court. An old man dressed in black sat on the throne in a state of deep thought, his chin resting on his fist.

The scientist threw himself to his knees and wailed, "Your Majesty!"

The man shuddered at this display and shook his head. "I'm not the Emperor. Do you think he sits all day in an empty room? His Majesty is detained. I was waiting for you. I am Mercurino Arbono Marchesi di Gattinara, Grand Chancellor of all the realms and kingdoms of the Emperor."

"Your Excellency," Taddeo said with a bow.

Prospero got back onto his feet and dusted himself. "I was told we were to present ourselves to the Emperor himself. When shall we return?"

"His Catholic Majesty does not have time to meet every Pablo, Pedro, and Pánfilo called into his presence. I have authority to act on behalf of the realm. We shall conduct our business now, if you please."

"Well," Prospero said, recovering his dignity. "Then I present myself and my protégé, Taddeo Cellini, at your service."

The Chancellor appraised them. "Hmm." He added in Latin, the universal language of Europe: "*Video barbam et pallium, philosophum nondum video.*" *I see a beard and a cloak, I have yet to see a philosopher.*

"*Nota bene,*" Prospero said. *Observe carefully.*

Gattinara smiled, revealing yellow teeth. It was a dangerous smile, the smile of a snake contemplating its next meal. "*Nullum magnum ingenium sine mixtura dementiae fuit.*" *One can't be a genius without being a little nuts.* "So far, so good. Perhaps you are a philosopher after all. Come with me, gentlemen. Let us take the air. The gardens are blooming."

He led them out into a sunny colonnaded inner courtyard at the rear of the basilica where a lush garden had been planted, a bright, colorful riot of bluebells, roses, and plenty of carnations. "Listen carefully," he told them. "At this time, four great powers control the world, each ruled by a great man. Charles V of Spain, the Habsburg lands, and the Holy Roman Empire; Francis I of France; Henry VIII of England; and Suleiman the so-called Magnificent of the Ottoman Empire. Christendom is divided against itself. This must not be. I have convinced the Emperor to reconsider his strategy. The conflict with France has therefore shifted from its focus on Navarre and Burgundy to a grander stratagem. Burgundy is a trifle, a pawn easily sacrificed; Italy is the grand prize. Control of my native Milan is critical to linking Spain and Franch-Comté with Tyrol, which would unite Spain, Italy, and Austria. Instead of playing Francis's petty game, we must play our own, for the biggest stakes of all— *Dominium Mundi.*"

"World empire," breathed Taddeo, struck by the boldness of the vision.

"An empire uniting all Catholics under a single monarch, a single banner, and a single motto, *Plus Ultra*—Even Further—to convert the pagans of the New World, Martin Luther's misguided Protestants, and finally the Turk himself. An empire bringing all mankind together to serve God. An empire of everlasting peace and strength!"

For thirty-five years, France and Spain warred over Italy like two tired, drunken boxers fighting over a beautiful but fractious woman who wanted neither one of them. During the previous war of 1521-26, a French army invaded Lombardy and conquered Milan, but was soundly thrashed by Imperial troops at Bicocca and Sesa. King Francis led the next invasion personally, inspired his men to heroic feats of courage, and got utterly crushed at Pavia. The French mode of warfare simply proved no match for the Spanish arquebusiers, who decimated their ranks with massed shot. Charles imprisoned Francis, who regained his freedom after signing the Treaty of Madrid, giving up all claims to Italy, Burgundy, and Flanders. Upon setting foot on French soil, Francis renounced the treaty, saying it had been made under duress. Enraged at this betrayal, Charles challenged him to a duel, which Francis accepted but later, after everyone pointed out how ridiculous the whole thing was, pretended never happened. If kings wanted to fight, they could settle their disputes in a duel of nations in which thousands died.

The next war started as soon as Francis could form a new alliance, the League of Cognac, which arrayed France, Venice, Florence, Milan, and the Papal State against the Empire. The war started when Burgundy, which Francis had been forced to guarantee to Charles, simply refused to be handed over. Henry VIII would have joined in but backed out in a huff because the treaty wasn't signed in England. Imperial troops again thrashed the French, took Milan and, in one of the war's worst atrocities, sacked Rome, which drew England into the war. Emboldened by this new ally, Francis sent another army through Genoa to Naples and laid siege to it. Things were now finally looking up for the French.

The fate of Italy hung in the balance.

"I'm from Venice," Taddeo said.

Prospero looked at him sharply. "But not I, Excellency. While it is my adopted country, I am originally from Florence."

"We're also at war with Florence," Gattinara noted.

"Oh. Right."

"I do not hold it against either of you. I believe the war will come to an untimely end soon. We are content to leave Venice be as long as she returns some territory that rightfully belongs to us. As for her ally Florence, we shall see."

"As a citizen of the world, your relations with Venice and Florence do not concern me," Prospero assured him.

To a large extent, the same went for Taddeo. His father was a patriot, but his primary loyalty was to his family and business. Gregorio supported the war so he could sell more wool to the army and tackle to the navy. Otherwise, he had no use for it.

"Now allow me to cut to the heart of the matter," the Chancellor said. "These wars are bleeding the treasury dry. We need money."

"But you have the gold of the Aztecs—"

"Spent."

"The Fuggers—"

"We have reached the ceiling of our credit with all the banking families."

"I see," Prospero said.

"You have a reputation as having knowledge of the transmutation of base metals into gold."

"It is possible, yes. Anything is possible. But very difficult."

"After difficulty, sweetness."

"It is no small task. It could also take a very long time."

"He who has the job started has it half done."

Prospero offered a pious look. "Plus there are the moral concerns."

Gattinara winced. "Like what?"

"The lust for gold has led many men down the wrong path," Prospero opined. "I could not make gold for you because God frowns upon such vanity. It would only jeopardize my everlasting spirit, and yours."

"Interesting. Well, then there is nothing more to discuss. Hmm?"

Taddeo let out a massive inward sight of relief he hoped didn't show on his face. He sensed the Chancellor missed nothing. One of those cunning men who sees right through people. Prospero had gotten them out of the impossible contract without calling himself a fraud. Now they could go back to raising money for their hot air balloon project, which had promise.

"We are learned men, at your service," Prospero pleaded. "Perhaps there is something else—"

"*Si tacuisses, philosophus mansisses*," Gattinara snapped, quoting Boethius. *If you'd stayed silent, you would have stayed a philosopher.* He turned his attention to Taddeo. "What about you, young man? Do you care to add anything, or are you going to just stand there fretting?"

Taddeo wilted under the man's fierce gaze. "*Scio me nihil scire,*

Your Excellency." *I know that I know nothing.*

The Chancellor laughed. "And that makes you far wiser than men older than you. It turns out we do have a philosopher in the room, and beardless to boot. I have a boy proclaiming philosophy and an alchemist who doesn't want to make gold. The universe is upside down today. Ah, well. It is no matter. We have retained another alchemist. One of the best, I'm told, and *in magicis expertus.*"

Prospero frowned. "An expert in magic, you say? And who is this fraud?"

"He's hard at work in his laboratory," Gattinara proclaimed with his devious smile. "Take a walk with me, and I will introduce you to your colleague. He's only two hundred paces from here."

They followed him out of the building. A squad of his personal guard fell into step behind them. The crowd outside had gotten word that the man they were cheering wasn't Michelangelo, only his kid brother, and had gone back to the jousting tournament. After weeks on the road, Taddeo enjoyed the sights and smells of city life, even the garbage and waste choking the gutters and the rat that raced underfoot. A woman walked by with a bucket of water. A crowd of boys ran past laughing. A woman stooped to collect horse dung from the street for her garden, offering a mesmerizing glimpse of full breasts bulging from her bodice. A farmer driving a wagon loaded with onions tipped his hat to Gattinara and wished His Excellency a good day.

"Here we are," said Gattinara after a short walk. "I'm told this building was once a temple dedicated to the goddess Diana." He gestured with his cane. "Shall we?"

Taddeo froze in the doorway. His heart pounded.

The building was owned by the Crown but had previously been unused, and was therefore abused by nature and various squatters over the years. Holes in the roof showered the space with a multitude of light beams. Pigeons trilled in the rafters. The stonework around the altar had been chipped raw by people seeking to decorate their homes. Pornographic graffiti covered the walls. Water pooled among debris in the corners, in which tiny plants struggled to survive. Smoke produced by a bank of furnaces hung heavy near the ceiling. Taddeo noticed almost none of these details.

Glass vessels, iron pots, scales, hammers, and mortars and pestles littered a series of wood tables scattered around the main floor. Leather-bound books, rows of iron and lead ingots, and crucibles filled shelves against the far wall. Mysterious substances boiled in pots and cauldrons. Water, sand, and ash baths stood ready for use. A distillery dripped liquid into a glass beaker. The air reeked with the tangy scents of ammonia and brimstone.

"I'm in Paradise," Taddeo said.

The Chancellor had spared no expense. The equipment here exceeded even their own workshop in *The Prometheus*. They could do real science here. Chemistry and metallurgy that could make people's lives better. Alcohol for the treating of wounds. Ammonia for scrubbing away harmful molds. Soap for hygiene, pure table salt for nourishment, mercury for treatment of the pox, charcoal for fuel, pigments for painting, dyes for clothes, medicines for curing, new forging techniques.

Gattinara nudged him. "You like it?"

"I love it."

"Prospero, allow me to present the Magus Myrddin Wyllt. Magus, I present Prospero Buonarroti, renowned inventor and alchemist."

The old giant in the dark cloak and tall conical hat stood from one of the tables, where he'd been reading a parchment scroll. He bowed low.

"We are already acquainted," Prospero said with a scowl. "How have you been, you fraudulent, science-hating, half-faced trickster?"

The Magus made a wagging gesture with his hand. *So-so.*

Something growled at Taddeo's feet. He looked down to see a mangy, feral dog glaring up at him like something out of a dark fairytale, and took a step back.

"Leo, behave."

As the dog slunk away, Taddeo located the source of the voice. The

57

Magus's assistant, whom he'd mistaken for a boy in his distraction, was a girl about his own age. She'd been feeding wood into one of the furnaces while pumping the bellows. Now she approached, sweating and dirty with soot, her red hair fraying from its ponytail to fall loose around her face.

She was the most beautiful thing he'd ever seen.

"I'm Marie Dubois," she said. She wiped sweat from her forehead with her gloved hand, leaving a black smudge behind.

They stared at each other for a moment. She was waiting for him to say something. He was trying to find the strength to speak without babbling algebraic formula to fill the empty space.

His attraction went beyond her appearance. There was something to this girl. It was the way she carried herself. She was like something out of nature. Not ugly, unpredictable nature. Nor like the neatly manicured gardens of Venice. Marie Dubois was like a wolf stalking sheep. Like a perfect tree in the forest, bathing in filtered sunlight. Like a riot of wildflowers in a meadow. Like a—

The dog growled again.

"Your Excellency," Prospero said, "I have changed my mind. I am happy to accept your commission, if you are still offering it."

Gattinara nodded. "I am indeed."

"Of course, we will require compensation. Twice what you are paying this man."

"You are certainly welcome to a percentage of the gold you make for us, which we will convert into the coin of the realm for you."

Prospero hesitated. "Well. Yes. But we still have our upfront costs."

"Which will be covered by the Crown, and to include materials, room, and board. Bring me receipts." The Chancellor smiled at them. The smile of a hawk swooping down on an unsuspecting rabbit. "It's thrilling to see such great minds working together for the greater good. Now I'll leave you to your work."

Cane tapping, Gattinara left the four standing in an awkward silence.

"I think we'll take the air," Myrddin said. "Come, Marie."

"Fresh air would be good," remarked Prospero, inspecting his fingernails. "It stinks in here."

After they'd left with their menacing dog, the scientist gripped his stomach. "Well, I am starved. How about you? I could eat a horse. *Fames est optimus coquus*." *Hunger makes the best cook*. He winced. "Lord in Heaven, now I am doing it. What a man, our Grand Chancellor, hey? A dangerous lunatic from heel to head."

"Why did you agree to work for him, then?" Taddeo cried. "We can't make gold!"

"And let that bamboozler Myrddin get all the action? Never! If he thinks magic can do it, science can do it faster, cheaper, better!"

"How do you know the Magus, Doctor?"

"That is a story for another day."

"Well, why do you dislike him so much? Can you say?"

"You do not already know? Your instincts as a scientist do not recoil in disgust at the very sight of him? The man makes a mockery of science! With all this hocus-pocus that violates the physical laws! And magic? Phooey! His magic is simply science ahead of its time. Spanish cannon struck fear in the hearts of the *Indios* because it appeared to them as magic. Is gunpowder magic? But instead of sharing his knowledge with the world so that everyone might benefit, this man calls it sorcery and would keep it to himself. Secrets only for a select few to benefit. Everything about the man is an illusion, a fake. I took the contract to prove to him that whatever he can do by means of his so-called magic, I can achieve by science. And after I learn this secret, everyone will make gold and be rich as Midas. The world will be plated with gold!"

"But you just said his technology is way ahead of ours. How can we hope to compete?"

"Am I not Prospero Buonarroti, inventor of Prospero's Clear Glass Mirror? Prospero's *Para Cadere*? Prospero's Steam Wagon? Prospero's Loom Automata—"

Taddeo knew he had to cut him off there, or his mentor would list every single one of his inventions, which could take an hour.

"Okay, okay. I agree. If it can be done, we'll find a way to do it. Now excuse me, Doctor. I must get my paper and pens from the wagon."

"You have an idea already? That is my boy!"

"I need to write to my mother and tell her where I am and that I'm safe."

"You are a worrier, like her. You are here now, no? Enjoy!"

While he collected his things from *The Prometheus*, Taddeo had to admit Prospero had a point. Even if the building was a dump, the laboratory itself was fantastic. He'd have the chance to immerse himself in science. The mind of Christendom often felt like a blank slate. When he told Gattinara he knew very little, he hadn't been joking. Knowledge was a fragile thing that rose and fell with the fortunes of civilization. Europe had forgotten so much that the Greeks and Romans had taken centuries to learn. The Muslim world, meanwhile, was way ahead in every field, though even they knew little of all there was to know. Given time and equipment, who knew what new processes and technologies a bright and open mind might discover? Perhaps he'd discover things that once would have been perceived as magic, and share them for the benefit of everyone, as Prospero quite rightfully said they should do.

Plus there was the girl. There was definitely more to her than met the eye. Who was she? How did she come to be with the Magus? Taddeo understood now what drove his attraction to her; the same as what drove his desire as a scientist to study the material world. Curiosity. He wanted to know her. The idea of discovering Marie Dubois excited him far more than any potential invention, no matter how remarkable, no matter how many lives it might improve.

Back in the laboratory, he found Prospero rifling through the equipment and the Magus's books. Given a moment of peace, he sat on a bench and began first to compose a letter to his father, wondering how he should explain his current situation.

Greetings and Salutations to my dear Father, to whom I pray this Correspondence finds in good Health and in charge of profitable Trade. Papa, I am honored to report that I have embarked on a bold

Endeavor—to produce Gold from common Ores for the Holy Roman Emperor to finance his Armies' continuing Aggression against Venice and its Allies in Italy.

Taddeo sighed and flung down his pen. He couldn't get the girl out of his mind.

He spied a pair of eyes in the corner and turned. Leo, the flea-infested mutt.

Taddeo held out his hand. "Hey there, boy."

The dog slunk close, head low and ears pulled back, and sniffed Taddeo's fingers before turning around and walking off.

"Yes. We're going to be friends."

The dog paused and turned its head to produce a little bark. After this happened several times, Taddeo realized the dog wanted him to come.

He stood and followed, hoping Leo would lead him to Marie. His hopes were answered.

She stood outside the city gate, facing the setting sun with her hat in her hands. The cool wind blew her hair around her head. He felt concerned for her safety out here alone. He touched the dagger on his belt for reassurance. Then he noticed the sword she wore on her own hip, which gave him the feeling she knew how to take care of herself.

She turned at the sound of Leo barking. "Oh, it's you," she said, her tone flat. "Greetings, Taddeo."

He nodded emphatically, unable to speak. The old fire burned in his cheeks. She remembered his name. That was a good start. After a few moments of staring at each other, she returned her attention to the sunset.

Leo bumped against his leg. Then did it again.

"Why are you here?" he blurted.

Her eyes narrowed. "The same as you. Ask yourself."

He nodded and blushed again.

"Why not tell you?" she said with a sigh. "We're here because of me. Myrddin didn't want to do this, but I somehow talked him

61

into it. I wanted to see the big city. This wasn't what I had in mind, though." She gestured toward the sky. "Now I miss the open road. I'm homesick for it."

He couldn't stop nodding. He clenched his eyes shut and willed himself to speak.

"What about you?" she asked.

Taddeo shrugged. He stared at his shoes. He kicked a pebble. When he looked back at her, she was frowning.

"Well, I guess I'll see you later then, Taddeo."

Leo nipped his leg. "We can't make gold," he yelped. "Prospero wanted to build a boat that could travel underwater. A boat with a glass window so he could study the creatures of the sea and hunt for lost treasure. He said with such a boat, we could find Atlantis. He believes it lies west of Portugal, in the great sea."

He paused, dry mouthed. When Marie didn't say anything, he went on, still speaking to Leo, "The problem was the project was going to cost a lot of money. Smugglers in Siena put out the word they were looking for an alchemist, and Prospero convinced them he could do it. He didn't even try, knowing it was beyond him. He had another idea, though, one based on the principle that all things are made up of the four elements—earth, air, fire, water. He believed fire could be separated from everyday substances, an alchemical concept. He told me what he wanted, and I built him a working device. It was a clay jar with a copper cylinder inside, with an iron rod inside the cylinder. A stopper kept the copper and iron from touching. Then we filled the jar at different times with wine, grape juice, lemon juice, and vinegar, anything acidic and therefore possessing the properties of fire. In each case, the device extracted *fulmen*, the essence of lightning, from the liquid into the iron. This *fulmen* could then be transferred as heat to plate metals onto other metals. Such as gold onto iron. We plated a chest of iron bars with a thin layer of gold. When the smugglers told us to pay ourselves from what we'd made, we insisted on payment in coin. It's not like you can buy a stay at an inn with gold bars and expect change. They paid us in florins, and we left town before they realized they'd been cheated. We built the underwater boat, but it sank to the bottom because of a leak in the air tank—a manufacturing error, not an engineering one, mind you, but unfortunate just the same, especially for our pilot. Prospero had it in principle, though. We never built another. That's what he's like. He goes from project to project, whatever interests him."

Still Marie said nothing. Leo stared back at him with rapt attention. Taddeo took a deep breath and added, "Prospero wanted to build his underwater boat, but the real genius was in the *fulmen* device. It produced very little fire, but a revolution can occur from such humble beginnings. One could dedicate a lifetime to its study and development. I'm dead serious when I say that little clay jar could change the world. If *fulmen* can be transmuted into heat, which is a type of energy, so can it into mechanical force and even light. Imagine a world in which public roads are filled with light at night, making them safer to travel. A world where no man need freeze in his own home during the winter. A world in which these devices spin looms, turn wheels, grind wheat, crush olives, anything. We would all have lives filled with hours of learning and leisure. There would be plenty of food and clothing for everyone. As every man would have everything he needed, and everyone would have equal access to it, there would be no more rich or poor, no more crime. No longer would mankind need to feed off the corpse of Rome. We would create a new civilization, a better world, a new era in the history of the world. And it would all start with this one event, this one device. That's the beauty and nobility of science. Its remarkable possibility. That's why I'm a scientist. Prospero is here because he considers your master a rival, but that's not why I'm here. I want to change the world."

Taddeo stopped, exhausted from the effort. Leo whined and lay at his feet, gazing up at him quizzically. After a few moments, he worked up the courage to look Marie in the face. The girl stared back at him with wide eyes, her lips slightly parted. He felt stupid telling her all that. How could he expect her to understand him when no one else did, including his own father? And did he really say, like an idealistic idiot, that he wanted to change the world?

He didn't know her. Besides that, she served Prospero's competition. Now she'd run straight to Gattinara, who'd have him and Prospero beaten, flogged, burned, maimed, or even worse.

He realized he'd made a massive mistake telling her these things, but a part of him didn't care. It had felt good to share his feelings with her. He considered it a major step in his relations with the opposite sex that he'd been able to speak at all in her presence.

"We can't make gold either," she said to his surprise. "I mean, the Magus can, but it's just an illusion. A trick. It looks real, but it's not."

"That's a shame," Taddeo said, back to stammering. "Prospero's tearing the laboratory apart trying to figure out what you're doing."

"That's an illusion too. We're not doing anything. We got those experiments going just to fool Gattinara into thinking we were making progress."

"Well, you had me fooled," he said with a nod.

"Our masters can't make gold. I guess this means we're both in trouble then."

"Marie," he said, relishing the word. "When I asked you why you were here before, I meant how did you come to be here. Who are you?"

Taddeo surprised himself how clearly he said it. Saying her name had unlocked some reservoir of courage.

Marie looked back at the sunset. The sun bled into the distant mountains. Soon it would be dark, and the world would sleep until morning.

Why did she look so sad? Had his question upset her in some way?

"Another time," she said. "I have to go, Taddeo. Night is falling."

She ran back toward the city. He watched her go until she disappeared beyond the gates. Leo circled his legs. Whining, the dog studied him from every angle before racing through the gate to catch up to his mistress.

The wind felt cold against his body, but Taddeo didn't care. He smiled, hugged his ribs for warmth, and started the long walk back to the laboratory.

Prospero was right about something else. Taddeo would know the one when he saw her.

~ Chapter V ~
QUID EST PHILOSOPHI LAPIS

The scientists worked day and night to convert the Roman ruin into a working laboratory. Taddeo mopped the floors and scrubbed the graffiti off the walls while whistling an Italian folk song that Marie later could not get out of her head. Prospero cataloged their materials and equipment and committed the distillation apparatus to the manufacture of what alchemists called *aqua vitae*, the water of life—i.e., liquor. Alchemy, Prospero declared in his cups—the man was always declaring something—had two branches, not one. Not only did alchemists seek the philosopher's stone, the catalyst that turned base metals into gold, but also the elixir of life, which gave health and long life to those who consumed it. *Aqua vitae* was not that elixir, but who cared? It got you drunk.

Marie wondered why they worked so hard to achieve a goal that appeared impossible. Prospero and Taddeo argued incessantly about the composition of metals and methods to break them down into their constituent parts. Whether the four elements that composed matter could be achieved in pure form. And which was the most important principle for certain ends—salt, mercury, or brimstone. They were particularly concerned with making a substance called Alkahest, a solvent that could dissolve anything into its constituent parts. Marie found the idea confusing. If it could dissolve anything, what vessel could contain it? When she voiced her concern aloud, Prospero said that would be a good problem to have, because it meant the main problem had been solved. After they burned a hole to China, he said, they'd look for a material that could not be dissolved. Marie had no idea what he was talking about.

She could see why Myrddin had committed his life to magic. Science made her head hurt.

The Magus loathed science. He wanted man to leave the natural world alone. He was an animist who believed that all things, even trees and rocks and rivers and thunder, had a soul. That made science a great destroyer, a challenger to the natural order of things, a weapon that would grow bigger and bigger in man's hands until he finally used it against himself.

Yet she could appreciate its meticulous and unforgiving demand for utter precision—similar to fencing—even what Taddeo called its nobility. God created the universe and owned it. Science was man's way of claiming it for his own, and only time would tell who'd have the last laugh.

Gattinara dropped in to check on their progress. Prospero had drunk too much *aqua vitae* and was sleeping it off under one of the benches. The Chancellor gave the place a cursory look and inquired to Taddeo how spending days cleaning the ruin contributed to the production of gold.

"A clean workspace is essential to great invention," Taddeo told him.

"Thus you shall go to the stars, my son," the man replied.

"I will settle for your satisfaction, Excellency."

"Such ambition is touching. Now pay heed. I am about to embark on a journey to negotiate peace with the Pope. Tell your master that whence I return, I expect to see results. I shall be gone no longer than two months."

Taddeo awoke Prospero and wrote high on the wall:

QUID EST PHILOSOPHI LAPIS

"What is the meaning of those words?" Marie whispered to Myrddin. She'd mastered many languages over the years but still could not read.

"'What is the philosopher's stone?'" the Magus said. "This is where trouble always begins. Asking questions that shouldn't be answered."

For the next three days, the scientists brainstormed possible answers, which they called hypotheses, and listed them on the wall in the same bold Roman capitals. They'd subject these hypotheses to a series of experiments. Their scientific method bound them try to prove these hypotheses *wrong*, which Marie found even more confusing.

Now came days of grinding, boiling, evaporation, distillation, measurement, and occasional explosions that shook the building. Finally, Prospero and Taddeo left to take the air, talking excitedly about the flammable properties of brimstone. Marie sat with Myrddin and let out a sigh of relief. Leo plopped down at her feet, exhausted, and promptly fell asleep. Marie took out Artemis and began sharpening it with a whetstone.

"Thank God they're gone," she said. "Their talk addles the mind."

"A dog chasing its tail forms a beautiful, elegant circle. But it's still a dog chasing its tail."

Leo opened one eye to gaze balefully at the wizard. Myrddin bent down to scratch him behind the ears. The dog groaned and returned to sleep, legs twitching.

"I can't sleep at night," Marie complained. "They're always at their labors."

Myrddin produced a long-stem wood pipe and filled it with tobacco. "The Tower of Babel wasn't built in a day."

"And why is Prospero always doing that thing with his hands?" she asked. "Like he's trying to cast a spell but can't remember the words."

The Magus lit his pipe and shrugged. "Everything is a drama to Italians."

"Gattinara doesn't do that. He's Italian."

"Yes," Myrddin said, his face thoughtful. "He's a carefully coiled snake, that one. A very dangerous man. I fear he missed his calling as an Inquisitor for the Church."

"Taddeo doesn't do it either. He's very controlled."

"Mm," Myrddin said, puffing away.

"I actually wish he were a bit more expressive."

"Do you?" mused the Magus.

"Forsooth, he doesn't seem to like me very much."

"I would say just the opposite. Marie, the boy is shy with women."

She said nothing for a time, processing her surprise. She knew the concept but had never seen it in practice. Most men either came at her like rutting goats or, like Prospero, looked like they wanted to give her a pat on the head when she spoke. But not Taddeo. Taddeo talked to her through Leo; now the dog had taken to following him around sighing. Even then, he only talked about science. At first, she'd thought him a stuck-up rich kid but came to believe he was simply oblivious to anything else. Now it intrigued her that he might be fond of her.

"You and Prospero don't seem to like each other. Am I right about that, at least?"

"Ah. Well. That is a long story."

"Pray, tell it to me, Myrddin."

"Then I suppose I must make it short for you. I was passing through Venice some years ago—this happened before you were born, child—and presented myself to the Duke. Prospero, obviously a younger man then but already an accomplished scientist, challenged me to a duel. And not just any duel. It was to be a duel of science versus magic, and may the winner rule the earth, or some melodramatic drivel. In the Duke's court, we fought. The scientist presented many fine inventions, including a clear glass mirror, riding machine powered by foot pedals, steam-powered number calculator, and, just for spectacle, a toy replica of Mount Vesuvius that erupted black foam. It went on for days. Then it was my turn."

Myrddin's long-stem pipe had gone out. He rubbed his thumb and forefinger together vigorously and touched the tobacco to relight it.

"What happened then?" she wondered. The Magus rarely talked about his past.

"Let's just say Prospero's inventions couldn't compete with a flying dragon made of fire."

"What did he do when he lost?"

Myrddin blew a perfect ring of smoke. "He called me a fraud. I am willing to concede that perhaps he had a point. After all, the dragon wasn't real. Then again, if I had conjured a real dragon, it would have torn apart half of Europe by now. But those people wanted to believe it was real because man craves something greater than material conveniences."

"Why? Aside from the model volcano, his inventions improved their lives. Yours provided a brief entertainment."

"More than entertainment, I should think," Myrddin said, indignant. "Mine inspired wonder. That's what magic does, you see. It didn't matter whether the dragon was real. Science may improve man's lot in life but will rob him of awe. The awe Adam and Eve felt when they first looked up at the sky, saw the sun, and mistook it for God. If all the mysteries of the universe are explained, what use will the children of Adam have for God? The sun, after all, is just the sun."

Marie finished sharpening Artemis and examined the sword's shimmering length with satisfaction. It served her well in her fight with Don Jorge. She had a feeling she'd be using it again in the near future. Next time she faced a skilled opponent, she'd know what to do.

When the scientists returned, now talking excitedly about the stabilizing, incombustible properties of salt, she looked at Taddeo in a different light. They were from different worlds, true, but she now found herself more open to understanding his. She lived in a very physical world; she'd never heard men talk so much. She also lived in a very ignorant world.

As she began to listen to what they were actually saying, his world opened up to her. When she overhead Taddeo talking about steam combustion, the manufacture of blown glass, and how to distill stale pee to make ammonia, she felt a strange yearning. When she watched him turn a cask of seawater into pure table salt through fractional distillation, it awakened a sense of curiosity she hadn't known she had. Wasn't this what Myrddin meant when he spoke of wonder?

Over the next few weeks, the scientists whittled down their list of hypotheses.

Marie sat with Myrddin. "They're failing. What are we going to do?"

"Probably be tortured and executed," he said. "That was just my first thought."

"Can't you do something?"

"I'm a thaumaturge, not a metallurgist. This form of alchemy is impossible even for magic. I can convince everyone they're seeing gold, but as soon as the Spanish change its form—melt it down into coin at the mint—the truth will be exposed." He paused. "You know, we could just leave."

"Leave?"

"Disappear in a puff of smoke and emerge from the ether anywhere you like. If you like cities, we could try London. Krakow. Paris. I've always wanted to see Mecca myself."

"I can't leave," she said. "I'd never be able to return. I swore an oath to the Emperor. He's my sovereign now."

Marie also didn't like the idea of leaving Taddeo and Prospero to Gattinara's tender mercies.

"Well, then, I suppose that settles it," the Magus said. "Our fate is in your hands."

"Do you believe in fate, Magus? That some things are meant to be?"

"It's an interesting question. Quite possibly another case of illusion being indistinguishable from reality. Are you hoping God has planned for us to get out of this mess?"

"Sometimes, I feel like providence brought us into the company of these scientists."

"I believe every enjoyable thing that happens to you appears meant to be when viewed in hindsight. But I shall think on it."

With that, the Magus crossed his legs, rested his hands on his knees with the tips of his index fingers touching the pads of his thumbs, and entered one of his trances. She knew further conversation with him would be impossible at this point. He was "working."

It was time for her to get to work as well. She stood and crossed the room to where Prospero and Taddeo sat staring at the wall with its crossed-out hypotheses reminding them of their failure. Their silence was worse than their noise.

"Gentlemen," she said. "Have you answered your question?"

Taddeo surveyed the inorganic acids arrayed in front of him in stoppered bottles, the result of endless hard work, and shook his head in intellectual despair.

"I will think of something," Prospero said, stroking his goatee.

"Maybe you should start thinking about faking it. Illusion."

Prospero put his hand over his chest. "Such a thing is beneath a real—"

Taddeo scratched his head. "It's possible, Doctor. Maybe we could get our hands on some electrum, a silver-gold alloy that appears to the naked eye as silver. Dip it in diluted nitric acid, and the silver will dissolve, leaving the gold."

"Similarly, silver could be extracted from silver-rich lead ore," Prospero chimed in. "Real gold, in some cases, from pyrite. We could also forge a rod that is half gold and half iron, paint it black, and dip into a solution that dissolves the paint, revealing the gold. Very easy."

"None of this helps us," Taddeo said. He gestured toward a nearby chest filled with lead rods. "*Signore* Gattinara expects all this to be converted into gold. Mass production."

"Then the game is finished," Prospero said. He looked at Myrddin, who had interrupted his meditation to saunter over to one of the furnaces, pull up the back of his cloak, and warm his arse. "Look at him. For two months, he has done nothing! He has it all figured out and sits at leisure, laughing at me. It is our duel in Venice all over again!"

"Isn't there some way to make Gattinara happy?" Marie wondered.

The scientist stabbed the air with his finger. "Eureka! That is it!"

Taddeo stared at him. "What, Doctor?"

"We will make him happy." Prospero's face lit up as he called out to Myrddin, "Do you hear that, you big phony? We will shower the man with so many incredible inventions he will have no choice but to be happy! What do you think of this, you old fraud?"

Myrddin cupped a hand to his ear. "Eh?"

"I said it is like Venice all over again! A rematch!"

The Magus waved as if to say, *fine, fine.*

"Taddeo, to work!"

Several days later, they heard the sharp tap of a cane accompanied by the tramp of booted feet. The Grand Chancellor and his guard had come. Marie washed her face and buckled her sword onto her hip. If the man attempted to arrest the Magus, she would defend him. As for the scientists, she felt conflicted. She didn't want to see them come to any harm, but she'd sworn an oath of loyal service to the Emperor, and Gattinara was his agent.

The old man entered wearing the simar of a cardinal of the Holy Roman Catholic Church—a black cassock with scarlet piping, shoulder cape, silk sash tied around the waist, and skullcap. His personal guard, dressed smartly in new black and red uniforms, formed a line against the wall behind him as he approached Prospero and Myrddin.

Taddeo bent his knee and kissed Gattinara's gold ring. "Your Eminence."

"I gather the peace negotiations went well," observed the Magus.

Cardinal Gattinara smiled like an old hawk with a belly full of field mice. "The Pope was most agreeable to our terms. He will trouble us no more with aspirations of becoming another Caesar. There is no Caesar other than His Catholic Majesty, Charles V, who is answerable only to God. Besides that, he ceded to us Modena, Parma, Piacenza, and Civitavecchia. And, you may have noticed, I got made a cardinal."

"Congratulations, Eminence," Prospero said, doing his best to play the toady. "Let us raise a toast to your stunning diplomatic victory." He handed him a slim glass, filled with brandy from the still, and watched him toss it back.

"Delicious." The smile vanished as neatly as cleaning a slate. "Now show me the gold."

Prospero presented Greek fire, a combustible compound used for thousands of years to set fire to enemy ships in naval warfare.

"Interesting that you should rediscover the lost recipe, but it is quite obsolete nowadays."

"Ah, yes, but this Greek fire burns a bright, sizzling green. It will strike terror into the hearts of your enemies! May I demonstrate, Your Eminence?"

"Certainly not. You'll burn the place down."

"Then allow me to demonstrate a superior analgesic. Most aspirin, made from the bark and leaves of the willow, requires a large quantity to be consumed, which can be upsetting to the stomach. We have synthesized a purer form of the drug, which makes it much more efficacious."

"My explicit instruction was to make gold, not cure headaches."

"Then perhaps His Eminence might find my cures to other common afflictions interesting." He swept his hand over a series of bottles filled with white powder. "This one is an antacid, ideal for relieving a burning gullet. This one prevents skin ailments from taking hold when one wears the same set of clothes every day. This one—"

"Where is my gold?" Gattinara snapped.

Prospero wiped flop sweat from his brow. "I could make you an underwater boat that can sneak up and place mines on enemy vessels. A hot air balloon from which your soldiers can drop bombs or observe positions. A—"

"Stop," the Chancellor said. He pinched the bridge of his nose. "Just stop." He turned to Myrddin, who stood waiting patiently by a large wood chest. "What about you? Did you succeed, Magus?"

"See for yourself."

He opened the chest. Gattinara peered in. His face reddened.

"Are you jesting with me, sir?"

Marie looked inside and saw scores of lead rods.

Myrddin appeared shaken. "The alchemical process isn't stable, as it violates the natural laws. The gold must have changed back to its original form."

"Ha!" Prospero barked and crossed his arms. "We shall call this round a draw!"

The Grand Chancellor fixed them with his glare. "Need I remind you gentlemen of the Papal edict banning the fraudulent sale of alchemical services? I would hate to see this become a matter for the Tribunal of the Holy Office of the Inquisition. As an officer of the Church, I could conduct the questioning myself here and now, assisted by your own equipment."

They shuddered at the idea. The Spanish branch of the Inquisition in Europe had been established fifty years earlier in response to reports of Jews professing to be Christian so as to remain in the country, but secretly practicing their faith. Soon, tribunals flourished in cities across Spain. The Inquisitors tortured suspects to gain confessions, seized property, and burned people alive. The Inquisition had spent its energy in most of Europe, but here in Spain, it was still alive and kicking.

Gattinara added, "I have made a considerable investment in you, however. I will give you one more chance. You have one week to make good on your promises. Do or die."

After the cardinal and his guard filed out of the room, Prospero grabbed the bottle of brandy and went into a corner to sulk. Taddeo sat by the furnaces and cracked open Bolos of Mendes's *Physika kai Mystika*, a practical guide to alchemy.

Marie looked at Myrddin. His face had turned the color of ash. "What happened?"

"Prospero wanted to see lead more than Gattinara wanted to see gold. His skepticism destroyed the illusion." He eyed Prospero with something like respect. "Remarkable."

"I'll be back soon," she told him.

She entered the street in time to see Cardinal Gattinara and his troop turn the corner. The streets had emptied as night approached. She ran to the corner and watched them march away. For a man with a cane, he was pretty spry. As she suspected, the Chancellor was returning to the basilica. If he reported to Charles, he might reveal what he planned to do with them if they failed. If he intended to do what he threatened, they'd have to make a run for it. Maybe Mecca wasn't such a bad idea after all. If Gattinara wanted to kill them, nowhere in Christendom would be safe.

Marie counted the seconds as the pacing guards crossed paths. Relying on her training as a ninja, she sneaked past with ease and returned to invisibility in the shadows. Inside, she heard the babble of conversation and musicians playing a *pavan*. Most of the great hall of the basilica stood dark and empty; a small party was being held in the nave at its center. She hugged the wall and waited for a bored guard to pass then tiptoed to the nearest column for a better look. Several dozen lords and ladies mingled in the space, drinking wine, dining from a buffet, and talking politics. Charles stood near the center of the room and listened politely as Francisco Pizarro regaled him with some violent tale of the New World, miming frantic sword thrusts. As she'd hoped, Gattinara approached and said something near the Imperial ear, but she couldn't hear what he was saying. They left Pizarro in the act of slaughtering his imaginary *Indios*. Then a bloated courtier in Imperial livery blocked her view, cocked his leg, and farted pure brimstone.

Marie left her vantage point and raced toward the rear of the building. She slipped outside into the garden and burrowed in the carnations just as Gattinara appeared with the Emperor. As she'd suspected, he was making his report on the alchemists.

"If they fail, I will add the girl to my guard," the Chancellor said. "The Magus will be turned over to the Inquisition on charges of practicing black magic. I haven't decided about the scientist and the boy yet. The boy shows promise."

Charles received this information with an impassive expression, his hands clasped behind his back. "We would much rather have additional funds in the public purse."

"If it doesn't work, I'll find another way. *Plus Ultra.*"

"If we do not replenish our coffers, we will be forced to conclude the war in Italy, and we will be no closer to our goal. The last time we did not pay an army, it sacked Rome. We would be most pleased if your alchemists persevered, as we could continue the war indefinitely."

"*Dominium Mundi*," the cardinal nodded. "With an endless treasury, all it would take is time to unite the peoples of the world under one monarch."

"Then we would wish that you make it so, Grand Chancellor," Charles said, stiff and droll as ever. "To that goal, we are quite dedicated."

Lying on her side among the plants, Marie thought about what Gattinara said. He wanted to offer her a position in his personal guard! Fine red and black livery, two squares a day, a roof over her head, and a chance to do what she did best for a man to whom she'd sworn eternal loyalty. In all her life, failure had never yielded so great a reward.

The two men talked about other matters, including the military situation in Italy, the potential loss of Naples, and whether it was time to crush the heretic Martin Luther and his followers. Gattinara told the Emperor the Pope had grown a beard in protest of the sack of Rome two years earlier, a most unseemly gesture for the pontiff, as canonical law forbade the clergy to allow their facial hair to grow. After that, Marie fell asleep.

When she awoke, she found herself alone. She stretched and re-entered the building, which stood empty except for a few weak fires burning in braziers mounted on the columns.

"Hey! Halt!"

Marie wheeled, hand on the hilt of her sword, as the guard jogged toward her with his halberd extended toward her middle. One thrust, and she was as good as dead.

"You're not supposed to be in here," he said. "You're under arrest."

"I like your hat," she said. "Those black plumes are lovely."

He grunted. "You're a woman."

She unsheathed Artemis. "I'll fight you for them."

Later that night, she entered the workshop, where she found the Magus sleeping on a bench by the furnaces with Leo sprawled across his chest. Prospero was nowhere in sight. Taddeo stood at one of the tables before a collection of equipment. Wielding tongs with leather mittens, he poured a stream of molten gold into a crucible.

"Is that gold?" She clapped. "Taddeo, you did it!"

Taddeo turned bright red and nearly dropped the crucible. "Illusion," he croaked.

"It's not gold?"

He nodded then shook his head. "It's some of the coin we raised before coming here," he managed. "We'll tell Gattinara we produced it. But it will be in such a small quantity that its value will be less than that of the lead from whence it was extracted."

"So you prove you can produce gold from lead, but it won't be worthwhile for Gattinara to have you do it. That's really smart, Taddeo."

Taddeo stammered for a while, shredding a simple thank-you before adding, "We'll tell the Grand Chancellor it was a joint effort. We'll all be set free."

Marie smiled. "That's very sweet of you. Thank you."

He clenched his eyes shut and whispered, "You're welcome."

By the time he opened his eyes, she was gone.

Slipping back out the front door, Marie recalled Cardinal Gattinara and the Emperor plotting their world empire in the basilica gardens, the key to which was gold in limitless quantities to field vast armies of Spanish arquebusiers, German *Landsknechte*—feared mercenaries recruited from Imperial territories in central Europe—and Italian *Condottiere* in a perpetual war. The Chancellor would not be deterred by Taddeo's ruse, she believed.

Myrddin would be forced to flee to escape the Inquisition, and once he got wherever he was going, he'd have to find and train a new bodyguard. Knowing him, he wouldn't mind either terribly.

The Magus had lived a very long time, possessed simple needs, and could escape life-threatening jams simply by disappearing; he'd learned to take everything in stride.

No, Myrddin Wyllt would land on his feet no matter what happened.

The main problem was Taddeo and Prospero. The idea of them coming to harm agonized her far more than she thought it should. So much so, in fact, that she decided to embark on a desperate course of action that might cost her everything.

Prospero sat on the temple steps with his back against a chipped column, gazing up at the moon.

"*Buonasera, bella*," he called. *Good night, beautiful.* "And where are you off to this fine night?"

"Taddeo has come up with a ruse to convince Gattinara to let you go."

"Ha! That is my Taddeo!"

"But it's not enough. Gattinara won't be satisfied."

"*Merda.* So it is true. We are finished."

"Not quite. I'll be back soon."

"What are you planning?"

Marie took a deep breath and said, "I'm going to rob travelers until I come up with enough gold to satisfy the cardinal. Just in case he doesn't buy the ruse. Then Gattinara won't kill us."

"Bravo!" The scientist clapped. "I wish Taddeo had such warrior spirit. You are not just a pretty face, are you? But why should you do such a thing for me?"

"I'm doing it for all of us. We're all in trouble."

"Tush," the scientist said. "I am hard on the man, but I know what Myrddin Wyllt can do. If he wanted, he could turn you into a little bird, and you both could fly away to Africa. So why?"

Marie said nothing. The question made her feel strange.

"Ah, *bella*. Do not be ashamed. It is a natural thing."

"Tell me," she said. She wanted to hear him say it.

"You are in love with me."

"No!" she cried. "Do you jest?"

"Okay, you are in love with Taddeo."

And she was. She realized it now. She felt an attraction to Taddeo as steady and true as the miraculous compass he showed her. Over the past two months, her heart had undergone a transformation as strange as alchemy. He could barely talk to her, but he had won her over, starting with telling her his passionate dreams of a future powered by electric fire.

Taddeo was handsome, though looks had almost nothing to do with what she felt. His mind was the most beautiful thing she'd ever connected with. Unlike every other man she'd ever met, Taddeo Cellini was kind, gentle, and brilliant.

It was all terribly confusing. The process of change was filled with turmoil, and she'd often seen herself reflected in the hapless ore boiling in the furnaces, experiencing the pain and pleasure of transformation. Was this love? She'd never felt this way before about a man. The more she changed, the less complete she felt. Now she couldn't do without him. If that meant giving up a position in Gattinara's personal guard, so be it.

"What if he doesn't love me?" she asked. Instead of her realization liberating her joy, she felt miserable. "He loves science."

"Of course he loves you. Look at you."

"When I first met him, he asked me who I was, and I ran from him. I ran because I may look like something to a man, but I'm really nothing. I don't think great thoughts. I can't even read."

"Taddeo is a prodigy, but he is still just a man. Men have a higher threshold for pain than women, but not as much endurance. If he loves you, he will not be able to hold onto it for very long. He will come around even though it feels impossible to you now. His shyness is not the problem; the cause of his shyness is the problem, see?"

"What is it?" she said with flash of jealousy. "Does he have a lover back home?"

"Ha! Sadly, no, *bella*. What he has is a very strong father who wants his son to be just like him. Here is a boy who wants to be free to learn and dream and create while his father, whom he worships, tells him he has to be something else. He is under a great deal of pressure to live up to the family name, understand?"

"Not really," Marie said, who was essentially an orphan. But she did know something about trying to impress the man who'd raised her.

"So you want to save him. Go then. Go rob some poor fools and take their gold, if you think it will help him. As for me, you need not worry yourself. I am like a cat. I always land on my feet."

"Maybe you should worry a little more."

"Bah! I will think of something."

"Do it soon. The cardinal is thinking about turning you over to the Inquisitors."

"But not today. Today, I have a warm, dry place to sleep and good food to eat, and I am alive and well. Today is all that matters. Tomorrow will take care of itself. Who knows? Perhaps you will rob the richest man in Spain and secure my reputation as the greatest alchemist in the world!"

Marie stared at him. "Why are you here? What do you want, Prospero?"

"I want to make something happen. That is always what I want."

It rang true to her. "I want the same thing." She chewed her lip. "I really, really want to do something. I just don't know what it is I want to do."

"We are passionate people. We have this in common. Kindred spirits, eh?"

She snorted. "Let's not get crazy—"

She whirled and caught the dart before it struck her throat.

Another buzzing sound like a mosquito. Prospero stiffened, a dart in his chest.

"*Così sia*," he gasped before collapsing into a heap and rolling down the steps.

She had to get back inside and warn Taddeo.

Then she noticed the second dart protruding from her shoulder.

"God's Wounds," she swore. Her vision swam.

Marie fell as brown half-naked figures emerged from the dark.

France

Chapter VI

A Royal Hunt

Marie awoke with a splitting headache in a drafty carriage that thundered across the countryside. Her captors had bound her wrists tight with rope. Prospero snored next to her with his head resting on her lap. She nudged him awake.

The scientist took in his surroundings. "Fie! Kidnapped!"

She glared at him. "Did you arrange this?"

"Of course I did not," he huffed. "What an outrageous accusation."

"It just seems like something you would do to get out of trouble."

"I cannot think of everything," he said with a frown. "Where is Taddeo?"

"I don't know. Maybe they didn't take him."

Prospero yawned and rubbed his face. "Well. In that case, I hope he figures out how to make gold, or his goose is cooked."

The horses shrieked. The carriage came to a shuddering halt. Marie heard heavy footfalls on the roof. Her captors chattered in a strange language. She reached for her sword, but her scabbard was empty.

The door opened. A brown face with glittering black eyes and a nose ring leered at them. Then it disappeared.

"Okay, that was odd," Marie said.

Prospero gasped. "An *Indio*! Are we across the sea, in New Spain? How is this possible?"

"I think he wants us to follow him."

Prospero sat up. "I know what you are thinking." He continued in falsetto, "'Oh, I would love to retrieve my sword and hack my way to precious freedom!'" He wagged his finger. "Do not entertain such notions until we have all the facts, *va bene*?"

Her eyes narrowed. "We'll see."

"I am quite serious, *bella*. No heroics. I will go first. Follow my lead. I know how to handle the noble savage. He is easily awed by a man of science."

Her leg had fallen asleep and now prickled with the sensation of pins and needles. She massaged it. Then she stepped out of the carriage and found her captors kneeling at Prospero's feet. They crossed themselves and kissed the crucifixes they wore around their necks.

"See?" the scientist said. "I have this situation well in hand!"

Marie counted five of them. She'd never seen an *Indio* this close. She gaped at their fantastic brown skin, long sinewy bodies, and shiny black hair. Half naked, they wore loincloths, seashell necklaces, armlets, and bits and pieces of European clothing—a doublet here, leggings there, even a codpiece. One of them had Artemis thrust into his girdle. They gazed up at Prospero and muttered in their strange tongue.

"Now observe," he said to Marie and added in a booming voice, "I command you to release us!"

The *Indios* grinned like wolves. One of them stood, bowed, and slapped Prospero on the back of the head.

"Occam's Razor!" he swore. "Was this needed?"

"Maybe that's part of their Prospero worship," Marie said dryly. "It's fitting, isn't it?"

"I do not like what you are implying, *bella*. I do not like it one bit."

One of the horses fell heavily to the ground, pulling its mate on top of it in a pile of flailing legs and hoofs. The others panted and trembled. They'd been ridden too hard and were blown. The *Indios* cut the throats of the fallen animals with knives and bent to drink the blood. After setting the remaining horses free with swats on the rump and sharp cries, two of the *Indios* ran off across the fields toward a distant farm while the rest slaughtered the carcasses for meat and piled fallen timber to start a fire.

"Bloody savages," he muttered as he emptied his bladder noisily against a carriage wheel. "Their mental processes are quite alien to us."

"I think we're still in Europe," she said. "In fact, I know those mountains. If I'm not mistaken, we're in eastern Spain, close to the border with France."

"We must have slept for days. No wonder I am starving."

"I hope you're hungry enough to eat a horse, my lord. Because I think that's what we're having for dinner."

"I like this new thing you are doing," he said with a grin. "Calling me a lord. This too is fitting for Prospero worship."

The *Indios* started their fire. They rubbed slabs of raw horseflesh with handfuls of dried herbs and dropped them into an iron skillet. Marie's mouth watered at the scent of frying meat. Slapping their chests with loud cries, the men took turns standing and pointing at Prospero and Marie, miming shooting them with darts from imaginary blowpipes.

"Har, har," Prospero said while Marie fumed. "It was hardly a fair fight, no?" He pointed at the horse meat. "By the by, I shall not eat such fare. It is beneath me. As your god, I command you to find something edible for my table."

One of the men mimed a slap. "*Pow*," he hissed.

The scientist shrugged. "All right, I shall try it." He accepted a steaming slab of steak, juggled it for a few moments to cool it off, and took a bite. "Hey, this is good!"

Marie tore into her own meal with her teeth. It *was* good. The herbs gave the meat a spicy, tangy flavor. She glanced at the man wearing her sword and narrowed her eyes as she chewed. *Soon*, she thought. *You will give her back to me very soon.*

The *Indios* who'd left earlier returned leading horses. They motioned for Prospero and Marie to mount one and doubled up on the rest. They rode for days, the men chanting songs from their homeland all the while. Marie didn't know their language, but the concepts were clear and universal. They sang about that which young men had sung throughout the ages: fighting and women. They sang about home. Marie sang an old French song about a girl who misses her lover who has gone off on one of the Crusades; she dies of homesickness in her own bed, in her own house, because her lover is her true home. The *Indios* wiped their eyes at the end while Marie thought of Taddeo with an aching heart.

Is he safe and well? she wondered. Gattinara seemed to like him; perhaps the Chancellor would find another job for him. Most likely, Taddeo was hard at work on some brilliant invention, happy to be immersed in his beloved science, and had already forgotten about her.

She couldn't bear to think about the alternative. That Gattinara had ordered him killed.

As for Myrddin, where was he right now? Astonishing the Muslims in Mecca? A small part of Marie hoped he would come for her. She missed him almost as much as she did Taddeo. Perhaps they'd teamed up and were even now in hot pursuit to rescue her! She hated herself for thinking such a thing. Some ideas, once conceived, could not be taken back and instead planted false seeds of hope. Hope she had no right to have.

No, like it or not, she was stuck with Prospero and these strange *Indios*, at least until she found opportunity to escape. Then she could return to Valladolid, reunite with Taddeo if he was still there, and attend a career in Gattinara's guard.

They crossed into France and halted at the ruins of an old monastery perched on a hill overlooking a walled town. In the distance, the vast blue waters of the Mediterranean Sea glittered in the morning sunlight.

She knew the town. Narbonne. It had once been a prosperous center for trade, education, and culture, but the River Aude changed course and the gradual silting along the shoreline ended its fortunes as a competitive port. The Black Plague and warfare had taken further toll. The town had bounced back in recent years, but like most towns, it was struggling.

It felt good to be back on French soil. Perhaps she'd go north if she escaped, not south. North to her village to find her mother.

They dismounted and stretched their legs. Marie tilted her head and closed her eyes. She felt the warm sun on her face. She listened to the birds sing in the trees. Prospero sat on a bed of moss, his back against a stone wall, and gnawed on heavily salted horseflesh.

Marie confronted the *Indios*. "Now what?"

They grinned and motioned for her to sit. Wait.

Prospero smacked his lips. "This is really quite good."

Marie paced in front of him. "You know, you could try taking this more seriously."

He looked up at her with bulging cheeks. "What do you want me to do?"

"You're a genius. Think of a way out of this!"

"Why? They obviously want us alive. They are feeding us. See?"

"We're their prisoners, Prospero. You could be a little more worried."

"You and Taddeo, always worrying. *Basta*. Look, I am alive and my belly is full. They have not molested us in any way. That is enough. Personally, I am curious who has gone through this trouble of abducting us from under the Emperor's nose."

Marie looked out across the shimmering blue water. "Of course I worry. I worry about everything. I want a future." She frowned in sudden anger. "You don't understand. You don't value your life as much because you've lived a long time."

"On the contrary, I have little time left, so every moment is precious to me. And I refuse to waste a single moment on worry."

"I haven't done anything yet," she confessed. "I'm not ready to die. I haven't really lived."

"You have already done more than most. I will tell you a little secret about me. When I was young, I played by the rules. I did everything they told me to get ahead. And I got ruined for it. Exiled from my home. My brother, Michelangelo, bucked the rules at every chance and got away with it. He told the Pope himself to go to hell, and you know what happened? He is now called *Il Divino*. How is this fair? Now I say to hell with all of it. None of it matters."

"What happened to you, Prospero? Why were you banished?"

The scientist flung the piece of meat on the grass and wiped his greasy hands on his trousers. "Fine, I will tell you the story. I will tell you how Piero di Lorenzo Medici, ruler of Florence, became Piero the Unfortunate, and Prospero became Prospero the nothing."

It was the first of the Italian Wars.

In 1494, Ludovico Sforza rose to become duke of Milan, a city dominating the rich northern Lombardy region of Italy. Alfonso II of Naples claimed Milan for himself. Ludovico invited Charles VIII, the king of France who had a thin claim to the throne of Naples, to invade. Charles assembled an army of twenty-five thousand men and marched across the Alps.

"The French passed through Italy as a knife through butter," the scientist said as he untied one of his shoelaces and set it on the moss in front of him. "One by one, the great city states declared their neutrality and allowed Charles VIII and his army to march south unmolested. As he entered Tuscany and neared Florence, Piero did the same. But Charles coveted Piero's castles in Tuscany to ensure his supply line back to France."

When the King of France showed up with his army, Piero called his counselors together and asked for advice.

He had the benefit of the sage counsel of Niccolò Machiavelli, who at the time was mentoring a brilliant, upcoming courtier named Prospero Buonarroti, son of a modest banker. At a young age, Prospero understood the game of power and how to play it—that power was its own end, the ends justified the means, and morality had been invented to keep the little people in line, not check the unsavory prerogatives of the rich and powerful. Prospero would later inspire Machiavelli to pen *The Prince* as much as the ruthless Medicis.

Prospero told Piero he had to offer battle and make it look good, even if it meant certain destruction of his army, as without it he would lose face, and the people would lose faith in his leadership. Piero said he couldn't stomach the needless waste of life for a lost cause, meaning he thought if he fought and lost, he would lose even more prestige. Machiavelli hemmed and hawed and played both sides, but Piero had already made up his mind. As the French neared Florence, he surrendered his castles to Charles VIII in exchange for guarantees of security.

"As I predicted, the people rose up in rage," Prospero went on as he tore a leather elbow patch from his doublet and put it next to his shoelace. "Piero had reduced Florence without a single drop of French blood being spilled. The mob chased the Medicis out of the city and sacked their palaces. As one of Piero's courtiers, I shared the same fate. We ended up in Venice, where Piero wasted no time blaming his failure on bad counsel, forever sullying my reputation. Not Machiavelli, mind you—he came out smelling like a honeyed peach, as always. And so I foreswore princes and kings and became a citizen of the world. It has done well for me all this time, so why should I worry now what will come?"

"What happened after that?" Marie asked. "Did the French take Naples?"

Prospero paused in his sharpening of a stone to gaze up at her with a frown. "I tell you my life story—from *here*," he pounded his chest, "and this is what you want to know? Who won the war? The pointless war that accomplished nothing just like every other idiotic war?" He waved his hand. "Do not answer that. Charles VIII took Naples as easily as he cowed Florence, sacked it, and started home. Now the city states finally discovered their testes and formed the League of Venice, raising an army that beat the French and ended the war. Spain invaded Naples to remove the French garrison and restore Alphonso II, and you know the rest of the story. The *idioti* have been fighting each other ever since, an irresistible wind pushing an immovable object forever and ever *ad nauseum*."

"What about Piero? Can you tell me what happened to him?"

"Ha! He wound up fighting for his new masters, the French,

and died fleeing a battle. He drowned in a river. God is great!" He hammered small holes into the leather patch with a rock and a small nail worked from the bottom of his shoe, and widened them with his sharpened stone. "So much French blood has been spilled on Italian soil, our wines taste like it. Listen. You told me you do not yet know what you want to make happen. I do. I want to create. That is all I want to do. Look what trying to control my fate did for me. Look what it earned Piero. To hell with it all! Just let me create."

"I know what I want," Marie said, struck by the realization. "I want to serve a cause bigger than myself. I want to change the world for the better."

"Aargh!" Prospero smacked his forehead with his palm. "Like Taddeo the idealist! Were you not listening to even one of my words?" He sighed. "Well, go ahead and do that then. It suits you." He finished threading his shoelace through the leather patch, knotted it, and handed it to her. "There. You wish to fight for our freedom, no? *Così sia*. Now you have a sling with which to throw stones at the *Indios* at range and kill them. Or perhaps you could strangle them with it, I care not which. Me, I will use this stone to cut our bonds."

The ground trembled. The *Indios* hooted and pointed at a distant dust cloud that rapidly grew larger. A muffled roar filled the air around them.

"I believe the mystery of our abduction is about to be solved," the scientist said as he freed their hands. "If you would liberate us, now would be splendid timing."

Marie handed the sling back to him. "I will abide. I guess I'm curious too."

He frowned. "You say this now? You could have said it sooner and saved me the trouble. I have ruined my doublet. See?"

Marie gaped at the approaching horde glimpsed through a rising wall of dust. Thousands of carriages and horsemen rode pell mell down the road, led by a single laughing rider. It was an astonishing sight; there must have been twenty thousand horses in the frantic endless train.

The horde swerved off the road and came to a crashing halt at the bottom of the hill. Horses reared and threw their riders. Carriages flipped and spilled luggage and howling men. A giant cloud of flour billowed upward. Women screamed from the vehicles in the rear. Flags and pennants waved and fell. The rest of the procession came to a weary stop. Men and horses panted and coughed in the dust. The wounded wailed in pain where they lay. Their leader galloped up the hill on his charger, beaming back at them while waving his feathered hat.

"Ha ha ha ha! We win the race!"

The man reached the top of the hill and flung himself from the saddle to strike a pose upon landing. Several heralds in blue and white livery dragged themselves broken and bleeding from the ground and toiled up after him.

"*Bon jour!*" the man called to Prospero and Marie. "We are most—"

He flinched as the heralds blared a ragged fanfare with their brass trumpets.

"*Dio Mio,*" Prospero said. "It is the King of France."

"In the flesh!" cried Francis I. He swaggered up to one of the *Indios*, popped a bon bon in the man's mouth, and patted his head. "Our savages are wonderful, are they not?"

Marie couldn't believe her eyes. Another great king of Christendom! Young like his rivals Charles V and Henry VIII, slim and athletic from constant tennis and hunting, Francis I could be considered strikingly handsome but for his long, large nose, which led some people to say he resembled the Devil.

"They are Caribs," Francis added. "An island people and most warlike. They eat their slain enemies! Ah, a purer life, for sure, free of the cares of State. We have often wondered what it would be like to live as a simple savage, maybe even a pirate."

"Your Grace," Prospero said in perfect French. "It is most—"

"Your Majesty," Francis corrected him coldly, his good humor vanished.

"You use the honorific of the Holy Roman Emperor?"

"We are the rightful Emperor, not Samson!" the king exploded. "He only got to be emperor because he had a bigger bank than ours for bribing the Electors! It was our crown, and he took it from us!" His rage passed as quickly as it had come, and he grinned while splaying his hand in front of his face to make his chin seem bigger. "We call him Samson because he has the jawbone of an ass! *Comprenez-vous?*"

"Delightful, Your Majesty," Prospero said.

"We defeated Henry VIII in a wrestling match, did you not know this? At our conference at the Field of the Cloth of Gold. What a party that was! We would have accepted Charles's challenge to personal combat and defeated him too, but that would mean stealing all the glory from France." He pointed to the horizon. "See, there! France is marching to glory!"

A long snaking column of men and horses, bristling with pikes and lances, choked the road heading east to Lombardy. An endless train of people, wagons, and baggage followed them—barber-surgeons, cooks, bakers, quartermasters, peddlers, pilgrims, and ladies-for-hire. After crossing the Alps, they would join the war against the Empire, which now hung in the balance. The Genoese admiral Andrea Doria had switched sides and pushed the French garrison out of Genoa. Imperial troops menaced Milan. In southern Italy, the French were close to capturing Naples despite an outbreak of plague and the treacherous Doria's removal of his naval blockade.

This fresh army would put Genoa in its place and retain Milan. It would strike a decisive blow for France.

"Are they not magnificent?" the king said.

"A truly inspiring vision of national strength," Prospero said, in full toadying mode.

Marie counted flags. She estimated the force to be about twenty-five thousand men. If she could escape, this would be valuable information for the Empire.

The French court, meanwhile, dusted itself off, licked its wounds, and began erecting a city of tents around the base of the hill. The din of shouting men, hammered pegs, and groaning carriages was deafening. Penants fluttered in the breeze. Surrounded by his fierce nobles, Chancellor Antoine Duprat, falconer, astrologer, treasurer, heralds, and other minions, Francis elbowed a retainer out of the way and strutted closer to Prospero and Marie.

"So you are the great spellbinder of which we have heard so much," the king said as he gave Prospero a thorough once over. "The man who wins all of Charles's battles for him." He sounded puzzled, as if he had expected someone more august. "You are the one called the Magus, no?"

"So that's why the Caribs were worshipping you," Marie muttered.

Prospero scowled. "I beg your pardon, Your Majesty. But I am not Myrddin Wyllt. I am Prospero Buonarroti of Venice." He added with a flourish, "At your service!"

"*Imbéciles!*" roared Francis, reddening. His court took a careful step away from him. He glared at the Caribs. "You brought us the wrong man!" The Caribs shrugged.

"Your Majesty," Prospero said. "Beg pardon, but these noble savages did not err. Their unfettered instinct discovered a true treasure for you, for I am a great scientist."

"A scientist, eh? So? Feh! The universities are full of such men."

Prospero grit his teeth. "I am the younger brother of the great Michelangelo."

"Why did you not say this at the outset?" cried Francis. "You have deceived us! And how fares the Divine One?"

"He is in Florence, building lavish tombs for aristocrats."

"A most excellent commission! Prospero, we would welcome you. We are a collector of great men, you see. All are welcome in the shining tent of my patronage. Musicians, dancers, singers, poets, painters, architects, and philosophers."

"I am all those things and more," Prospero said. "A real bargain."

"We are a bit of all these things as well." The king now gazed upon Prospero as a kindred spirit. *Which they are,* Marie thought. *Two overgrown children.* "We know your name from somewhere.

Ah! The inventor of the clear glass mirror, no?"

"Your Majesty is well informed," Prospero grated. "But I have invented many—"

"We use ours all the time! Surely, the most glorious invention of the age!"

Prospero opened his mouth but, expending great effort, wisely closed it.

"All learned men are welcome into the favor of the Crown," the king said. "We nourish as well as extinguish. So tell us what a Florentine from Venice is doing in Samson's service, since both these states are treasured allies of France in this holiest of wars."

"Alchemy, I am afraid, and very much against my will. I said to him, 'I am very sorry for you, but it cannot be done.' But he insisted. I am a great man, but he is greater. I was pining for freedom in my workshop when your men rescued me from that droll, unhappy existence. I was like a plant yearning for the sun and found it in your august—"

"*Oui, oui.* And what is the Magus doing for him?"

"The same, Your Majesty." Prospero added smugly, "But he made no progress either. Alchemy is a fool's dream, like the Kingdom of Prester John. It cannot be done."

"Alchemy! What a joke! Ha, ha, ha! That can only mean one thing. Samson is running out of money." The king appeared to notice Marie for the first time. "God in Heaven. And who is this ravishing creature who transforms my leaden spirit to golden joy?"

"May I present the *gentildonna* Marie Dubois," Prospero announced.

Marie bent her knee. "Your Majesty. I am most—"

"Ah, you are French! Rise, girl, so we may recognize you. Mmmm," he crowed, eyeing her heel to head. "*Enchanté.* We have decided that you please us." He took her hands in his and kissed her fingertips, his eyes going moony. "We hope you will forgive us for the rude manner in which we invited you here."

Marie blinked. "Um. It's okay—"

"Okay. Okay. It is okay!" He laughed and clapped his hands. His courtiers stiffened to attention. "We will go hunting with our new friends! Then, tonight, we wish a ball. We wish a ball to be held right down there in that field, under the stars. Make it so!"

"We are in luck," Prospero hissed at Marie while hundreds of retainers dropped what they were doing and scrambled to the preparations.

Marie walked over to one of the Caribs and held out her hand. "I want my sword back."

The *Indio* scowled and glanced at Francis, who motioned for him to give it to her.

"A woman who fights like a man," laughed the king. "Such is the *Renaissance*! Modern times, eh? You are like our Joan d'Arc, the Maid of Orléans." He eyed her with open lust and said gravely, "Similarly, you will inspire a king and a nation."

Marie put Artemis back in its rightful scabbard. "Thank you, Your Majesty." She felt better already with its familiar weight on her hip.

The hunters gathered, hardy peasant folk clad in leather and carrying bows and heavy boar spears. Dozens of hounds flowed around their knees and bayed for blood. Pages dressed in bright livery carried cudgels with which to kill rabbits and other small game. Some held horns, which they would blow during the hunt to signal the other parties in the thick forest. The French lords and knights, looking fierce with their taciturn Gallic faces and ornate armor, had already mounted under colorful pennants. Grooms fussed over the mounts. The royal falconer appeared with his *gerfaucon* balanced on his leather-clad arm. A train of servants brought bracing cups of spiced wine for the nobles. Francis gallantly called out for the servants to tap a keg of beer for the hunters, who responded with a ragged cheer for the King.

Several grizzled senior huntsmen disappeared into the woods with specially bred scenting dogs. They returned to describe the lay of the land and tracks, droppings, broken branches, and other deer sign they'd found. The assembly divided into hunting parties.

The King, of course, chose the most promising ground for himself. Marie kept pace with Francis and his nobles while Prospero lagged in the rear on his lurching mount.

Francis's senior hunter halted once they reached a deer trail. He showed the king signs of a herd passing through and in what direction they were going. The party again waited while his dog raced about, its nose buried in the forest floor, and picked up the scent.

The dog jerked its head and barked. Prospero adjusted the binocular vision on his glasses and said, "I see deer. Red deer, to be precise. A whole herd of them."

Francis didn't wait for the dogs to be staged in relays along the path of the herd, which allowed fresh hounds to join the chase until the deer were exhausted and turned at bay. He spurred his mount and took the lead. "After them!"

The hunting party fanned out and plunged into the brush with manly shouts while the hounds clamored ahead. One of the hunters paused to give a deep, booming blast with his horn. The horsemen flew past the hunters. Marie notched an arrow in her bow. Prospero pocketed his glasses and raced after the party, riding through a cluster of branches and coming out spitting leaves.

The horse panted and trembled between Marie's legs as it galloped across the forest floor. The herd of red deer came into sight. She began to steer with her knees. The other riders were behind her now. Her horse snorted. The endless green flashed past. Then they left the trees and entered a meadow washed in bright sunlight. Snarling dogs held a stag at bay against a pile of rocks.

Marie and her horse bore down on it at the gallop. As she prepared to release, she felt struck by the majesty of the animal. The beast had a natural nobility and regal bearing greater than Charles V and Francis I put together. No wonder it was popularly believed the stag had a bone in its heart that didn't allow it to suffer fear. Then she remembered Myrddin's words: *We need to eat.*

Still she didn't release. Instead, she reined in. The kill belonged to Francis as the leader of the hunt.

The king arrived with his train and dismounted. He whistled in admiration at the number of tines in the stag's antlers. A page offered him a lance, but he shoved the boy aside, drew his sword and approached the animal at a crouch. The stag, advancing and retreating to avoid the snapping jaws of the hounds, regarded this new threat with flaring nostrils and wide black eyes.

The stag charged. Francis sidestepped and thrust his blade into its heart as it passed. The antlers caught his side and threw him to the ground with a burst of breath. The animal continued to bound away, the sword dangling from its ribs, until it collapsed with a final gasp.

The hunters hauled Francis to his feet. The nobles offered their congratulations for such a fine kill. Prospero rode up and joined Marie.

"Very good," he sighed. "He killed something. Now we can get out of this horrid wood."

"That was really fun," she told him with a grin.

"Chasing animals around trees is fun?"

"It was one of the most satisfying things I've ever done."

He snorted. "Says the virgin."

"You're an arse, Prospero. I felt truly free. It was like fighting Don Jorge all over again."

"And you almost died doing that, no? How freeing that would have been, I wonder. Similarly, the King almost freed himself from his earthly existence fighting that stag. He risked political turmoil, civil war, losing the war against the Empire—not to mention his life—for a cheap thrill."

Francis called to her, "You should not ride so reckless. You could have gotten hurt!"

"Is he serious?" she muttered before calling back, "*Oui*, Your Majesty!"

The king cleaned his bloodied sword on a page's tunic. "You should not be riding in the forest at all. It does not become you. We should like to see you in a gown tonight."

"I haven't worn a dress since I was nine. May I ask why it's important I do so now?"

"Of course!" Francis said. "Ha, ha! The answer is because it is our good pleasure."

"I don't even have a—"

"The gentle lady shall be radiant so attired, Your Majesty," Prospero cut in. "She will be the moon to your sun."

"Moon to my sun," Francis said. "Hm. We like that. May we steal it for a poem?"

"It is I who stole it, Your Majesty," Prospero toadied. "Great minds often have the same thoughts." He turned his head and muttered to Marie, "You should not have ridden in front of him. Kings are a lot like stags themselves. Very twitchy. In any case, you were not planning on attending the ball looking like that, were you?"

A ball, Marie thought with a smile. *I'm going to a ball.*

The hunters arrived panting and began the unmaking, the meticulous slaughter of the deer followed by rewarding the dogs with a share of the meat. Grooms watered the horses at a nearby stream. Servants poured wine and unwrapped loaves of bread and wedges of strong cheese. After eating her fill, Marie found Prospero sitting with his back against the trunk of a tall oak, whittling pieces of wood to make odd tiny sculptures. The carving reminded her of the Magus's staff with its little slumbering faces.

"Myrddin was once imprisoned in an oak tree just like this one," she said, running her hand along the rough bark. "He slept in its trunk for hundreds of years."

Prospero paused in his work with a frustrated sigh and glared up at her. "Seriously? Please. How is this even possible?"

Marie shrugged. "The man does magic. I guess that makes anything possible."

"Science makes everything possible. Observe."

He assembled the tiny wood pieces together into a whistle and blew into it. The whistle produced a loud fart. He took it apart and tuned the wood with his knife. After several tries, it sounded: *Aaaaank, aaaaank, aaaaank!*

At the sound, the hunting party stiffened and grew quiet. The hunters scanned the trees and readied their bows. Even the dogs froze and sniffed the air. It struck Marie as a funny prank; she cupped her hand over her mouth to hold back her laughter.

Then a distant brace of ducks answered the hail call. Marie gasped. She'd witnessed her share of miracles in the company of the Magus, but she'd never seen a man speak to animals in their language.

"I said hello. Now I shall tell them I am a poor, lonely girl looking for some company." He blew a nasal *Quooooooooooonk.* "And, 'Look, I have found food for us to eat!'" *Diddiduddadiddit!* "Now I shall plead with them to come." *Conk, conk, conk, conk, conk!*

A brace of ducks rose above the trees, swerved at the call, and flew straight toward the meadow. Marie loosed as the others did and struck a bird from the sky. The rest of the ducks flew away fast with angry quacks. The hunters laughed at their luck.

"This was not luck!" cried Francis. He shoved his fussing physicians aside and strode to where Prospero was sitting. "See? It was the work of my magician!"

"Scientist," Prospero corrected and handed him the whistle. "Now here is how you make—"

Francis put it to his lips and wailed on it. It sounded like a duck being murdered in its sleep.

"Subtle works best, Your Majesty."

"We shall be the greatest hunter of the age! Even Henry VIII cannot compete with us now. And that stiff prig, Charles! Ha, ha, ha, ha!" Then he winced at the pain in his ribs.

And with that, he declared the hunt at an end. The hunters cheered. Five lads began a *caccia*, a hunting song, adding in sounds similar to barking dogs, shouting men, and the horn blasts. Francis repeatedly regaled them all with the tale of how he felled the stag, though they'd seen it firsthand. The nobles smiled at the appropriate places in the story and frowned the rest of the time.

"At least we shall eat well tonight, eh?" Prospero remarked.

Marie nodded in silence, deep in thought. Like Francis wincing over his aching ribs after a joyous kill, she felt sad now after the elation of the hunt. She missed Taddeo. She missed him much as the lonely wife in her song missed her Crusader husband. Part of the pain she felt was due to the physical distance between them and the uncertainty whether she'd ever see him again. The rest was because of the impossibility of them ever having a future together even if they were to be reunited. They were separated by distance, but more importantly, by class.

Prospero was right about one thing; she'd already accomplished much in her short life. Today, she went hunting with a king! But no matter how closely she flirted with the sun, she could never truly join its orbit. God had seen fit for Marie to be born among people of lowly status. Women like her had been put on the earth to work to enrich their betters, including people like Taddeo's family. Even if she joined Gattinara's guard, she'd never be considered anything other than lowborn. What hope could she have that a rich boy like Taddeo would ever consider her as anything other than a servant, perhaps a roll in the hay?

Maybe Prospero was right about something else. Maybe he'd been right to say to hell with all of it. Kings and serfs, rich and poor, highborn and lowborn. What others called a vagrant, he called a citizen of the world. Maybe society was just another illusion, and the only important thing was for individuals to try to be happy as best they could according to their own rules. The big question was whether Taddeo felt the same way. Was he the type of man who'd buck the rules for love? Prospero said he was ruled by his father. Even if he loved her, did he have the strength to say to hell with his family? Did Marie even have a right to ask such a selfish thing?

She felt she'd never sleep well again, tormented by such ideas.

Tonight, the King of France would host a ball in a field under the stars, and she'd eat and drink her fill with lords and ladies. Thinking of Taddeo's absence, it all soured in her mind.

"They'll rescue us," Marie told Prospero. "I know it. They'll come."

"Oh, Lord," the scientist said. "Let us hope not, okay?"

As they neared the city of tents on the hill overlooking Narbonne, riders shouted the news that a fleet of foreign vessels had been spotted. Royal Guard troops marshaled in neat formations under their flags on the beach; the nearby town shut its gates in panic.

Marie watched the ships plow the sea with their oars. "Who is it? Have the Spanish come?"

Prospero put on his glasses, adjusted the binocular vision, and grunted in surprise. "Some things must be seen to be believed."

He handed her the glasses. The sudden leap in vision gave her vertigo, but the scientist steadied her until she recovered. She focused on a large sleek galley streaming across the smooth waters with a rhythmic clack of oars, its deck swarming with dark-skinned sailors and blue-coated soldiers. A shirtless brute pounded a drum to pace the rowers.

She looked up and sucked in her breath.

The mast flew the red flag with a crescent symbol. The flag of the Ottoman Empire.

For the first time in history, the fierce Turk, who'd conquered most of Hungary in just the past few years and now menaced central Europe, was coming to France.

~ Chapter VII ~
A Hero's Quest

Taddeo piloted *The Prometheus* out of Valladolid's northern gate, brought it to a wheezing halt, and gave Don Jorge and his troop of lancers a little wave. They didn't return his salute. Instead, they stared in stunned disbelief that the Almighty God in His infinite wisdom suffered such a mechanical monstrosity to exist in Christendom. A small babbling crowd gathered to witness the excitement. Cardinal Gattinara arrived to bless the assembly before warning them of the consequences of failure, adding a quote from Anacharsis, "What hurts, often instructs."

Taddeo grinned. He'd been kicked awake by the Cardinal's guards, thrown in the stocks, brutally tortured, and then released. His body hurt everywhere, particularly his feet, which had been burned and now screamed at every step. He'd never been so happy. He was happy because Gattinara had paroled him to aid Don Jorge in recovering the woman he loved.

After Prospero and Marie disappeared, the Chancellor at first believed the alchemist had simply run off and brought the beautiful girl to warm his bed. Don Jorge would catch him easily and bring him back to face the Crown's judgment. Then he learned one of the royal guard had been wounded in the basilica; he swore he'd been jumped by ten men. An insomniac shopkeeper had seen men carry a sleeping man and woman into a carriage outside the workshop. A farmer reported that while urinating against the side of his house, he saw this same carriage fly by in the moonlight, piloted by half-naked devils capering on the roof.

"Only one breed of man acts like that," Gattinara said upon hearing this. "The French."

The entire city had woken to an uproar of strange rumors. The tales grew larger as they passed from one mouth to the next. Panicked mobs gathered in the street ready to hunt witches. The Devil, they cried, had come to Valladolid.

After Taddeo had been dumped groaning at his feet, Gattinara asked him if he had anything useful to say that might spare his life.

"Yes," Taddeo gasped, lying curled in a fetal ball. "Please let me go and find her."

"Your ambition is a neverending source of surprise to me, my son. I have not yet decided whether I find it bold or simply naïve. Then again, if Don Jorge had you along to bring Prospero back without violence, that would be preferable to being handed his head, as a dead man can't make gold. I shall therefore grant you parole, but note you are still under arrest. You must swear you will not seek to escape Don Jorge, and you will return to finish your work once the Crown recovers your master." Like Beelzebub, he held up their contract and shook it, smiling his cold smile. "Do not think of crossing me. There is no place you can go where my agents will not find you. Now, do you swear, or should the Inquisitors torture you some more?"

Taddeo shivered in pain on the floor. "I swear it. Thank you, Your Eminence."

The cardinal shook his head. "I have a soft spot for you, my son. I don't know why." He watched Taddeo feebly reach for his hand. "What's wrong with you now? Oh, all right." He stooped to allow the boy to kiss his ring. "Go with God."

Now, finally, Taddeo was ready to begin his quest to find her.

Don Jorge signaled it was time to get moving. Taddeo powered up the steam wagon and waited for the engine to build enough energy to turn the wheels. The cavalrymen waited with an incredulous look.

Myrddin arrived to see him off. Leo swirled around the man's legs, sniffing the ground and whining.

"I wish you were coming," Taddeo told him.

"Gattinara forbade it. I must produce his gold or be tried by the Inquisition."

"I know. That's why I wish you were coming."

That, and being alone with Don Jorge and his terrifying battle scar for the next few weeks didn't appeal to him.

"Regardless of where Don Jorge wants to go, follow Leo. He knows where your master is."

"How?"

Myrddin winked. "Magic, my boy."

"Right. But how?"

The Magus sighed. "Okay. Have you ever seen Leo eat or defecate?"

"No. He's a very private individual."

"He's also not real. He's Marie's ghost dog. A familiar I created from a drop of her blood and animal dung to keep her company. They are psychically connected. Whatever she feels, he feels. And no matter what the distance between them, he will find her. Just follow his nose. If Marie is with Prospero, you will find them both."

"That is the strangest thing I've ever heard, but I'll trust you." The wheels began to roll. "*Grazie, mago.*" *Thank you, magician.* "Good luck to you!"

"I hope you find her," Myrddin said, which made Taddeo smile. The man knew whom he was truly seeking. The one he would risk everything to save. Maybe the wizard was more human than he seemed.

He turned in the seat and shouted, "Marie's real, though, right?"

Myrddin cupped his hand to his ear. "Eh?"

He was already too far away to repeat himself. He simply waved, and the Magus raised his staff in reply. *The Prometheus* chugged down the road in high gear, belching smoke and vibrating on its shock-absorbing springs.

"Try to keep up," Don Jorge growled.

The lancers cantered ahead. Within an hour, they left him in the dust.

He was now alone with only Leo and his memories of Marie to keep him company. The dog led him north. Then east. Then north again, following the old Roman roads.

After several days of almost constant driving, Taddeo arrived in Navarre, a harsh, mountainous region bordering France. He saw signs of devastation everywhere. The war had spilled across the border and with it murder, rape, and famine. He passed towns filled with corpses and clouds of flies, fields burning, castles smoking on distant hills.

Many of his contemporaries would have considered such scenes unfortunate but an inevitable fact of life. Taddeo refused to accept it. On one thing, he and Prospero agreed one hundred percent: War benefited few people and was a pointless nightmare for everyone else. The peasants of Navarre were hardy folk living in isolated communities. Because two powerful men with fancy titles and money hated each other, now they died by the thousand; one day, soldiers showed up, hacked everyone to bits, burned the houses, and left. The world would have been better off if Charles and Francis had gone through with their duel like men and killed each other. With them out of the way, maybe the people here could rule themselves in peace.

The countryside became colder and more desolate with each passing mile. Leo never tired. He'd plodded through half of Spain with his nose skimming the dust. Riding night and day with little sleep, Taddeo began to lose track of time. Overall, it was a pleasant journey; it was a nice change not to have a mad scientist shouting at him. Then one day, while snoozing at the tiller, he started awake to find the Magus smoking his long-stem pipe in the seat behind him.

He screamed. "You shouldn't sneak up on people like that!"

Myrddin blew a perfect O of smoke. "Maybe I didn't sneak up on you. Maybe I was always here but invisible. Maybe you're not here, and I'm dreaming you. Maybe—"

"Okay, that's enough, *mago*," Taddeo said. "You're scaring me a little."

"The next one was a good one."

"I don't need to hear it."

Myrddin shrugged. "As you wish."

Taddeo glanced at the rear view mirror—he'd finally found an effective application for Prospero's clear glass mirror that didn't involve people staring at themselves—and saw the Magus's cart bouncing along behind them. Myrddin had somehow hitched it to the wagon.

"So why are you here?" he asked Myrddin.

"Why are *you* here?"

"I'm going to save Marie. I love her."

Saying the words loosened a massive knot in his brain. He could even breathe easier. In fact, he felt light as a feather. He turned to Myrddin with a grin.

"Then you're insane," the Magus said.

Huh? Love is insane?"

Isn't that obvious? I thought you were supposed to be smart."

Taddeo frowned and descended into the carriage to shovel more coal into the firebox, which heated the water in the boiler to make steam, which in turn moved the pistons. He returned to the driving bench and sat next to the Magus.

"Okay, tell me. Why do you call someone in love insane?"

"You already answered that yourself. You said you were here because you're going to try to rescue her. You're risking your life to save a girl you barely know."

"You don't understand," Taddeo sulked. "I have feelings for her."

"So you put your trust in illusions after all."

"My feelings are real enough!"

"Don't be offended. I think the whole human race is insane. Women suffer childbirth and give their lives to their children. Men and women marry for life when they will inevitably want to be with other people. A brave soldier gives his life on the battlefield so some rich and powerful man who doesn't even know his name can be a little more rich and powerful. And they all die believing they will wake up and live in eternal happiness for the rest of eternity. Is this not insane?"

"Fine, then! I'm insane. Okay?"

"Insane enough to die for her?"

Taddeo felt his resolve crystallize. "If I must," he said bravely.

"That's good, because you're about to be attacked."

The engineer stood and scanned the surrounding hills. "I don't—"

Angry cries echoed across the rocks.

Taddeo snatched the arquebus from the gun rack behind him. "Crap."

The bandits swarmed off the hills on all sides, shouting to build up their courage and reduce Taddeo's, though he didn't need the help. His bowels had already turned to water. He retrieved his bandolier and pulled it across his chest. The first of the bandits ran toward the side of the steam wagon, brandishing spears and scythes and pitchforks.

"Shit!" Taddeo gripped the wood handle protruding from the breech of the swivel gun and aimed its barrel directly at the center of the group with a shaking hand. Crossing himself in the hope of divine aid, he touched the powder in the priming plan with the burning match at the end of his *botefeux*. The *peterero* roared and shook with a flash of light. Through a haze of smoke, Taddeo counted six men lying on the ground.

The rest converged on *The Prometheus* from all sides. He looked at the cannon in mute longing but didn't have time to reload it. He was down to the arquebus, his dagger, and one worthless pipe-smoking magician.

"You know, you could lend a hand," Taddeo pleaded. "At least grab the tiller and steer!"

"I wouldn't dream of it," Myrddin said. "I'd rather die than use this infernal technology."

"Which is what's going to happen to us if you don't help! They're going to kill us!"

"What do you mean, *us*? I'm practically immortal."

"Can't you do your magic? Throw fire at them or something?"

"I swore an oath not to do harm to any human being."

Taddeo shook his head in disgust. "Then what good are you?"

Arrows thudded into the sideboard. One whistled past his head while he primed the pan with gunpowder from his horn. Blowing off loose powder, he righted the matchlock gun and poured more down the muzzle from a little wooden tube he yanked from his bandolier. He found the procedure briefly comforting. It reminded him of measuring out powders into test tubes back at the laboratory. Then he remembered he was going to shoot and kill someone with it.

Myrddin surprised him by laughing, a wheezy cross between a cough and a sigh. "What good am I. What good am I? What a wonderful question. I shall think on it."

And with that, he went into a trance.

The steam wagon swerved off the road. Taddeo corrected course and put the tiller between Myrddin's knees. He dropped a ball and paper wad into the barrel and rammed the charge home with his scouring stick. Then he presented his gun and pulled the trigger.

The burning tip of match cord plunged into the priming pan. The gun fired with a *crash*. One of the bandits flopped to the ground with a large smoking hole in his chest.

Two hairy hands gripped the side of the driver's bench. A snarling face appeared. Without thinking, Taddeo thrust the butt of his gun into the face with a meaty crunch. He heard shouts from behind and glanced in the rear view in time to see a line of roaring men catching up to the puffing wagon. Taddeo stomped his foot against a lever.

For a moment, nothing happened. His hopes sank. Then something clanged deep in the bowels of the vehicle, something else spun and clacked, and a box opened at the rear of the wagon. Dozens of caltrops spilled onto the road. The line of men went down howling.

Taddeo turned to ask Myrddin again for his help, but the wizard sat still as a rock with his eyes closed, hands resting on his knees, his pipe gone out. A trio of faces appeared at the edge of the carriage. One of the men yelped and fell, Leo's jaws clamped around his ankle. Taddeo presented his piece and told the other two to jump, or he'd shoot. One nodded and disappeared. The other, a boy about Taddeo's age, continued to pull himself up while his comrades cheered him on.

Taddeo didn't have time to reload. He could only watch in terror as the boy gained his feet holding a sickle. He drew his dagger and probed more than thrust, afraid of actually cutting him. It was one thing to shoot a man at range; stabbing him in the heart while looking him in the eyes was something else entirely. A rock flew past his head as a reminder to kill or be killed. If he were murdered, he'd never rescue Marie, and the Magus would be proved right, which was almost as bad.

Shutting one of his eyes while squinting with the other, he extended the point of his dagger. The boy reflexively raised his hand to defend himself. Taddeo felt the blade penetrate skin and skid along bone. The boy shrieked and gaped at his bleeding hand.

"I'm sorry!" Taddeo said, horrified at the sight.

The boy reached out to grab the dagger. Taddeo cut him again. The boy screamed like a pig being slaughtered, tears flowing down his cheeks. It was pitiful.

"*Basta!*" cried Taddeo, tearing a page out of Prospero's book and kicking him in the nuts. The poor lad tumbled over the side; a moment later, the wagon lurched as its wheels navigated a bump.

Taddeo reloaded his arquebus and pointed it at his remaining foes, who tapered away. They leaned on their knees panting and watched him go.

Taddeo took little satisfaction from his victory. The violence had been sickening. These men weren't bandits, they were farmers. They weren't evil, they were starving. Desperate enough to kill for food.

Taddeo turned and saw another man climb onto the driver's bench. A tall, gaunt warrior in old chain mail, his cheeks sunken and his eyes crazed with hunger. The knight drew his sword with an exhausted sigh. Taddeo presented his arquebus.

"Don't make me shoot you, Don—excuse me, but what is your name, noble sir?"

"Just kill him," Myrddin said.

The knight raised his sword to strike. Taddeo shot him point blank. The lead slug punched a hole through his sternum. His body toppled off the carriage to land in a lifeless heap on the hard earth.

Taddeo quickly reloaded his piece, but there were no other foes. *The Prometheus* continued its chugging progress down the road. The sun came out from behind the clouds, its light warm on his skin.

He shook his head in despair and said, "If they'd just asked me for food in the first place, I would have given it to them. It was pointless. Stupid and pointless."

"You didn't have enough to feed all of them. If it's any consolation, they wanted to eat us."

"Oh, now we're an 'us.'"

"Perhaps using that word was stretching things a bit," the wizard conceded.

"You want to be an 'us'? Next time, help me out."

"You said you were willing to die to save Marie, but you weren't sure because you hadn't been tested. Now you know you really are willing to risk everything. Besides, you did just fine with your technology."

"I only survived because they were a bunch of starving farmers. They couldn't hit a barn with those bows."

"Nonetheless—"

"I don't want to go through that again." Taddeo hugged his ribs. "I can't."

"I was going to say, you can take further comfort from the fact they will eat very well tonight," Myrddin told him with a friendly pat on his shoulder.

Taddeo felt sick. "Please stop."

"No, I mean it. You placed a veritable feast on their table. You're a hero."

He lurched to the rail and vomited over the side. Every time he closed his eyes, he saw the boy crying over his bleeding hand. The boy was about Taddeo's age. They even looked alike. But one had been born to a merchant family in Venice and the other to a peasant family in Navarre.

Taddeo spit twice and wiped his mouth. "Is this how it's going to be then? I do all the work to bring you to Marie?"

"Nonsense," Myrddin said. "I can transverse time and space. I would have caught up to her by now if I weren't forced to ride in this ridiculous machine."

"Then why don't you?" Taddeo wanted to know.

"I told you already. I swore an oath not to directly harm any man. So when we do find her, you will have to kill her captors and rescue her. Plus you're using my dog. Now you know the answer to the question you first asked."

"What question?"

"Why I'm here, of course."

Taddeo thought about it. "So if we give up *The Prometheus*, you could get us there faster?"

"Certainly. Unless you'd rather fight your way across southern France."

"Prospero is not going to like it. Especially leaving all the tools and materials in the workshop."

"If you leave your machine, I can carry all that junk."

"It weighs about a ton."

"No matter."

"But how will you do it?"

Myrddin rolled his eyes. "Magic. I do magic."

The steam wagon rolled to a stop behind a stand of trees. Taddeo climbed down to the ground, where Leo welcomed him with a red grin. The wizard unfolded a small burlap sack and entered the carriage, from which emerged a neverending din of rattling and clanging. Taddeo scratched the dog behind the ears and taught him what he knew about thermodynamics while he waited. The wizard emerged with a full sack held over his shoulder and set it on the ground, where it sank into the dirt.

Taddeo frowned at the sack. "That's it? You were in there over an hour!"

Myrddin gestured toward the carriage. "Let me know if I missed anything important. I only grabbed what I thought were essentials, but I couldn't be sure of everything."

Taddeo climbed aboard and looked around. The entire space was empty. Even the spider webs were gone. He emerged scratching his head in disbelief. "Is this illusion, or is it really happening? I can never tell with you."

Myrddin smiled and tapped his long nose. "Now he gets it."

"But what you did violates the laws of physics. Laws that are immutable."

"Magic isn't governed by the natural laws. Did I ever tell you that you remind me of a boy I mentored long ago? It's true. A boy who became a king."

"I don't want to be a king."

"That's why I like you better than I did him. That being said, he was my friend."

"I want to be with Marie."

The Magus scowled. "Oh, boy. Here we go again."

"Tell me about her, Myrddin."

"You love this girl and you want me to tell you who she is?"

"Come on. You've known her longer than I have."

"What do you want me to tell you? She's a passable cook and an excellent bodyguard."

"Yes," Taddeo said dreamily. "And?"

"And? And that's it. What?"

He broke his reverie with a frown. "Do you even know what love is, *mago*?"

"I'll have you know I am very fond of Marie," the old man blustered. "Here, I will demonstrate to you I am quite capable of affection."

He sat on the ground and whistled. Moments later, a large rabbit bounded forward with bright eyes, its ears pulled back and its nose twitching. Leo stiffened but stayed put.

The hare hopped onto the wizard's lap. Myrddin stroked its fur. "Yes, you are a beautiful bunny," he cooed. "Yes, you are." The rabbit shivered in terror. "Would you like to come with us and see the world? Would you like to be my new familiar?" He looked up at Taddeo with a smug expression. "There. See? This animal is responding to my love." He cupped its head, twisted, and snapped its neck. "Now let's get a fire going and cook it for our supper before we get back on the road. I'm famished."

When Taddeo didn't move, Myrddin cocked an eyebrow. "*Now* what?"

"Do you think Marie loves me back, *mago*?"

The Magus appeared to find the question intriguing. "Would you continue to risk your life making this journey if she didn't?"

Taddeo considered it. What if this were all for nothing? What if he rescued her and found the courage to confess his love, and she laughed in his face? It was probable; after all, they lived in different worlds. He lived a life of the mind. He considered his body an inconvenient cage with more limitations than advantages. It was what made him brilliant. Marie lived in the physical world. She experienced it to the fullest in every moment. There was something about her that reminded him of a cat.

Besides that, they lived in different social classes. He'd grown up a pampered city kid, wise beyond his years but ignorant of the simple things that made country folk tick. He knew he respected them; they worked with their hands, they made things, they grew their own food. If the world ended tomorrow and threw mankind back into a state of brutal savagery—Myrddin's idea of paradise—men like Taddeo would be useless. The bottom line was humanity didn't need banking or trade or elites running things, it needed people who could work and fight and survive despite endless hardship. People like Marie.

The girl he loved was going to reject him. It was the most

probable outcome, assuming he could rescue her at all, which was similarly unlikely.

Taddeo looked at Myrddin. "Yes, I would still try to save her."

The Magus shook his head. "Completely insane."

They ate the rabbit and prepared for the next phase of their journey. Taddeo looped his powder horn, canteen, and a sack of food across his chest and hoisted the arquebus over his shoulder. *This is turning into a real adventure*, he thought, happy to be alive and well enough to consider it such. Myrddin was right about one thing, though; the whole thing was quite insane. Marie Dubois likely didn't need rescue. She would find a way to escape on her own. He knew she'd fought Don Jorge and almost won. Marie was a fighter; she didn't puke over the rail after a fight.

When he turned around, the steam wagon was gone, along with Myrddin's rickety cart.

"Now what have you done?"

"I put the vehicles in the sack with Prospero's other junk. I don't mind carrying it." He gestured to the road with his oak staff. "Shall we?"

Taddeo hurried after him. Leo led the way with a happy wag of his tail. "I'd still like to know how you do what you do, *mago*."

"How do you *think* I do it? Hint: I've told you before. Many times."

"I'm talking about how it actually happens. What is the mechanism and its rules?"

"There you go again, trying to turn magic into science."

"Prospero says you are simply a scientist like him, but privy to technologies way beyond our time."

Myrddin squinted at him. "Very clever. Your master is a brilliant man. And quite right. I'm actually a traveler from the distant future. A golden age when mankind has used advanced technology to solve all its problems."

Taddeo stared at him wide eyed. "Is that true?"

"Of course not! Listen, if you want to know how I do what I do, why don't you learn?"

"How am I supposed to do that?"

"You have a bright mind and a good heart. I could teach you."

"You're speaking in jest. You really would?" Taddeo's eyes narrowed. "What's the price?"

"Just two little things. First, you must renounce science. To a true wizard, it is a dark art that only brings trouble to man. Second, you must give up all this youthful idealism about changing the world for the better. A true wizard is above such earthly passions."

His heart sank with disappointment. "In other words, you want me to be somebody I'm not. I could never honestly swear to do those things. You might as well ask me to give up loving Marie."

"Yes, thank you, I forgot. You'd have to do that too."

"I don't even understand the point of having so much power if you can't use it for good."

"If you try to use magic to make the world a better place, you only make things worse. That's why it's only for the select few who can handle it."

"Then what good is it?"

"Another excellent question. Would the fact I'm immortal and get to do pretty much anything I want strike you as a suitable answer?" Before Taddeo could reply, Myrddin showed him the staff carved from the tree where he'd been imprisoned. "See the faces of these sleeping babes in the wood? I am beginning to remember now, just as I remembered the boy who became a king. These are the faces of men I once knew and called my brothers. Men who did what you propose. They tried to make the world a better place and tangled with forces they couldn't control."

"Then I will do it with science," Taddeo declared. "If the rich are well mannered and cultured and generous, and the poor ignorant and brutish and cruel, then wealth is the key to good. Technology can create wealth. If it is shared equally, everyone will become good."

"I'm impressed. You're even more insane than I'd first thought. Ever since man invented fire and tools, his problems started. Before that, back when the giants walked the earth, he lived in a natural state as part of the animal kingdom. He didn't think, he did. He didn't ponder the meaning of life or ritualize the reality of death. He lived in harmony with nature. He looked up at the sun and saw a god; the universe filled him with awe. Every moment, he was fully aware, immersed in the world, connected to everything. Seriously, can you name one case where technology ever did anyone any good?"

"What about agriculture?"

"Yet people are still starving. If you make people's lives better, they will produce more people. Men will multiply until there are no more trees or stones or water left. The more he gains, the unhappier he will be, wanting more. And God will no longer recognize His creation."

"But you would have us swinging from trees like monkeys! Without art or music or learning! We're not animals, *mago*. We're humans, established in our unique place in the Great Chain of Being. We're capable of great things, but we suffer. Progress eases suffering; one day, there will be no more famine or pestilence or war. You wring your hands and wish we could go back to the time we were living in caves. I live in the real world, and I'll do everything I can to make it a better place. No, I think it's best if I refuse your offer, and we keep things as they are. I'll be your bodyguard, and you'll be my guy who carries stuff and starts cooking fires by rubbing his fingers together."

"I believe the word is 'porter.'"

A long moan of pain sounded from the nearby woods. It ended in a guttural growl.

The wizard and the boy looked at each other. Taddeo shivered; it was a horrible sound.

"Some strange animal?" he asked.

Myrddin pointed. "Oh, dear. Look there."

Men staggered out of the trees, their flesh pale and slack, their limbs stiff and twitching. They sniffed the breeze, taking little bites out of the air, and fixed their glittering black eyes on the magician and the scientist. After the first few, dozens more stumbled moaning out of the woods.

"*Mago*, what did you do?"

"Me? I didn't do anything."

"You think science did this?"

Taddeo recognized the men he'd killed back at the running fight for control of *The Prometheus*, led by the old knight, who limped along with a giant ragged hole in his chest. He even saw the boy he'd stabbed and thrown off the wagon, lurching and swaying with his broken spine. Many others had come as well. All the war dead of Navarre, it seemed, had returned to life, including rotting, bloated, grimacing monstrosities that been dead a long time. Their incredible stench made him gag. Leo ran cowering behind Myrddin.

Taddeo gulped. "God did this. He's punishing me for killing those men."

Myrddin shook his head. "Sonny, if God did this to every man who had to kill someone in self defense, there'd be no room on earth for the living. No, this is magic. Powerful magic. The magic of Arabia. These men have become ghouls."

"So what do ghouls actually do?"

"The same as when they were alive. They're going to try to kill and eat us."

Taddeo raised his matchlock gun and fired a shot. One of the creatures toppled over, its chest shattered. Moments later, it slowly rose to its feet.

"Try aiming for the head," the Magus suggested.

"Are you sure?" cried a panicked Taddeo as he reloaded the gun.

"No. It's just a hunch."

He pressed the trigger and ignited the powder with a loud *bang*. The ghoul's snarling face exploded in bloody fragments, and the corpse dropped to the ground. This time, it didn't rise.

The wizard clapped. "Ha! I was right. Go get 'em."

"We're surrounded. There must be a hundred of them. And I only have nine shots left."

They were doomed.

"You could try to fight your way out, but they will follow you to the ends of the earth."

"Another feeling?" asked Taddeo as he reloaded again.

"No, I know that for sure."

"Maybe they're after *you*, not me. Did you ever think of that?"

"Don't be ridiculous," Myrddin said with a snort. "Why would someone want to kill me?"

Taddeo fired and dropped another ghoul.

Myrddin patted his shoulder. "Good shot. Keep it up."

"Why don't *you* do something?"

The Magus stiffened and placed his hand over his heart. "I swore an oath—"

"Come on! They're already dead! They're dead men possessed by magic!"

"Oh. Well. All right then. Bear with me. I haven't done this in a while."

"Taddeo watched him crouch for battle. The old man was just limbering up but already out of breath. His joints creaked. *Oh, God*, thought Taddeo. *Look at him. We're definitely doomed.*

The Magus ran into the midst of the ghouls, surprisingly nimble and light on his feet. He touched their foreheads with the tip of his staff as they reached out for him with chomping jaws. And each one he touched, died. Died and stayed dead.

Wow, thought Taddeo. *The old coot can really move when he wants.*

One of the ghouls staggered howling toward him; Taddeo put it down with a shot through the skull and reloaded. The creatures swarmed the Magus, who laid them out in piles at his feet. But their numbers began to tell.

The last score of the noxious things put their hands on him.

"Oh, dear," Myrddin said as they bit into his flesh.

The ghouls tore him apart and devoured everything in big bites—flesh and blood, organs and bones, hair and clothes. Nothing was wasted. And when they were done, nothing was left.

The wizard hadn't made a sound as he died.

"*Mago!*" Taddeo cried in horror.

He couldn't believe it was true. Myrddin Wyllt, the ageless

spellbinder, was no more. So much for being immortal.

Their stomachs bulging with wizard flesh, the ghouls turned as one to fix those black eyes, bright with evil intelligence and shiny with raw hunger, on Taddeo. He counted eighteen of them. Eighteen ghouls he'd have to shoot down with seven balls.

As the ghouls lumbered closer, they gripped their stomachs. The light in their eyes faded. Their moaning grew louder, more needy, more pitiful.

They began to belch up Myrddin's remains onto the ground.

Everything came up—flesh and blood, organs and bones, hair and clothes—into steaming piles in the tall grass. It was a nauseating sight.

Then, one by one, they wilted and collapsed with a sigh and died.

Nothing stirred. Myrddin was gone.

"Goodbye, *mago*," Taddeo said.

He was about to say he would miss him, but he had to think about that. The man was positively frustrating, his way of thinking diametrically opposed to Taddeo's.

He decided he'd miss the old man after all.

And he would continue his quest to save Marie. Without the steam wagon, unfortunately, as he had no idea how to get it out of Myrddin's old burlap bag. No matter. Like these ghouls, he'd follow his quarry to the ends of the earth. No matter what it took, no matter how difficult the test, he would find Marie and rescue her.

This was his journey, and he'd have to face it alone.

"I'm sorry this happened to you, *mago*. I'll take good care of her." He thought for a moment. "You know, there was one important thing you taught me, and that's—"

The piles of vomit began to flow toward each other. Whatever magic the wizard had conjured before his death was still happening. Taddeo crouched and waited.

Blood sought blood. Bones joined to bones. Clothing stitched to clothing. Hair fixed to flesh which wrapped the organs which sucked in the blood, and clothing covered it all. The creature lurched into an upright position, taking the form of a tall man.

Myrddin appeared to be reassembling himself.

"*Mago!*" Taddeo shouted.

At last, the old wizard stretched and bent to pick up his staff. "Good, you're still here. Are there any more ghouls? Ah, well. I suppose that's for the best. Now stand back." He shook his cloak, spraying bits of bits of rotting flesh.

"I'm glad you're alive. I was sure you were dead."

Myrddin picked up the sack and threw it over his shoulder. "You were? I'm pretty sure I told you I'm virtually immortal."

"You had me worried just the same."

"As for me, I'm intrigued."

"Why is that?"

"The presence of those ghouls means there's a powerful magician in these parts, and he's trying to kill us."

Taddeo liked the sound of that. Myrddin referring to them as an *us*, that is.

Chapter VIII
A Grand Ball

Marie stepped from behind the dressing partition and confronted Prospero, who'd been pacing the tent waiting for her to finish dressing.

"If you laugh, I'll hurt you," she said.

Prospero took a step back, briefly stunned, and did a slow clap. "*Bella, bella, bella.*"

She wore an elegant blue gown accented with a darker blue high standing collar that framed her face and chest down to her cleavage. Long decorative sleeves, splitting away at the elbow to touch the floor, added another splash of elegance. Beneath the dress, she wore a corset that accentuated her slim waist and made her feel like someone was sitting on her stomach. The getup was less comfortable than even her old metal cuirass.

The scientist looked dashing as well in a black-and-white striped satin doublet embroidered in gold. He'd set his white-feathered hat at a rakish angle on his curls. A gift from his new patron, King Francis I.

"The Duchess Anna Jeanne de Pisseleu loaned me the dress herself," she said. "Is it nice?"

"I did not know you were even capable of vanity."

Marie glared at him. "I've never been to a ball. I want it to be special."

"*Bella*, she gave you one of her best gowns."

"Oh." She felt a swirl of butterflies in her stomach, the excitement of making her grand entrance observed by the finest people of the realm. "That was nice of her."

"Did you ever hear the expression, 'Keep your friends close and your enemies closer'? She's the king's mistress. You might be a rival. A rival and a friend."

"A rival for *his* affection? Ha!"

"Do not rush to judgment. There are women all over France who would kill for the chance to be the king's bedmate. It is not a bad life, you know. You lie with the king a few times each month, and you will live well as long as your looks last. Even after that, you may earn a pension."

"I'd rather hang myself. In any case, I've pledged my heart to another man."

"A mistress of the king goes everywhere he goes. She often serves as a confidant and advisor; with a little pillow talk, she can influence royal policy. And she will attend balls and games and parties all the time."

"That's not for me," Marie said, though a little less convincingly this time.

"No matter. She set you up to fail to enamor the great king."

"She did?" Marie looked down at herself. "Is there something wrong?"

Prospero went to the dressing table and picked up a mirror. "Allow me to acquaint you with one of my most popular inventions."

Marie saw herself and gasped. "I look *amazing.*" Like something out of a fairy tale. She fluttered about, inspecting herself from every angle. "What's wrong with how I look?"

"Your hair, simply put, is like a nest for rats. If you appear at the ball looking like this, you will be quite radiant but also play the fool."

She touched her hair. "Oh." He was right. It didn't look like Anna Jeanne's hair had.

"Luckily for you, I am also a genius of fashion." He patted the stool set before the dressing table. "Sit, *bella*, and I shall style it for you."

The scientist propped the mirror on the table so she could observe what he was doing. Picking up a boar hair brush, he hacked at her tangled, curly red hair. Marie winced but held her tongue; he seemed to know his business. A part of her also liked being fussed over.

This done, he braided and wound the braids into coils on the sides of her head.

"Do women really do this every day?"

"Even more than this."

"But the party's already started! We're missing it!"

"You will make a much grander entrance if you arrive just a little bit late. This, my dear, is *sprezzatura*. There. It is done." He added in booming Latin, "*Ecce domina!*" *Behold the lady!*

Marie leaned toward the mirror and studied her appearance. The transformation was amazing. She'd become the fairy tale princess of her daydreams.

Prospero smiled. "And for garnish..."

He placed a gold necklace around her neck. It tickled her cleavage.

"Oh, my," she breathed, her lips parted. It was beautiful.

"It once belonged to a very rich Spanish lady, but do not tell anyone that."

She stood and twirled around the room, miming the exchange of pleasantries with fine people. But something was still missing. "Would Taddeo like me like this? Is this what he wants?"

Prospero laughed. "Of course, but I suspect Taddeo does not care what you wear. He loves you for what you are, not how you look in a dress. To him, clothes do not make the woman; they keep out the cold. I am sure, however, the outfit would impress the boy's father. You look like a proper lady. The kind Gregorio expects his son to marry."

"Marry?" Marie blushed at the idea.

"But..."

"But what?"

"You move like a wolf that smells blood. Watch carefully." He slapped his face to bring blush to his cheeks then walked across the tent light on his feet, hands clasped in front of his stomach. Lips pursed in a tight smile, his eyes flashed back and forth to take in every detail.

Marie watched the ridiculous display. "This is how women act?"

"It is called grace, and one must have it to play in high society. Speaking of which, do you know how to dance?"

"I can do the *branl*—"

"That is excellent! But this is the French court, my dear, not a barnyard hootenanny for country bumpkins. You must learn proper dances. Lord and lady dances. Ah, this blushing of yours is quite attractive. Try to be embarrassed while you are dancing."

"I'm not embarrassed. I'm angry."

"Just the same. It is a pity I do not have time to facilitate further transformation. Observe the dancers. Pay attention to the steps." He crooked his arm. "Shall we?"

Marie took his arm. "Prospero, do me a favor at the party. Don't mess things up by doing that thing you do."

"I do not know what you mean."

She tightened her grip on his arm. "And thank you. For helping me. You're a good friend."

"It is our great pleasure," he said, quoting Francis.

Marie allowed him to escort her through the camp toward the sounds of conversation, laughter, and buoyant music. She barely heard it over the blood crashing in her ears. Tonight was a challenge she'd never faced before. It set her nerves on edge. With Don Jorge, she'd fought to win. When she'd stood in the stirrups on her galloping mare and closed in on the stag at bay, she'd played to win. Now she found herself thrust into a new type of game in which she didn't even know the rules. She didn't know how to win; tonight, she would fight to avoid losing. She felt hot and more than a little light headed at the prospect of mingling with aristocrats.

But she couldn't walk away. Marie had spent her entire life wondering how the rich lived and wishing she could join them. Tonight, for just one night, she'd live this dream and pretend she had everything. Security, food, warmth, and love in endless abundance.

At last they came upon the glowing field. Couples danced to the music of a band that included a lute, cornett, recorder, viol, and tambourine on an improvised stage. Others mingled outside the dance area while servants circulated among them bearing silver trays loaded with flutes of wine. Francis's stag roasted whole over one of the fires; pots of mutton, game, and spring vegetables boiled over other pits.

Be ever vigilant for threat, the wisdom of her *sensei* intruded. *It only takes a moment to die.*

She scanned the assembly, looking for traps. There—a lady curtsied. Marie didn't know how to do that. Accepting a glass of wine from Prospero, who was babbling something about Francis being a friend of science, whatever that meant, she saw another lady curtsy and studied the technique. After a while, she realized she in turn was being watched. Ladies and the king's mistresses appraised her heel to head, while young, dashing courtiers and knights smiled and cocked an eyebrow. She turned away to study the dancers.

Prospero called it a *galliard*, a courtly and formal dance to triple-meter music. It was quite beautiful; the hundreds of dancers flowed together in a meticulous choreography. The man bowed, the woman curtsied. They stood very straight, side by side and holding hands, and skipped about before breaking away. The man danced alone until it was the woman's turn to prance around the man. Then they held hands and circled each other, first clockwise, then counter clockwise. It looked like a lot of fun; she itched to join the dance. Marie glanced at Prospero—who was slurping his wine and pontificating about building Francis something called an *air force*— and wondered if she should ask him to dance with her.

A chill along her spine alerted her to an unseen threat. She wheeled as two men approached. The first, dressed in a simple long-sleeved black tunic, turban, and trousers, bowed low and intoned:

"Dear lady, allow me to introduce the leopard of strength and valor, the tiger of the forest of courage, the hero filled with holy zeal, the lion of the restoration of dominion, the precious pearl in the ocean of all power, the champion of the faith, *Vezir-i-Azam*, *beylerbey* of Rumelia, Pargali Ibrahim Pasha."

"And I am Prospero Buonarroti," Prosper declared, puffing out his chest. "The lion of learning. Occupation: scientist. At your service!"

The herald asked him who was right, Aristotle or Plato, which Prospero began answering before the man could specify about what. Free to speak to Marie unmolested, Ibrahim Pasha presented himself.

Tall, slim, and bit stiff in his posture, he was a swarthy handsome man with a short-cropped beard that tapered to a point at his chin. He wore a shiny, sky-blue, close-fitting *kaftan*—a long-sleeve buttoned coat that flowed to his ankles. The jeweled hilt of a curved sword protruded from his red silk sash. His fingers glittered with gold rings. Baggy red trousers and curled slippers completed his ensemble.

She'd heard about him. He was born the son of a sailor in Greece. At a young age, pirates captured his ship, murdered his father, and sold him as a slave to the Manisa Palace, where the Ottoman princes received their education. It was there he befriended Suleiman, son of Selim the Grim. They spent their days engaged in wrestling, archery, horsemanship, and philosophy. When Suleiman became crowned Sultan, he brought his friend with him to Istanbul as a trusted adviser. Ibrahim's talent led to his rapid promotion and culminated in his appointment as Grand Vizier of the Ottoman Empire. And so a Greek slave rose to become prime minister of one the greatest empires on the earth.

Ibrahim inclined his head. "Marie Dubois, it is an honor to make your acquaintance."

"You know my name."

He nodded again. "Now we know each other."

"You missed my implied question. How do you know me?"

"It's the obligation of every man to learn the identity of the most beautiful woman at a party."

"You flatter me, sir." Marie blushed despite herself. The clothes, atmosphere, and pageantry had gone straight to her brain. Everything seemed more important, more dramatic; after a single glass of wine, she'd become drunk on the party itself. He was indeed a dark and handsome specimen, and quite charismatic. She sensed Ibrahim Pasha was another Gattinara, however—extremely ambitious, cunning, and dangerous. Men like him played chess with nations and for incredible stakes. They dealt in peoples, not individuals. She reminded herself to tread carefully.

He smiled. "I sought you out. How do you say it? We are in the 'same boat.' Strangers in a strange land."

Suleiman the Magnificent's great-grandfather had conquered mighty Constantinople, taking down the last bastion of the decayed Byzantine Empire and making it his capital with the new name of Istanbul. Suleiman's father brought the Middle East under virtual Ottoman control. Suleiman, inheriting a standing army one hundred thousand strong, would prove to be even greater than his predecessors. His first campaign resulted in the capture of Belgrade. A year later, he took the island of Rhodes from the Knights Hospitaller.

In 1525, King Francis I was defeated at Pavia, his army annihilated. Charles imprisoned him in Madrid, where he was forced to sign a humiliating treaty requiring him to cede Burgundy, over which Charles had claims, and renounce his own claims in Italy. While he languished in his Spanish cell complaining he'd lost everything save his honor, his mother, Louise de Savoie, sent an envoy to Suleiman requesting support against the Habsburgs. Suleiman agreed to an alliance.

A year later, the Ottoman war machine advanced into Hungary and destroyed its army at Mohács. Suleiman was stunned this large nation—once led by the likes of the fearsome Matthias Corvinus with his vaunted Black Army—had sent such a small, inadequate force to be slaughtered by his guns. News of the defeat of the Shield of Christendom would later terrify all Europe. The next day, Suleiman wrote in his diary:

The Sultan, seated on a golden throne, receives the homage of the viziers and the beys. Massacre of two thousand prisoners. The rain falls in torrents.

Ibrahim had distinguished himself in the battle as one of Suleiman's generals. He held the title *Serasker*, which meant he could command the Army in the name of the Sultan.

The Grand Vizier told Marie, "In my country, we have a saying: '*Gözden uzak olan gönülden de uzak olur.*' Which means: 'Who is far from the eye is also far from the heart.'"

"We have a similar saying in Christendom: 'Out of sight, out of mind.'"

"Exactly. An alliance is like a garden. It must be watered. And so I am here."

Marie found the French-Ottoman alliance puzzling; the two nations had almost no common interest, as far as she could tell, other than destroying Charles, which they would try to do anyway. It even confounded the French. Earlier in the day, Marie and Prospero watched the longboats launch from the Turkish galleys. Wrapped in a fur-lined cloak, Francis waited on the beach under his coat of arms decorated with gentle *fleur de lis* and fierce lions, which embodied the royal motto, "We nourish, and we extinguish." The proud regiment of his royal guard stood behind him under banners that whipped and cracked in the wind. African giants rolled out a red carpet and formed an honor guard on both sides of it. Drums rattled on the French side. Ibrahim Pasha stepped out of the boat and marched smartly up to Francis. While the heralds began their longwinded introductions, the solemn diplomatic proceedings were interrupted by the arrival of several hundred louts from the town. Armed with rakes and pitch forks, they declared themselves ready to die as heroes for France in her defense against this Turkish invasion.

It had taken the diplomats the better part of an hour to sort it out. It was terribly embarrassing.

"But I do not wish to speak of politics," Ibrahim said. "I

would speak to you instead of a man in whom we have a strong common interest."

Marie sucked in her breath. "You know Taddeo Cellini?"

Ibrahim smiled. "I was speaking of the Magus Myrddin Wyllt."

"Myrddin? How do you know him?"

"Only by reputation, I'm afraid. I'm a great admirer. It's a pity Francis didn't acquire him, despite the indignity that would have involved. I would have enjoyed meeting the man."

"Why did Francis go through all this trouble to try to abduct him? He never said."

"You have served Myrddin Wyllt, yet you do not truly know him. The man is immensely powerful. Such power is reserved for sultans, and even sultans do not have his power."

"The Magus?" Were they talking about the same Myrddin Wyllt? "But he's an illusionist for the most part. His magic is basically harmless. We're hungry half the time."

"Then he has fooled you with his greatest trick of all. He's a master sorcerer with enormous power over the elementals and all living things. So tell me, Marie Dubois. Where is our friend now?"

Marie realized this was not a social call. The man had an agenda.

"Mecca," she said, feeling trapped.

Ibrahim laughed, but his eyes were cold.

"So there you are!" cried a familiar voice. Francis swaggered up to them laughing. "We would dance with you." He wagged his finger at Ibrahim. "We saw her first!"

The Grand Vizier bowed. "As the alternative would be to risk an international incident, I defer to Your Majesty on the matter."

"Great Pasha, you are ever the cunning and able diplomat." The king eyed Marie heel to head with a stunned expression. "My God, you are like a delicious bowl of cream. I could eat you!"

"Your Majesty flatters me," Marie said, bewildered by the verbal assault.

"That is our pleasure." Francis returned his attention to Ibrahim. "The party will end soon, and we may speak privately of my hopes for a grand partnership between our two great nations."

"Very exciting, Your Majesty. It is said, 'It takes two hands to make a sound.'"

"What? Well, *oui*, that is quite right!"

"Goodbye, Marie Dubois. It is also said, 'Patience is bitter, but its fruit is sweet.'"

Francis laughed as he took Marie's hand and led her away. "Have you ever heard his herald introduce him? They have another saying: 'The Turk says little but acts grandly.' We think it might be the other way around." Smiling impishly, he guided her into the dance area. The musicians began to play a song suited to the *pavane*, a very slow and stately dance in which the couples lined up behind each other in a processional.

"So what is your opinion of the great Pasha?" Francis asked her as they stepped in unison. "As a man?"

"Slippery," she said without thinking.

"Ha, ha! How witty! You know, that town over there was once part of the Emirate of Cordoba. Pepin the Short, Charlemagne's father, took it from them. Now it is ours. There probably has not been a Muslim here in eight hundred years before the Pasha graced us with his slippery presence. But such is life. History is always in the making. It is the present, not the past. Is that not so?"

"Indeed, it is, Your Majesty."

"And we are the players dancing on life's august stage. Such as our vanquishing of the noble stag today. The Hector of deer. That was one for the history books."

"You seem to be recovering well from the hurt the stag inflicted upon you."

"Bah," Francis said. "We simply drank until we stopped noticing the pain. We have suffered far worse wounds in battle against men. But let us speak of pleasure, not pain. We wish you to visit us after our meeting with the great Turkish Pasha."

Marie almost stumbled. "Visit?"

"Give this password to the guards: *l'amour.*" Love.

The dance ended. Four men took the stage and launched into a *chanson* about the Battle of Marignano fifteen years earlier, in which Francis, leading the French horse, smashed the Duke of Milan's line of Swiss mercenaries and won a great victory. While they sang, they took turns miming the trumpet blasts sounding the charge, the thunder of the hoofs and the clash of arms, the rout and victory. The song ended in a triumph.

Francis applauded. "Very wonderful!" He turned to Marie. "It was our first campaign. We were but twenty years old and had only just been crowned king."

After the party, Marie found Prospero near the ruins of the monastery, gazing up at the sky with his strange spectacles. Still tipsy from all the wine, the dancing, and the king's heady offer, she twirled around him in a solo *galliard*.

"Dance with me, Prospero!"

"Can you not see I am very busy now with my research?"

"Come on! I have itchy feet." She stopped prancing. "What are you doing?"

"I am studying the moon. Care to see?"

Marie looked up. "Aye, it's beautiful tonight."

"Do you remember how these lenses made you see far-away things as if they were right in front of you?"

"You can do that with the moon as well?"

"Of course," Prospero said. "The moon is a thing."

He put the glasses on her and guided her head until she saw part of the familiar pattern of the man on the moon. It was shockingly close.

"It's falling on me!" she cried. "Or am I flying?"

"Neither. You are still here."

She relaxed and enjoyed the view. "The king invited me to his bed."

"My girl is finding her way in the world. It brings a tear to my eye."

The man was serious. In his mind, she'd outgrown her childish desire to serve something bigger than herself and had decided to take care of number one. After all, being the king's mistress offered a life of luxury and leisure in a world of poverty. Protection, help, money, status.

All she had to do was renounce her feelings she still had for Taddeo, her friendship with Myrddin, and her oath to the Emperor.

All she had to do was prostitute herself and become someone she wasn't, and she could have everything she ever wanted.

She lowered her head and fiddled with the magnification the way she'd seen Prospero do it. The king's tent resolved into focus at the bottom of the bill. A squad of bored halberdiers in decorative armor guarded it. She expected the king to have a visitor. After a short wait, Ibrahim Pasha appeared alone, spoke to the guards, and entered the tent.

Her eyes narrowed. Everyone has a nemesis. Myrddin had Prospero. Charles had Francis. This man, she suspected, was hers.

"I'll return soon."

"Just lie back and think of France," Prospero advised.

Marie walked down the hill and approached the guards. One of them eyed her up and down. "What can I do for you, milady?"

"Lady Dubois is here to see the King," she said.

"He's busy." He stared at her. "On your way, miss."

"I am to see both gentlemen. The King and his guest, the Turkish prince."

The guards exchanged lascivious grins and ogled her. "Password?"

"*L'amour.*"

They laughed. One of the oafs made a sweeping gesture toward the entrance of the tent. "Of course it is. *Entrez vous*, milady."

"*Merci*," she answered demurely and went in.

The tent was like a palace in itself, with multiple rooms and servants. Floor to ceiling tapestries, which served as partitions, depicted the heroic deeds of Francis's noble ancestors. She slipped between the nearest tapestry and the tent wall and traced the perimeter of the royal pavilion until she heard men's voices. She peered through a crack where two tapestries adjoined to glimpse King Francis and Ibrahim Pasha sitting on couches.

"Our needs are simple," Francis said. "We wish for our merchants to be free and safe to buy and sell in your ports. For an embassy and a Christian chapel to be built in your capital with the understanding my subjects may be free to practice their faith within your borders. And that certain sites considered holy to the Catholic faith be entrusted to our care."

"Your Majesty mentioned money earlier," Ibrahim prompted.

"A donation to the Crown would free our hand in diplomacy to continue to secure alliances with England, the Italian states, and the northern princes in the Holy Roman Empire. We are thinking one hundred thousand ducats. The grand strategy is beginning to bear fruit. Our armies fight Charles in Italy. The German princes press him in the north. And your armies engage him from the east. With a little more pressure, we would see the Empire utterly broken."

This was a different side of Francis, Marie observed. Gone was the impulsive, fun-loving king. This man was a shrewd head of state. The alliance started to make more sense to her now. Besides the commercial advantages, she understood the strategy. France, virtually encircled by the Empire, had in turn ringed the Empire with enemies.

"And what would the Sultan hope to gain by agreeing to these expanded terms?"

"A steady friend in the West. New trade through the port of Marseille. An ally in the struggle against your enemy and mine. Were you to peel Austria from the Habsburgs, we would not object. Its loss would be a devastating blow to the Empire, possibly resulting in Charles's impeachment, possibly even ending it as a political entity."

After which time France will come forward as the next Defender of the Faith and unite the Christian world to fight the Ottoman invader, Marie thought. Francis was playing a long game.

"Very well, Your Majesty," Ibrahim said. "I will take your terms to the Sultan, who may find them agreeable. As a gesture of good faith, the Army is already marching against Austria. We will take Vienna by winter."

The words rang Marie's ears like a bell. The Turks marching on Vienna! The capital of Austria and homeland of the Habsburg dynasty! Marie couldn't believe what she'd heard. The Emperor must be warned; his army was embattled in Italy, leaving the eastern frontier open to Ottoman invasion. She pinched her nose and stifled a sneeze. The air behind the tapestries was filled with dust. It had gotten all over Marie's dress; the Duchess was not going to be happy.

"That is most pleasing to our ears, Ibrahim Pasha. Between our two mighty nations, we will tear our friend Charles V to shreds. But to revisit our terms, do *you* find them agreeable? It is well known the Sultan acts upon your counsel."

"We might have to haggle a bit on the details like customs fees, but in principle, I agree. Our interest is in reducing the Holy Roman Empire. Everything else is a trifle."

"*C'est bon!* As for the mundane details, our chancellor, Antoine Duprat, will negotiate on behalf of the Crown." Francis began to rise.

"There is one more small matter, Your Majesty, which requires discussion."

The king returned to his seat with a sour face. "*Oui?*"

"It was understood you would capture Myrddin Wyllt for the Sultan. This was not accomplished."

"We shall try again. He is just a man. It is our pleasure that he be captured."

"He is not just any man. It is vital that France deliver him to us. Alive or dead, it does not matter."

"We said it shall be done. It shall be done because we wish it." Francis was a man who believed things happened simply because he wanted them to happen.

"We might also discuss the scientist and the girl you did manage to take."

"What would you have us do with them?"

The Grand Vizier shrugged. "I care not what you do with them. Do what pleases you."

"Ah. That is good."

"You can hang them, flay them, draw and quarter them, burn them at the stake. Whatever style of execution is in vogue in this country. It does not matter to me as long as they die."

Francis sulked. "But we have taken a liking to our new friends."

"The girl must die. I smelled Myrddin on her. We may talk about the scientist later."

The king inspected his nails. "We have particularly taken a liking to the young lady."

Ibrahim sighed. "Then kill her after you bed her, Your Majesty. I would have your word on that. The relations between our great nations depend upon it. An alliance that benefits France."

Francis looked down at this lap with a sad expression. Then he shrugged and smiled. "*C'est la vie*. Very well. It shall be done tonight. Both of them will die."

"Your Majesty is powerful and wise."

"We nourish and extinguish," the king said.

That was more like the Francis she knew. She resisted an urge to lunge into the room and crack their heads together. What a pair of jerks!

She emerged from the tent moments later. One of the guards raised his eyebrows. "My, milady, that match was short."

"They king could not rise to the occasion."

After turning the nearest corner, she broke into a run. There was no time to waste. She found Prospero on the hill stargazing with his glasses.

"Back already?" the scientist asked. "Are you unwell?"

"We have to get out of here, Prospero. Tonight."

He lowered his head to stare at her through his glasses, which made his eyes appear comically large. "In the name of Copernicus, why would we do that?"

"The king plans to—"

"What?" He adjusted the glasses, looking past her shoulder. "It simply cannot be!"

Marie wheeled. She saw nothing in the darkness beyond the campfires. "What is it?"

Prospero's look of surprise turned into a frown. "Not what. Who. The Magus comes."

She followed his gaze and saw a speck of light. "Myrddin's here? Let me see!"

He handed her the glasses, but still she saw nothing. There! Myrddin strode along the road, the tip of his oak staff glowing bright as a lantern. Taddeo marched at his side, toting an arquebus. Leo trotted ahead of them wearing a foolish grin.

"That man is going to ruin everything," Prospero said, flapping his hands. "He is trying to get in on my action. Francis is *my* patron. I found him first!"

"Taddeo is with him!" she said. She bounced from foot to foot, too excited to stand still. "He came to rescue me!"

"How is this joyful news? Did I mention there is no Inquisition in France? We have a good thing here! Are you really that much in a hurry to go back to the Emperor and die in some dungeon because we cannot make gold for a madman?"

"I swore an oath—"

"*Mama mia*, woman, do you think Charles gives a crap about your heartfelt oath of loyalty? Francis is our friend. He is offering everything we could ever want."

"He's also planning to kill us. I heard him say it to Ibrahim Pasha in his tent."

"What? That makes no sense. Why would he do such a thing?"

"We're to be executed after I sleep with him."

"Then do not sleep with him! Is this so hard for you?"

"There's no time to argue. We must make haste. It's happening tonight whether I sleep with him or not. Every minute we delay, we risk him realizing I'm not coming."

She hoisted her skirts and ran down the hill.

Prospero gave chase. "Hey! We must talk about this!"

Her mind flashed to Taddeo, her brave and intrepid Taddeo, marching to her rescue with an arquebus on his shoulder. "He came for me!" she yelled into the night. "Taddeo came!"

"Yes," Prospero huffed behind her, "this is very nice for you, but—"

"Blah, blah, blah," she called back to him.

Marie skipped into her tent and bounced off the chest of a giant African wearing a red vest. She swung her fist toward his face, but he caught it in his massive hand. Two other turbaned giants lit a lamp on the dressing table. A pale glow filled the room.

The African raised his scimitar. "Nothing personal, love. It's just orders."

Marie clenched her eyes.

Make it quick.

"You are not being rational, *bella!*" Prospero raced into the tent and barreled into the assassin, who staggered with an *umph*, his weapon flying.

She drove her palm into the man's nose, which spurted blood on her dress. Anna Jeanne was going to have a fit. "Get his sword!"

To Prospero's credit, he scooped up the scimitar in an instant. Then he fled into the back of the tent and left her to fend for herself.

The first giant stumbled away from her holding his nose. The others drew their swords and advanced with angry growls.

Marie arched away from the first sword cut, the blade whooshing past her throat. She ducked as the next giant swung his scimitar in a gleaming arc toward her neck. Overturning the dressing table to buy time, she kicked the stool high in the air, caught it and smashed it into the face of one of the assassins, shattering both. She drove the shards into both sides of his bull neck. He gurgled through a fountain of blood and fell with a heavy thud.

"I will be there in a moment!" Prospero called. Marie glimpsed him hunched over a table in the back of the tent, attacking a piece of metal with a hammer. "Keep the knaves busy!"

The man with the broken nose wagged his head to clear it. Marie smashed the clear glass mirror and flung handfuls of glass shards into his face like shurikens. He howled at this fresh pain. Dislodging the nearest tent pole, she struck him with it several times about the face and neck before it snapped over his head.

Prospero banged with his hammer. "Almost done, I assure you!"

The other African ran at her with his sword poised to strike. Marie wheeled and hurled her makeshift spear at him. He dodged, but she'd bought enough time to lunge into her dressing area.

Artemis whispered from its worn leather scabbard and hummed in her hand. Marie and the giant hacked at each other. The sharp ring of steel filled the tent. Sparks flew from the blades.

"*La!*" she hissed.

She feinted and thrust her blade into his chest. He fell with a groan.

The last giant, his nose broken and his face bleeding from a dozen cuts, grabbed her from behind. She spun away, but he caught her dress, flung her high into the air, and smashed her against the ground with the sound of ripping fabric. Artemis flew from her hand.

It was like getting hit by Don Jorge. She felt the impact everywhere, the pain overridden by the desperate need to breathe.

Now she lay on her back unable to move.

The African picked up his comrade's scimitar and positioned its point over her heaving chest. He raised the sword to strike.

"Now it's personal," he said.

Goodbye, Taddeo—

"*Basta!*"

The man's head popped off his body with a grisly *snip*. Blood geysered in the air. The decapitated corpse stumbled, the tip of the sword swaying perilously in front of her throat.

Then it collapsed to the side, revealing Prospero holding a giant pair of scissors.

She let him pull her to her feet. "You had a sword! Why didn't you just fight them with it? I was almost killed!"

"This is a vastly superior offensive weapon." He admired his bloody scissors before tossing them away. "Look at this mess. It is terrible. Francis will not believe a mere girl did this. But I—am I not the greatest scientist of the age? It is exactly the kind of thing I might do! I will be blamed!"

"Aargh!" Marie said in a rage. She tore off the bloody remains of her dress and strode behind her dressing partition wearing only her corset and the gold necklace. She pulled on her clothes. "You're impossible!"

She was squaring her wide-brimmed hat on the way out of the tent when a squad of royal guard tramped onto the scene.

"*Merda*," Prospero hissed behind her.

"Prospero Buonarroti, Marie Dubois, in the name of His Majesty, King Francis, I hereby place you both under arrest," their captain said. "Come peacefully, and we will not harm you."

She studied the fine plumage cresting the man's helmet.

Prospero raised his hands. "We—"

Marie leaped high into the air with a scream and brought Artemis down against the captain's head. The blow cleft his skull and sent the plumes flying. Then she was among the French singing her death song, hacking and thrusting and lopping off limbs in a *galliard* of blood and howling men. All the training she'd received had finally fused into perfect violence. Prospero ran back into the tent to get his scissors. By the time he returned, Marie stood surrounded by corpses sprawled on the bloody grass. She tucked an ostrich plume into her hat band.

Around them, the camp roused at the noise.

The scientist looked down at the bodies. "Perhaps we should go now."

"Are you sure you want to leave your loving patron who's trying to murder us?"

"I just want you to be happy, *bella*." As they left, Prospero cast one last shivering glance over his shoulder and added, "Just remind me never to make you angry."

Chapter IX

RING OF FIRE

Taddeo missed *The Prometheus*. All of its inconveniences seemed nothing compared to this hard, neverending march along the stone road. His sore feet stung with each step. His shoulders ached from carrying the arquebus. His eyes drooped with fatigue. To make things worse, Myrddin whistled the same grating tune hour after hour. He said it was Welsh.

Nonetheless, when the sun went down, Taddeo wished they could press on. As if in answer to this thought, Myrddin rubbed his fingers together and tapped the end of his oak staff, which glowed a feeble red. The Magus blew on it until the gnarled wood burst into incandescence.

Then more marching through black forest so thick that no moonlight penetrated its canopy, the night quiet interrupted only by their footfalls and the distant thrashing and cries of strange beasts. Taddeo withdrew into his mind. He imagined finding Marie tied against a tree with heavy ropes and taunted by evil, leering pirates. In his fantasy, he didn't stammer or study his shoes. He shot the pirates down, swept her off her feet, and kissed her.

They emerged from the forest as if from a cave. The moon loomed bright in the sky, washing the world in its gray light. Leo led them up a rocky hill covered in pines and evergreen shrub. As they topped the rise, a sea of campfires spilled across the landscape. The hazy outlines of hundreds of tents revealed themselves. The army lay sprawled around the base of a hill dominated by the ruins of a monastery. He did a few quick calculations. If ten men occupied each campfire, and as many fires were set on the far side of the hill as within view on this side, then about two thousand men rested here. Possibly a thousand fighters.

His body stopped on its own. His shoulders sagged.

Leo paused when he realized Taddeo wasn't following.

The exhaustion Taddeo had been delaying finally caught up with him. "I thought we'd find Marie and Prospero tied up in a barn somewhere. That's a French army!"

"On the bright side," Myrddin said, "now we know roughly where Marie is."

"How are we ever going to get her out?" Taddeo looked down in despair at his trusty arquebus, completely unsuited to the scale of the monumental task.

"Are you giving up the quest?"

"No." He steeled himself. "I'll figure out something. It's like Prospero always says." He stabbed the air with his finger and added, "'There is always a way!'"

"So what's your plan?"

"The plan is to come up with a—what's that?"

A spark streamed through the night and arced toward the French camp. A tent burst into bright flame. Another spark fell, then another.

"Fire arrows," Taddeo said. "But just one archer. Who in his right mind would be attacking a whole French army on his own?"

"I think we've located Marie," Myrddin said.

Fire raced among the tents. The flames illuminated the underside of a drifting veil of smoke. Taddeo heard men shouting, the sound tinny and distant. Drums pounded. A trumpet blared.

"Any ideas yet on what you want to do?" asked the wizard.

Taddeo set his jaw. "We're going to walk straight through that camp and rescue her."

Myrddin nodded. "Very sound."

Transversing time and space, they entered the French encampment. The east side was in chaos. Coughing men-at-arms ran in all directions. *Gendarmes* strode through the chaos shouting at the cowardly enemy to show himself. Lines of men formed bucket brigades. A man and woman staggered past stark naked, laughing and passing a bottle and crying out, "It's the end of the world!" A fire arrow flickered overhead. Screaming horses stampeded through the burning tents. A handsome man of obvious rank, dressed in bedclothes and surrounded by half-dressed officials, raised his fists and stomped his feet as he watched his massive pavilion collapse in flames.

Taddeo did a double take as they passed. "Wow, I think that's the King of—"

Blinking with vertigo, a man-at-arms watched a boy, tall old man, and a mangy dog appear to walk toward him with massive strides. He raised his crossbow. "Halt!"

"We have an urgent message for the commanding general," Taddeo said.

The man aimed the crossbow at his chest. "That's exactly where I'm taking you."

Myrddin held out his hand and wiggled his fingers. "Sleep."

The man fell into the doorway of a tent, already snoring.

Taddeo grinned. "You helped!"

"Don't get used to it."

The smoke thickened as they reached the edge of the camp. He winced at the searing heat. Men, tents, trees, and grasses burned in a massive wall of fire.

Behind them, French troops formed ranks to repel an attack.

"We're trapped!" Taddeo cried.

Myrddin sighed. "All right, I'll help once more, but that's it, okay?"

"Whatever you say, *mago*. Just get us out of this."

"Don't be so hasty. There's a price. You must give up Marie."

Taddeo blinked. "What?"

"No, I'm just jesting with you. All you have to do is follow me into the fire."

Leo tilted his head at the wizard and whimpered.

"No way!" Taddeo coughed. His eyes stung.

"You have seen me shortcut time and space. Pack your abominable vehicle into a Hessian sack. Start fires with my fingertips. Attract rabbits with a whistle. Yet you still don't believe in magic. I'm not asking for blind faith, sonny. Empirically, as a matter of fact, I can do magic!"

Taddeo couldn't stand the heat any longer. His skin felt taut as a drum. He either had to trust the Magus or retreat and surrender to the French soldiers, who were in the mood to hang someone.

He followed the wizard into the flames. He entered a blinding field of white.

The heat and light and noise suffocated him. He flailed and cried out.

I'm okay, he realized.

The heat had lost its intensity. The smoke no longer choked him. Surrounded by the pure glow, he followed the shadowy form of the Magus through the conflagration.

And emerged on the other side falling to his knees hacking, his clothes smoking.

Myrddin patted his shoulder. "You did very well."

Taddeo coughed up a mouthful of soot and spit. "You mean there was a chance," he said hoarsely, "I could have burned up and died?"

"Well. Um." The wizard pointed. "Oh, look, it's Marie and Prospero."

The boy picked up his arquebus, still hot to the touch, and peered into the dark.

"I don't see—"

The arrow whistled through the air. Taddeo glimpsed its point flickering toward his face before Myrddin reached out and snatched it.

"*Cristo santo*," he breathed.

"See what happens when you save someone's life once?" the Magus said. He tossed the arrow over his shoulder. "One finds himself feeling responsible for it. It's a slippery slope."

"Marie!" Taddeo called out. "Don't shoot, it's Taddeo and Myrddin!"

The wizard reignited his staff to provide a beacon. They hurried through an uncultivated field overgrown with grasses and wildflowers. The shouts and roar of the flames receded behind them. Two figures emerged from the gloom.

Marie wore a wide grin that mirrored Taddeo's. Bow in hand, splattered heel to head in French blood, she was even more beautiful than he remembered. He knew he looked pretty dreadful, his hair singed, his face and doublet blackened with soot.

He wanted to tell her about the incredible adventure he'd had. Fighting a running battle with bandits in the war-torn wasteland of Navarre. The slaughter of the ghouls. The long march. The rush through the French camp. The walk through fire. He opened his mouth but nothing came out but a hoarse croak. His throat felt better after a long pull on his canteen.

Smiling again, he said nothing. He decided to let his presence speak for itself. He handed the canteen to Marie, who accepted it with her own smile.

While she drank, he noticed she looked a little higher in the chest and thinner about the waist then he remembered. The realization she was wearing a corset under her clothes nearly made him swoon.

Leo barked happily and wagged his tail at the reunion. He circled Taddeo's legs several times before knocking him down into the wildflowers and licking his face.

That was when Taddeo realized Marie liked him the way he liked her.

He scratched the dog behind the ears. "I love you too, Leo."

Prospero helped him to his feet. "You have done well for yourself coming to find us, my daring protégé. But as you can see, we have rescued ourselves. After the king ordered our execution, our lovely friend here went on a murder spree."

Marie took another nip at the canteen, swished the water around her mouth, and spit, still smiling. Once again, she reminded

Taddeo of a cat.

"I suggested she shoot a fire arrow at her tent to destroy the evidence and sow confusion. A single arrow." He glared at her. "Not ten!"

"I got a little carried away," she admitted.

"Do not make her angry, Taddeo. You would not like her when she is angry." The scientist rubbed his hands together. "So. We are all here."

"Aye," Marie said. She looked at the wizard as if she wanted to hug him.

Myrddin returned the look. His hands jerked at his sides. He glanced up at the moon. "We'd better get moving."

Prospero eyed him with a sniff. "I was just going to say that. It is like you rudely interrupted me while I was actually saying it." He turned to Taddeo. "So where is *The Prometheus*? We will make good our escape in the wagon."

"I won't ride in that odious machine again," Myrddin said, looking down at Prospero.

"And who invited you? So, Taddeo. Where did you put my precious?"

"The Magus is carrying it in his sack, Doctor."

Myrddin patted the bulging sack and nodded with a slight smile.

Prospero regarded the oily burlap sack with its mysterious black stain and offensive odor. The blood drained from his face. "You cannot carry *The Prometheus* around in a bag! It is degrading!"

"Doctor, please," Taddeo said. "We don't need it anyway. We can walk faster than we can ride if we go with the Magus. He can shortcut space and time."

"*E tu, Bruto?* You have been around this charlatan a few days, and already you are eager to abandon the rock of science for hocus pocus and mumbo jumbo!"

"But you said yourself that what the Magus practices is actually science but on a more advanced level."

Eyeing the bulging sack, which allegedly contained his steam wagon in violation of every known law of nature, Prospero stroked his goatee, no doubt now finding his earlier claim dubious. The wizard looked back at him with his bemused expression and cocked an eyebrow.

"Perhaps I did say that, Taddeo. But that does not mean I do not loathe the man. I would not stoop to transverse space and time with the likes of *him*!"

"That's okay," Myrddin said. "I can only do it with one person anyway."

"That is very sad for you. We all have our limits. Return my marvel and take back your girl—before she gets angry and slaughters another army—and we will be on our way, and good morrow to you, sir!"

Taddeo sagged. Marie pleaded with the Magus with her eyes.

Myrddin sighed. "I would be proud to ride in your abomination, Prospero."

"It could be arranged," Prospero sniffed.

"Now that that's settled," Taddeo said, "where are we going?"

"We can't go west for obvious reasons," Marie said. "South is the Mediterranean. North keeps us in France. We have to go east into Italy. Agreed?"

"The ground here is too soft for *The Prometheus*," Taddeo chimed in, finding it easy to talk as long as he addressed Prospero. "The Alpine road leading to Lombardy can't be more than two miles southeast of here. I'll go with the Magus and get the steam wagon up and running on the road. By the time you and Marie arrive, Doctor, we'll be ready to move."

"No, Taddeo, it is I who must go and keep this old fraud company," Prospero said with the air of one making a noble sacrifice for a friend. "You have endured him enough. If he will ride in my wondrous chariot, it is only fair I condescend to transverse space and time with him. You escort Lady Slaughterhouse. Get to us as fast as you can. We will be ready for you."

"Godspeed," Marie said.

The wizard and the scientist left them with a final wave.

"How is this transversing anything?" Prospero said. "It is just walking!"

And then they were gone, Myrddin's torch a dot of light in the distance.

Taddeo let out a long sigh of relief. The ensuing quiet brought an incredible sense of peace. He smelled the wildflowers. Marie toyed with a button on her jacket while she stared at him.

He pretended to find the stars interesting. "Um. Well."

Then she stood right next to him, her face so close he could smell her unique scent, feel her moist breath on his face, sense the heat radiating from her body.

The girl touched her lips to his cheek and moved her face from side to side, tickling him. Then she pulled away, leaving him spellbound.

This, he thought, *is what transversing time and space should feel like.*

"Thank you for coming for me," she said.

Still he couldn't look at her. She tilted her head.

Taddeo held out his hand and brushed his fingertips against the back of her hand.

She smiled and took his hand in hers.

"You're welcome," he whispered.

They walked hand in hand across the field and through the distant woods. At dawn, French cavalry would be hot on their trail. Still, they took their time.

For a while, they enjoyed the quiet. Then Marie related the wondrous things that had happened to her while they were apart. The Carib tribesmen, the arrival of the king, the hunt, the ball, meeting the Grand Vizier of the Ottoman Empire and her spying, ending her tale with the arrival of the Turkish assassins and French troops. Taddeo shook his head in wonder.

"And what about you?" she asked him. "Did you have any adventures?"

"It wasn't so bad," he managed. He said nothing more. He

wanted her to talk. He wanted to share her silence. Either was fine, as long as he didn't have to ruin the moment by hearing himself think or speak.

Marie squeezed his hand. He squeezed back.

They heard *The Prometheus* before they laid eyes on it. Then they cleared the treeline and saw it parked on the road, puffing steam.

Prospero greeted them with his hands planted on his hips. "There you are, Taddeo! What have you done to my baby?"

"What's wrong, Doctor?"

"There are arrows sticking into it everywhere, that is what is wrong! There is dried blood on the driving seat! And my hookah has a crack in it!"

Marie's eyes filled with worry and wonder, but he pretended not to notice. He didn't want to talk about killing that boy and the others. When Marie told her story of fighting ten men-at-arms during their escape, it sounded like high adventure, the stuff of legend. When he thought about what he had to do to stay alive during the running fight with a ragged bunch of starving farmers, he remembered it only as pointless horror.

"I ran into a little trouble on the road."

"A little?" Myrddin snorted. "I was there. The boy singlehandedly fought off thirty—"

"It's not important," Taddeo said quickly. "I apologize for the damage, Doctor."

Marie stared at him wide-eyed.

Prospero nodded. "All right then. Take the tiller. You will drive."

Taddeo suppressed a smile. Prospero almost never let him drive the wagon.

They climbed aboard. He released the brake and put the steam wagon into gear.

"I can't believe you actually met the King of France," he said. "What was he like?"

"Selfish, frivolous, and a little crazy," Marie told him.

"Yes, a truly a great man," Prospero said. "A real friend of the arts."

"Except for the part where he ordered our execution. That wasn't so friendly."

"Why did he want you dead?" Taddeo wondered.

Marie answered, "The Ottoman ambassador asked him to kill us because we know the Magus. But what he wanted most of all was the Magus himself."

The three of them turned to the wizard for an explanation, but Myrddin lay sprawled on the back bench under the gun rack, sleeping with Leo draped across his stomach.

"It's worse than that," Marie added. "The Turks are marching on Vienna."

"The Sultan too is a great friend of the arts," Prospero noted.

"There's nothing we can do about any of this now," Taddeo said. "The *mago* is right; we need to sleep. I'll take first shift at the tiller. You go ahead and get some rest, my love—that is to say, my dearest, I mean, Marie—"

She smiled, looking as though she might kiss him again. Instead, she curled up on the bench and fell asleep instantly.

Always the cat.

Taddeo piloted by moonlight. If they survived the next twenty-four hours, they would enter the Alps the day after that. Then Italy and safety.

Unless they ran into the rear of the French army that Marie said had marched this way just a short time ago...

Unless the French pursued them into war-torn Lombardy and killed them there...

Unless...

None of it mattered now. For once, he had no interest in worrying. The future would take care of itself. Right now, he felt filled with contentment.

When he couldn't keep his eyes open anymore, he woke Prospero, curled up next to Marie, and fell into a deep, dreamless sleep.

He woke with a start in bright sunshine.

"Trouble has arrived," Prospero said. "The French kind."

Taddeo stared at him bleary eyed. "Can we outrun them?"

"Not this time, my friend."

He nodded and sat up. "I'll load the guns."

Marie stood on the bench with an arrow notched in her bow. Prospero returned to the tiller, driving the steam wagon directly toward the line of armored horsemen that blocked the road. Leo leaped into the air, jaws snapping at a ball that Myrddin made appear and disappear.

The French had somehow gotten in front of them. There was no way to turn around.

Except they weren't French.

"Doctor, stop the wagon."

"One should never surrender without at least firing at least one shot," Prospero chided him. "If only Piero had listened to me—"

"They're not French. I recognize that man's armor. The Old Guard of Castile. It's Don Jorge."

Prospero cut the engine and pulled the brake lever. *The Prometheus* shuddered to a halt.

Don Jorge raised the vizor on his helmet and said: "Ha. Found you."

"Good day to you, sir!" Prospero declared. "Prospero Buonarroti, at your service!"

"You're under arrest," Don Jorge told him. "Cardinal Gattinara would like a word."

"*Merda*," Prospero hissed.

Don Jorge eyed Marie. "Fight another duel, Marie Dubois? You're covered in blood."

"From killing the French," she told him. "How did you find us? What are you doing here?"

A slight smile cracked the knight's typically fierce expression. "We were looking for you. Then we saw smoke on the horizon." His horse bent its head to crop the grass growing on the side of the road. He leaned and patted its neck. "We'll head toward it and have you back in the warm glow of the cardinal's love in no time."

"I wouldn't do that," Taddeo said.

Don Jorge appraised him briefly. "So you found her." He grinned at Marie. "After a full day being questioned by Inquisitors, the only thing he said was he wanted to go after you."

Marie glanced at Taddeo, who blushed furiously.

"And he found you before we did," Don Jorge added. "It looks like we should have stuck with him. But I'm in charge now. We're going west. Turn this horror around, and off we go."

"That's suicide!" Taddeo insisted.

"Listen to him, Don Jorge," Marie said. "He's right."

"Have no fear, children. I told you we saw smoke on the horizon. An Imperial army has invaded France and sacked Narbonne. If we head west, we should run right into it."

"That wasn't an army," Marie said. "That was me."

The knight slammed his mailed fist into his thigh and roared with laughter. "You? If it were anyone else, I would call them a liar. So what's to the west then that has you in a panic?"

"The King of France and a regiment of royal guard. I fired the camp during our escape."

Don Jorge threw back his head and laughed again. "You are an interesting girl, Marie Dubois." His grin faded to a scowl. "Ah. I think I see your French friends now."

Taddeo wheeled. A small cloud of dust hung over a distant point in the vast landscape behind them. It grew larger by the moment.

Prospero adjusted his glasses. "He is right. I count sixty men on horseback. About ten lances." Ten knights, twenty archers, and thirty *coutilliers* and other retainers.

Marie looked at Don Jorge. "What are we going to do?"

"Oh, now I'm in charge, is that it?"

"Don't you want to be?"

"I am in charge," he said flatly. "I'll tell you what you're going to do. You're going east to Italy as fast as this monstrosity will take you. What I'm going to do is hold the French here as long as I can."

"But that's suicide too!" Taddeo said.

The knight shrugged. He had a job to do, and killing and dying went along with it.

Taddeo estimated their distance from the column and the relative speed of the horses versus the steam wagon. "May I suggest then riding ahead of us about a thousand paces into those trees yonder? The enemy will catch up to our wagon around there, and if you charge them in the flank or rear, you'll have the element of surprise."

The knight shook his head. "A warrior maid and a boy general." He wheeled his horse. "Come on, lads. You heard the kid. Follow me!"

"Don Jorge," Marie called. "I thank ye for this."

"My duty is to keep the four of you alive. But now that you mention it, seeing as I'll be saving your life, I will have my plume back when I catch up to you later."

Then he rode off after his men, crossing a field of golden wheat.

Marie crossed her arms. "He'll have to fight me for it."

Her eyes betrayed her worry. Don Jorge was almost certainly riding to his death.

Its panting breath quickening, *The Prometheus* steamed down the road. Taddeo descended into the carriage, surprised to find it exactly as it had been before Myrddin packed it into his bag. He shoveled coal into the firebox and returned to the driving bench to load the guns.

The column closed fast. He'd miscalculated their speed. They'd have to fight the French before Don Jorge could execute his ambush.

He turned to Myrddin. "What about you? Are you going to help?"

The wizard squinted up at him with irritation. "Again?" The expression turned into an ingratiating smile. "How about I strike them down with a big, fat thunderbolt?"

"You would do this?"

"Of course!"

"But what about your oath?"

"Who cares about that? First, I'll destroy the French. Then I'll make you taller and better looking. I'll make sure you never have to work another day in your life. You won't even have to get out of bed to make a bowel movement. I'll live *just for you*, Taddeo. In fact, you won't even have to live at all, just lie in bed, and I'll fill your head with dreams of perfect—"

"Never mind," Taddeo said. "I'm sorry I asked."

"Oh, you wish to take responsibility for your own life instead of taking me up on my generous offer to live it for you? Well then. Good luck to you!"

Taddeo looked at Marie, who shrugged and offered him a smile. "I guess that leaves us," he said, his fear of death overriding his innate shyness. He swallowed hard. "Are you ready?"

She held up her longbow. "I've got fourteen arrows left."

He gripped his arquebus. "Seven shots. Plus the cannon."

"The knights are wearing plate," Prospero said from the tiller. "Make your shots count."

Long-range fire would be useless. Once the knights got close, he and Marie would have to shoot them in just the right places. By then, their archers would be in range. They typically fought dismounted but would be deadly at close range.

"Aim for the joints and weak spots in the armor," Marie told Taddeo. She tapped his body to show him where, making him tingle. "And hold your fire until they're almost upon us. I'll take out any archers that come near." She looked at his gun. "Are you skilled with that?"

"I can shoot," Taddeo said.

Fighting farmers armed with sickles and spears was one thing. These were well fed, heavily armored French *gendarmes* mounted on powerful destriers. Professional killers, born and bred. Hardened and remorseless. In the old days, a knight was worth any ten infantry, maybe more. Stronger bows and gunpowder weapons began to even the odds. But then stronger armor was developed. Knights still held the edge in any fight.

And they stopped at nothing.

The only thing that could save Taddeo and his friends was Don Jorge. He just hoped the vaunted Spanish knight proved as good as everyone said he was.

The Prometheus chugged down the road at full speed. Pennants streaming, the French cavalry pounded after them in an orderly steel column. The knights' beaked helmets, massive plumage, and velvet coats made them appear like colorful birds of prey.

Their leader raised his visor. "Stop in the name of the King!"

Marie stepped onto the roof of the carriage, but Taddeo stayed her with a touch. "Let me get them off the road first. It'll slow them down."

"You can do that? How?"

He stomped a lever at his feet.

Something clanged. Something else whirred. A box opened under the backboard.

Caltrops spilled bouncing across the road. The first ranks of French horsemen went down as their horses fell or reared. Taddeo winced, appalled at the terrible but necessary harm he was doing to the poor animals. The next riders in line, unable to change course in time, also went down in a flurry of screams and crashing metal.

Marie flashed him an approving smile. "Taddeo *pour la victoire.*" *Taddeo for the win.*

The rest of the column swerved off the road. Marie leaped onto the carriage roof. She notched her bow as the first riders caught up to *The Prometheus.*

The archers came first, flying out on the flanks. Taddeo ducked as arrows and crossbow bolts snapped past his ears. The archers were unused to shooting while riding, and the rough ground ruined their accuracy. It didn't stop them from being terrifying, however.

Marie pulled the bow taut and took aim.

"*Salut!*" she cried as she loosed.

Taddeo saw an archer lean from his saddle and spill onto the grass.

She loosed again. A second archer threw his hands in the air and fell off his horse with a feathered shaft in his chest.

She was *singing.* Taddeo had never heard anything like it before.

Her third arrow glanced off a *gendarme's* ornately embossed breastplate and up into the exposed underside of his chin.

Prospero was right, Taddeo thought. *She's a killing machine.*

The French veered away to avoid Marie's withering fire before returning. Some of the archers, armed with wheel-lock pistols, opened fire with loud bangs and puffs of smoke. The air filled with the hum of shot. Taddeo discharged his arquebus and dropped one of them. Marie loosed, and another spilled out of his saddle to lie writhing in the mud.

The next wave of archers caught up to the steam wagon and emptied their pistols. Marie ignored the metal buzzing past her head. She released shaft after shaft with devastating effect.

Then she dropped her bow and dusted her hands.

"*La.*" She drew her sword and regarded Taddeo. "*Voici, monsieur.* The knights and their *coutilliers* will try to board now. I'll fight them. You cover me, I cover you."

Taddeo nodded in wide-eyed terror.

The French flanked *The Prometheus* in heavier numbers. Some drifted close to board while others sped ahead to take a shot at Prospero. The balls smacked into the paneling behind the scientist's head. Arrows thudded into the sideboards. Another struck his hat and sailed away with it.

The scientist patted his curls. "Archimedes' Tub!" He turned to Taddeo. "I must remind you even I cannot drive and die at the same time."

Taddeo sighted down the barrel of the swivel gun. "Not now, Doctor." He touched the burning tip of his *botefeux* against the priming pan.

The *peterero* belched grapeshot and smoke in a blinding flash of light. The smoke drifted to reveal a group of riderless horses.

He pumped his fist. "*Per la vittoria!*"

Myrddin, sitting with a heavy leather-bound book open on his lap, wiggled his pinky in his ear after the blast of the cannon.

"I'm so sorry to disturb your reading with my struggle to survive, *mago.*"

The wizard's lips curled into a slight smile as he returned to his book.

Marie hacked and thrust as French *coutilliers* grabbed hold of the wagon and tried to pull themselves up over the edge of the carriage roof. They were lightly armored but still formidable. Taddeo rushed to cover her. He lowered his muzzle as two helmeted heads popped up.

"Let go, or I'll shoot you both," he said.

"The King will do worse to us if we do," one of them said.

Taddeo nodded. "*Così sia.*" He ignited the powder in this piece and fired. The gun butt jerked against his shoulder. A smoking hole appeared in the man's helmet with a metallic *thud*. Then it was gone.

He put his boot against the other helmet and pushed as hard as he could. The Frenchman wouldn't budge. Against all reason, the soldier hoisted himself up.

The only way to stop him was to shove a dagger into his face. Taddeo reached for the blade at his belt with a trembling hand.

A sword flashed and withdrew in one clean motion. The *coutillier* dropped away with a brief scream to fall under the carriage wheels.

"Reload your gun," Marie said with a wink. "I'll handle the wet work."

He nodded, paling, then flinched as a pistol ball clanged off the exhaust pipe. He called on all the saints as he reloaded.

"If only we had a giant magnet," Prospero yelled back to him.

Marie moved like a dancer. She hacked at helmets and upturned swords that now rose on all sides of the wagon like a flood of steel.

He whistled. She glanced at him. He tilted his head. *Look over there.*

Don Jorge was coming.

The troop of Spanish cavalry left the wood at the gallop and crossed the wheat field in seconds. They lowered their lances as one.

"SANTIAGO!" they roared, calling on Saint James.

"For Spain!" Don Jorge cried.

The charge hit home. The line crashed into the flank of the French column. Men toppled, their chests pierced or shattered. Horses reeled shrieking. The air filled with screams. The Spanish threw away their broken lances, drew their broadswords, and waded into the press, lopping off heads and limbs.

Half the French raced toward this new threat. Their horses stomping mud, the knights traded blows in a swirling melee. Taddeo saw Don Jorge stand in his stirrups and cut an opponent almost in half. Then he lost sight of him amidst the roaring metal men.

Taddeo raised his piece and fired at a *coutillier* who had pulled himself up onto the carriage roof. The ball glanced off his helmet with a loud *clang*. The man stumbled backward and disappeared over the edge.

Ten riders were still in pursuit. Five *coutilliers* climbed onto the roof. Marie met them with steel while Taddeo frantically reloaded and Leo puffed out his chest and barked.

"*La!*" She slashed at their blades. "*La!*"

Taddeo whistled and presented his gun.

She jumped to the side to give him a clean shot.

"*Basta!*"

Prospero barreled past with a metal tube stoppered at the back like a giant syringe. He ignited the tapered tip at the front with the *botefeux* and plunged the stopper. A stream of phosphorescent green fire leaped across the soldiers' heads and chests.

The men flailed in agony. One by one, they staggered off the carriage like human torches and crashed to the ground. The rest of their pursuers slowed. They were giving up the chase. Seeing their comrades burned alive had taken the fight out of them.

"Greek fire," Prospero said. He dropped the tube onto the driving bench, where Myrddin still read his book while steering the steam wagon with one stockinged foot. "And a brilliant green. Did I not say it would be a most brilliant, sizzling, warlike green, my protégé?"

"Yes, Doctor," Taddeo said. A wave of exhaustion passed over him as he realized the fight was over.

Marie nudged him and smiled. "We work well together."

Taddeo ran to the edge of the steam wagon and vomited over the side.

"Yes, not bad for a couple of scientists, eh?" Prospero said. He cupped his hands around his mouth and called, "Hey, where are you going, Frenchies?" He dismissed them with a wave of his hand. "Bah! Look at them flee like little Gallic chickens! Bock, bock!"

"Let's not get carried away," Marie said. "We had the elevation, their horses were tired, they were floundering in the mud, their archers had to shoot from horseback, only a few could come at us at once, none of their knights made it onto the wagon, Don Jorge arrived in the nick of time—"

"Yes, but aside from that—"

"Besides all that, we were just plain lucky."

"Yes, well, it may be as you say, but we still did very well. Eh, Taddeo?"

Taddeo didn't answer as he watched the ground roll by. Marie was right; they were lucky to be alive. He looked up and saw a large walled city in the distance.

They were passing Marseille.

Ahead loomed the Alps. And Italy.

He was going home.

Italy

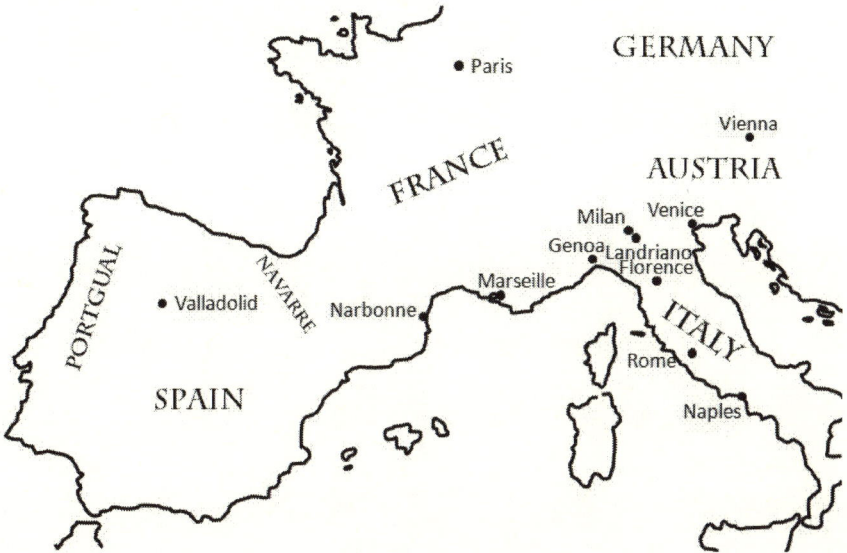

Chapter X
LEGION OF ITALY

The moon hung full and low as *The Prometheus* chugged through the mountains. Taddeo and Marie huddled behind the tiller, wrapped in a heavy wool cloak while Leo slept at their feet. Prospero and the Magus had turned in and now shook the carriage with their snoring. Outlined in hazy moonlight, the hulks of the Alps loomed around them. Glass oil lamps fitted with mirrors, mounted on the front of the carriage, lit the cracked road and gleaming particles of snowfall. Taddeo listened to the steady gasp of the steam engine. Aside from an occasional deer or hare darting across the road, it felt as if the entire world were asleep except for them.

Marie snuggled against his arm and rested her head on his shoulder. Her rhythmic breathing signaled that she too had fallen asleep. A deep and warm sense of contentment filled Taddeo's chest. He ached to tell her he loved her. To hear her say the same. For the past few days, they'd barely exchanged a word. There was too much work to do, his terrible shyness had returned, and it often proved impossible to get a word in with all the bickering between the scientist and his arch nemesis. She'd matched his silence with her own, though he often caught her watching him—her eyes bright and a slight smile parting her lips—particularly when he was building an invention on the fly, such as the carriage lamps. They began to anticipate each other's needs without words.

Although he wanted more, he felt happy and was even grateful for his shyness. So many ideas and feelings burst through his head, he feared once he started speaking, they would all come out in a flood and make him sound like a madman. It was bad enough he'd lost his lunch in front of her after the running fight with the French. He'd dropped some serious *sprezzatura* points on that one.

The Prometheus picked up a little speed as the grade began to decline. They'd entered Italy and would cross the foothills of the Alps by morning. Already, he felt like he'd come home. He pictured the steam wagon continuing east without stopping. First came hilly Piedmont, filled with industrious people dedicated to cattle and winegrowing, including its famous sparkling wines. Then Lombardy and its plains, one of the most populous and richest regions in Europe with its great cities, universities, and industries. And after that, the Republic of Venice, the great trading center. He felt close enough to his native land he could almost smell the Great Lagoon, hear the endless hammering and sawing of shipbuilding, and taste his mother's *cicchetti*.

The Floating City was built on one hundred twenty small islands linked by canals and bridges and packed with houses built on wooden piles petrified by the neverending flow of waters rich in minerals. Founded by refugees fleeing the horrific German and Hun invasions during the fall of the Western Roman Empire, Venice remained part of the Eastern Roman Empire for centuries, and as a result enjoyed enormous trading privileges in the Near East. The city, which became a city-state as its autonomy increased, grew rich in trade in grain, salt, silk, spices, and other goods. Pilgrimages and Crusades into the Holy Land launched from its ports.

In 1203, the Fourth Crusade intended to sail for Egypt from Venice but, running out of money, decided to sack Constantinople, capital of the Eastern Roman Empire and Christendom's greatest city, instead. A flood of Byzantine refugees, many of them philosophers, artists, architects, and scholars, took refuge in Venice. The Eastern Romans recaptured the great city but lost it to the Turks in 1453, resulting in another wave of refugees. These men brought with them the stored knowledge of the Greek civilization, contributing greatly to Europe's *Renaissance*, which began in Italy. And Venice, in acquiring Crete, Cyprus, and other islands and territories around the Mediterranean, became an empire.

When Taddeo saw the winged Lion of St. Mark on the flag of the Republic, his heart swelled; when he heard a band play "Judith Triumphant," he wiped a tear from his eye. His family could trace its roots back to the founding of the city. A distant ancestor in the Cellini clan designed the great engineering plan to divert the rivers flowing into the Great Lagoon to create a natural defense for the city against land-based attacks. Taddeo's palatial house, with its views of the Rialto Bridge spanning the Grand Canal, was one of the finest in the city. His father Gregorio served as a member of the Great Council, on which all the noble families sat, as well as the Senate it elected. When Taddeo closed his eyes, he could see his father in a smoky study surrounded by sharp-eyed merchant lords, discussing supply and demand. Taddeo had the same blood as his forebears. One day, he would take his place in that exciting world, and these and other worries would be his. His blood held rights, and those rights carried responsibilities.

He couldn't help but see himself as a steady disappointment to Gregorio in that respect. Taddeo excelled at math but cared little for accounting. He was a dreamer; for him, the little worms that produced silk were far more interesting than the finished product's prices and trade routes. Whether other planets like Earth existed out there in the cosmos kept him up at night, not interest rates and credit risk. He didn't have a ruthless nature suited to business or politics; he didn't enjoy competition.

In fact, capitalism interested him only as a stage of social evolution. It offered the possibilities of much greater production compared to the feudal system it displaced, true, but it ultimately replaced one master with another, a master with even greater wealth to use against the oppressed. Taddeo rejected Venice's brand of republicanism in which only the richest and oldest families could vote or hold high office. He saw a future in which men ruled themselves, and all men were equal. Technology would make this future possible by producing vast surpluses of goods such that none would ever want.

These worries had turned his stomach into knots since he'd left home. He had a limited time to make his mark in science. After that, he had to begin learning the intricacies of the family business and court a gentlewoman from a strategically important family. His father depended upon it.

He was so close to home now, but he didn't want to go home.

The girl sitting next to him made all these worries disappear as if by magic. In everything she did, Marie Dubois exhibited a freedom of spirit, thought, and action he'd always dreamed for himself. She was like a perfectly finished design, his feelings for her like an exciting new project filled with possibilities. The obstacles to him loving a woman like this, once insurmountable, seemed unimportant now. He knew in his heart that if it came to giving up everything—even his birthright—to be with her, he would do it. This was true alchemy, he believed. The more valuable pursuit of such transformation was internal, not external. Love was the most precious possession in the world, and no amount of gold could buy it. It either happened, or it didn't, and if it did, it could be pure magic. A miracle as real and pure as when he walked through fire.

Taddeo gazed up at the moon and wished this night would never end. They'd have to stop somewhere in Piedmont to take on coal and provisions. After that, he wanted to keep driving forever. To Persia, even. Maybe see India. Perhaps take the Silk Road all the way to great Cathay, as another notable Venetian, Marco Polo, once did to attend the court of Kublai Khan.

The steady pant of the steam engine lulled him into a doze. The distant babble of voices woke him. He lay on the back bench wrapped in the cloak, early morning sunlight warming his face.

Marie sat behind the tiller. The moment he saw her tense expression, he sat up and gazed across the foothills of the Alps. Ahead, the road climbed a hill, revealing nothing of what lay beyond.

The rising run blazed along its crest.

What had Marie worried revealed itself instantly when he simply turned his head. On both sides of the wagon, ragged horsemen picked their way through the rocks, pacing *The Prometheus* as it labored up the incline. Leo followed his gaze and growled. Beyond the distant hills, columns of smoke twisted in the sky, a reminder they'd entered a country embroiled in endless war.

Where were Prospero and the Magus? Marie tilted her head toward the carriage. Still sleeping. He nodded and studied the nearest riders with Prospero's binocular spectacles. At the moment, they stayed about a crossbow shot's distance from the wagon.

Taddeo recognized them as *Reiters*, German mercenary cavalrymen lightly armored in crested morions and chainmail blackened against rust. Their appearance, coupled with their ferocity on the battlefield, inspired the French to call them *Diables Noirs*, or Black Devils. Each carried a heavy boar spear and kept multiple wheel-lock pistols holstered within easy reach at his saddlebow, the long straight butts terminating in large round pommels they used to club their foes at close range.

The presence of German soldiers in Italy was hardly remarkable. Foreign armies had defiled these rich lands for years. But whom did they serve? Living in Imperial territory, most Germans fought for the Emperor, true, but France hired them for its own armies as well. Either way, it spelled trouble. After all, Taddeo and Marie were on the run now from both sides of the conflict.

The question was whether the Reiters would attack. For now, they appeared content to simply keep pace with the wagon.

"I think we could take them if we have to," Marie said.

The Prometheus crested the hill.

Below, a vast army spilled into view.

Taddeo whistled.

Marie: "Um. Never mind."

Taddeo muttered a passage from Boccaccio's *Decameron*: "*Noi abbiamo costui tratto della padella e gittatolo nel fuoco.*" Roughly translating as, *Out of the frying pan and into the fire.*

It was an army of ragamuffins, their tents scattered across the plain under a smoky haze from hundreds of cooking fires. A portion of the camp consisted of a ring of wagons, gun limbers, and cannon, inside which hundreds of tents and makeshift huts, supported by pikes, had been erected. Captains drilled loose formations of soldiery. Drummer boys practiced sounding the advance. Laundry women hung up shirts to dry in the shade of poplars. *Stradioti*, Balkan mercenary cavalry who fought like Turks, raced back and forth, contesting who could score the most tent pegs with the tips of their lances.

When Taddeo saw the yellow-and-black Imperial Eagle banners thrust into the ground in front of the command tents, he confirmed what he'd already figured: They'd found the Emperor's main army in Italy. He blew a sigh of relief. If it were French, riders would soon bring word to arrest the fugitives of the King's justice. Seeing as it was Imperial and so far from Spain, it was likely operating outside the Emperor's direct control. That meant whoever commanded this army probably was not on the lookout for any missing alchemists.

Not that they were in the clear. As far as the army ahead of them was concerned, they were no one special, and therefore could be casually robbed and murdered depending on the whims of whoever was in command of this mob of killers. The entire region had already been depopulated by marauding armies. Two years earlier, men like these sacked Rome, plundered the Vatican's gold, and kidnapped the Pope for ransom. The Reiters on their flanks were likely waiting for their surrender so they could be first at the spoils.

Taddeo and Marie couldn't fight their way through. They'd have to talk their way out.

Moments later, he was shaking Prospero awake and babbling their troubles.

The scientist yawned. "Then it is hopeless. So I shall sleep a bit longer—"

Taddeo shook him again. "Doctor, we need you!"

Prospero started awake. "Need me? For what?"

"We need you to be impressive. Can you do that?"

A grin spread across his mentor's face. "But of course! This I can do." He sat up, bits of straw falling from his curly hair, and thrust his finger in the air. "I shall impress them into submission. I shall impress them to their knees!"

As Prospero climbed the steps, Myrddin appeared next to Taddeo. "Shall we?"

"Are you sure? I wouldn't want to force you into some sort of obligation that might make you uncomfortable."

"Are you kidding? Prospero is going to impress someone. I wouldn't miss that for the world."

They ascended to the deck. Prospero stood behind the tiller looking ahead bold and cocky as a general. As the steam wagon rolled into the heart of the camp, the soldiers trickled away from their duties to watch it chug past with their mouths hanging open like drawbridges. Soon, hundreds, thousands gathered around—Landsknechte with their garish rags, Spanish arquebusiers in dark doublets, enigmatic Stradioti brandishing Turkish scimitars, flamboyant Italian Condottiere in highly polished armor, and bejeweled Croats.

The soldiers exclaimed in a dozen languages and dialects. Then they gasped and broke into spontaneous applause.

Prospero turned and winked. "Impressive enough for these ruffians, it seems. Child's play."

Taddeo sighed. "Doctor." He pointed over the scientist's head.

Prospero looked up and scowled. Silent fireworks burst in the air, fanning sparkling streams of red, blue, and yellow light. Behind him, Myrddin muttered and weaved his hands.

"Stop that!" he snapped. "Now you are just being childish!"

Myrddin crossed his arms. The fireworks faded away. The soldiers grumbled and rapped against the sideboards with their weapons.

Prospero glared at him. "See what you have done?"

"*Mea culpa*," the Magus said.

"We'd better stop," Taddeo advised. "They're getting angry."

He brought *The Prometheus* to a long shuddering halt and wilted under the glare of thousands of soldiers.

Prospero, however, still had plenty of panache upon which to draw. He looked down his nose at the flea-bitten louts. "What is this army and who is its commanding general?" he said in halting German. "Speak, knaves! I have urgent business to discuss with him."

The Landsknechte burst into laughter. The Condottiere inspected their nails with disdain. The Spaniards, who didn't speak German, shrugged.

"We are the Legion of Italy, and we serve the Prince of Orange, mighty lord," one particularly brutish specimen said with a mocking bow.

Taddeo gasped. Next to him, Marie frowned. Philibert of the House of Châlon, Prince of Orange—the Flemish Imperial province comprising Holland and Zeeland—had a reputation for unparalleled brutality after the sack of Rome two years ago.

Men like these hadn't sacked Rome. *These exact men* had sacked Rome.

Originally a favorite of Charles V, Pope Clement VII announced for Francis in the previous war after the French took Milan, then switched back to Charles after France lost the war. Following Francis's release from imprisonment and founding of a new alliance against the Empire, Clement switched sides again and joined the League of Cognac, which led Charles to remark with his customary blandness that the Pope was more wolf than shepherd.

While the French advanced on Milan, the ragged Imperial army in Italy, unpaid for months and close to starvation, mutinied and demanded their general, Charles III, the Duke of Bourbon, lead them straight to the comparatively easy, rich spoils of Rome. Yes, Rome was the center of the Catholic world, but the Pope had declared war on the Empire and must be punished. Fearing his own troops, the Duke wisely saw the merit of the new war strategy.

In May 1527, the thirty-five-thousand-strong Imperial army

stormed the walls and overran the militia. Charles III wore a brilliant white cloak during the assault so he'd be readily visible to his men and inspire great feats of bravery with his own. It also made him visible to the Roman gunners, who shot him out of the saddle. The Prince of Orange assumed command as the Landsknechte went berserk, slaughtered a thousand prisoners, and sacked the city. The Pope's Swiss Guard fought heroically on the steps of St. Peter's Basilica; the last of them sacrificed themselves to buy time for the pontiff to escape the city via an underground passage. Unchecked, the Emperor's mercenaries laid waste to Rome. They stole holy relics, broke open the tombs of saints, burned libraries, and squeezed the rich until they coughed up every penny they owned. They violated the nuns and danced drunk in the smoky blood-splattered streets wearing the vestments of cardinals. Bodies rotted in the gutters; the dead choked the Tiber River; the survivors fled howling into the countryside. The Landsknechte found the Pope, who'd been hiding in disguise, and ransomed him for a fortune. The nightmare went on for eight long months and ended only when the food ran out and plague struck.

Many saw the sack of Rome as God's judgment against the corruption and excesses of the Church, but most of the Catholic world reeled at the shocking news. To Taddeo and Marie, the Prince of Orange was a bloodthirsty monster.

"Well then," Prospero brazened it out. "Take me to him at once! I bear a message for the commanding general from the Holy Roman Emperor—"

The Landsknechte gave three cheers for the Emperor as they swarmed over the side of the steam wagon, scooped up Prospero, and tossed him shrieking into the crowd. A dozen massive troopers caught him and bore him away on their shoulders while singing a patriotic song.

"Poor bastard," Myrddin said. "I should have let him win our duel in Venice."

"He'll be all right," Marie said.

"Let's hope so," Taddeo added. "Because if the Prince doesn't like him and whatever message he invents, we're dead."

The excitement over, the soldiers drifted away. A burly Spaniard hammered at the side of the steam wagon with the pommel of his sword. "Get this thing off the road."

Taddeo bowed. "At once, sir."

"Who are you?" The soldier squinted. "You sure as hell aren't soldiers."

Marie stiffened. "I will fight any—"

"We were sent by the Emperor to help," Taddeo cut in. "Whatever you need." Leo barked as if to support his claim.

The Spaniard jerked his thumb to indicate a collection of tents at the edge of the camp. "We got thousands down with the fever. One out of three men is dying in the dirt. Can you help with that?"

Taddeo presented Myrddin. "This man is a physician. He can cure any known disease. He'll have those men back on their feet in no time."

The soldier spit. "Fine."

Taddeo shouldered his arquebus. "Time to make yourself useful, *mago*."

The wizard glared down at him from his imposing height. "You need to quit volunteering me for work, sonny."

The boy feigned shock. "But you swore an oath not to harm a human being."

"That I did. So?"

"Mind you, I'm not asking for your help. But if you don't pitch in and help heal those men, these soldiers are going to cut us to pieces. And you'll be responsible because you could have prevented it, and hence violate your most sacred oath against giving harm."

The Magus's lips moved as he went over the logic himself. He closed his eyes and pinched the bridge of his long nose. "Damn it."

Myrddin touched his shoulder. "Thank you, Myrddin."

"Just remember you're *my* bodyguard, all right?" he growled. "Not the other way around. And you—" he added, glowering at

Taddeo, "you only get to play that card once."

"As you wish," Taddeo said with a bow.

A band of drunk Landsknechte leered at Marie and laughed. They wore heavily plumed hats, hose, and jerkins or doublets pulled over brightly colored rags. The rags were the clothes of men they'd killed; besides great tears from mortal cuts, the clothes typically ripped because their new owners were so large, resulting in a puffed and slashed look that was now being imitated in civilian fashion throughout Europe. Even the hose they wore did not match from one leg to the other.

Their bizarre appearance belied the fact they were the fiercest fighters in Christendom. Short swords and maces hung from their belts; some carried a *zweihander*, a terrible two-handed sword, while others leaned on pikes and long ash staves with ribbons and fox tails tied at the top. Grotesque codpieces suggested monstrous genitals. Men like these died like flies on campaigns. They didn't expect to live long, and they lived as if every day were their last.

"Hey, girlie, fancy a drink?" said one particularly ugly hatless rogue.

Taddeo gulped and fingered his arquebus. Myrddin crossed his arms. Marie sighed and adjusted her sword on her hip.

"I'll be right back." She marched up to the German. Smiling demurely, she took the tankard from his hand and downed it in a single swallow.

The giant grinned down at her. "Now what do I get?"

Marie slammed the tankard into the man's face, making his head vibrate. The Landsknechte roared with surprise.

The ruffian's face darkened. He rubbed his chin. "*Ach!* Now I'm going to have to—"

She swung the tankard over her head in a wide arc and smashed it over his head. Blood poured from his scalp. He winced.

Then he grinned as if the blow had been a mere tap. He clenched his fists with a harsh laugh.

And fell over like an oak.

Marie bent to see if he were still alive.

"Don't worry about him, lass," said one of the Germans. "Rupert's head is hard as a morion." He rapped his knuckles against his helmet.

True enough, the rogue snored peacefully with a little smile on his big ugly face.

Another giant stepped forward and glared down at her with his fists planted on his hips.

"You can fight, girl, but can you drink?"

"Like the ocean drinks a river," Marie answered.

The Landsknechte huzzaed and begged her to share some ale at their canton.

"This is one of those offers that can't be refused," she told Taddeo and Myrddin. "It'll give me a chance to reconnoiter and maybe convince someone in charge here that we need to march to Vienna and aid it against the Turks. I'll meet you back at the wagon tonight for supper."

Taddeo's heart ached as he watched her go. The night before, when they'd nuzzled together under the bright moon, already seemed a distant memory. Filled with contentment, he'd wanted to drive on forever, he remembered. Just a few hours later, his bubble had already burst.

Myrddin filled his pipe with tobacco. "You asked me what Marie is like. That is what she's like. A free spirit in a world of rigid conformity. Knowing this, do you still love her?"

"Yes," Taddeo said. "I do. I love her."

The Magus nudged him. "Then you should be happy right now, not sad, eh?"

"I get your point, *mago*. I just don't want anything to change."

"What has changed?" He blew a smoke ring. "Now if you'll excuse me, I have to go to the sick tents and cure twelve thousand men with typhus, all thanks to my good friend Taddeo."

He was alone now. There was much to be done. *The Prometheus* needed coal and provisioning. He needed to buy new powder and shot for his arquebus. But none of these ideas inspired him. He just wanted to stand there and feel sorry for himself.

He'd never felt so tired.

"You any good at that?" a soldier asked in lyrical Spanish. "Whatever did you do to it?"

While he'd been pondering, five Spanish arquebusiers surrounded him, eyeing his weapon. Compared to the Landsknechte, the Spaniards dressed modestly in dark brown doublets with a red X across the front and stiff ruffles around their necks.

"I added an attachment at the end of the muzzle for my dagger," Taddeo explained. "On the way here, I was forced to stab a boy trying to rob me. I figured if I could stab someone from a distance, it'd be safer, and I wouldn't have to look him right in the eye while he died."

He paused. To professional soldiers like these, he must sound like a coward. But the mustachioed men simply stared back at him and nodded.

"A practical invention," one said while the others muttered their assent. "It gives you the option to thrust with the knife or swing with the butt. Turning the gun into a spear could be particularly handy when you're up against cavalry with nowhere to go, eh? And this?"

"This is just a shoulder strap that makes it easier to carry."

"Hard on the shoulder and back for a long march," the soldier said skeptically.

"But for a short walk, it allows me to use both hands for other things." He flexed his hands.

"Interesting," the men muttered.

"When I have time, I intend to upgrade to the new wheel lock design," Taddeo told them. "What I'd really like to do is make a gun that loads from the rear instead of the front. Henry VIII uses one for hunting. But I'd make a special cartridge that has the primer, powder, and shot sealed in paper. A firing pin would penetrate the paper and strike a percussion cap. Then *bang*. A rotating bolt would seal the breach after firing."

The men peppered him with technical questions. His answers ignited a dozen minor side arguments about how to make the gun lighter and safer to use, streamline the laborious loading process, and improve accuracy over longer distances.

Spain had been in a state of virtually perpetual war since 1494, resulting in the closest thing to a standing army in Europe west of the Ottoman Empire. These men were professional military, veterans of endless campaigning in Italy. They'd shredded the French at Pavia and Sesia. Their success with mass firearms was revolutionizing warfare in Europe.

Somehow, he'd managed to impress them.

"Who are you then?" they asked him. "Some nobleman's son?"

"Me? I'm not an aristocrat. These improvements are my inventions. I'm a scientist."

The men laughed. "Come and drink wine with us then, *científico*."

"Maybe just a little," he replied.

They found out he was the eldest son of Gregorio Cellini of Venice and offered him endless credit, selling him new powder and shot for his matchlock gun at a grossly inflated price. Taddeo bought himself a leather jerkin to wear over his doublet and Prospero a new feathered hat. It was a tradition, they said, for a newcomer to issue a challenge to shoot at targets, and the loser had to buy drinks all around for the platoon. Taddeo, considering himself a good shot and eager to please his new friends, agreed. The men laughed, rushed into a tent, and dragged out a skinny boy named Félix, who arrived sporting a lazy eye and a bucktoothed grin.

"We can always wager a little more than a few drinks," a Spaniard suggested.

Being a city boy, Taddeo knew a con when he saw one. The goofy-looking kid was no doubt a dead-eye shot. He counted the men and figured he could stand them all a drink on his father's credit, assuming he lost. When he refused to increase the wager, they sagged a little.

"*Científico*," one muttered to his comrade, tapping his head.

Taddeo found he wanted very much to win, however. It wasn't often one got the chance to put his skills as an arquebusier against the finest marksmen in the world.

"Gentlemen, you may load your arms," one of the Spaniards said.

Félix gave Taddeo his bucktoothed grin and loaded his arquebus by feel alone. Taddeo tried to match his speed, but his hands kept shaking. He almost forgot to blow the loose powder off the gun, which left unattended could have caused it to blow up in his hands.

The boy snickered, his head bobbing, and gestured for Taddeo to take the first shot. The men gave him a monopod, a forked stand on which to rest the muzzle of the heavy gun. As he was used to shooting without it, he hoped it would give him a nice boost in accuracy.

The man-sized target had been placed a hundred yards across a field. At this distance, he knew, the average marksman hit the target only half the time. The arquebus was considered accurate up to three hundred yards, but only if one were shooting at a barn.

Blowing air out his cheeks, he aimed down the barrel. Continuing to exhale until his body had perfectly stilled, he pulled the trigger. The match dropped into the priming pan, which ignited the powder with a *crash*. A massive cloud of gunsmoke erupted from the muzzle.

A hundred yards distant, a soldier got up from a ditch, dusted himself off, and approached the target. He gave a thumbs-up.

Taddeo turned wide-eyed and nodded to Félix.

The boy laughed, placed his gun, and fired. Moments later, he hooted as he was given a thumbs-up. The Spaniards cheered, placing new bets among themselves. Taddeo caught enough of what they were saying to understand his already long odds were being lengthened.

He reloaded as the target was moved to one hundred twenty-five yards. At this range, a man might hit four out of ten times.

He sighted down the barrel and waited until his trembling body achieved a moment of stillness. He fired. He squinted through the haze.

A hit!

Félix frowned, placed his gun, and fired.

The bullet snapped through the target with a puff of dust.

"Let's spice this up," a Spaniard said. "Make them take a drink!"

The arquebusiers laughed, pushed cups of strong red wine into their hands, and shouted at them to down it fast. Hoping it might still his nerves, Taddeo tossed it back and swallowed it with a gasp. The alcohol rang his head like a bell.

It produced another strange effect. He felt perfect certainty he would hit the target while at the same time hardly caring if he missed. He casually placed his gun, sighted, and fired.

He pumped his fist. "*Per la vittoria!*"

The bucktoothed kid reloaded his piece, his face flushed now, and fired again. Hit.

"Drink! Drink!"

The Spaniards forced another cup on them. Taddeo drank it down greedily. He'd never known wine had such a powerful effect on bolstering courage. No wonder Prospero so often sought its medicinal qualities. It was amazing.

He laughed at the thought of Prospero, though he wasn't sure why. The Spaniards laughed with him and shouted their bets, their eyes gleaming with excitement.

Fire. Hit.

Once again, the boy matched him.

After another cup of wine, he tried to calculate his odds. The target was approaching two hundred yards, at which range a skilled arquebusier might hit a man-sized target perhaps one out of four times, one out of three if he had luck on his side.

He'd crossed some sort of threshold as far as the wine's effects, which he continued to catalog in his mind. His head felt thick and heavy. He knew it would be impossible for him to hit the target at this point but no longer cared in the slightest if he didn't. He was having too much fun to mind losing a silly bet. The gun was practically firing itself at this point anyway.

He felt something nudge his leg and looked down to see Leo gazing up at him with a worried expression, whining and thumping his tail against the ground. "It's okay, boy," Taddeo told him. "Go back to the wagon and wait for me there."

Seeing him sway on his feet while talking to a dog, the Spanish cried fresh bets, clubbing each other with fistfuls of money. Scores of soldiers from other units had gathered to watch the show. They slapped down their coins and squabbled over the odds in a dozen languages. Taddeo laughed at them, making them all dive for cover as he swept the crowd with his muzzle.

"You want to see something? You want to see a true marksman in action? Watch this!"

He threw away the monopod and presented. He'd show them how to shoot without the use of a crutch! The image of an outsmarted Myrddin pinching his nose and saying, "Damn it," crossed his mind and made him laugh out loud. He fired at the same time.

Crap, he thought as he sobered fast. The ball had sailed off into the blue.

The bucktoothed kid snickered. "What a pity."

A moment later, a goose fell out of the sky and smacked into the target board, which toppled over.

Taddeo gasped, unable to believe the blind luck of the shot. Then he laughed and declared, "Gentlemen, dinner is served!"

"*El Diablo!*" howled Félix. He threw down his matchlock and stomped into his tent as half the soldiers swept Taddeo off his feet and hoisted him onto their shoulders. They jogged him around the camp, chanting, "Santiago! Santiago!" while the rest stood glumly until he shouted at them to tap a barrel and put it on his credit. Their faces brightening at the news, they huzzaed and joined the parade, waving swords and pikes and firing guns into the air. *Stradioti* waded into the press on prancing chargers, clashing their scimitars against their shields. A military band led the procession, playing a ragged parody of a marching tune.

The mob passed Marie standing at the center of a large crowd of Landsknechte. Taddeo blew her a kiss with both hands. "I love you, Marie Dubois!"

She stared back at him dumbfounded as they swept past en route to the wine sellers. The Germans cheered and raised their tankards.

Prospero found him still deep in his cups early that afternoon, pontificating to a group of drowsy arquebusiers roasting the goose on a spit while Leo lay on his back, sunning his belly.

"So I was like, 'All celestial objects are in constant motion, and that motion can be expressed mathematically,'" Taddeo told the Spaniards. "And then Giovanni was like, 'Well, we tried that, but our model doesn't work, so God must be intervening to keep the heavens stable.' And I was like, 'That's ridiculous! If the model doesn't work, it's wrong and must be revised—using mathematics!' And then he was all like"—he switched to a mocking falsetto voice—"'I'm going to report your heresy to the Bishop!' And I was like, 'Go ahead! Do it!'"

Prospero whistled and shook his head. "Taddeo, Taddeo. While I am happy to find you at last exploring the joys of the grape, it deeply saddens me you have wasted your virginity on this camp swill. Fortunately for you, I have distilled a pure analgesic for your use."

"Doctor!" cried Taddeo, jumping to his feet. "I bought you a new hat! Pablo, Ambrosio, Diego, Cristóbal, everyone—this is Prospero Buonarroti, my mentor! He taught me everything I know!" He gave Prospero a bear hug. "I love you, man. You are just incredible. I mean it."

Prospero patted his protégé's back. "My poor Taddeo. Now I know your wits are gone. Can you walk? I need you to come with me."

"That," answered Taddeo, "is a great idea."

But walking turned out to be much harder than he'd expected even with Prospero holding him up. His vision swam. Groups of soldiers hailed him and raised their cups in salute.

"How much wine did I actually *buy*, Prospero?"

"You do not want to know," the scientist answered. "And I am not entirely sure. But I might point out half the army is lying in the grass stinking drunk."

"I'm going to be in so much trouble with my father."

"You may take solace in the fact that eventually the sellers ran out of wine."

"Where are we going? I want to see Marie. My dearest, my shining star, my wondrous delight—"

"I do not believe you would make a favorable impression on the young lady at this moment. I am taking you instead to see the Prince of Orange."

"But he's a monster! He's going to kill us all!"

"Ah, he is not so bad."

"If you say he's a 'friend of the arts,' I'm not going."

"Even better than a friend," Prospero declared. "This one is a true lover of the arts."

The commanding general of the Legion of Italy was a young handsome man dressed in gilded plate armor and helmet topped with a generous bouquet of plumage. They found him sitting astride a tall horse, glaring imperiously into some private horizon, prepared to strike whomever displeased him with the gleaming sword he held in his hand.

"Ah, *heer dokter*, I see you have returned with your prodigy," said Philibert of Châlon, the Prince of Orange.

Taddeo felt himself visibly wilting under the man's martial gaze. This was the brutal general who'd sacked Rome. Then he realized the Prince's horse was built of wood, and the Prince himself was posing for a painter laboring over a portrait.

"Your Imperial Highness," Prospero said with a slight bow. "May I present Taddeo Cellini."

Taddeo executed his own awkward bow and almost fell over. He felt sick.

Whatever you do, don't bring up Rome. Don't even say the word. Don't even think it—

The general jumped down from his wood horse, provoking a frustrated sigh from the painter. "Your master tells me a French army passed through this way. About twenty-five thousand fighting men, isn't that right, *heer dokter*?"

Prospero clicked his heels. "That is correct, Your Imperial Highness."

"Our men are ragged, but their swords are sharp. We also have the advantage in firearms." Philibert removed his gloves and waved them at a fly buzzing around his face. "But there are more of them than there are of us, and numbers usually win battles. That is true, is it not?"

"It is so true it should be a Commandment," Prospero assured him.

"Quite. Three days ago, we broke the siege of Genoa and pursued General Odet until we caught up to him just a league south of here. That's where you'll find his dead army rotting on some nameless hillside. We outnumbered them. Half of the poor sods were so weakened by plague they could barely put up a fight."

"In which case, the slaughter was an act of loving mercy, Your Imperial Highness."

"As you say. The war is at a critical juncture. We have recovered Milan and Genoa. The French have an army somewhere in Lombardy, another on the verge of taking Naples. If we can defeat the army here in Lombardy, I believe the Emperor can end the war on favorable terms." He set his mouth in a hard line. "But this time, *we* will be outnumbered. And every day, more of our men fall victim to this deadly fever."

"The *mago* is curing the sick," Taddeo said. "I believe he'll do a lot of good. If he can cure them, many of your men will be back on their feet soon."

"Magus, you say? A wizard is here?"

"No one special," Prospero said with a dismissive wave of his hand.

"He's healing the sick even as we speak," Taddeo said.

"If you don't mind me saying, you don't look so well yourself, lad. You look a tad *green*."

"I'm drunk, Your Greatness."

The Prince of Orange sighed. "Of course you are. Intoxication appears to be a soldier's entire entertainment. When he's not gambling and whoring."

"As a trained physician, I was going to heal the sick myself," Prospero cut in with a frown, but added magnanimously,

"Nonetheless, I am grateful for the Magus's assistance. He is my helper, you see. Every hero needs a sidekick."

"Very good. So tell me about your invention that will help us find this French army."

"Invention?" Taddeo belched.

"We need a practical demonstration of the principle of using heated air to raise reconnaissance airships," Prospero told him. "Can you do this for the general?"

"Absolutely." Then he bent and vomited on the Prince of Orange's boots.

"Ah," said Philibert as a dozen toadies cried out in horror and rushed from all sides to clean up the mess. "Well."

"I'm really sorry about that."

"You are ill. Perhaps another time—"

"I can do it," Taddeo said, waving. "I'm okay, I'm okay, I'm *okay*. Your Imperial Highness."

Feeling a little better, he staggered off toward *The Prometheus* and returned with an armful of materials, which he dropped on the grass. Within minutes, he constructed a boxlike frame of thin sticks covered in silk on all sides except one, which he placed over a small fire.

The box slowly levitated. It hovered over the ground.

One of the Prince's guardsmen crossed himself. "Magic," he muttered.

"Not magic." Taddeo pumped his fist. "*Science*."

"Heated air rises," Prospero explained. "On this principle, we could build airships."

The box wobbled and fell on the fire, bursting into flame.

"It's like Rome," Taddeo blurted before he blacked out.

He woke groaning on his cot in *The Prometheus*. Marie sat on a stool next to the bed. She sponged his aching forehead.

"I'm dying," he said.

"You're not dying," she assured him. "You just feel like you're dying."

"Was I run over by a horse?"

Marie smiled. "Taddeo, you drank too much. You slept an entire day. This is one of Prospero's potions. It will make you feel better." She handed him a cup of water mixed with a bitter analgesic powder, which he drank in sips.

He gripped his aching head. "I barely remember a thing. Did I do anything stupid?"

"Well, I understand you won a shooting contest against the best marksman in the Empire."

"I kind of remember that—"

"Then you bought wine for half the army."

"That part is a little hazy—"

"Then you blew your biscuits on the commanding general's boots."

He blanched. "I did *what?*"

"And you invented something. Something amazing. While you were drunk."

He opened his eyes. "I invented something?"

Marie stood and offered her hand. "Come and see."

He eyed her hand for a moment. "Did I—did I say anything strange to you yesterday?"

"Nothing I would consider *strange*," she said with a mischievous smile that made him shiver. "Could it be I find it strange you're talking to me at all?"

Taddeo blinked. She was right. He'd either gotten over his shyness or was simply too hung over to feel shy. Either way, he welcomed it. He took her hand.

"I want to take this opportunity to tell you how fond I am of you, Marie."

"Should I tell you as well? I think we already know, Taddeo."

He smiled and squeezed her hand. She squeezed back and opened the door.

The bright sunlight struck his eyes. The first day of summer was just days away; the day was hot. He staggered after her, moaning like a ghoul.

As his aching eyeballs adjusted, he made out the shapes of a crowd of men. They slowly came into focus as giant Landsknechte squatting in the dirt and humming to themselves.

They were *sewing*.

A hundred of them sewed buttons onto sacks of Hessian material. Another score buttoned the pieces of sack cloth together under Prospero's direction. Leo raced playfully around them.

The scientist swaggered toward him, wearing his new hat set at a rakish angle. "Taddeo, our bold vision of scientific progress is being realized. What you see is the construction of an airship that will take the first man up into the ether. I call it, 'Prospero's *Volantes Sacculum Gas*'!" Latin for, *flying gasbag*.

Taddeo nodded then winced at the sudden motion. "Okay, let's get to work, Doctor."

"That is my boy!"

Within two days, they constructed the hot air balloon from empty meal bags provided by the army's quartermaster and buttons donated from the jackets of the soldiery. Launch was imminent. Prospero stuffed handfuls of Don Pedro's silk into his doublet and trousers—just in case they had it in principle but not in reality—and tied his binocular glasses around his neck with a piece of string. Taddeo watched the hot air inflate the balloon's material like an anxious father watching his son take his first steps.

All the Landsknechte came to see the show. "The crazy man is going up in the gasbag," they said, elbowing each other. "He's nuts!"

Taddeo caught Marie's eye, and they exchanged a knowing smile. Last night, he'd desperately wanted to kiss her. They'd taken a walk outside the camp and into the woods. The air was warm and aromatic with the scent of trees and other green things. Nocturnal animals scurried through the brush. The moon was growing thinner by the night. In a quiet meadow, they looked up at the endless field of stars. He told her he believed each of those points of light was a ball of fire just like their sun, but so far away they appeared to men as pinpricks of light. That meant the universe was much bigger than the Earth-Sol system regardless of whether the sun rotated around

Earth or vice versa. Surely, many of those foreign suns had their own planets. Maybe some of them were like Earth. What were the people on them like? Were they even people? Would men ever cross the void and meet them?

He'd lost his train of thought when she put her arm around him and rested her head on his shoulder, a simple romantic gesture that brought him swiftly back to Earth and its own fascinating possibilities. He held her close and pointed out the constellations. He related the myths of the ancient Greeks and how the constellations came to be. The gods, it turned out, were a cruel bunch with a peculiar sense of justice. All the while, he plotted to kiss her. The timing, however, had to be perfect. He pictured himself doing it several different ways, each with more *sprezzatura* than the last. His heart galloped at these fantasies.

Do it now, he'd told himself, *or you'll never do it.*

He was right. He never did. The moment passed, and the next and the next, and then it was time to return to the camp.

Twelve hours later, as the balloon slowly filled with hot air, Taddeo stole another glance at Marie and cursed himself again for his cowardice. Why did love have to be so darn challenging? Just four months ago, during a bout with insomnia, he'd stayed up all night to produce a general solution for a special case of the fourth-degree polynomial equation. *That* had been one of the hardest things he'd ever done, yet it was mere child's play compared to the astounding complexity involved in kissing a girl.

Myrddin appeared at his side. "In case you were wondering where I've been for the last three days, I've been healing thousands of sick men so these soldiers didn't kill you."

"*Mago!* I told you not to sneak up on me like that."

"Did I really sneak up on you? There is another possibility we haven't yet explored, which is that I'm not real and exist only in your head. After all, I perform magic, and that's impossible, right? So you must be hallucinating."

"But everyone sees you, *mago*."

"Ah. That is because they are in your head too. You are actually in an asylum in the twenty-first century, living in a dream world of your own fanciful construction. I, Myrddin Wyllt, am a symbolic manifestation that the last shred of your rational mind created to shake you out of this stupor—by convincing you what you are seeing can't actually be happening." He shook his head, suppressing a smile. "It's sad, really." He frowned at the swelling balloon. "Is that an airship?"

"What?" Taddeo was still shuddering. "Um, yes. It is. Do you like it?"

Myrddin clapped his hand on the boy's shoulder. "I absolutely hate it. If man were meant to fly, God would have given him wings."

"This from a man who can actually fly."

The wizard considered this. "Okay. Fair point."

"So did you actually cure them? We might be marching soon."

"Some. Most, in fact. The ones who were too far gone I simply put out of their misery."

Taddeo gaped. "You did what?"

"I'm just jesting."

"Most people smile when they're joking, *mago*."

"But that would spoil the illusion."

Philibert arrived in a galloping train of heavily armored men and horses and dismounted. He eyed the hot air balloon with a dubious expression.

"You there!" he called. "Taddeo Cellini, is it?"

"At your service, Your Imperial Highness."

"Will this blasted contraption fly?"

"It's designed to fly. Whether it will fly, we're about to find out."

Taddeo had lost most of his fear of the Prince, having figured Philibert wasn't really in charge of the army any more than he'd been in charge of it during the sack of Rome. He hadn't presided over the slaughter; he'd most likely tried to stop it. But the mercenaries weren't afraid of him and didn't respect him, and as a result considered his orders optional. Most of the time, they simply marched around looking for the easiest loot and beat the French when they had to while Philibert tagged along hoping they didn't get him into too much trouble.

The Landsknechte hollered their delight as the balloon rose above the basket and yanked at the tethers. A company rushed to grab the ropes before the airship ripped its stakes and sailed away. Prospero waved at the men, gave Taddeo and the Prince of Orange a thumbs-up, and climbed into the basket.

"Today, we shall make history," he declared. "For the first time since Icarus, a man shall take flight. Gentlemen, you may release the *Volantes Sacculum Gas*, which I hereby christen, *The Aeronaut*!"

The mercenaries let go of the ropes with a ragged cheer.

"Good luck, *herr* crazy man!"

"Break a leg!"

The crowd grew quiet as the balloon rose into the air, ropes dangling from its sides. Prospero waved down at them. Taddeo watched him go with a mix of pride and worry.

Marie ran at him, Leo yapping at her heels, and threw herself into his embrace. The momentum spun them in a circle, laughing.

She planted a loud kiss on his cheek. "You did it! It's incredible! Can I go next?"

His face tingled. "Of course you can," he told her with her a stunned smile.

"*Herr* crazy man!" the Landsknechte called to Prospero. "*Feuer!*"

Taddeo froze.

Feuer was German for "fire."

He looked up. Prospero stood in the basket. Behind him, tongues of flame leaped out of the firebox, surged up the ropes, and caught on the sack cloth. The fire spread fast.

Taddeo waved his arms. "Doctor! Doctor!"

Prospero couldn't hear him. He scanned the horizon with his glasses.

Marie cupped her hands around her mouth. "Prospero! You're on fire!"

"Just like Icarus," Myrddin observed.

The Aeronaut was already falling.

As the last of the material went up, the balloon collapsed and entered freefall.

And down it went.

"Doctor!"

"Wow," Myrddin said.

The Landsknechte scattered as the groaning airship, trailing flames and a long stream of thick black smoke, crashed to the earth with a massive blast.

Taddeo and Marie ran toward the inferno, but the intense heat halted them in their tracks. They retreated as a wave of sparks and burning bits of sack cloth blew against them.

Prospero stepped out of the pall, coughing and patting himself. Black soot covered him. His doublet still smoked in places.

"Doctor! Are you all right?"

"Of course! See?" He slapped his bulky chest. "Silk!"

"You had me worried there."

They hurried away from the blazing wreck. Prospero grinned like a madman.

"I could see scores of leagues in all directions, even further with my glasses. There was Genoa in my palm. With my specs, I could see all the way to Milan. It was quite exhilarating. Even my swift plunge back to the earth gave me interesting insights into gravity."

"I suppose we should have tried to fireproof the fabric somehow," Taddeo wondered. He rubbed his chin. "Alum, maybe."

"An engineering issue," Prospero noted.

Taddeo cleared his throat. "Well."

"Prospero, you have impressed me," Myrddin said. "If only you'd done that in Venice, you might have won our duel."

"Oh, yes, certainly," the scientist grumbled. "I design an airship and make history by flying it, and all you or anyone else wants to see is it crash in a big fiery ruin."

"May I interrupt?" the Prince of Orange asked. He waved smoke from his face with a handkerchief. "Aside from being historical and entertaining, it was also an unfortunate waste of time and resources."

"Not at all, Your Imperial Highness," Prospero told him. "I have located the French. I estimate them to be fifteen leagues to the northeast, camped near Milan."

"Milan, you say? In what direction are they headed?"

"They are going precisely nowhere. They are encamped. You passed right by each other. Proverbial armies passing in the night. Perhaps they intend to lay siege to Milan. Perhaps they have already recaptured it. Who knows what they are thinking? They are French."

"Well," the Prince said. "I suppose that's well done then."

"Did you hear that, lads?" a mercenary bellowed. "*Herr* crazy man has found the Frogs for us!"

The Germans filled the air with a bloodthirsty shout. Some started up a marching song and others joined in. They clapped and pounded the earth with the butts of their pikes to keep time.

"*Hut! Dich! Baur wir komm!*"

The Landsknechte chanted that when they marched into battle. *Look! Out! Here we come!*

Philibert raised his hands in a futile effort to quiet them. "Now, men. This is most excellent news. On the morrow, I will issue new orders after I've considered my strategy."

The mercenaries had already dispersed to strike their tents, collect gear, and otherwise prepare for a long march.

The Prince sighed. "Well, I suppose we could—"

Trumpet blasts signaled the army to break camp.

Taddeo, Marie, Prospero, Myrddin, and Leo climbed aboard the steam wagon, which had been refueled and provisioned. And more: The rig had been retrofitted to transport a specially designed bronze cannon in a new wood frame enclosure on its roof.

The Prometheus was now a tank.

Taddeo started the engine while Prospero got behind the tiller and released the brake.

"Today was a good day," the scientist said.

Military bands struck up a marching song and led the way out of the valley and toward the plains of Lombardy, where the French waited for them near Milan. *The Prometheus* fell in line with the long column of men, horses, and wagons clogging the dusty road heading east.

The soldiers sang hymns as they marched to war.

Chapter XI
The Battle

The Imperial army marched for two days in sweltering heat and dust. Troops of mounted Reiters flew ahead of the column to scour the countryside for provisions, information, and easy loot. From her perch on the driving bench of *The Prometheus*, Marie turned and looked back at the long column strung out behind, bristling with pikes and flags. They were a terrifying sight until she remembered they were on her side.

A soldier ran alongside the steam wagon and tossed a *gulden* onto the deck, crying his thanks. Prospero picked it up, bit it to test whether it was counterfeit—inferior metals hardened the coin, while pure gold was relatively soft—and, thus satisfied, pocketed it.

"That's another one you saved from the fever," Marie said to Myrddin, who lay sprawled out on the rear bench with his hands clasped over his chest. "See? When you do nice things for people, they appreciate it."

The wizard opened one eye and regarded her with a nettled stare. "I saved his life. He gave me a coin. Tell me. Is that *truly* appreciation?"

"Well, tush! What do you want?"

"An excellent question! What I want is nothing, actually. Nothing at all." He shut his eye. "To think, if only I appreciated their appreciation, we might all be happy." The eye opened again. "You, for some reason, appear to be very happy."

"I have goose bumps," she said. "This is it, Myrddin. The final battle of the war. The battle that will decide who will be master of

Italy. I can feel it. And we will be there! Fighting for a good king, all of us bonded in brotherhood by war and a common cause that is just. Deciding the outcome of the fight, though the odds be against us, with bravery and might of arms!"

Prospero stared at her. "Christ, please tell me you do not honestly believe all that."

"If you don't, then why are you here?"

"These ruffians have seen fit to provide us with safe escort to Milan. From there, we shall return to Venice and reopen our workshop. I am a scientist, you know, not a conquistador."

Marie pointed to the bronze cannon resting on the roof of the carriage. "Then why did you ask the Prince for materials to build that if you intend never to use it?"

The scientist smiled. "My poor naïve child, have you not noticed that everyone is trying to kill us everywhere we go? A cannon will make even a knight think twice before wasting our time with violence. The minute we escape this parade of homicidal drunkards, we will turn the cannon around so it faces behind us. Then let us see who dares give chase to *The Prometheus*!"

"You have no honor, Prospero Buonarroti."

"You say this like it is something bad."

"There is a clear right and wrong—"

Prospero waved his hands. "Not interested!"

Myrddin said, "For once, I agree with Prospero. Chivalry makes sense only in bad literature. As soon as we can, we should get away from these fools and resume our old safe life."

"Wandering aimlessly around Christendom, always hungry, sleeping on the cold ground or in some stranger's lousy bed, performing cheap illusions for coins," Marie intoned, laying out for inspection the long bleak remainder of her existence.

"Yes," Myrddin said with a nostalgic sigh.

"Taddeo, what about you?" she said, nudging him. "Don't you find all this exciting?"

The boy leafed through the handful of bills he'd received from the wine sellers. "My dad is seriously going to kill me. How am I going to explain this to him?"

"*Bella*," Prospero said patiently, "leave the boy be. I need to know something from you. See these men marching all around us? They are all here because they are getting paid in coin and loot. That, and they see no future for themselves other than having a little fun before bleeding to death on some battlefield. You? You are not even getting paid. So why risk your neck?"

"I told you once. I want to fight for something greater than me. For an ideal."

"Where does this ideal exist? Allow me to ask a more practical question. What do you think will actually happen if the Emperor wins this battle?"

"He will be master of Italy."

"And what will that accomplish? How will your lot be any better than before?"

She crossed her arms. "You don't understand. It's an idea!"

"Then—"

"What about the Turks? They are even now marching on Vienna! If they capture the capital of Austria, they could winter there and in the following year, threaten all of Christendom! Ha!"

"She's right," Myrddin said.

"If the Imperial army is victorious, we can rush to Austria's aid. Otherwise, all of central Europe will be enslaved to the Sultan!"

The wizard bent to scratch Leo behind the ear. "But, again, it's not our problem."

Prospero nodded. "Mark this occasion, Magus. For once, we agree on something."

"The occasion is duly marked."

"Oh, never mind!" She turned her back to them.

Individually, the wizard and the scientist could be insufferable. Together, on the same side of an argument, they became impossible.

How could she make them understand these events gave her life meaning? That these past months had stirred her soul and made her feel a deep connection to a larger whole?

She'd taken plenty of risk during that time, but she'd lived more deeply than she ever had before—

Trading blows with Don Jorge in front of the Imperial court—

Chasing down the stag in the forest—

Fighting the Turkish assassins—

Firing the French camp—

Standing on the roof of the steam wagon, loosing arrows against sixty French riders—

Now two great kingdoms clashed while the Sultan threatened them all.

It was all terribly exciting, and she wanted to continue playing the game no matter what the stakes, regardless of what the penalty was for losing.

For all his faults, she reflected, *King Francis was right about one thing. History is not some past thing; it is now. A neverending play on a grand stage, and we are the players.*

Myrddin and Prospero seemed happy to stay out of history's way in exchange for a little peace and quiet, but Marie couldn't be content with that. She'd had enough peace and quiet in her short life. She wanted action. She wanted to force history to go where she wanted.

Was such a grand prize not worth the ultimate risk? To attach oneself to a cause and really *do* something? Right now, she had it in her mind to save Europe from the Ottoman yoke.

Flags flashed along the line as the colonels of the regiments signaled it was time to stop for the night. *The Prometheus* slowed to a halt. Marie watched the ragged column disintegrate into thousands of individuals wandering about babbling, brawling, and emptying their bladders. Some pitched tents where they stood while others lay on the ground or wandered off in search of shade. Men took off their jackets and entered the nearby woods with axes to cut firewood, leather bags to collect water, bows to hunt small game to eat.

Myrddin stood, stretched, and scratched his arse. "You know,

Prospero, this contraption of yours really is an affront to God, but overall it's not a bad way to travel. I could get used to it."

"It astounds me how you say these things with a straight face," Prospero answered. "This, from a man who takes a short walk and somehow ends up in another country. God approves of violating the immutable laws of physics He created?"

Ignoring their neverending squabbling, Marie grabbed the rungs of the ladder and hopped to the ground. Prospero followed, rattling some coins in his fist.

"By Epicurus," he proclaimed, "the touching gratitude of the army shall not go to waste this night. I am going to see if I can buy us supper with the money and a decent wine to go with it."

Marie took a *batzen* from him. "And I'm going to buy a drink of ale from the Germans."

Prospero tossed her a second coin and raised his hand in a gesture of benediction. "Go with God, my child. Try not to butcher anyone."

Taddeo dropped to his feet next to her. "Hey, listen, I have to do some maintenance on the boiler. The extra weight of the cannon is murder on the engine. Then I need to write a letter to my father. After that, I was just wondering, do you want to take a walk or something? It really is a lovely night."

Marie's heart broke. "What happens next is not up to me, Taddeo. You need to think about what you want."

"Huh? What do you mean?"

"I'm serious. Just think about it."

"Um. Did I do something wrong, Marie? I'm sorry I didn't support you when you were arguing with Prospero. I guess I was pretty distracted by my problems. I just don't know how I'm going to explain to my—"

"I like it when you say my name," she blurted and ran away, her eyes stinging.

She felt ridiculous but couldn't help herself. The truth was she'd been avoiding him ever since they broke camp.

They'd fallen in love with few words spoken and had learned to communicate with subtle glances and gestures, creating a language all their own. Now that he'd gotten over his shyness, however, they were free to use nearly every word in seven languages.

Just talking by itself was problematic. In a typical conversation, he might describe an experiment he'd devised to try to measure the soul by weighing a man before and immediately after his death, and then subtracting the difference to calculate the weight of the departed spirit. What could she say to match that? *That's great, my love—can I help by killing someone?*

Look at the cannon on the steam wagon! Taddeo and Prospero couldn't simply mount a light cannon on the roof and let it be, oh no. Taddeo had to *design and build a special three-barreled cannon*, the large mobile base supported by springs. The barrels were strapped together. Once one barrel fired, a metal stick was used to lever the assembly up and turn it via a rotating mechanism so the next barrel would be at the top to shoot. It'd get too hot to fire repeatedly, but it wasn't intended for that. It was intended to fire three shots in rapid succession. A battering ram to knock down whatever was in their way and keep moving. It was a sight to see.

In contrast to these fabulous inventions her beloved continually produced, Marie didn't feel very interesting. She felt herself growing increasingly shy; what if he found her dull?

Even worse, now that they were actually on speaking terms, eventually they'd have to talk about where their relationship was going, and then things would get very complicated. She guessed a man and woman falling in love might enjoy talking about exploring the future as a couple, but for her and Taddeo, it could prove disastrous. They'd have to talk about the fact she was low-caste and penniless. They'd have to face the enormous expectations his family placed on him about whom he should marry.

They'd talk and talk some more, and their fairy tale romance would be over. Just like that. They would literally talk it into an early grave.

Besides all that, Marie wasn't sure she even wanted the

relationship to progress in any traditional sense. Although many men waited until their mid twenties to tie the knot, girls got married as young as fourteen. They produced a baby every year—with only perhaps one out of three of these children surviving their first few months—and kept house while obeying their husbands in all things. And Marie, a girl who'd seen the world, would be confined to four walls and a roof.

The pressure to live an ordinary life according to one's station was intense.

Marie wasn't sure that was the life for her. She knew the sexes were not the same but craved the same opportunities as men. She dreamed of bigger things than were allowed by her birth.

But she didn't know what she wanted.

One thing she *did* know was she wanted to be with Taddeo. She needed him. That was certain. But she wasn't sure she wanted marriage and everything that went along with it.

She slowed her pace and walked along a grassy hillside covered with a riot of wildflowers, rabbit holes, and the half-buried bones of men felled in some old battle. The tall grass was alive with buzzing and hopping bugs. The humid air had begun to cool as evening approached.

At the top of the hill, Marie found Myrddin crouched over one of the holes. He was whistling.

"What are you doing?"

The wizard squinted at her. "I'm trying to catch something for supper." He rubbed his hands together. "Imagine Prospero's face when he returns with his expensive camp food and learns I've already prepared us all an exquisite four-course meal!" He cackled and shook his head.

Marie smiled. She'd never seen the Magus have so much fun as he did antagonizing Prospero and Taddeo.

"Myrddin..."

"Yes, my child?"

"Did you really mean what you said about wanting to go back to our old life?"

He rose to his feet with a grunt. "The good old days. Things were certainly simpler then, and safer, wouldn't you agree?"

"If that's what you really want for us, why do you keep showing me all these exciting things? You even lied about being an alchemist so I could enjoy city life for a while. Why?"

"Well." The Magus scratched his nose. "That's a good question. I suppose I keep thinking if I indulge you, you'll eventually get sick of it all and come back to me on your own."

"You really believe that?"

"When you tire of all this horrid adventure, you'll come back, and things will go back to the way they were before." His smile faltered. "Am I wrong?"

"Oh, Myrddin." She rose on tip-toe to kiss his hairy cheek. It was heartbreaking to hear him talk like this. "What if I don't want to go back? What if I can't?"

The Magus stared at her with a mournful look. "You mean you might want to leave me forever?"

"I don't want to *leave*, Myrddin. But things change. Today, tomorrow—it's like the King of France said, these are the good old days, don't you see? Things just change. At some point, I may not want to be your bodyguard anymore. I'll want to find my own way and live my own life."

"You may not like what you find. Prospero's right. It's a dangerous world out there."

"I know, Myrddin. I've traveled much of it as your bodyguard, remember?" She hugged his arm as they strolled toward a copse of olive trees. "I can't just walk away from everything that is happening to us. Remember our talk about fate? Whether some things are meant to be—like meeting the scientists? I believe everything that has happened to us has been meant to happen." They paused, taking in the spectacular view of the army milling about the plain and settling in around their fires. Beyond, the sun hung low over the distant purple hills. "Similarly, we will survive this battle, and we will go to Vienna to save it from the Turk. I honestly believe this."

Myrddin stroked his beard. "Interesting. Do you feel your fate has a divine author, or is it simply some force in the universe responding to your projected desires?"

"I can't say. I just feel it." She glanced at his profile. "And it's not just my fate. It's yours. It's our fate and the scientists' fate, all intertwined."

He frowned. "Well, there you're wrong, see. My fate, if I have one, is mine and mine alone. You kids need to learn that I may help if I choose to help, but I am not obligated to do anything for anyone."

"Do you really believe that?"

"Of course I do! You kids today think everyone owes you something!"

"Myrddin, why does Ibrahim Pasha want you dead?"

"That is a very good question you should ask him."

"Taddeo told me about the ghouls. They were hunting you, not him, weren't they?"

"Probably," he admitted. "But what does that have to do with anything?"

"Okay, let's add it up. Prospero and I were kidnapped. Taddeo was tortured by the Inquisitors and had to fight his way into France through bandits and ghouls. King Francis ordered the execution of Prospero and me. Turkish assassins nearly cut off my head. And then we fought a battle against twenty French lances. Do you see what I'm getting at?"

"Of course! There can be no other conclusion. The Pasha has a wizard in his service."

"No, Magus. I'm saying all those things happened because Ibrahim Pasha wants *you*."

Myrddin muttered to himself as he went over the logic. "Damn it."

"Don't you think you're at least a little responsible at this point for what happens to us? Given the fact we're almost always on the verge of dying because someone very powerful is trying to kill *you*?"

"Maybe," he admitted.

"It's fate," she told him. "And fate never allows you to stay in the same place."

"Fate can be a real flapdoodle," he observed.

"*C'est la vie, magicien.*"

He put his large hand on her shoulder and squeezed affectionately. "Speaking of which, do you believe you and Taddeo are fated to be together? And if you do, shouldn't you do something about it?" He winked. "Or do you expect fate to do all the work?"

Marie stared at him in wonder, feeling struck. "You're amazing, you know that? Sometimes, you—" She pretended to strangle someone. "And then, other times, you—" She brought her fingertips to her lips and kissed them. "You said the perfect thing just now. I love you!"

She ran back toward the steam wagon. Behind her, Myrddin crouched over another hole, whistled, and reached in to grab a hare by the scruff of its neck.

At that moment, Marie realized the old rascal had tricked her with another illusion—he'd simply been trying to change the subject and get rid of her—but no matter. As Myrddin often said, illusions and reality informed each other. Sometimes, in fact, they turned out to be the same thing.

Whatever his motives, he'd said the one thing she'd needed to hear. She and Taddeo *were* fated to be together. Why had she allowed herself to get so gloomy?

She flew past Leo, who lay outside the steam wagon whimpering with his head buried in the weeds, and climbed the ladder up onto the driving bench. Then down into the carriage.

Her smile faded. She rubbed her eyes, unable to believe what she was seeing.

Taddeo, her beloved Taddeo, lay on his cot, shirt and jacket open to expose his chest, surrounded by beautiful women dressed in sheer silk wraps and apparently nothing else. Their flawless skin shimmered in the light of the oil lamps.

The women were sultry and exotic, with dark slanted eyes and long, lustrous black hair spilling free across their shoulders or tied into various styles of buns and braids. One sat on the edge of the workbench, surrounded by tools, scrap metal, and wood dust, her smooth legs kicking empty space, while the others knelt on the floor around the cot. They ran their long red fingernails playfully across Taddeo's chest while the most beautiful of the lot straddled his hips and ground herself gently against him, her robe open to expose small, pointed breasts. She giggled, speaking in a strange lyrical language Marie had never heard spoken before, and traced a heart shape over his chest with her finger. Though the language was alien, the meaning was unmistakably clear: *mine*.

Marie blinked away tears. How could she have been so foolish? Taddeo—her Taddeo, her shy boy, her beloved, her man—was a horny, frisky, randy, cheating old goat!

The woman sitting on Taddeo flung off her robe and arched her back while he stared up at her with wide eyes. Marie could only watch too, forgetting her jealous shock as she stared at the exotic girl's perfectly sculpted body with fascination.

The others laughed and touched their bodies. The air thickened with a musky, sexual odor that was vaguely female, vaguely animal, and made Marie's senses swim.

One of the women noticed her and made a flinging gesture. *Get out.*

Marie backed toward the ladder. "I'm sorry." She wiped tears from her cheeks with a loud sniff. "I—I—oh, Taddeo!"

Then she noticed the large golden-furred foxtail fluttering behind the naked girl.

"*Wait*," Taddeo whispered in a small voice.

"What are you?" Marie said.

The woman raised her finger to Taddeo's lips. *Shhhhh.* Behind her, the tail wagged playfully behind her rump.

Marie's eyes narrowed. Her hand dropped to the hilt of her sword.

"Get your hands off my man, thou harlot," she snarled.

The air in the cramped wagon became stifling hot and wet. The women flung themselves onto all fours and grinned up at her. Their naked leader traced another heart on Taddeo's heaving chest.

Mine. Her lush scarlet lips parted in a feral smile. A droplet of drool dripped onto his skin and joined the thick sheen of sweat covering his body.

"One must be careful with others," she said in a guttural voice.

Marie drew Artemis as they pounced hissing with hands splayed into claws. She punched the first woman in the forehead with the pommel, provoking a livid shriek that swept through her body like a hot wind. The second fell away in a tangle of limbs, howling as a spurt of blood splashed searing hot into the air.

Then they were upon her in a fluttering crowd, shrieking and clawing as she repeatedly shoved them back and cut at them. It was like fighting a dense, blinding flock of pigeons. Fingernails raked her neck. Sweat trickled stinging into the scratches.

The soft, creamy limbs gave way to golden fur and scrabbling paws, the beautiful hissing faces to snouts lined with sharp teeth. After a confusing swirl of movement, the silk robes at last fell away to unveil a pack of foxes scurrying past in a mad break for the exit. Each boasted a set of nine quivering tails. Marie kicked and stomped. The little gold foxes shrieked like women as they escaped out the hatch.

Outside, Myrddin's voice boomed: "Be gone, *Huli Jing!* Be gone!"

Taddeo groaned on the table, drenched in sweat from heel to head. Marie rushed to his side and rained kisses on his flushed shining face.

"Are you all right, my love?"

"They bewitched me. I couldn't move. I could barely breathe. I had to do exactly as she commanded me."

Myrddin came down the stairs and regarded Taddeo. "That ridiculous shyness of yours finally came in useful."

"No, I resisted." Taddeo turned to Marie. "I thought of you, and I resisted."

"Hmm," the wizard said. "In any case, it's a good thing you didn't give in to them. If you'd made love to one of the fox-women, she would have cracked open your chest and eaten your heart during climax." He scratched his nose. "Possibly your liver too."

Marie shuddered as she remembered the girl tracing her fingernail across Taddeo's chest in a heart shape. *Mine.* "They were so beautiful and...compelling and..."

"Gone. I banished them back to Cathay."

"What *were* they, Magus?"

"Fox spirits, and very old," the Magus answered. "They are known as *Huli Jing* in China, *Kitsune* and *Kumiho* in other parts of Asia. As you saw for yourself, they take the form of beautiful women when they want to seduce young men. This is strong magic."

"But why Taddeo?" she wanted to know. "Why did they come for him and not you?"

"The only way I can describe it is long exposure to magic causes it to rub off on some people. You and Taddeo are susceptible. Prospero not so much, I would venture to guess."

Marie nodded. "I understand. Ibrahim Pasha said he could 'smell' your magic on me."

"Well, he was being literal."

"That's how I was able to understand her language."

"Correct again."

"All right. So why didn't they attack you?"

"My magic protects me. It doesn't protect you. Like the ghouls, the fox-spirits went for what they saw as an easier target."

She squeezed Taddeo's hand. "Not that easy." Then she glanced at the Magus and tilted her head toward the recovering boy. "I guess someone here needs to admit some responsibility, hmm?"

Myrddin rolled his eyes and blew air out his cheeks. "I'm sorry this happened to you, kid."

"It's all right, *mago.*"

"On the plus side, you can now brag you resisted the seduction of the *Huli Jing*, the most powerful succubi in Asia. I doubt there's another man alive who could make such a boast."

"That would be really great if I knew someone who was actually aware they even existed."

"Marie here knows. You can brag to her."

Prospero called down to them through the hatch: "Dinner is served!"

They sat on the driving benches and ate by the light of oil lamps and the glow of hundreds of fires. Around them, the soldiers listened to the crackle of the flames, sharpened their blades, and rested for the long march ahead. At this proximity, they knew, there might easily be a hard bloody fight at the end of it. Some prayed, some settled debts, others wandered off in search of female companionship. Despite all the jokes about the French, despite the fact the Frogs had lost battle after battle due to poor leadership and blind faith in obsolete modes of war, no one disputed they were tough as nails and hell to beat. Tomorrow or the next day, many Imperialists would lie dead or dying on a smoky field.

Prospero ate the supper he'd pieced together around the camp; Myrddin chewed on his hastily cooked rabbit—his diabolical plot to serve a four-course meal having failed—and spit the bones over the side. Taddeo and Marie, now sporting a golden-furred foxtail hanging from the back of her wide-brimmed hat, picked at both meals before curling up together under a cloak.

She felt the warmth of his body against her back and nuzzled against him.

"Do you love me?" Taddeo whispered in her ear.

"I do," she said.

"I need to ask you another question. It's kind of important."

"I'm listening."

"If we survive the battle tomorrow, would you marry me, Marie Dubois?"

She turned and stared into his eyes from inches away. "That's a little sudden."

"The way things are going, life may be short."

"If I marry you, will I be able to continue living my life the way I want to live it?"

He smiled. "I wouldn't have you any other way."

She smiled back. "Then I would marry you, Taddeo Cellini."

"If I were to be disowned by my family and find myself without a penny to my name, would you still love me and be my wife?"

"As long as I have you, I will love you forever."

"Then I would marry you too," he said.

"Don't we need a contract?"

"What is in my power to give shall be yours. What is in your power to give shall be mine."

"That works for me."

Taddeo offered his hand. "Then shake on it." While they shook, he added, "That's the *impalmamento*. The contract is now sealed."

"Oh, I think we can do better than that, don't you?"

They kissed. It was clumsy and alarming and overwhelming. Lovely and warm and intoxicating. Dangerous and awkward and historic.

They kissed. They kissed. They kissed.

They kissed while the army slept around them.

At last, drunk on their kissing, they fell asleep as well.

Just after dawn, they woke to a swarm of Reiters pounding into the camp grim faced and bloody. Marie stood and hailed them for news.

"The French," one shouted back at her. "Thick as fleas in yonder town."

They'd gone into the town to reconnoiter and blundered into a squadron of French cavalry watering their horses in the *piazza*. The Germans emptied their pistols, bolted, and ran into another squadron racing toward the bridge to trap the Imperialists on the eastern side of the river. The Reiters charged and after a short, sharp skirmish, they'd broken through to safety.

There would be no marching today. The French, it seemed, had come to them.

The free mercenary companies, each four hundred strong, assembled under the Imperial eagles. The ragged formations tightened into squares under the bawled commands of their captains. Nearby gun crews strained at the limbers. Priests moved from one gun to the next to bless the great iron muzzles with dashes of holy water. Drums pounded martial rhythms to stir the blood for the killing.

The heavily armored double-pay men, the most experienced warriors in each Landsknechte company, took positions at the front of the square to lead the attack (and at its rear to keep the rest from running away). The pikemen, of course, occupied the first few ranks. The halberdiers and berserkers with their *zweihanders* arrayed behind them, prepared to rush out from the sides to flank the enemy if the opportunity presented itself. The *schützen*—arquebusiers and crossbowmen—skirmished from the flanks and middle of the formation.

The mercenaries crossed themselves, prayed, fingered their talismans, threw pinches of dust over their shoulders for luck, kissed the hems of their banners. They cracked nervous jokes. Veterans gave last-minute advice to the new recruits. Some of the regiments broke into ragged hymns, adding to the incredible din.

The captain of the company nearest *The Prometheus* glared at his men with his one good eye and boomed, "God be with you men! Now let's make some coin!" His fighters replied to this inspiring speech with a boisterous roar. They stomped the ground with the butts of their pikes, staves, and guns. Someone called out, "Look out! Here we come!" Despite the anxiety typical of the hours before a battle, the men appeared to be in good spirits. The fact they'd given the French a good thrashing not far from here, four years ago at Pavia, was not lost on them.

Marie watched it all with pulse-pounding excitement.

"And now," Prospero said, "it is time to get the hell out of here."

"What? We can't just leave!" she cried.

"Yes, you are right, of course," he said, stroking his goatee. "We will need to first devise a proper ruse. Perhaps a diversion."

"If you want to go then go. I'm staying. This is my fight."

He frowned. "Not this again. Do you have any idea what is about to happen here?"

"I swore an oath—"

"Oh, come on! You are nothing to the Emperor! Why should he be everything to you?"

"Do you think we met by accident, Prospero?"

"I do not understand what you are asking."

"I believe we were meant to be together on this battlefield. I believe we will win here today, and then we'll march on Vienna to save Christendom from Turkish invasion."

Prospero stared at her for a long time saying nothing. Finally, he turned to Myrddin and said, "You, of all people, I should be able to count on to talk some sense into these youngsters."

Marie turned to Taddeo. "What about you? Do you believe in fate, my love?"

"Absolutely not," he replied. The very idea made him shudder.

She frowned, taken aback. "You don't believe we were fated to be together?"

"Listen, my dearest, if all things are fated, it would mean everything we say or do is preordained and that we have no free will as human beings. And if that's true, then God must be the author of our actions, but then why would God punish people who sin if he predestined them to sin? Wouldn't that make God the actual sinner, which would nullify the very idea of morality? Think about it: Why would God make people who would never enter Heaven? Or, for that matter, who die in pain in childhood or suffer a long life in endless poverty? Why are we held responsible for our actions at all if God is pulling our strings as if we were so many puppets? The idea of God not being loving and merciful but instead the cruel author of the meaningless lives of tiny beings—ignorant, suffering things who have no choice about what happens to them, like bugs in a glass jar—is too horrible to even contemplate."

"Oh," she said. "Um."

"Then there are the social ramifications! If you are born rich, does that mean God likes you since he fated you to be born that way? And just the opposite—if you are a poor, wretched peasant, does God hate you? It reinforces a cruel social order based on divine right, which is more than just the right of kings to rule. It's the right of a whole social order based on legitimized oppression. It's the moral justification for a small minority of people lucky to be born rich to forever exploit and dominate the great unwashed. Do you know what I mean, my shining star?"

Marie didn't know how to respond. It had all sounded so much better in her head.

"Well," she said. "I—"

"On the other hand, I do believe our fates, so to speak, are now joined. So if you stay and fight then I must stay and fight too."

Marie smiled, her chest filling with heat. "I so can't wait to marry you."

"Though I'm completely terrified by the idea of having to fight again," he added.

Prospero's face reddened. "Taddeo, I am warning you, if you persist in attaching yourself to this suicide attempt, I am going to tell your father that you are an unruly boy!"

"If you do that, he'll make us come home and end my apprenticeship," Taddeo shot back. "And you'll be out of a job, Doctor."

The Imperialists filled the air with a full-throated roar. The enemy had entered the field, rank after rank of cavalry, infantry, and artillery advancing under the blue and gold banners of the Kingdom of France.

They took up positions on the gentle slope of the opposite hill.

"Fools," Prospero muttered at the impressive sight. "All right, Taddeo. If we must stay and fight a battle, we may as well try to win it. I see the Prince. Let us aid him with a strategy."

"At once, Doctor."

Marie buckled on her cuirass and followed.

A group of ruffians waved at her. "Brunhild, Brunhild!" She recognized Rupert, the giant she'd felled, now grinning with a shiny purple egg on his forehead, and some of the other Landsknechte she'd befriended over pints of bitter ale. They'd started calling her Brunhild, a German name meaning, *armored warrior woman.*

She waited for them approach as Prospero and Taddeo strode on without her. "Hail, brothers."

"Come join our company and kill the grape-stompers with us today!"

Marie clapped them on the shoulders. "I will fight with you." After the oafs had a chance to nudge each other and grin happily, she added, "In fact, tell your captains I will join the Blood Flag today."

"No!" they cried. "Please do not do this!"

"Tell the captains of the companies I want them to create a Blood Flag made up of men from every company, assembled here by the steam wagon. Trust me when I say I will not only fight with you today, I will lead you all to certain victory."

They watched her go with awe-stricken expressions before running to find their captain. She caught up to Prospero and Taddeo as they came upon Philibert of Châlon breakfasting at a buffet set up in a colorful open-air tent, surrounded by his usual entourage of toadies and servants. Several mercenary colonels were just leaving, wearing broad grins.

The Prince of Orange fumed. "Damned mercenaries! Demanding double pay just before the battle joins! They do this to me every time! I'm not a general, I'm a banker!"

"I'm not getting paid at all," Prospero muttered.

"Ah, *heer dokter*!" the Prince cried. "Look, everyone, and mark him well, for here is a true patriot and friend of the Crown. So tell me, *dokter*, you are from these parts. What is the name of yonder town?"

"That would be Landriano, Your Imperial Highness," the scientist said with a courtly bow. "How may I be of service?"

"You could tell me if there's a church there."

"A church, Your Imperial Highness? I should think so."

"The imperatives of state, you know..."

"I am afraid I do not follow."

The Prince of Orange sighed. "We're running a little short on funds. We're going to have to melt down the church plate if we're going to pay the men a single *real* after this."

"I understand. But first, we must win the battle, is that not so? For that purpose, I have come to aid you again in your hour of need." He paused to pluck a handful of grapes from a bowl on the buffet table. "May I? Ah, delicious." Munching with his mouth full, he continued, "First, we must discover how our foe is arrayed. I suggest probing the French line with light cavalry and plotting the size and disposition of their forces on a map."

Outside the tent, an artillery battery fired with a massive *BOOM*, hurling round shot and canister at the opposite slope. The French guns replied like distant thunder.

"This is most interesting," Philibert said. "Do go on."

"After we reconnoiter the enemy forces, we shall seize the initiative and launch our assault at the weak point in their line, like Alexander of Macedon, with the objective of breaking it. Like so." He arranged the grapes on the tablecloth, green for French, red for Imperial. "A *feint* will draw the enemy's reserves to the opposite flank while our artillery softens the line where we intend to break through. Our objective is to deliver overwhelming force at this one point. The infantry will advance, testing, testing, then WHAM!" He slammed his fist against the table, sending the grapes flying. "At the critical moment, heavy cavalry emerges on their flank, crushing them via an enveloping maneuver!"

The Imperial batteries shook the tent with their barrage. The French artillery responded with distant booms and local concussions followed by screams. A wave of acrid gun smoke rolled across the buffet, sending the Prince's toadies into a coughing fit.

They'd wasted enough time here. Marie tugged at the scientist's sleeve. "Prospero..."

Philibert nodded. "It's an excellent plan, *heer dokter.*"

"Thank you, Your Imperial Highness."

"You may lead the attack."

The blood drained from Prospero's face. "You want *me* to lead the attack? As in personally?"

"Someone give this man a sash befitting his rank."

"But Your Imperial—"

"May God grant us victory today, General Buonarroti!"

"—Highness, I am hardly worthy—"

Marie gripped the back of his doublet and pulled him out of the tent.

"This is no way to treat your commanding officer!" he yelled.

"We have to get back to the steam wagon now."

They jogged along the ranks. The soldiers let up a warlike shout as they passed. Trumpets blasted across the line.

"I feel like Caesar," Prospero said, pausing to acknowledge the men's homage with a wave.

"Hurry up, *arschloch*!" one of them shouted. "The line is about to advance!"

Marie grabbed him by the scruff again and forced him to run.

"Taddeo, you will be my second in command," Prospero huffed. "Your first task will be to find some signal flags and figure out how to use them. Then I can issue my orders."

"The battle's already started," Marie said. "The strategy is we hit them first, and we hit them hard. As for orders, there is only one. Take your steam wagon, drive it straight at the enemy line, and fire your cannon at it. Give them the grape with all three barrels. Do you think you can do that?"

Taddeo nodded. "Consider it done, Marie."

She wanted to kiss him again, but there was no time. They exchanged a quick smile instead. She prayed they would live long enough to exchange their vows as they'd promised.

"And where will you be?" Prospero asked as he fixed his new red sash across his chest.

"Right behind you," she said. "Leading the Blood Flag."

"Well, whatever that is, it sounds very safe," he said with obvious sarcasm. "I will see you in Dante's *Inferno*, I suppose. In the middle ring of the seventh circle, the one reserved for suicides."

The new Blood Flag, four hundred strong and bristling with a riot of bright red banners, cheered at the sight of their Brunhild. Typically, the Blood Flag consisted of a special suicide squad within each company, chosen by dice and tasked with charging tough enemy positions. They died like flies. Marie had asked for a company-strength Blood Flag to use as shock troops and had gotten one entirely from volunteers. Being the darling of the Landsknechte had its advantages. A bigger bunch of murderers, arsonists, and thieves you never saw, true, but they could be extremely chivalrous.

Marie scanned the battlefield. A little valley separated the two hills along which the armies sprawled, populated by a few farms and a large flock of bleating sheep that appeared oblivious to the screaming shot being lobbed over their heads. She fixed her gaze on a block of French soldiers forming under a copse of olive trees.

There. That is where we'll break them. Rupert handed her a small shield, which she fitted on her arm before addressing the men:

"My brave brothers, do you see the *arschloch* in yonder wagon?" She pointed at Prospero standing in front of the tiller. He saw her pointing and saluted. "We are going to follow the wagon to the enemy line. After it fires its cannon, we will charge, kill any French left standing, and break the line. Understood?" As they roared, she drew Artemis and held it gleaming over her head. "Then follow me to victory! *Marsch, marsch!*"

The Prometheus rolled toward the French line, breathing gusts of steam. Taddeo scrambled across the gun emplacement on the roof, loading the bronze barrels with grapeshot. The company tramped down the hill after it to the rhythmic pulse of fife and drum, the men already chanting, "*Look! Out! Here we come!*"

Marie had heard that war carts had been used at the Battle of Ravenna about twenty years earlier during another episode in the neverending Italian Wars. The two-wheeled carts, pushed by a man behind, carried up to three swivel-mounted heavy arquebuses. Apparently, they'd failed miserably as a weapon—the French won the battle in the end—but *The Prometheus* was no cart. Mantlets, of course, were nothing new; large shields, mounted on wheeled carriages, had long been used in siege warfare. *The Prometheus* combined the defense of the mantlet with the firepower of the carts and independent mobility. She believed the steam wagon would give the assault a much-needed edge. They might all die in the attempt, but if they broke the line, the rest of the army could expand the breach, perhaps allow cavalry to pour through.

The battle would be won, and those who died for this victory would become legend.

The valley was fast becoming a very dangerous place. Little puffs of smoke sprouted along the ridge as distant artillery pounded. Shot whistled through the air. The sky darkened from smoke clouds drifting across the Sun. On her left, French *gendarmes* charged into the withering massed volley fire of Spanish matchlocks and scattered, leaving the field strewn with dead and dying. A riderless horse, wild eyed and snorting, flew out of the chaos at Marie; Rupert pulled her out of the way with a chuckle. She saw a farmhouse burning.

The Germans waded into the flock of bleating sheep at the bottom of the hill, swatting at them with the flats of their swords to push them aside. They began to climb the slope toward the French line, the rest of the Landsknechte toiling at their heels, still chanting. The French infantry waited on the high ground, shouting taunts and insults.

Round shot ripped through the air over *The Prometheus*, plunging into a mass of infantry behind. The vehicle shuddered as another shot tore into its side with a spray of splinters.

"I'm just curious if this was what you wanted," Myrddin said.

Marie took a sharp breath. "Taddeo's right. You do sneak up on people."

"You were happy the battle was coming. I was just wondering if you're still happy now that it's here and everyone's dying."

"I'm not *happy* about it," she replied. The truth was her very blood sang.

On the right of her Blood Flag, French infantry charged downhill toward the Imperial line. Guns popped. Pikes cracked as the two dense masses of men plowed into each other.

"Fire at will!" an officer screamed before a wave of black smoke covered them all.

"Is this cause of yours really worth dying?" Myrddin wondered.

"If I must," she said bravely.

"What about Taddeo? I suppose it's worth him dying too?"

Her heart galloped with alarm. *The Prometheus* had taken another hit and was burning and listing. The wood frame enclosure on the roof had been blown away. Prospero was nowhere to be seen. Taddeo stood crouched behind the gun, hatless, his hair flying. He rested a quadrant on the barrel as he lined up his first shot. She breathed a sigh of relief.

The truth was it wasn't worth him dying. None of it was. Let Francis have Italy, let the Turk crush Germany with its yoke. None of it mattered. Just let him live.

She felt her legs weaken and struggled with the urge to get Taddeo and make a run for it.

"You know," Myrddin said, "I could say a simple *abracadabra* and whisk all of us far away from here in an instant."

Marie grit her teeth. For better or worse, they were committed now. They had to see this through. "Myrddin, go back to where you came from and let me work. Please."

"Back to Prospero's machine? Impossible. A man could get killed over there."

"I hear Mecca is nice this time of—"

"On the other hand," the wizard said as he opened a parasol and raised it over his head, "things are about to get very dicey right here."

The air hissed. Marie raised her shield as a cloud of crossbow bolts fell out of the sky and cut down the men around her. Rupert collapsed at her side, pierced through his thick skull. Two of the bolts thudded against her shield. Several bounced off Myrddin's ridiculous parasol.

The officers bellowed at the men to *tighten up, tighten up.* Stepping over their screaming comrades, the mercenaries closed the gaps in the line.

Another rain of bolts fell into the mercenaries. Every Frenchman at the top appeared to be firing at them. Dozens of her comrades howled in horror and pain as they fell. The air appeared to be alive with a withering rain of death.

Ahead, the steam wagon, afire and billowing black smoke, had almost reached the top. A French ball punched through the sideboards with a burst of smoke and splinters. Taddeo stood tall on the gun deck, ignoring the whistling shot and humming crossbow bolts while Leo raced barking around his feet.

He doesn't care about the Emperor or who owns Italy or even the Turks. He's doing this for me. The thought filled her with pride, love, worry. And terror.

"Now, my love!" she cried. "Fire!"

Taddeo did nothing.

He can't hear me, she realized. *He's waiting for the signal and can't hear me.*

She took a deep breath and emitted a high-pitched shriek piercing enough to break glass. The mercenaries around her winced. Taddeo turned and gave her a thumbs up.

Taddeo shouted the battle cry of the Venetian Republic, "Marco! Marco!"

And lowered the *botefeux.*

The cannon discharged with a deafening *BANG* that made her teeth vibrate. Smoke cascaded over the mass of French infantry. The cannon lurched against the springs and settled back into position. Taddeo frantically rotated the next barrel into place then sighted and fired another blast of grapeshot.

Then she lost sight of the wagon in the smoke.

Myrddin tossed the parasol. "Well, I guess I'll leave you to it. Good luck!"

She turned to bid him farewell, but he'd already disappeared.

Taddeo's cannon fired a third time and fell silent.

He's done his part. Well done, my love. Now it's my turn.

"Brothers, follow me!" she screamed. "To glory!" She flung aside her shield and raced toward the enemy line while ululating a blood-chilling cry. "To victory!"

The Germans raised their *zweihanders* and surged after her. "HERE WE COME!"

The Imperial army cheered as they saw the red banners of the Blood Flag mount the hill.

Marie halted at the top. It was horrible.

The mercenaries paused as they realized there were few opponents still on their feet and willing to fight. Taddeo's three blasts of grapeshot, fired at point black range, had torn the French apart. Men rolled screaming in the bloody grass. Others lay dead in heaps. Scores fled toward the rear.

The ground shook as an endless column of howling Reiters and Stradioti thundered into the breach. The horsemen enfiladed the disintegrating French line on either side.

The Germans looked at each other and shrugged. "Did we win?"

Marie looked across the field of dying men. "TADDEO!"

More companies of Landsknechte arrived and rolled up the line. Imperial cavalry emptied their pistols into the hapless French before darting away like wasps. The French flank collapsed. The center followed. Marie watched as a company of Spaniards, having overrun a nearby artillery battery, turned the pieces around and opened fire on the approaching French reserve and put it to flight. Disordered retreat turned into rout. The entire army was on the run.

"TADDEO!"

The Imperial infantry planted their standards at the top of the hill. The battle was won. Over the cheering, she heard the steady chug of the steam engine. Battered and charred, *The Prometheus* limped through the drifting clouds of smoke.

Marie wiped her eyes with gladness.

Please be okay, she prayed. *Be okay, and I'll never ask you to do that again, I swear it.*

Around her, the Germans mumbled in confusion. They looked up at the sky.

She did too. And saw it.

Something was *falling.*

The object trembled in flight, trailing tongues of flame and little bursts of smoke that thickened into a wide billowing tail.

Marie and the Germans followed its descent in awe.

When the rebel angels fell from Heaven, it must have looked like this.

"Look out, lads!" someone cried.

The mercenaries scattered as the thing struck the hillside. The earth trembled. A geyser of dirt soared into the air and fell like rain.

The impact left a smoking crater.

The mercenaries gathered around in a state of wonder.

The Prometheus continued its approach. Still no sign of Taddeo. Marie's heart pounded hard against her ribs, torn between the spectacle and her hope to see her love safe and sound.

One of the soldiers peered into the hole. "*Herr* crazy man?"

Marie saw a flash of green that devoured the man in a single gulp before returning to the smoking pit. The mercenaries crossed themselves. Marie caught the strong briny smell of newly caught fish.

"*Dämon,*" they muttered.

They backed away from the hole slowly, quietly.

"*Galia est pacata!*" Prospero called to them from the tiller of the battered wagon, looking smart in his red sash as he quoted Julius Caesar: *Gaul is subdued.* "*Veni, vidi, vici.*" *I came, I saw, I conquered.*

Taddeo stood at his side, grinning with a bloody bandage wrapped around his head. Marie's heart flooded with relief.

Then the monster, drawn to the sound of the scientist's voice, emerged hissing from the hole.

"*Joy,*" it said, its voice a wispy throaty sigh.

A wave of impressions washed over Marie's shocked mind.

It was big. It was repulsive. It was beautiful.

She thought back to the stag she'd hunted with the King of France. The creature wasn't just beautiful. It was *regal.*

First came the great grinning reptilian head with its liquid black eyes, wide flaring nostrils, goat's beard, and pair of curved horns sprouting from its skull and framed by a pair of ears shaped like a cow's. A forked tongue darted between two massive sharp fangs; catlike whiskers swayed along its upper lip. A long slim serpentine body followed, supported by four short thick legs terminating in claws, and balanced by a long tapering tail that swished behind it. It shimmered across the ground, its jade green scales shining like emeralds.

The creature flowed in a circle, its eyes never leaving Marie, until it lay coiled. It licked its lips and grinned at her. Unable to move, scarcely able to breathe, she watched it settle on the grass while her mind reeled from the vision of a great storm that covered the world.

The rain never stopped while the dragon danced and laughed. The brown waters rose and flooded the plains and cities. Only the peaks of the mountains remained, upon which the waves heaped millions of drowned men, women, and children. She saw the bloated bodies tumble in the surf.

The Germans shouted and clapped their hands to scare the monster away. Marie snapped out of her trance and tightened her grip on her sword. Water seeped out of the impact crater and splashed around the creature's clawed feet.

Whatever the thing was, it was very old. Very powerful. And it controlled water.

"What is it, Brunhild?" a crossbowman asked her. "What is that thing?"

"It's a dragon," she answered.

And took a flying leap—

Artemis gleaming in her hand—

Singing a single high-pitched note—

The monster swatted her out of the air.

"Love," it said.

Marie spun through empty space and landed hard in the muddy grass. The dragon peered over the edge of the hill and looked down at her the way a man would regard a fly that required further swatting. Its nostrils flared as it smelled her.

Her, or more specifically, the essence of Myrddin on her.

It's come for me, she realized.

The creature began to slink along the ground toward her. A wave of water flushed down the hill. The Blood Flag recovered from its stupor, shouted a war cry, and charged.

The sheet of water slammed into her. The companies of Landsknechte behind her fell cursing and tumbled back down the slope in the muddy torrent. The corpse of a French knight rolled past, metal harness and flailing limbs tangled in a blue and gold banner. She held onto an exposed root until the wave passed. The water around her turned red.

She regained her feet in time to see the last of the red banners fall. The dragon had torn her Blood Flag company to shreds in seconds.

It shuddered, ejecting a score of crossbow bolts from its hardened skin like so many toothpicks, and fixed its godlike gaze on her again.

Then grinned, its whiskers quivering.

The Prometheus plowed into the monster, which writhed in a frenzy under the heavy wheels. Its tail caught in one of the axles and forced an abrupt turn that sent Taddeo and Prospero over the rail to land in a howling slide down the muddy hill.

"Lucky," it groaned.

The steam wagon hit the slope and slid on the muck. Mud sprayed around its wheels. The vehicle spun twice. Top heavy, it tilted; the cannons toppled off and flew away. *The Prometheus* continued its sideways skid down the long incline, dragging the dragon with it, until it came to a splashing halt in the middle of a newly formed lake.

The dragon rolled out from under the wagon and blew mud from its snout.

Thousands of soldiers converged on the thing with their pikes.

Marie knew they didn't stand a chance. The dragon would kill them all. And then it would kill her to satisfy its master.

"Myrddin," she hissed. "Myrddin, if you can hear my prayer, I need your help!"

"What have you youngsters done now?" he said at her side. "I was only gone a quarter hour!"

She pointed at the creature, which had risen to its feet and was now inspecting its tail.

"Ye Gods," Myrddin said.

"Happiness," the monster sighed as it fixed him in its glare.

"What do we do now?" Marie asked the wizard.

He paled. "I suggest you run. Fast. Now."

"But—"

"Go, child!" The wizard raised his staff and advanced, chanting in the old tongue.

The tip of the staff burst into flame. The dragon retreated from its glare, hissing and spitting jade sparks.

"I banish you!" Myrddin roared. "Return! Return from whence you came!" The light flared even brighter until it consumed him.

"Friendship," the dragon moaned as it writhed in the glow.

Shielding her eyes against the light with her hand, Marie did as Myrddin told her. She ran.

But not away from the fight. She ran into the thick of it.

The sky darkened as black clouds formed over their heads. Flashes of light pulsed in the murk, followed by deafening thunder Marie knew was the dragon's roar.

"I banish you!"

Lightning writhed and swished and arced toward the tip of the wizard's staff. His chanting became lost in a sudden blasting wind.

Myrddin was going to die, she believed. How could one defeat a god?

She reached *The Prometheus*. Taddeo and Prospero were gone. Climbing onto the roof, which sagged and cracked under her feet, she leaped—

Screaming, while Artemis sang in her hand—

The blade hissing through the dragon's slender neck—

Cutting the beast in two—

And landed with a splash, the monster's head falling into the water at her feet still wearing its serene expression.

The light in Myrddin's staff faded to a dull red glow.

"What have you done?" he cried.

"I killed it." Every nerve tingled at the realization she was still alive.

"This was one of the original children of God! I was going to banish it!"

Marie reached down and picked up the beautiful head. Raised it high for the Landsknechte.

The Germans roared and shook their weapons at the sky as if daring more dragons to fall.

After this, she knew, these men would follow her anywhere.

Even to Vienna.

Chapter XII
A Special Day

Taddeo tapped the chisel with his mallet, dropping tiny curls of wood on the ground at his feet. With each tap, he created another scale in the dragon's hide. The bas-relief was almost done and ready for painting.

It had taken a hundred men hauling on ropes to pull the wreckage of *The Prometheus* out of the swampy lake in which the dragon had died twitching. The waters were found to have miraculous powers. Its consumption healed wounds and cured diseases.

While the Imperial army rested over the past week, Taddeo and Prospero restored the vehicle to working condition. After four days of hard work, the roof had been rebuilt, the walls replaced, the boiler cleaned and repaired.

Working with his hands helped him forget the horrors of the battle and put off his worries. After the main work was done, however, he needed something else to occupy his mind. Something bigger. He had a vision of transforming the steam wagon into a mobile work of art.

For days and nights, shunning food and sleep, he transformed one of its sides into a bas-relief depicting Marie's fight with the dragon. Myrddin was there too, raising his fiery staff as lightning writhed and crackled in the air around him. Taddeo's arms ached and his hands frequently cramped, but he worked through the pain, avoiding the future.

Avoiding thinking about how angry his father was going to be with him.

In the past few months, Taddeo had participated in the fraudulent sale of alchemical services to the Holy Roman Emperor, been arrested by the Spanish Inquisition, fought the King of France, helped the butcher of Rome win a battle, and pledged marriage to a low-born girl whose occupation might best be described as a cross between cutthroat-for-hire and vagrant.

Not to mention run up an enormous bill his father would have to pay to the wine merchants for a day's debauchery for the Imperial army. Gregorio was definitely going to hate *that*.

Taddeo had written a letter to him explaining everything but believed events had gone too far for amends. By becoming betrothed to Marie, he'd crossed the line separating independence and rebellion. Likely, Gregorio would cut him off and give his birthright to his brother Agostino, who had a mind for business.

Perhaps that would be for the best. A part of Taddeo actually found this idea liberating. Up until now, his patrimony and its responsibilities had defined his life. Once he accepted it was gone, he would truly be his own man for the first time, answerable only to himself.

But that presented new worries. Even bigger worries.

Prospero returned from his errand and paused to take in the bas-relief. "Remarkable."

Taddeo wiped sweat from his forehead. "That is kind of you to say."

"It is remarkable, that is, that you are still wasting time on your art project when there is so much more reconstruction to be done on my precious! Is this what I pay you for?"

Taddeo selected a gouge with which he would finish the fine detail of the monster's tail. "Actually, Prospero, my father pays *you*. As for me, I've lived in poverty ever since I've known you, as every penny we earn goes to our projects. And since when is art ever a waste of time?"

The scientist nodded. "*Dalla bocca dei bambini.*" *From the mouths of babes.* He eyed the bas-relief. "Too bad the Magus is not present to enjoy your extraordinary rendering of his nose."

Prospero was anxious to finish work on *The Prometheus* so he could return to Venice. He'd had enough adventure, he'd explained. Summer had come to Italy, the war neared its end, amorous women were everywhere, and the world was beautiful. Time to go home before his luck ran out and he somehow managed to ruin his welcome in even more of Europe. In Venice, he'd raise capital to build airships or whatever else struck his fancy. The realms of science remained filled with possibility.

Once his mentor left, Taddeo's independence would be complete, a heady prospect that filled him with new worries. Where would he and Marie live after they'd tied the knot? How would they earn an income?

Would they survive Vienna?

He'd promised Marie she could continue to live her life on her own terms, which apparently involved fighting a war. After slaying the dragon, she told the army she would lead it to Austria and drive the Turk back into Asia. The men roared their approval. They'd have followed her to Jerusalem at that point. To Hell, even. Vienna was small change.

To Taddeo, however, Hell and Vienna had a lot in common. Europe was still reeling from the elegant destruction of the Hungarian army at Mohács, but even now, most people regarded the Turk as an uncivilized barbarian. Taddeo's family did business with them, and he knew how good they were at war. The Sultan maintained a standing army of nearly a hundred thousand men, many of them dreaded Janissaries, elite troops raised from childhood to fight. His artillery included two hundred massive siege pieces that could pound a city's walls into rubble. Guns just like these had helped Suleiman's grandfather take Constantinople, which had stood for more than a thousand years.

The Turks were tough, and they were ruthless. The battle for Vienna would very likely be one of the bloodiest ever fought.

He paused to flex his hands. These hands were meant to create, not destroy. He wanted to save men from ignorance and poverty and oppression, not kill them.

"Look at you," Prospero said. "Standing there, you remind me of my brother painting the Sistine Chapel. Did I ever tell you I modeled for the prophet Isaiah?"

Taddeo smiled. This was about the highest compliment a man could get from the scientist.

"You are just as obsessive and worrying as he was," Prospero explained.

They jumped as the air filled with a massive roar. The howling of the Landsknechte inspired fear even in their friends.

The soldiers were cheering. Endless cheering from thousands of throats.

"What's happening?"

"The homicidal maniacs are worked up about something. Perhaps your fiancée killed another dragon." The scientist put on his binocular glasses and gazed across the valley. "I see a train of people, flags. Someone of importance has arrived. Perhaps I should introduce myself."

Taddeo resumed his tapping. "I'd stay away from any more generals. The Prince knows how effective *The Prometheus* was in the battle. He'll put another cannon on the roof, one with six barrels this time, and turn you into a mercenary."

"As you can imagine, that is not for me. But you never know from whence a lucrative commission will come. Everyone with money is a potential patron. Write that down. Perhaps I will design a fleet of such armed vehicles and revolutionize modern warfare. You should start thinking of such things. Why not come along? Take a break from your opus."

He finished the dragon's tail. "No, thanks. I'm still working through some issues here."

"The future will take care of itself, my boy." Before Taddeo could respond, the scientist added, "You might consider a bas-relief on the other side of my precious, depicting me leading the attack in *The Prometheus*."

Taddeo nodded. "That's a good idea."

"Be sure to include my red sash in the detail. *Arrivederci!*"

Taddeo said nothing. He didn't want to think; he wanted to immerse himself in the act of creation.

But he frowned at his project until his shoulder muscles burned from holding the mallet over the gouge for too long without striking. He'd lost his rhythm. Perhaps the time had come when even this labor couldn't save him from his worries.

Maybe he needed a bigger project. Prospero was right; he needed a commission. If he survived Vienna, he would find a rich progressive duke and offer to electrify his city with *fulmen*. He'd begin his life's work to create a happier, more peaceful world.

"Did you miss me?"

Taddeo jumped again. Myrddin stood next to him wearing a sly smile.

"I told you not to sneak up on people, *mago!*"

"Did I sneak up on you, Taddeo? Did I? *Hmm?* Think about it."

"Where have you been?"

The wizard frowned at the bas-relief. "Ye Elder Gods, is that me?"

"Yes, *mago.*"

"Is my nose really that big?"

Taddeo shrugged, confirming it.

"Humph," the Magus said. "Well, if you must know where I was, I was in mourning."

"Who died?"

"The dragon died! Why does no one care about the dragon?"

"Well, it *was* trying to kill Marie. And you."

"If the moon was about to fall on you and you destroyed it with one of your obscene inventions, would you not feel sorry for its loss?"

"I guess I see your point," Taddeo said.

"The death of such a fine creature demanded more than mourning. It required penance. I spent the week on a mountaintop meditating on how the world keeps changing for the worse. The old ways are fading. The old things are dying. Even the Old Ones are packing it in."

"Who are the—"

"It's your world now. All yours. Enjoy it!"

"What are you saying, *mago?*"

"I'm leaving. I've had it with the world. I don't know why I bothered to wake up. It wasn't so bad in the tree."

"You *could* stay and try to help," Taddeo said.

"That again!"

"I mean—"

"You youngsters have to learn to fend for yourselves, or stay out of trouble!"

"You say the world's getting worse, you have the power to make it better, but you don't use it. Then you complain about it."

"*De ore infantium,*" Myrddin said. *From the mouths of babes.* "Nonetheless, the world must find its own way, sonny. And you must find yours." He looked past Taddeo's shoulder. "And over there, I see the one thing in the world that matters to you."

Taddeo wheeled, expecting to see Marie, but saw only an empty expanse of green field.

When he turned back, the Magus was gone.

He laughed. Myrddin's parting shot had been the simplest illusion of all. Yet like all the wizard's tricks, it had been educational.

Without thinking, Taddeo had realized the one thing in the world that mattered to him.

And in realizing this, all his worries melted away. Because nothing else mattered.

Absorbed in his work, he'd seen little of his beloved over the past six days. He now wanted to see her and tell her he too would follow her anywhere. Even to Hell. Even to Vienna.

He returned to the bas-relief and raised the gouge and mallet. First, he'd finish his project. Then he'd show it to her. Then he'd kiss her.

They would kiss, and kiss, and kiss.

A shadow fell across the sculpture.

"Remarkable," said a voice.

Taddeo turned and saw Don Jorge.

"Ha," the knight said. "Found you."

"Don Jorge! You're alive!"

But barely, it seemed. The man's armor, while cleaned, was battered, and his head and one eye were covered by a massive stained bandage.

"Looks like Marie Dubois owes me my plume back. I take it that's her in your sculpture?"

"Yes," Taddeo said. "She killed a dragon."

"So I hear. All the men are talking about it. I wouldn't have believed a word of it if it weren't our dear Marie Dubois. It's exactly the kind of thing she would do."

"I'm glad you're alive. What are you doing here?"

The knight grinned. "The cardinal requests the pleasure of your company."

Taddeo's heart sank with terror. Gattinara had been true to his word; there was no escaping the man. He sighed and put on a brave face. "Lead the way then."

Don Jorge gave him a quick once over. "Surely, you're not going to enter the presence of the Grand Chancellor of the Holy Roman Empire looking like *that*."

Taddeo washed his face and combed his hair while the knight chatted away, informing him about the coincidence that led to this happy reunion. The Emperor himself had arrived in the camp on his way to Bologna, where he intended to sign a formal peace treaty with the Pope while his aunt, Margaret of Austria, negotiated peace terms with Francis's mother in Cambrai—their sons hating each other too much to work things out themselves. The knight said the Emperor sought virtually the same terms as in the Treaty of Madrid signed after the last war; in other words, the last war had essentially been refought.

Taddeo shook his head in disgust. *That's just great*, he thought. The countless thousands dead or maimed, the waves of plague depopulating the land, the towns burned and economies ruined, had all been suffered to change exactly nothing. But he cared about none of it right now, his thoughts focused on Marie and Prospero. Had the cardinal arrested them? He knew better than to ask Don Jorge. Despite being a bit of a gossip, the knight would tell him nothing, he knew.

He'd have to find out from Gattinara himself.

He changed his shirt, put on his best jacket, and said he was ready. Don Jorge gave him a brief unsatisfied inspection, shrugged, and led him down the hill into the sea of drab tents that filled the valley. They passed French prisoners hauling firewood, Spaniards arguing over a game of cards, laundry women laughing at a mercenary's drunken serenade. A tinker from Milan banged his pots to draw attention to the quality of his wares. Stradioti groomed their horses. A squad of Landsknechte nudged each other and eyed him as he passed.

They left the camp and proceeded up the opposite slope toward a vast and colorful open-air tent protected by a phalanx of stalwart royal guard. Richly dressed lords and courtiers babbled and picked at a sumptuous buffet loaded with roast pig, seafood, and delicacies. The atmosphere was jubilant. Victory was in the air. Taddeo's stomach flipped in terror. The last time the Grand Chancellor had given him an audience, he'd been lying trembling on the floor after being tortured by the humorless Inquisitors.

The bulk of courtiers clustered around a man with a large bearded chin that could only belong to Charles V, the Holy Roman Emperor. Taddeo stared at him, star struck, until the Emperor's eyes flickered to fix him with a startled gaze.

Gattinara emerged from the crowd in his black and red vestments, propelling himself with his cane. He smiled his cold, mirthless smile. "Master Taddeo. You seem surprised by our fortuitous reunion. Coincidence is merely God's will, is that not so?"

Taddeo bent his knee to kiss the man's offered ring. "Your Eminence."

"Rise, my prodigal son. Walk with me. Your staring is making the Emperor nervous."

He followed the Chancellor out of the tent and back into the bright sunshine. They gazed across the Imperial encampment that stretched between the two hills. The soldiers milled about on their errands. Thick black smoke billowed along the summit of the opposite hill, where the French dead were being burned in piles.

"It's good to be back in Italy," said Gattinara. He breathed deep and wrinkled his nose as a waft of mercenary stink rose up on a chance breeze. "It's good to be home."

"It is," said Taddeo, who felt homesick.

"The war is coming to an end, young man. Soon, Italy will be under our thumb, the Pope will know his place, and we will have a free hand to root out and destroy the divisive heresy of Lutheranism at last. With enough money, we could bring France to heel. Keep the English out of Europe. Drive the Turk back into Asia Minor. Recover Jerusalem." His eyes gleamed. "Understand?"

"Yes, Your Eminence."

The Cardinal's face darkened. "So where is my gold?"

"It can't be done. I'm sorry, but it just can't."

"I kind of figured that after my second alchemist disappeared. I'm not an idiot!"

"We tried everything, but we failed. You see, there are seven metals in alchemy." He counted off with his fingers: "Gold and silver, of course, plus mercury, copper, tin—"

"You once told me that you know nothing. Through diligent study and experimentation, not to mention my considerable expense, you have confirmed it. Is that not so?"

Taddeo deflated. "It is, Your Eminence."

"Yet even a crooked log can make a fire. In Latin, *aeque pars ligni curvi ac recti valet igni*. Failing to produce gold, you managed to win the war."

"I did my part in the battle, Your Eminence."

"Your part delivered Italy to the Emperor! Did you think this would escape my notice?"

"No, Your Eminence."

The cardinal tapped his nose. "Nothing escapes me. I see everything. In fact, I understand you're getting married soon. Is that not so?"

"It is, Your Eminence."

"Marie Dubois has turned out to be much more intriguing and capable than I had initially given her credit. I suppose you will hear soon enough that she leads her own regiment now."

Taddeo stared at the man. "She *what*?"

"That business with the dragon made an enormous impression on the men. One of the mercenary colonels died during the fighting; his regiment elected her its leader just this morning."

"That's amazing."

"I assume you know that now she wants to take the army to Austria."

"Marie overheard the Ottoman Grand Vizier plotting with the King of France. The Ottoman Army is on its way to Vienna right now."

"We have confirmed this information. The emperor's brother has sent letters begging for help. From his council in Prague. In Bohemia." Gattinara was referring to Ferdinand, Archduke of Austria, appointed by Charles V to manage the Habsburg territories Austria and Slovenia; he was also nominally King of Hungary. The cardinal shook his head. "The next letter we get will probably be from Cuba, where he will bravely direct the defense of his realm."

"Without help, the Austrians don't stand a chance."

"Be that as it may, this army is not going to Austria."

Taddeo gasped at this news. "Why not?"

"Italy is key to everything, Master Taddeo. Imperial control of Italy will forever bring peace both to this country and to Europe. If this army left and were destroyed by the Turks, France would have the opportunity to undo everything we've gained here. Ferdinand must take care of his own."

"But…" He didn't know what to say. Vienna was doomed.

"The army will instead march south to raise the siege of Naples and bring Florence to heel. Then, perhaps, we will move against the Turk."

"But it will be too late then! Surely, you can do something, Eminence."

"Oh, but I am," the cardinal said. "I'm going to send Marie's regiment. I'd also like to send seven hundred gunners so we can field-test their new wheel-lock muskets."

"They'll be slaughtered!"

"Only if it is God's will, my son. And God's on our side, so there. In any case, *Signora* Dubois told me she plans to go, and I assume you will want to go with her. If you manage to succeed in your encounter with Suleiman, I will reward you beyond your wildest dreams. If you even merely survive, I will appoint you to an important post in the Imperial court."

The words barely registered. Taddeo blew a sigh of relief. Marie was all right. For now.

"Of course," Gattinara added, "you will want to be married before facing such danger."

"We haven't made any arrangements beyond the contract," Taddeo stammered.

"I have." Gattinara squinted in the sunlight. "My eyes aren't what they once were, but I believe I see your bride approaching now."

Taddeo wheeled. "Say *what?*"

The cardinal chuckled. "It appears to be your ring day, Master Taddeo. *Nec mortem effugere quisquam nec amorem potest." One cannot flee death or love.*

The procession wound through the camp. Minstrels and military bands led the way with their happy if somewhat martial music. The regimental colonels swaggered after them, followed by smiling laundry women and camp prostitutes bearing the bride's chalice and a stack of cakes. The standard bearer of Marie's regiment came next, the dragon skull mounted over a blood-red banner. Leo tagged along, wagging his tail proudly.

At last came the bride accompanied by a grinning Prospero looking smart in his red sash.

Marie Dubois was radiant in a simple blue dress, a wreath of wildflowers, and herbs woven about her flowing red hair and the veil covering her face. Blue was the color of purity, the flowers and rosemary meant luck and fertility, and the veil, a Saracen tradition brought back by the Crusaders, symbolized purity and protected her from the evil eye.

Even at a distance, her beauty was stunning.

The mercenaries stood and doffed their helmets and hats as she passed. Soon, the entire army crowded around to see the dragon slayer on her wedding day. The Imperial court left the tent and formed a semicircle behind Gattinara.

"*Dio Mio,*" Taddeo whispered.

The one thing in the world that matters to you.

It was her. And nothing else mattered.

"It's custom for the groom to buy a drink for the other men at his *matrimonium,* since he is denying them a potential bride," said Gattinara. "But I heard you already did that."

Taddeo could only nod dumbly, awed by the vision of his approaching bride.

"You might need this," Don Jorge said with a nudge. He gave Taddeo an exquisitely carved gold ring. "It once belonged to Moctezuma, or so Don Hernando Cortés told me."

Taddeo stared at the ring in his palm and nodded his thanks before returning his gaze to his beloved, who now stood at his side. Through the veil, he could see her smiling.

"Surprise, honey," she said.

The camp was completely quiet except for the chirping of the birds.

"Taddeo Cellini," said Gattinara, "in the presence of the Emperor and all these witnesses, do you wish to have this woman as your wife, to love her and honor her, to keep her and protect her, in health and sickness, and to stay away from all women except her, as long as you both live?"

"I do so wish it," Taddeo said, finding his voice at last.

"Marie Dubois, do you wish to have this man as your husband, to love him and honor him, to obey him and serve him, in health and sickness, and to stay away from all other men except him, as long as you both live?"

She smiled at Taddeo. "I do wish it."

"Then join hands."

Marie took his hand and gave him a leather cord, which he wrapped around their joined hands to symbolize their union.

Gattinara added, "You may exchange your vows, which the Holy Church will ordain."

Taddeo licked his dry lips. "I take you, Marie Dubois, to be my wedded wife, to have and to hold, from this day forward, for better or for worse, for richer or for poorer, in sickness and in health, until we depart this world, and to that I swear to be true."

"I take *you*, Taddeo Cellini, to be my wedded husband, to have and to hold, from this day forward, for better or for worse, for richer or for poorer, in sickness and in health, to be loving and giving, in bed and at our table, until we depart this world, and to that I swear to be true."

"The ring, if you please," the cardinal said. He blessed it and returned it to Taddeo, who placed it on the ring finger of Mare's right hand as was custom.

"I give you this ring to wed you, my body to worship you, and all my worldly goods to support you," he said.

One of the laundry women brought forward a silver cup, from which they both drank. The wine shot to Taddeo's brain, making him feel even giddier.

"By my authority as a notary, I pronounce you man and wife," Gattinara said. "By my office as a cardinal in the Holy Roman Catholic Church, I bless this marriage."

Several of the colonels wiped tears from their eyes and sniffed.

Gattinara added: "You may kiss the bride, my son."

Taddeo raised Mare's veil, still awestruck.

They kissed.

The moment stretched for an eternity while the army roared.

They kissed.

And over the roar, he heard a single note that went on and on, cold and sweet and metallic and beautiful, like an angel singing in the ether.

They kissed—

The sound became more intense until it was piercing. Taddeo and Marie parted in a daze and looked around. The sound wasn't in his head; everyone else heard it too. The wedding guests shielded their eyes against the bright light as they looked up at the sky.

Taddeo watched the majestic creature descend singing out of the sun.

"How about that?" Don Jorge said. "Dragons really are real."

But it was no dragon. Taddeo only caught a glimpse as it fell, but that glimpse told him everything.

He'd seen its like before but only in art. His mind flashed to a statue carved into St. Mark's Basilica in Venice and the Republic of Genoa's coat of arms.

The majestic creature had a lion's body and the head and feet of an eagle, and was supported by a massive wingspan.

Griffin. Beautiful and powerful. The king of the beasts.

Taddeo almost smiled at a sudden thought. If another monster had come, that meant the Magus was here. Myrddin had come to his wedding.

The claws splayed as the creature fell. The wedding guests scattered. Don Jorge stepped in front of the Emperor—who was observing its flight with detached amusement—and shielded him with sword drawn.

The griffin hadn't come for the Emperor, Taddeo knew.

A strong cool wind swept over them. The sky darkened as the griffin swooped down.

There was only one thing to be done.

"A sword!" Marie screamed. "Someone give me a sword!"

Taddeo pushed her to the ground.

The claws gripped him.

They lifted.

Vienna

AUSTRIA

● Vienna

● Mohács

Venice

HUNGARY

● Belgrade

ITALY

Istanbul

OTTOMAN EMPIRE

~ Chapter XIII ~
THE GRAND VIZIER

The Ottoman Army began its long march against Austria in April. The long column that snaked out of Bulgaria included Sipahi cavalry, elite Janissary infantry in their blue tunics and tall white hats, Akinji marauders, provincial infantry, artillerymen hauling five hundred guns, and administrators and support personnel.

A second army followed close behind, consisting of an endless wagon train, massive animal herds, and two hundred fifty thousand teamsters, bakers, traders, imams, tentmakers, leatherworkers, drovers, carpenters, and blacksmiths.

By the end of June, this vast host neared Belgrade.

Sultan Suleiman led the army personally. One hundred thousand strong and virtually unbeaten in the field, his finely tuned military had become a juggernaut. In this campaign, it would be venturing farther than ever along what long ago had been termed the Highway of Holy Struggle.

He intended to winter the army in Vienna before sweeping across Germany the following year. On the banks of the Rhine, he would built a monument to Islam. First, the Balkans, then Hungary, then Germany. Soon, all Christendom would lie prostrate at his feet. After that, who knew? The blood of Genghis Khan flowed in his veins. He dreamed the same dreams as Alexander the Great. The entire world would be his, perhaps, if Allah, the Most Gracious, the Most Merciful, willed it.

After all, the Ottomans could be delayed, but they had

never been stopped.

Two hundred fifty years ago, Ertuğrul, chief of a wild band of four hundred horsemen from Turkestan, arrived in western Anatolia to support the Seljuk Turks against the Byzantine Empire. For his service, the Seljuks allowed him to establish an emirate on the Byzantine border.

His son, Osman, declared independence from the Seljuks during the invasion by the Mongol hordes. He armed the refugees flowing into his emirate from the east and marched them against the declining Byzantine Empire to the west, expanding his holdings.

Henceforth, the Turkish dynasty would be called Ottoman, or of the House of Osman.

Osman's son conquered all of western Anatolia. His grandson crossed the straits and overran the Balkan Peninsula from Romania to Greece. Fearing the strength of his nobles, Murad I built a slave army, including the vaunted Janissaries, from captured prisoners. To maintain this force, Murad II instituted a tax on Christians, which could be paid by giving a male child to the Army.

The Crusader armies continued to come from Europe, but the Turks not only held onto their territory, they expanded it. In 1453, they captured Constantinople, the greatest city in Christendom, and made it their new capital. By 1517, they'd conquered Egypt and the Middle East from the Sassanids. By 1526, Suleiman, the tenth sultan the House of Osman had produced, had captured Rhodes and most of Hungary.

Now the Empire boasted a population of twenty million. The Ottoman Army threatened central Europe; the Navy had made the Mediterranean Sea an Ottoman lake. Not since Rome had Europe seen such capable administrators, such a large and disciplined standing army, nor a people so quick to embrace science, notably advances in modern warfare.

But they could not conquer the weather.

The sky darkened and rain fell as the army marched through Serbia. The next day, it fell harder. By the third day, it became torrential. No one had seen its like since the days of Noah.

The river waters rose, spilled over their banks, and flooded the countryside. The roads disappeared beneath running water. The land became a fetid swamp.

On a rocky hill overlooking the struggling columns in the river valley below, the Magus Myrddin Wyllt sat in the lotus position, sheltered by a massive leaning boulder.

He waited.

He'd had every intention of being helpful, but not in the way Taddeo had hoped. Instead, he'd disappeared to keep him and Marie out of trouble with the monsters the Asiatic magician conjured from the higher realms. By staying away, the youngsters would be out of danger except for the kind they appeared to continually seek out on their own.

The only problem was he'd indulged a sentimental urge to see them married; he'd attended the ceremony in the guise of a barn swallow and stayed just long enough for trouble to come knocking. The griffin snatched Taddeo and was now somewhere over Bosnia.

The wizard had followed the creature. He wanted at last to get a look at his adversary. After landing on this ancient hill, he decided that he would teach the Turks a lesson. He'd answer fire with fire, or, in this case, water with water. He invoked the charm of creation.

Day after day, rain lashed the Ottoman Army. Thunder pounded the heavens. The pack animals died in droves. Moisture ruined powder stores. Grain spoiled. Wagons and heavy guns became stuck in the endless morass. During the worst of the flooding, soldiers climbed trees to avoid drowning in the deluge. Then a bridge washed away during a hurricane, taking scores of men with it.

"Oh, darn," the Magus winced, remembering his vow. "Sorry about that."

The cold wet soldiers grumbled. The campaign had already tested their endurance, and they hadn't even crossed the imperial border yet.

A league distant, Pargali Ibrahim Pasha, Grand Vizier of the

Ottoman Empire, sat on a stool in the open doorway of his dry and brightly illuminated pavilion, playing a haunting cadenza on his violin to the accompaniment of thunder. He loved the violin, the dark queen of musical instruments. So dexterous, it could be used to play sequences of notes of almost any complexity and at almost any speed. So expressive, it came closest of all instruments to the human voice.

Played properly, it could even produce a scream.

The violin trilled in his hands.

The dark bird appeared in the gray roiling sky, singing its crystal note.

Ibrahim's solo lilted to a soaring crescendo.

The griffin fell through the rainfall and landed softly on taloned feet, its head held high and its wings still flapping as a brake. Singing its piercing note, it strode majestically to Ibrahim Pasha and shuddered to dry its feathers.

The Grand Vizier lowered his violin. "Have you brought something for me, my old friend?"

The creature cawed, a strident sound like a herald's trumpet.

"Then let's see him."

The griffin lowered its head and vomited a slime-covered form onto the ground.

Ibrahim inspected the fetal thing and frowned. Then shrugged.

"Interesting," he said and nodded to his servants, who picked up the coughing figure and brought it into the pavilion while he resumed playing to please the griffin.

The boy awoke to music and the patter of rain in a room whose walls appeared to be constructed of heavy carpets and ornate tapestries depicting exotic caravans and battles. He stared at the two salaaming African giants in a daze, unable to remember his name.

I was getting married, he thought.

The men drew a steaming bath for him and left. He peeled off his wet clothes, sank into the hot water, and sighed. The heat and violin music lulled him into a doze.

Three beautiful dark-skinned women appeared, scantily clad in veils and silver anklets and bangles that tinkled as they moved. He yelped with shyness and sank into the water up to his eyes. Laughing, they dropped rose petals into the water and coaxed him to give up his limbs one by one for scrubbing. Then all three washed his back while singing in their exotic language.

Meanwhile, it all came back to him with a long despairing sigh; he'd been kidnapped from his own wedding. He was still alive and, so far, treated well by these strange people; there was that at least. And at last, he'd learn the identity of the Asiatic magician who wanted to destroy the Magus.

The women laid out clean garments for him and withdrew. Once he was certain they'd gone, he stepped out of the tub and put them on. He eyed himself in the mirror and thought he looked fairly dashing in his kaftan, baggy trousers, and red silk sash. Then one of the servants appeared, shook his head at his posing, and gestured for him to follow him into another room.

A tall slim bearded man sat in a jeweled chair, dressed similarly to Taddeo but wearing a large turban. His hand rested near the hilt of a saber thrust into his sash.

He's a Turk, Taddeo realized. And a rich one at that.

"Do you speak the language of the old empire?" the man inquired in Latin.

Taddeo nodded.

"Then I welcome you to my humble tent. Please feel at ease; you are in no danger." He considered his words. "Unless you displease me, of course, in which case I may have you flayed alive for ninety-nine days." He smiled again. "But I'm sure that won't happen." His face darkened. "Will it happen?"

"Um. No?"

"Allow me to introduce myself. I am the *Vezir-i-Azam* Pargali Ibrahim Pasha."

Taddeo couldn't believe his ears. This man was Mercurino Gattinara's counterpart in the Ottoman Empire, the highest minister of the Sultan's government.

He bent his knee and bowed his head. "Your Excellency."

Ibrahim nodded his approval. "You are well mannered. And apparently educated. I suppose that's a beginning. Now tell me your name."

"Taddeo Cellini, Excellency."

"Of Venice? I know your people."

"My father is Gregorio."

"Of course. We do some profitable business with his traders. Come. Refresh yourself."

The Grand Vizier gestured toward a nearby banquet table laden with fragrant dishes of roasted pigeon, *lavash* bread, lentil and cracked wheat salads, and much more. It smelled amazing.

Taddeo dug in. After three days of fasting, he was starving.

"The cuisine of empire," Ibrahim noted. "One of the benefits of ruling half the world is you have your pick of good food."

Taddeo paused from his meal. "Should I wait for you, Excellency?"

The man laughed. "I can't eat with an infidel. However, in His infinite wisdom, Allah does not forbid providing hospitality to non-believers. Go ahead, I've already dined."

"Thank you, Excellency."

"Perhaps we could talk while you eat. I'm very curious why you're here."

"You brought me here," Taddeo said, his mouth filled with spiced ground lamb.

"The griffin was supposed to deliver Myrddin Wyllt."

He sucked the juice from his fingers. "I'm not him."

"That, at least, is known." The Grand Vizier stroked his beard. "If the griffin brought you here, there was a reason for it." His eyes narrowed. "You know the Magus."

Taddeo shoveled stewed vegetables into his mouth with a piece of flatbread. "For the past few months. He's my wife's master."

"Your wife is the lovely Marie Dubois? A most curious woman. Allah willed that she kill several of my retainers and burn down half the French Royal Guard encampment."

"We just got married. You kidnapped me from the *matrimonium* ceremony."

"How rude of me," Ibrahim answered. "It is said, 'A fire burns if close, a beautiful woman if close or far.' True, eh? So. Would you happen to know where Myrddin Wyllt is at this moment?"

"I don't. He said he was tired of the world and wanted a break. I'm sorry."

"Did you believe him?"

Taddeo wiped his mouth. "Yes? I had no reason not to believe him."

"Ah. So. Enough talk. We'll speak again tomorrow once you've had a chance to collect your memories, anything that could be useful to me. You might be interested to know I've decided to allow you to remain alive out of respect for your father."

"You also want me as bait for the Magus. You're hoping he'll come for me."

"Yes. Yes, that's quite right."

"Which is good, because being bait for the Magus is much more likely to keep me alive than being Gregorio Cellini's son."

Ibrahim laughed. "I'd hate to have to bind such an interesting young man in chains and keep him in a cage like a monkey. Surely, it would stifle that bright mind of yours. Do you agree to be paroled in exchange for your word of honor you will not try to escape?"

"I swear it." Taddeo had been terrified the man was going to kill, torture, or jail him—or worse, turn him into a eunuch. "Can I ask you a question, Your Excellency?"

"And confuse the minor liberties of your parole with extreme impertinence? Why not?"

"Why do you keep trying to kill the *mago*?"

Ibrahim smiled. "Because he is the only man who can stop me from conquering the world."

Outside, the rain poured down.

The next morning, the servants kicked Taddeo awake. He leaped out of bed shouting with terror. The men laughed, folded his cot, and began breaking down the tent around him. He barely got dressed before they threw a cloak over him and the tent came down, exposing him to the downpour. Through miming punctuated with a few light slaps to the head, they instructed him to help load the Grand Vizier's possessions onto carriages drawn by trains of strong white horses.

Taddeo carefully tied and carried an armful of parcels while Ibrahim observed him with growing impatience from one of the carriages. When he returned for more, only a depression of wet flattened grass remained where a veritable palace of fabric had stood. One of the servants salaamed, swatted him, and pointed to the Grand Vizier's carriage.

"Come on, boy," Ibrahim said. "You're holding up the *jihad*."

He stepped inside and sat opposite the Grand Vizier and one of the beautiful servant women. Taddeo found it difficult to adjust to his new status, which was something of a cross between an infidel, a slave, and an honored guest.

Taddeo brushed rain from his cloak as the carriage lurched through the mud. "Can I ask you another question, Your Excellency?"

"It is said, 'It is not disgraceful to ask; it is disgraceful not to know.'"

"Where are we?"

"A question truly worthy of my time. We are at the frontier of the Ottoman Empire."

His heart sank at the news. He was so far away from everything he knew. From Marie.

"But we're going to Vienna," he said with hope.

Ibrahim glared at him. "How is it a boy knows our business so well?"

"Marie snuck into King Francis's tent and overhead you speaking with him."

"Ah. 'The Devil is no match for a woman.' Yes, we are going to Vienna. Why are you so eager about it?"

"Marie will be there."

"That is too bad for her. Will Myrddin Wyllt be there as well?"

"It's possible. Why do you think he would want to stop you from conquering the world?"

"He might not," Ibrahim conceded.

"He doesn't. He doesn't care much about anything. That's his biggest problem."

"Statecraft is like chess, my friend. One must make decisions based on worst possible outcomes. Even if there is only a small chance of the Magus interfering, I must assume he will do so and plan accordingly."

Taddeo's heart lightened at this news, which also meant as long as there remained an even remote chance of the Magus coming to his rescue, he would be suffered to live.

"If you can do magic, are you like the *mago*?"

"No," the Grand Vizier told him. "Only the *Sihirbaz* is like the *Sihirbaz*. He is a master sorcerer, the reason the Druids worshipped trees, the last of an ancient race who knew the Old Ones. One day, I will tell you another name by which he is known."

"How did you learn magic then?"

"Everything passes along the Silk Road linking China to Europe, including magic. There are even traders who specialize in it. My agents buy everything."

Ibrahim patted the servant girl's knee, which prompted her to feed him some grapes from a bowl. After popping a few into his mouth, she caught Taddeo looking and fed him one. He plucked one of the grapes and fed it to her, an egalitarian impulse that earned him a frown from Ibrahim. In the Grand Vizier's service, one did not feed the help. The help fed you. The stability of an empire of millions rested on ideas as simple as this.

The rain stopped as they caught up to the Ottoman Army. Taddeo heard the shrill marching music of the mehters first, platoons of colorfully clad musicians playing bass and kettledrums, triangles, cymbals, wind instruments, horns, and staffs with small bells attached. He parted the heavy curtain and watched the pageant of the march from the carriage window. Despite the wet and cold, it was a spirited army. The fierce Janissaries stepped proudly in perfect unison under bright banners and flags, a stark contrast to the filthy rabble that normally constituted a European army. These men, who had marched thousands of miles and called one another *fellow traveler*, had conquered Arabia and Egypt, Persia and Hungary, and now menaced central Europe. Dressed in blue coats and white felt hats, they splashed down the waterlogged road in their knee-high boots, voices lifted in some martial anthem.

"What are they singing, Excellency?"

"'Turkish nation! Turkish nation!'" the Grand Vizier said, his eyes blazing with fierce patriotism. "'Treasure your independence. Overwhelm the motherland's enemies, and make the cursed ones gnash their teeth in despair at your feet.'" He nodded. "It's a good song."

They stopped to water the horses on the swollen banks of the Danube. Branches and debris swept past. A Turkish galley stroked the river. Taddeo asked Ibrahim for some materials for a project. The Grand Vizier assented, curious about Taddeo's skills with magic.

"Not magic, Excellency," he explained. "Science. A minor project to pass the time."

"I have no use for science. Science diffuses power. Magic, like religion, concentrates it."

During the next leg of their journey with the army, Taddeo got to work while the Grand Vizier taught him Turkish. Every man, Ibrahim believed, should learn the language of the Ottoman Empire, which he regarded as the new Latin.

Taddeo liked the vocal harmony of the language and its high frequency of soft *zzz* and *shh* and *sss* sounds. He had an ulterior motive to his learning, however; he wanted to understand everything said around him. Even words could be weapons, and he intended to resist when the time was right. He yearned to get back to Marie; his heart ached to see her face, hear her voice, feel her lips against his. But he felt an even bigger responsibility to save Europe.

In any case, these aims were one and the same now. Anything he might do to help save Vienna would also save Marie.

Practicing his verbs, he cut a large circle of leather and sewed arrow shafts into the material as if they were spokes in a wheel. Then he added an actual wood wheel spoke as the handle, bent a ring of metal around it, and added a clasp.

"What does it do?" Ibrahim said in Turkish.

Taddeo understood the question. "It's like an awning you carry in your hand that keeps the sun and water off your head. And it retracts into a walking stick, see? You simply move the metal ring to the top and clasp it in place using this mechanism, which makes the leather and arrow assembly rigid. The rain strikes the leather and slides off."

The Grand Vizier dismissed it with a gesture. "Feh. It is like a parasol, which keeps the sun off one's head. This is a device for a woman. A man needs no more than a cloak to stay dry."

"The convenience of my device doesn't distinguish gender, Excellency."

"How can a man fight with sword and shield while carrying around such a thing? Convenience is useful in that it distinguishes wealth and class and therefore power. But some lines cannot be crossed, or a leader should lose respect. It is said, 'For a lean ox, there is no knife.' But the one that is fat must look over his shoulder at all times."

"Maybe there's enough for all of the oxen to eat the same," Taddeo ventured.

"Maybe some of the oxen will be flayed alive for the pleasure of the Sultan," Ibrahim said.

Taddeo kept his mouth shut until they reached Belgrade.

During the next two months, the Ottoman Army's march brought it to Mohács in southern Hungary. Taddeo learned the Grand Vizier's language and customs and wondered why Myrddin hadn't yet fallen into his devious trap by attempting a rescue.

His homesickness grew worse. He missed everything about his old life now, even his bossy mentor, even the irritating wizard.

At night, he dreamed about Marie, whom he missed most of all. Occasionally, Myrddin appeared in his dreams as an owl and promised that he would soon be delivered from his bondage. Taddeo put this down to wishful thinking. He didn't believe in the prophecy of dreams.

They reached the plains of Mohács in August on a rare warm, sunny day. The vast encampment stretched across the flat landscape. The army stood at attention, row after row of cavalry, infantry, and cannon arranged in neat formation on the bones of the Hungarian royal army it slaughtered in this very place three years earlier. Taddeo lost count of the red flags that rippled in the wind and identified the various companies and divisions. A column of Sipahi thundered past on prancing horses, their chain mail jingling. Pennants streamed from their green lances.

Spirits soared across the army now. If standing on the site of their amazing victory weren't enough, the endless rain had finally stopped. The Janissaries shook off their funk. They were the elite shock troops of an invincible war machine; what was a hurricane or two to them?

"At last, the sun shines upon us," Ibrahim remarked. "God is great."

Taddeo inhaled the warm, humid air and sighed.

"Come and meet the Sultan," the Grand Vizier said.

He paled. "Me?"

"Be polite, and don't turn your back on him, or he'll have golden screws, inlaid with rare pearls, inserted into your skull as a lesson in manners."

He smiled at the Grand Vizier's dark humor.

Ibrahim laughed and said, "I'm not joking."

It was on this note that Taddeo met one of the strongest rulers in the world, whose empire sprawled across three continents. At that time, perhaps the strongest since the Caesars.

His stomach flipped as they approached the massive red and gold open-air pavilion. Inside, the Sultan sat on a golden throne resting on a polished and carpeted cedar dais, attended by a throng of nobles and courtiers.

"See, Taddeo, there is the Sultan, Khan of Khans, may God be pleased with him."

Suleiman the Magnificent was a slim man with a long neck, sensitive face, and aquiline nose adorned with an incongruous horseshoe mustache. He wore a massive white turban on his head that reminded Taddeo of Prospero's balloon, decorated with an aigrette of peacock feathers fastened into place by a diamond clasp. Emeralds and rubies sparkled on his fingers. A giant jewel-crusted scimitar rested against the throne as a reminder to his supplicants not to displease him.

The Grand Vizier spread his arms and paid homage to the Sultan, who smiled at the sight of his old friend. After an intricate exchange of courtesies, Suleiman's eyes narrowed as they took in sight of the wide-eyed Taddeo.

"Who is your new page?" he said in his soft but deep voice.

"My new *Janissary*," Ibrahim corrected with a smile. "He cuts down his enemies with his wit."

"Speak, boy," the Sultan said. "I will survive the exchange."

Taddeo bent his knee. "Your Majesty," he said in Turkish.

"You have him well trained, Ibrahim."

"He arrived that way."

"Did he? Perhaps I should make *him* King of Hungary."

The army forced a ragged cheer as a column of armored horsemen rode into the camp, led by a stocky noble clad in furs and sporting a massive beard that balanced a receding hairline.

"That would be the warlord János Zápolya," the Grand Vizier murmured. "The man who would be king. Leave us, Taddeo, but don't stray far. You're about to see a king crowned and grovel in a single ceremony."

Escorted by the general of the army, Zápolya swaggered into the presence of the Sultan. His paused as he noticed his boots had tracked mud on the imperial rug. He bowed awkwardly before the throne.

After destroying the Hungarian Royal Army, Suleiman executed his prisoners, advanced to the capital of Buda, and sacked it before withdrawing from the country with a hundred thousand captives, as a revolt in Persia demanded his immediate attention. And so Hungary, which had defended Christendom against the growing power of the Ottoman Empire for a century, found itself without a king, its capital in ruins, the flower of its nobility slaughtered.

With the Turks out of the country, the Austrian Archduke Ferdinand and János Zápolya, Count of Zips and governor of Transylvania, claimed the throne and settled their dispute with combat. After two crushing defeats by Count Nicholas von Salm, Zápolya fled to Poland and threw in his lot with Suleiman, who was only too happy to make him a puppet king as a way to solidify his control over the sprawling country.

The Sultan commanded silence. He stood and welcomed the Count, who gave his kiss of submission and in return received four ceremonial robes, which a servant placed on his shoulders one atop the next. Zápolya chafed; he hadn't come for robes. Then his eyes lit up. Another servant had brought an iron crown on a pillow, which Suleiman placed on his balding head.

Moments later, clouds passed over the sun and thunder growled in the heavens. A great wind lashed the army with rain. Suleiman eyed the sky with distaste and wondered why Allah, the All Powerful, the Most Merciful, was making this so hard. Taddeo and the Grand Vizier looked up and muttered together, "Myrddin."

Taddeo deployed his umbrella, which had seen a lot of use during the journey, and noticed Suleiman staring at him with amusement.

"A man is as wise as his head, not his years," the Sultan said.

For the next two weeks, they passed sacked and abandoned towns and villages. Most of the population had fled to Vienna and Poland, leaving behind the old and sick to be slaughtered by the Sultan's thirty thousand Akinji horsemen—unpaid pillagers whom the Germans called "sack men"—and Zápolya's bloodthirsty patriots. Ranging far ahead of the main army, they plundered the countryside, fired whole villages, and murdered the innocent wherever they went.

The Grand Vizier's carriage rolled through a village turned into a charnel house. Crows and starving dogs had picked through what was left by the time the Sipahis cantered through. Most of the homes had been burned to the ground before the incessant rain extinguished the fires. Taddeo crossed his arms and shook his head in disgust.

Ibrahim shrugged and said, "To make *menemen*, one must break eggs. Be grateful to Allah, the All Beneficent and Source of All Peace, that He has not willed you to be an egg."

Within three weeks, this vast host would be knocking on Vienna's door. Taddeo had seen what the Ottoman Army could do. Of all the Grand Vizier's enslaved monsters, it was the greatest, and it could not be resisted.

Yet for the first time in months, he was happy.

Every league through this cold ruined country brought him closer to Marie.

~ Chapter XIV ~

BRUNHILD'S BASTARDS

he Imperial Dragon Head Regiment marched out of Italy along a dusty road in the heat of July, led by Marie Dubois and the hawk-faced Count Nicholas von Salm, a gray-haired, seventy-year-old veteran of the Italian Wars.

Salm was a decorated hero of the Empire, a living legend. At Pavia, he'd crossed swords with King Francis. In Hungary, he destroyed Janos Zápolya's army in two crushing engagements and chased him into Poland, earning the throne for his master, the Archduke Ferdinand. In numerous campaigns, he'd fought hard and emerged victorious.

Peace had never agreed with him, and the years appeared to melt away the closer their little army got to Vienna. His eyes twinkled at the thought of taking a crack at the Sultan. His presence on the battlefield alone would be worth two regiments.

He clucked disapprovingly at Marie and told her to put her cloak on. In the mountains, a cold could be serious. During a siege, fatal.

"And eat more," the hero of Pavia said. "You're too skinny."

Marie didn't answer, still brooding. For nearly two weeks, she'd sat in her tent at Landriano staring into space, still wearing her wedding dress, while the army crowded weeping outside. She slept rarely and fitfully, racked by feverish dreams. No longer did she dream of swordplay in dusty training yards and misty woods. Now she dreamed of Taddeo pushing her to the ground before the monstrous bird swept him away, its piercing song drowning out her long scream of anguish.

Again and again, the dream came, and she was forced to watch her beloved disappear into the clouds. Again and again, she was powerless to save him.

Then one night, Myrddin appeared in the guise of a barn swallow and told her that Taddeo was a captive of the Turks and was even now on his way to Vienna.

Marie believed in the prophecy of dreams.

When she awoke, she summoned the captains and told them to replace the regiment's losses with the hardest men in the army, men who became angry when they should be afraid. She called the regimental treasurer and told him to spend their money on the most highly skilled armorers, blacksmiths, bakers, and other tradesmen he could find in Milan. She feverishly reviewed maps and lists of ordnance and provisions.

Pargali Ibrahim Pasha had tried to have her killed. He'd plagued her with monsters, driven away her master, invaded her liege's lands. And then he'd stolen her husband on her wedding day. Was even now holding him captive suffering God knew what tortures.

She would make him pay for every torment, and get her husband back alive.

While sitting in her tent for ten days, Marie had punished herself for her folly. All her life, she'd dreamed of giving herself to a cause she could believe in. She thought she'd found it in knightly service to a great king who would reward her deeds with a warm paternal love. But Prospero, damn his eyes, was right. It all meant nothing. The only cause worth fighting for was herself and the man she loved. Nothing else mattered, and she'd lost him.

When Myrddin told her in the dream that Taddeo was on his way to Vienna, the two things that made her feel complete no longer competed. If she saved Vienna, she might save him. She swore that if she succeeded, she would give up her adventuring and help Taddeo pursue his own dreams. First, however, she had to fight the Turk.

Horns blared as the regiment marched out of the Imperial encampment. They were the best of the best. Brunhild's Bastards, the other soldiers called them. A Blood Flag regiment.

Gattinara kissed both her cheeks during the sendoff, blessed the army in Latin, and promised double pay and a large bonus if they survived the siege. He presented her with a purse of gold and an even greater gift—Count Nicholas, one of the Empire's best commanders.

After leaving Italy, the little army bivouacked for the night in a valley sandwiched by colossal mountains that loomed over them in the dark. The mercenaries prepared to sleep on the ground. They were marching fast and would be on the road again before dawn.

After grooming and feeding her horse, Marie wandered among the campfires to gauge the temper of the men. They were a sober lot; this long, hard march saw little drinking and clowning. Absent was the usual camp gossip and bitching about their officers. Surrounded by piles of gear, the mercenaries cooked their meals, sharpened their blades, and quietly spun tall tales about the fierce Turk. They stiffened and hushed as she approached. She said nothing, her expression perpetually grim. They were more afraid of her right now than of the Sultan's army. She touched their shoulders lightly as she passed, melting their tension and fears and leaving behind a fierce and quiet devotion.

At the rear of the army, Marie found *The Prometheus* parked among the camp followers. Firelight flickered across the bas-relief. She hadn't seen it before and sucked in her breath in astonishment at the artistry. She brushed her fingers against the detailing. There she was, fighting the dragon. The play of light made the scene come alive. In Taddeo's loving tribute, Myrddin perpetually waved his staff at the beast, she forever about to strike it dead. She stared at the masterpiece for a long time, reliving the excitement of the day, until a buxom laundry woman with flushed cheeks left the wagon, fixing her hair and softly singing an Italian love song.

Marie entered and found Prospero cross-legged on his rumpled cot. Dressed in a turban and kaftan like a Turk, he smoked his hookah while reading a large leather-bound book. He looked up and smiled.

"Ah, *bella*, it is nice to see you again."

"Prospero Buonarroti, you were supposed to go to Venice and deliver Taddeo's letter to his father. What are you doing here, and why are you dressed in that getup?"

He blew a smoke ring that briefly reminded her of Myrddin. "I sent the letter on by messenger. I am coming with you to find Taddeo."

She blushed. "That's very noble of you. Thank you."

"I cannot return to Gregorio and tell him I lost his son to a flying monster. My reputation is on thin ice in the city as it is."

That sounded more like the Prospero she knew. "How noble," she repeated in a different tone. "So what are you doing sitting there dressed like a Turk?"

"Just checking the fit," he replied. "I've grown a little around the waist since I last wore this disguise in the Levant."

Marie caught his plan. "Excellent! You'll be able to slip in and out of the Sultan's camp undetected! Perhaps even bring back Taddeo!"

Prospero toked on his hookah. "Ah, no. That would be far too dangerous for me."

"Then what's it for?"

"When the Turks sweep over the wall, I intend to blend in and praise Allah all the way back to Venice."

She gasped. "Have you not even a speck of honor, Prospero Buonarroti?"

"Once again, I cannot tell if you intend to insult or praise me. I am here to help you recover Taddeo, not get sabered in my invaluable brain. Sometimes I believe you want to see me killed for some ridiculous cause! If I am alive, I can help you. If I am honorable and dead, I cannot. Do you speak Turkish?"

Marie shook her head.

"Well, you may well observe that I am fluent! In fact, I speak eighteen languages not counting my native tongue, as befitting—"

"That's good—"

"How many does Myrddin Wyllt speak?"

"I don't know. Nine or ten."

"Ha!"

"Then again, his languages control the elements."

"Repeat after me: *I teslim!*"

"*I teslim,*" she said hopefully. "What does it mean?"

"It means, 'I surrender!' Now this: *Eğer beni kurtar, ben senin için dans edecek.* Which means, 'I will dance for you if you spare me.' I know many more helpful phrases like these."

"Aargh!" she cried and stomped out of the wagon.

Marie returned to her campsite fuming. Leo lay sleeping, his leg kicking as he dreamed about rabbits. Count Nicholas, wrapped in a heavy wool cloak, drowsily regarded the fire he'd made. He gestured to a pot hanging over the flames.

"I made you some cheese soup."

"I'm not hungry, *Feldherr,*" she said, addressing him using the honorific for a senior Imperial field officer.

"During a march, you need to eat to keep up your strength. You eat whenever you can. During a siege, you need some fat so your body has something to fall back on while you starve. When people get hungry enough, they'll eat anything. Horses, cats, dogs—"

Leo opened one eye and said, *oooo, woof.*

"We'll have enough food. I saw to it."

"You have enough to feed this regiment for a while, but what about any other troops that will be there with us?"

"I hadn't thought of that," she admitted.

"That's forgivable. You're still learning. Good shoes, dry powder, dry socks. Eat and sleep every chance you get. Stay clean. These are the simple rules that have kept me alive all these years. In any case, the siege may not last long. The Sultan won't stay the winter. He's no doubt scorching the country, and his supply lines will be overextended."

"So he'll give up after a few weeks."

"Or he'll take the city. There is no other possible outcome."

Marie gave him a shy sidelong glance. "I hear the Turks are good."

"The best," Nicholas said with a grin. He pulled his peaked

wool sleeping cap over his gray locks and curled up on his side. "But we're better."

"You're going to sleep?"

"Eat your soup."

"We should talk strategy, *Feldherr*."

He yawned and closed his eyes. "We're going to kick the Sultan in the balls. There's your strategy."

The old veteran shifted as he tried to find a comfortable position for sleeping. Finally, he farted loudly and settled with a tired but happy sigh.

"*Feldherr?*"

The man snored in reply.

Marie forced down a little soup. Then she lay on her back and looked up at the stars, which gazed back cold and uncaring.

Myrddin, where are you?

She fell asleep in an instant.

She stood at the opening of a massive cave, its mouth as tall as a cathedral, the moss-covered dark rock soaring up into darkness. Mist covered the scene like a veil. The moon painted the heavy fog that drifted across the moors bright silver. Strange animals groaned and shrieked on the heath. This was a very old place.

Warm firelight illuminated the cave walls, inviting her to enter. Runes appeared to dance in the flickering light. Cave paintings depicted men with spears hunting giant beasts. She stepped across a carpet of rotten vegetation that covered the cave floor, her boots crunching on the bones of small animals. The air had a strong earthy smell here, minerals and soil and damp wood. She ran her hand along the crude carvings. Pulled back in surprise.

She wasn't in a mountain, she knew.

She was inside a giant tree.

Something coughed deep inside the cave. Her hand dropped to the hilt of her sword. The realism, that sense she was actually here, was so much like her training dreams. She didn't want to fight tonight, but curiosity drove her forward.

She walked deeper into the hollowed wood. The passageway narrowed and curved. Gravity bent with it until she found herself descending in awkward spirals.

Deeper and deeper into the earth.

The ground pulsed under her feet. The tree was alive.

At the bottom, she found a large chamber. A bright little campfire burned at the center, where Myrddin sat roasting a rabbit on a spit.

The Magus hadn't been imprisoned in a real tree for eight hundred years. He'd been imprisoned here, in this fantastic place.

She ran to him. "Myrddin!"

"Hello," the wizard greeted her. "Sit with me. I was about to have my supper."

She sat on the other side of the fire. He removed the spit and pulled steaming pieces of rabbit onto a plate, which he handed over. "Eat. You need it."

"You're back here," she said. "Are you a prisoner again?"

"No, poppet. I came of my own volition this time. My little oasis."

"Why did you leave?"

"If I stayed, Ibrahim Pasha might have sent more children of the Old Ones after me, which meant they would have come after you. I'm staying away to protect you. Why did you kill the dragon, Marie?"

"I was trying to protect you. For you, I would kill all the dragons in the world."

He frowned at the flames. "It's all a mess. It's always better if I just stay away."

"Will I ever see you again?"

"You told me you wanted to find your own way in the world. You were right. It's time you got started. You don't need an old fart like me around."

"It's too hard to be alone."

"You must be strong," the Magus told her. "Tonight is the start of your final training, but you will have to do it on your own. It will be your hardest test. The spiritual warrior's greatest battle is always against himself. You must conquer yourself."

"Tell me about Taddeo. Is he—"

"He's fine."

"But are you sure?"

"I'm sure."

"Why can't you bring him to me?"

"Ibrahim Pasha is too powerful. He has the Book of Power. He has the magic of Asia."

"Are you sure they're not hurting him? He's not suffering, is he?"

And she finally did something she couldn't do with anyone else. She cried. She went to Myrddin and hugged him, her shoulders shaking as she poured her tears into his warm cloak. She'd never felt this alone before. She missed Taddeo. She wanted him back.

The wizard patted her awkwardly on the head. "I'm not very good at this kind of thing. Why are you crying? I just told you he's fine. They're actually treating him rather well."

"You wouldn't understand," Marie said.

"Why does everyone think I have no emotions?" he wondered. "I have emotions. I'm just not sure how one is supposed to express them. In any case, it's not very wizardly."

"Just be quiet, okay?"

He said nothing. He held her against his large bony shoulder.

"I love you, Myrddin," she murmured. "I miss you."

"You will find your own way. You must come to understand the one thing that is most important to you and fight for it. That is how you will learn to fight for yourself."

"If I'm not here, who's going to protect you?"

The wizard kissed the top of her head and said, "Child, I never needed a bodyguard."

She awoke on the hard ground. The fire had gone out. Around her, the camp stirred. Nicholas peeled an eye open to observe the paling sky and muttered an obscenity in German.

Marie smiled at him. She felt amazingly refreshed. Better than she'd felt in weeks. "Rise and shine," she told the man who'd captured King Francis.

"*Ja, ja*," he grumbled and spat a ball of phlegm into the smoking embers of their fire. "Away we go. *Marsch, marsch*."

While she ate a large breakfast under Nicholas's approving eye, she thought about her dream. Myrddin had tricked her for years with one of his greatest illusions. *He'd never truly needed a bodyguard.* He needed human companionship.

He needed *her*.

"Don't stay away for long," she said aloud. She hoped he could hear her, wherever he was. Whatever they'd thought, they still needed each other. "I'll be here, waiting for you."

"*Mein Gott*, girl," Nicholas said. "I'm just going past yonder tree to urinate."

The roads filled with refugees the closer they got to Vienna, a horde of weeping women, children, and old men hauling their pitiful worldly goods on their backs or in rickety little wagons drawn by mules. The Turks had swept through Hungary, the peasants said, laying waste to the country. Some major towns held out, but most had given up without a fight and accepted the Sultan's sovereignty.

And the sack men were everywhere, looting and murdering.

The Imperials marched against the current, heading inexorably toward the black clouds on the horizon. They crossed themselves and sang hymns, certain Vienna had already fallen. Marie urged the regiment forward, unable to control her excitement. Every passing minute brought the man she loved ever closer. Him, and the man who was her nemesis.

They found Vienna intact but in turmoil. The suburbs were on fire. Pikemen dragged chests and furniture out of the larger houses. Some of the chests fell and broke open, and soldiers crowded in to grab a share of the spoils while excited dogs yapped and nipped at their boots. Laughing arquebusiers rolled wine barrels down the street. A squad smashed a window and tossed torches inside to set the building alight.

"This is a disaster," Marie said to Count Nicholas, who cackled.

"It is good tactics."

She watched a crowd of soldiers chase a squealing pig down an alley, chickens stuck on their sword points. "Drunken looting and wanton destruction is good tactics?"

"They're razing the buildings outside the walls. Can't let the Sultan use them as cover for his troops to advance. We need clear lines of fire."

"Of course," she said. "I'm sorry, I'm—"

"Still learning. Aren't we all. It's a shame to lose such lovely buildings, though." He sighed wistfully, lost in some distant memory. "The corn market, the city hospital. At my age, one grows fond of old things. But time grinds everything into dust."

A dashing young aristocrat rode toward them whooping. He cleared a path through the soldiers with the flat of his sword. Marie and Nicholas reined in their horses and waited for him while the regiment tramped past like a living river.

The boy waved the blade over his head in a glittering arc. "Isn't it all just wonderful?"

"*Ja, ja,*" Nicholas said. "It is terrific. Who are you?"

"Count Ruprecht, at your service. By God, you're just in time. The Turks are coming!"

"That they are, son."

"It is an honor to finally meet the great Count Nicholas von Salm. We're going to teach the Sultan a thing or two, what?"

"Oh, you bet. We're going to punch him in the nuts."

The young count smiled impishly and led them into the city, babbling and pointing out its defenses. Vienna had been turned into an armed camp. Companies rushed down its narrow streets on martial errands. Everywhere, laborers dug the stones out of the streets to blunt the effect of the enemy's shot, removed shingles from the roofs to minimize the possibility of fire, and dug lines of entrenched earthworks behind the city wall.

"What's our strength?" asked Marie.

"Milady! This regiment brings us to twenty thousand infantry, two thousand horse and seventy-odd cannon. The Sultan has a hundred thousand at his command!"

"Most of them are cavalry and not very useful in siege craft," Nicholas muttered. "The key is whether he was able to get his wall breakers across Hungary. If he brings his big guns, we're screwed."

They watched the regiment and its baggage pile into the city square. The men fell out of formation and milled about. They were exhausted after their long, hard march. Many looked at Marie with tired faces. Her heart swelled with pride at the sight of them.

They needed to believe they could win. They needed hope.

She drew Artemis and stood tall in the stirrups.

"Dragon Head, heed me!" she called. Every head turned and regarded her, and she felt the tingling excitement at being a part of history in the making. "It has been a long hard march. This is the city we have come to save. More than a city, it is Europe. It is Germany and Spain. It is Italy and France and England. It is Christendom. The Sultan has come to rule it all. He has come to put a yoke on it. Grind it under his heel. Make it his slave."

The mercenaries grumbled. They didn't like the sound of that.

"Only you, my brave soldiers, stand in the way of this unhappy fate! Only you can save your fellow men from servitude. Your women from the carnal lusts of the sack men. Your children from captivity and slavery. It is here we will throw the Turk back into Asia. It is here we will stem the tide. This is the place. This is our time in history. Now let the Sultan hear us!"

The men stared back at her with fierce expressions.

"My beautiful regiment," she cried, "are you with me?"

The soldiers responded with a half-hearted cheer.

Count Ruprecht waved his hat. "Huzzah! Well put!"

Marie frowned at the tepid response. She added, "And don't forget we're getting double-pay for this job and a nice fat victory bonus, my lovely boys! Do your job well, and you'll have a full belly, plenty of wine, and a warm bed for months to come!"

The men glared and roared like men possessed. Spittle flew from their mouths.

"That's more like it," she said as Nicholas guffawed.

"You *are* learning," he told her.

"Personally, I liked the first part better," Ruprecht said. His face beaming, he added, "Isn't this terribly exciting?"

Marie learned her head toward him and dropped her voice to a whisper. "It kind of is."

Nicholas shook his head. "*Mein Gott.* Crazy kids."

The count said he had to escort Nicholas to a war council led by the commander of Vienna—His Grace Philip, Count Palatine of the Rhine and Duke of Pfalz-Neuberg. The Archduke Ferdinand, still in Bohemia raising troops, would not be in attendance. As for Marie, she wasn't invited.

After they rode off, Marie dismounted and pushed through the mercenaries thronging the square until she reached the steps of St. Stephen's, a massive Gothic cathedral built of limestone with a impressive southern tower that soared nearly five hundred feet. At the top of that tower, she knew, she'd gain a strategic look at the entire city and its environs.

Her legs ached by the time she reached the top, where she found an open-air room used by the fire watch. She watched dark masses of infantry circulate along Vienna's narrow arteries. Tiny figures toiled to erect palisades behind trenches cut in jagged lines behind the city's old walls; others bricked up its gates, sealing the defenders inside. Smoke billowed from the burning suburbs. The eternal Danube flowed past without a care for the wars of men. Wide stretches of woodlands and quaint farms, emptied of people and livestock, filled the southern vista.

Marie leaned against the window and closed her eyes. The cool breeze brushed her face. Around her, the sky continued to dim, and she remembered riding *The Prometheus* into Italy, snuggled against Taddeo's shoulder. She'd felt like they were the only two people in the world.

You're so close now, my—

"Christ," Prospero gasped behind her. He staggered up the last

276

few steps and fell to his knees. "That is a climb."

"I will thank you not to blaspheme in my presence," another voice huffed. "Yet again."

The two men rested their hands on their knees until they caught their breath, giving Marie the opportunity to study Prospero's companion, a large man in black robes with an expressive fleshy face framed by curly hair. Prospero appeared small next to this giant.

"Prospero Buonarroti, what are you doing here?"

"Looking for a safe place," he said gravely, "to become extremely drunk. Marie Dubois, allow me to present the monk Martin Luther."

"*The* Martin Luther?" she gaped.

"I am he. I can be no other."

Everyone knew who Martin Luther was. His challenge to the Catholic Church had divided the Christian world over the past ten years. He was one of the most dangerous men alive.

In 1516, Pope Leo X authorized the sale of indulgences in Germany to raise money to rebuild St. Peter's Basilica in Rome. While some princes banned these sales in their territories, the Archbishop of Mainz allowed it as long as he got a cut to pay down the debts he'd incurred to buy his lofty church rank. Catholic doctrine held that man could not reach Heaven through faith alone but had to further justify himself to God through charity and good works, which included giving money to the Church. So the Church began selling tickets to Paradise.

Martin Luther, a law student who became a priest after a lightning bolt nearly struck him off his horse, found the practice offensive and contrary to God. He believed faith in Jesus Christ alone was enough to justify man before his creator. Trying to buy God's favor with good works, in fact, was itself sinful. He wrote *The Ninety-Five Theses* refuting the sale of indulgences, copies of which spread and were read all over Europe. He became an overnight celebrity and his views expanded. The turning point came during an interview in Augsburg, when he told the papal legate he considered the papacy itself to be the Antichrist. It was right there in II Thessalonians 2.

The Pope responded by issuing an edict, *Exsurge Domine*, which stated Luther risked excommunication if he didn't recant his controversial views. Luther countered with his own work, *Why The Pope And His Recent Book Are Burned*. The Pope responded with *Decet Romanum Pontificem*, exiling Luther from the Church. In 1521, at a general assembly, or Diet, of the states of the Holy Roman Empire at Worms, the Emperor Charles V declared Martin Luther to be a criminal to be arrested or freely killed by any citizen in his domains.

Marie drew her sword. "The Emperor has been looking for you."

"We're all Christians here," Martin said, paling at the blade aimed at his throat.

"I'm a good Catholic. You're a notorious heretic and an outlaw."

The monk glared at Prospero. "You told me it would be safe here. Did Satan bid you lead me up all those cursed stairs just to fall into a trap?"

"It *is* safe. It is." Prospero glanced at Marie. "Mostly. But my friend is a redhead and therefore predisposed to violence." He offered an ingratiating smile. "*Bella*, I told him he could hide here for a while. Do not make me break my word. Put up your sword."

"*Your* word," she snorted. "I gave *my* word to serve the Emperor. It's against the law to give this man anything." But she put Artemis back into its scabbard with a scowl.

"Save your energy for the Turks. You will like this man once you get to know him. He has a grating personality, but one grows fond of him."

"Sounds familiar."

Prospero beamed. "He is a freethinker like me."

"What are you even doing here?" she asked Martin.

"I became separated from my protectors, and the Lord bid me hide from the authorities."

"I mean in Vienna."

"I was in Ulm, on my way to Marburg to produce a unified doctrine among my brethren in the Protestant states, and decided to come and pray for Vienna's deliverance."

Protestant. Marie recognized the term. In 1526, the Emperor suspended the Edict of Worms, which allowed the princes of the Empire free choice of religion. A bloody revolt had just been crushed in Germany, and the Empire faced the prospect of a long costly war against France and its allies. Charles wanted unity. Luther spent the next three years translating the New Testament into German and working with his followers to establish churches.

But now the wars between the Empire and France were coming to an end. The Archduke Ferdinand, representing his brother Charles, had recently resumed the Edict of Worms. All states in the Empire, he declared, should return to Catholicism and destroy the heresies in their midst. A majority of German states endorsed the decision, which made it official.

Six princes and the representatives of fourteen Imperial Free Cities stormed out of the Diet and wrote a letter of *protest* against the decision, which they delivered to the Emperor. These men became known as *Protestants*.

"I once preached that the Turk was a tool of Satan sent to destroy the Antichrist in Rome," the monk said, "and that we should not wage holy war against him, but the Emperor is right to wage a secular war in defense of his country. So I'm here to ask God for aid."

"Theology gives me a headache," Prospero said. "It is like watching a dog chase its tail." He uncorked one of his bottles of *aqua vitae*. "Perhaps we should all just have a drink."

Martin fell to his knees and clasped his hands together. "This is no time for revelry. Join me for a night of fasting and prayer. God must hear us all."

Night fast approached. Marie needed orders about where to place her men. She had to make sure her quartermaster fed them and saw to their quarters. The provisions they brought had to be properly stored and put under constant guard.

"Oh Lord, Jesus Christ, Son of God," Martin prayed, his eyes clenched shut, "I am beset on all sides by the most vile devils, lunatics, heretics, and heathens."

"To hell with it." She accepted Prospero's proffered bottle and took a swig.

"*Dio Mio*," Prospero said. He looked past her shoulder. "Pray harder, Martin Luther."

A lurid red glow seeped across the horizon.

Southern Austria was on fire.

The Turks were coming. An unstoppable juggernaut burning up everything in sight. Soon, they'd arrive in all their strength.

"Do you believe in fate, Martin?" she asked.

The monk opened an eye, irritated at having his prayers interrupted. "Only in spiritual matters. In the secular world, men are free to make their own decisions."

"I once believed this was all meant to be. I'm not so sure anymore."

Perhaps she and Taddeo had not been fated to meet. Perhaps life was random and full of risk. Maybe she'd end up like the French girl in her song, dying in her own bed of homesickness because her home was far away in the heart of her lover.

"In this world, we're on our own unless we call upon God for help. Now, if you don't mind, I'd like to get back to the important conversation I was having. With *God*."

Perhaps the monk was right. It was commonly believed that all power came from God and that God interceded in human affairs. Even magic was an instrument for siphoning God's might—didn't Myrddin receive his power by invoking angels? That meant magic was all around, and anyone could use it. The world as she saw it was filled with mystery; people lived surrounded by powerful invisible forces. So she prayed. She prayed for Taddeo. She prayed for all of them.

But what if the protectors of Vienna worshipped the same God as the Turks, who were praying just as hard for their own victory?

God defended the defenseless. He championed the weak. She found some solace from that. Because Vienna, ringed with its decrepit walls and manned by fools outnumbered five to one by the best military in the world, was the very picture of weakness.

If not the weak, God surely championed love. She hoped that mattered here. She didn't care about saving Europe or punching the Sultan in the nuts. She wanted to see her man back safe.

"Martin Luther?"

An exasperated sigh. "Yes, girl."

"Save a prayer for my husband. He's being held by the Turks."

"*Bella*," Prospero said. He rested his hand on her shoulder. "We will find him."

She wiped her eyes. "Are you telling me to have faith? You, of all people?"

"No, I am telling you to trust in the undeniable fact of my genius."

She smiled. Grating, yes. But one grew fond of him.

The next morning, Marie awoke with a groan. She held her head delicately, as if it were made of glass, and started at the sight of a sea of white tents sprawling across the countryside as far as the Leitha Mountains.

"They're here," she croaked.

The larger tents housed important officials, the largest—obviously the Sultan's—being a red and gold pavilion, big as a castle, with spires capped by massive knobs of gleaming gold. Columns of horsemen and blue-coated infantry circulated among the tents. Workmen dug trenches in front of three hundred cannon, their crews at attention and ready to fire. Turkish galleys glided along the Danube, completing the envelopment and cutting Vienna off from the outside world.

"What was in that bottle?" Marie moaned. "My head is splitting. I slept half the morning."

"I suppose I should have warned you that *aqua vitae* is an extremely potent intoxicant."

"Potent? I slept through the deployment of the Ottoman Army!"

"I will give you an analgesic."

She looked around. "I see Martin Luther has flown the coop."

"Evidence God does respond to prayers. My prayers, anyway."

"How are we going to find Taddeo among all those people?"

"Through hard work," he said with a yawn, "seasoned with a splash of genius."

She gripped her skull. "My poor head. Even your yawn was horribly loud."

He produced a clear glass hand mirror. "Vanity, thy name is woman. Allow me to reacquaint you with one of my finest inventions."

"Not now, Prospero. I especially do not want to see myself, feeling the way I do right now."

"Oh, *bella*. You are too beautiful to be so worried about your looks, even when your face is pale and tinged green like a living corpse. Now, take note."

The scientist angled the glass until the sun caught it just so and produced a burst of glare. He then held up a playing card, which he used as a shutter to block the sun's light from reaching the mirror. By moving the card, he exposed and covered the glass repeatedly in rapid succession.

"What are you doing now?"

"I am talking to Taddeo."

"What?" She clutched his sleeve. "Where is he?"

"Do you mind? I said I am talking *to* Taddeo, not with him. There is a difference."

"I don't see you talking at all."

"Taddeo and I created an alphabet in the varying duration of bursts of light. Alternately, sound. It is a secret code known only to us. If he is in the Turkish camp, he is surely looking at the city right now. He will receive my message and answer when he is able."

Instead, a Turkish cannon fired, followed by the rest in rapid succession. The bombardment filled the air with tense sporadic thunder for an hour. The stone balls smashed through roofs, splashed in the muddy streets, and splintered against St. Stephen's stubborn walls. Screams rang out from around the city. A man wailed in pain in the street below.

"Oh God," Marie cried as the barrage went on and on. "It's horrible. Make it stop."

It had turned her hangover into a blinding headache.

Then, mercifully, it ended. The salvo was not the beginning of a general attack, but instead the Turks saying, *Merhaba! (Hi!)*

As the smoke settled, three richly dressed men approached the city under a white flag of truce, Christian prisoners released as emissaries from the Sultan with terms for the city's surrender. Give up now, they said, and none would be harmed. Give up now, or within three days, the Sultan intended to breakfast in the smoking ruins of Vienna. None would be spared, and the city would be so completely obliterated that no one would know where it had once stood.

That was the Sultan's message to the defenders of Vienna.

After an hour, three Turkish prisoners, similarly dressed in fine raiment, were sent back. They carried no message at all. That was Vienna's answer to the great Sultan: nothing.

Within minutes, the sky darkened with Tartar arrows, which hissed and fell across the city.

Prospero eyed her. "Do you see what I see?"

"What is it?"

Deep in the Turkish camp, near a pavilion second only to the Sultan's in size and grandeur, a little star of light winked back at her.

~ Chapter XV ~

THE GREAT GAME

The smoke of the guns drifted across the field as the Tartars launched another shower of missiles onto Vienna. Taddeo's heart pounded in sync with the Ottoman regimental drums as he angled his mirror and sent the message: IS MARIE OK?

He froze. Ibrahim swept past with his fierce retainers and disappeared into his opulent tent.

Still he didn't move, afraid to even breathe. At last, when it seemed he was in the clear, he turned back toward the church spire that stabbed at the sky like a giant needle.

A light flashed at the top. Prospero was replying:

—AND THE MAINTENANCE TOOK ALL DAY STOP IN YOUR ABSENCE I MUST DO EVERYTHING STOP BESIDES THAT PROMETHEUS NEEDS A NEW BOILER STOP PERHAPS IT IS AN OPPORTUNITY TO REDESIGN—

The message ended there. Seconds passed. Then Prospero added: MARIE WANTS TO TALK TO YOU STOP.

His heart expanded. He angled the mirror and messaged:

TELL HER I—

The quirt cracked against his wrist. He dropped the mirror with a yelp of surprise and pain.

"What are you doing?" Ibrahim said.

Taddeo rubbed his wrist. "I was communicating with my wife."

"I thought you couldn't do magic. Tell me how this is possible."

"The mirror. It catches the sun at a certain angle, creating a flash of light. The number and length of these flashes is related to an alphabet. A code."

The Grand Vizier's face darkened. "And what did you say?"

"I was trying to tell her I'm okay."

"Did you transmit any military information?"

"Excellency, I know nothing I could tell them that they can't see with their own eyes."

The man's expression softened. "A code communicated with light. Interesting. You continue to be a most curious boy, Taddeo." Behind him, thousands of archers notched in unison and sent another wave of arrows over the city. "You may finish your dialog with your wife."

"Thank you, Excellency."

He knew Prospero was watching him right now with his binocular glasses. He picked the mirror out of the grass and sent: I AM SAFE STOP I LOVE YOU WIFE STOP.

Ibrahim observed his movements with acute interest. "What language are you using?"

"Latin."

After a few moments, Prospero relayed Marie's message: I WILL COME FOR YOU STOP.

"What did you say?"

"I told her I'm safe and that I love her."

"And her reply?"

"That she would come for me."

"That," Ibrahim said, "would be most interesting. Walk with me."

They strolled toward the front line, where the archers were withdrawing to allow the cannon to resume their work. They stopped near one of the batteries, which fired with a crash, its shot whistling into the city and landing with a cloud of dust against the stone tower from which Marie and Prospero had signaled him.

"This is just the preamble," the Grand Vizier told him with a sweeping gesture. "Our infantry prepares for the assault. We will attack Vienna within the hour and take it."

Taddeo pictured waves of howling Turks storming the walls with ladders, pouring into the city streets and sabering everyone in sight. "I wish you wouldn't."

"They ignored the Sultan's offer of peace and insulted him. I believe you have learned in your brief time with us that one simply does not do that. If they'd surrendered, there might have been no bloodshed, and even now, you'd be happily coupling with your lovely wife."

Taddeo said nothing. The Turks had come here for a reason, and there was nothing he could say or do that would stop them. It was hopeless.

"You should join me," Ibrahim told him.

He started. "*Join* you?"

"Of course. I would rather have such a bright young man as a friend than an enemy. Become my slave, and I will train you to become an Ottoman vizier. One day to become Vizier of Science."

The long line of cannon continued to pound Vienna. The stone balls exploded against the walls and plunged deep into the city. Taddeo was too amazed by the offer to notice.

A life of riches and power could be his. He saw himself working with Turkish astronomers to map the stars. Electrifying Istanbul with *fulmen*. Designing automated factories in which unskilled labor could dramatically increase the output of goods. Building a fleet of steam wagons on good roads to efficiently haul goods to the farthest reaches of the empire. An empire of peace and plenty.

In the most cunning way possible, he could destroy the Ottoman Empire from within. With science. He'd give the common man wealth, leisure, and learning, and in time, the common man would demand his liberty. The Sultan would fall, replaced by a democratic government backed by strong institutions led by educated, informed citizens.

And the revolution would spread across Europe. And beyond.

All this would mean betraying Marie, however. Taking part, in fact, in her destruction.

"I couldn't, Excellency," he said. "My wife is in that city. My loyalty is to her above all."

"Who loves a rose would bear its thorns," Ibrahim said with a sympathetic nod. He stroked his pointed beard. "Perhaps there is a solution. I would give you a chance to save Vienna, Europe, your wife."

Taddeo gaped in astonishment, unable to speak.

"Do you play chess?"

"I do, Excellency."

"We will play three games. For each game you win, I'll delay our attack five days. If you win all three, I'll give you your freedom. If I win any of the three, you will enter the service of the Ottoman Empire."

Taddeo considered the wager. Even if he only won once, it would buy five days of respite for Vienna's ragtag defenders. But it was fairly possible he might win all three games and delay the attack for two whole weeks, not to mention earn his liberty.

He couldn't fight with a sword, he was a lightweight with alcohol, and he stumbled around women, but he was a goddamn wizard at chess.

And if he lost, he'd send for Marie and Prospero, and they'd live in one of the finest palaces in Istanbul, with thousands of servants waiting on them hand and foot.

"What if the game ends in a draw?" he asked shrewdly.

Ibrahim smiled. He clapped his hands. Servants brought a table, comfortable chairs, and an ornately carved wood case, which they opened to reveal hand-carved pieces of African ivory and a brass board trimmed with gold.

Taddeo inspected the pieces, which depicted Ottoman and Hungarian armies. The delicately painted Ottomans, played as White, consisted of the Sultan and Sultana, viziers, Sipahis, cannon, and Janissaries. On the Hungarian side, played as Black, a king and queen, bishops, knights, castles, and feudal levies completed the set.

Ibrahim gestured to the empty chairs. "Shall we?"

Taddeo sat and watched Ibrahim hold up two fists.

"Forgive my skepticism, but I'd like to see both pieces first, if you please."

The Grand Vizier grinned and opened both hands, revealing two Black pieces. Like Myrddin, the man's best tricks didn't involve magic.

"A simple mistake," Ibrahim said.

"Let's try that again, Excellency."

This time, the choice was honest. Taddeo picked. He got Black.

Ibrahim arrayed his pieces. "Allah has willed that I play as Ottomans. It's only appropriate, no?" He eyed his Queen with distaste before placing her on the board. He obviously thought the most powerful piece should be depicted as the Grand Vizier, not the Sultana.

Servants brought parasols to block the sun's glare and a bowl of apples to refresh them. A nearby cannon discharged a round toward the city walls.

Taddeo smiled as he set up his Hungarians. This was the kind of war he liked. A romantic duel of nations without the torched cities, the chaos and despair, the spread of plague, the men dying on the battlefield. No innocents died in chess. Only egos were slaughtered. It was a contest of two minds locked in a pure battle of wits with endless possibilities. He'd once tried to calculate the number of possible moves, but the figure proved beyond him. There were more possible chess moves than there were drops of water in all the oceans in the world.

Winning required a grasp of both strategy and tactics. Of vital concern was maximizing options by controlling as much space on the board as possible, in particular the four central squares that often proved key to victory. Seizing and maintaining the initiative was critical to force the opponent to respond to threats rather than develop their own. Since White played first, it held an advantage over Black, particularly when both players were evenly matched. Taddeo would have to play dynamically to wrest the initiative.

The Grand Vizier smiled. "Shall we begin?"

He opened with the Queen's Gambit. They skirmished across the center of the board. Taddeo developed slowly, thinking seven moves ahead, watching his opponent and positioning his pieces like a coiled snake, full of potential energy.

Ibrahim was very careful, however. And very good.

Servants brought two cups of foamy, hot, brown liquid called *kahve*—coffee. The beans were ground to a fine powder and boiled with cardamom, Ibrahim told him. Taddeo found it bitter but strangely pleasing. He'd often heard wine was an acquired taste, though he'd never acquired it. But this he liked. It invigorated his mind and made him want to talk.

"Can I ask you a question, Excellency?"

"It is said, 'No one will give milk to a baby who does not cry.'"

"Why do you want to conquer the world?"

The man started. Apparently, the question never occurred to him.

Taddeo added, "You already have more wealth and power than you could every use. You don't need more. Look at all the horror and bloodshed caused by this war. It's pointless."

Ibrahim moved a piece. "An empire cannot stand still. It must expand or die. In the game of nations, every threat must be extinguished, or there can never be any security. By playing this game well, and through the will of Allah, a single family that once ruled a tribe now rules an empire of millions."

Taddeo moved his Knight. The Grand Vizier watched his hand move as a cat notices a mouse scurrying across the floor.

"But when is it ever over? Does the misery ever end just so a few rich and powerful men can get even richer and more powerful— power and money they use only to promote even more misery?"

"In his wisdom, Allah has placed East and the West on a board much like this one. A board spanning continents, with nations as pieces. And so we must play, and only one side may win. This is life. If you are to become a vizier serving the House of Osman successfully, as I do, this should be the first thing you learn."

Taddeo said, "Black wins in four moves."

BLACK TO PLAY AND WIN IN FOUR MOVES.

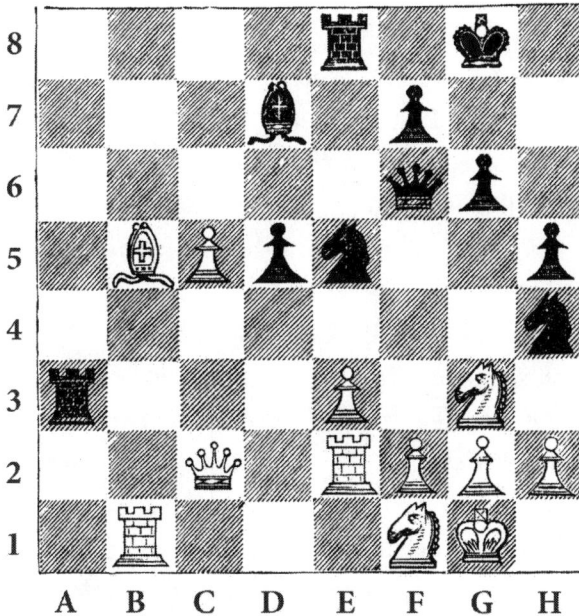

"What?" The Grand Vizier's face darkened, his eyes flickering as he scanned the pieces repeatedly. He quickly grasped his predicament and now searched for a way out.

This is what he saw:

Black to play Queen F6-F3, threatening checkmate within one turn. White to take the Queen with the Pawn at G2. Black to take the Pawn with his Knight, E5-E3. Check. White King moves to H1. Black Bishop enters the killing zone, D7-H3, then to G2.

Checkmate.

The firing had stopped. Taddeo glanced up at the city and was alarmed to discover he could no longer see the church tower. A massive haze of dust and smoke hung over Vienna like a shroud. His ears rang from hours of pounding by the Turkish artillery.

Ibrahim frowned. "I resign." Then grudgingly smiled. "It was a good game."

A light winked in the gloom as the church spire slowly

materialized out of the dust.

"Another message? What did she say?"

Taddeo smiled. "She said, 'Still here.'"

The Grand Vizier nodded. "You may reply that so are you. Tell the indefatigable Marie Dubois that you have won our wager, and that I am a man who keeps his word. For five days, we will not attack. In five days, we will play again for the same stakes."

In the tower, Prospero received Taddeo's message and relayed Marie's:

YOU ARE A HERO STOP I LOVE YOU END.

To Prospero, she said, "This doesn't make any sense."

The scientist nodded, clearly baffled. "To me as well. Why did Taddeo bother winning? Have you ever been to Istanbul? It is quite cosmopolitan."

"It's a trap. We're being set up somehow."

"Why must you be so cynical?" Prospero wondered. "Taddeo and me, we are valuable men."

"Prospero, you know how I feel about my husband. He's a great man. But no one is that important. Something is going on. This is how Ibrahim Pasha works. He's a trickster. He comes at you sideways."

"Being Myrddin Wyllt's servant, you would know such things. So if it is a trap, what is the trap?"

Marie crossed her arms, looking down at the Ottoman camp. "I don't know!"

"The Pasha says they will not attack. He wants us to know that. For what purpose?"

"You're the genius. You tell me."

"Perhaps we should just be thankful we will not be killed for five days?"

Using Prospero's binocular specs, she watched Taddeo walk smiling through the Ottoman camp. Her heart pounded.

He was the captive, and here he was risking everything to save *her*.

That's love, she thought. *Putting someone else first. The man truly loves me. My husband.*

He'd given up everything for her. Fought for her. Was even now putting his future on the line to keep her safe.

If we get through this, Taddeo, it's your turn. We'll serve science. No more adventures.

"Perhaps I can help," said a voice at her side.

Marie turned and threw her arms around the man who'd materialized out of thin air. "Myrddin!"

"Plato's Beard!" Prospero swore. "How does he do that?"

Over the next three days, the Austrian guns engaged the Turkish artillery in a duel of shot. Shrill whistles and the tangy, acrid smell of gunpowder filled the air. The ground turned to mud in the rain during the day and hard as rock with frosts at night. It made the Turks miserable.

On St. Michael's Day, the defenders of Vienna released several prisoners with a message for the Sultan, who'd sworn to breakfast in the smoking ruins of the city within three days. The Viennese let him know that they'd made him breakfast, but it had gone cold, *ha ha, boo hoo.*

If his breakfast had gone cold, said the Sultan, perhaps he would see it warmed. Within the hour, his Tartars launched fire arrows over the walls. Smoke billowed out of the burning city.

Then the fifth day arrived, as Taddeo had known it would.

At dawn, he wrapped himself in a warm cloak and took a stroll through the camp. He listened to the Turkish feudal levies complain about their officers and the weather, both of which, the men believed, had been inflicted upon them by Satan.

These men were not his enemy, he believed. If that were true, then who was?

Was it the Grand Vizier? He didn't think so. Overall, the man had treated him well. Besides that, he was an accomplished musician, able poet, powerful statesman, and something of a philosopher. Taddeo wished Prospero could meet him so he could see what a real friend of the arts looked like. Ibrahim kept an impressive library and an amazing table; if Taddeo ever escaped the Turks, he was going to miss the food. He played an incredible game of chess. Despite the constant menace the man exuded, Taddeo had begun to find him likable. Someone he could admire, even. A more kindly, forgiving version of his father.

Ibrahim Pasha was an opponent, yes, but not an enemy.

No, his enemies were as always the only things in the world that could inspire genuine hate in him: poverty, superstition, ignorance, and disease.

As Vizier of Science in the Ottoman Empire, he could fight them in open battle at last.

The offer still tantalized him.

The blast of a nearby cannon jarred him from his thoughts. He watched its gunners reload with practiced ease. A company of dirty men trudged past, carrying pickaxes, shovels, and lanterns. They looked like gravediggers. But something wasn't right about them. Something—

"*Woof, woof,*" said the dog at his feet, its tail thumping the ground.

"Leo!" Taddeo flung his arms around him. "How are you, my old friend?"

The dog raised his paw and made a *so-so* gesture.

"Come on. It's almost time for my game with the Grand Vizier. You can meet him."

Leo whined and followed meekly.

They found Ibrahim picking at a luxurious banquet table while nearby, musicians played a lilting tune. Taddeo introduced Leo, who drooled at the sight of all the food.

"I smell Myrddin on him," Ibrahim said.

"He's Marie's ghost dog. A familiar. The *mago* created him from a pile of dung."

"The family resemblance is striking."

"Marie must have released him to keep me company. Is that all right?"

"As long as I don't have to see him, hear him, or smell him, I don't see why not."

"Thank you, Excellency."

"Speaking of magic, have I ever showed you my collection of grimoires?"

"No. I would have thought your magic books would be carefully guarded."

"Normally, that is true. But today is a special day. We play again for the same stakes. Soon, you will be my protégé. And as my protégé, you will learn magic, as I did."

"I'd be honored to see your collection."

The Grand Vizier brought him into his pavilion and muttered, "Open in the name of Heaven." A hanging rug rolled itself up to reveal a small compartment with a comfortable chair, writing desk, hookah, and three bookshelves filled with scrolls and worn leather-bound volumes. "This," Ibrahim said with pride, "is my private library. You can tell a lion from where he dwells."

"Why are you showing me this?" Taddeo wondered.

"It is said, 'If Allah closes the silver door, He will open the gold door.' It is my hope that by showing you this golden door, you will enter willingly."

He understood now. The Grand Vizier was trying to weaken his resolve so he would put less effort into today's chess game, perhaps give it up entirely.

Which meant that the delay was working. It had hurt the Turks.

A general in gold chainmail entered the tent, bowed low, and hissed near Ibrahim's ear.

"You will forgive me, Taddeo, but I must attend a war council. Vienna's plucky defenders sank a galley in the Danube. The Sultan's patience is wearing thin. I can barely restrain him."

"Can I look at the books?"

"You may, but beware. Do not read any aloud. I don't want to return and find a homunculus ripping apart my tent. And keep a tight leash on your beast. Be *extremely* careful."

Taddeo ran his fingers along the cracked spines of the volumes in wonder. Some of the books were hundreds of years old. Others, thousands, written in ancient languages nigh forgotten. All of them concerning access to the divine power. "I will."

"Need I provide some obligatory warning about being flayed alive and devoured by hungry ants?"

"I'll be careful, Excellency."

"Good, then. I shall return when I am able, and then we may play our game."

After the Grand Vizier left, Leo licked his chops and said, "We're in luck. Now's our chance, kid."

Taddeo gaped at him. "You can *talk*?"

"Of course I can," the dog said. "I'm Myrddin. I thought you knew that."

"I had no idea! You shouldn't be here!"

"Oh, so when you thought I was Leo, you give a big hug. You find out it's *me* and first thing, you try to get rid of me."

"I'm happy to see you, *mago*. Really."

"Humph," Myrddin said. "Now help me find the book."

"But what the hell took you so long?"

"We really don't have time to revisit your keen sense of entitlement."

"Do you know how long I've been a prisoner of the Turks? Because of *you*?"

"Okay! It's all my fault! I'm sorry! There! Now can we look for the book?"

"What are you talking about?"

"The Book of Power. Written by Asaph ben Berechiah, Vizier of King Solomon, who could control reality using his knowledge of the Great Name. It was buried with Solomon and discovered by Babylonian philosophers who were repairing the dead king's tomb. Angels appeared, translated the text, and gave them power over Creation on the condition the philosophers keep the knowledge secret only to a select few. It was the same deal I got."

"Again, what are you talking about?"

"This book is the main source of Ibrahim's power. Most of the rest here are for show. Eternal mysteries of the frauds." The dog sniffed around the books and sneezed.

"Don't do anything crazy, *mago*. First of all, he's been hoping you show up so he can try to destroy you."

"That two-bit phony doesn't scare—"

"Secondly, I've got the situation here well in hand."

"Then you're an even bigger fool than I—*woof!* Here it is. Hidden in plain sight, of course." Myrddin dragged a thick book from a middle shelf with his jaws. He hoisted it onto the writing table and opened it with his paw, his long tongue hanging out of his mouth.

"See, we're playing this chess game, and if I win, the Ottomans won't attack for five days."

"Can we please talk about something important?"

Taddeo frowned and crossed his arms. "It must be killing you. The one time you actually want to help, and I don't need it!"

"Just give me a moment to find what I'm looking for, and I'll get you out of here."

"Didn't you hear? I don't want to go. If I leave, they'll attack the city and kill everyone!"

"Ah. Here we are. The spell of creation." Myrddin barked. "Fascinating!"

"What's fascinating?"

"The spell Berechiah describes as allowing him to defeat genies and teleport thrones is the same as I learned in Wales as a boy when I found the runes in the old cave." He uttered the spell, which sounded like gibberish to Taddeo's ears. "Got that? If you're staying, Taddeo, remember these words. It might save us all."

"Were you in the city? Did you see Marie?"

The dog glared at him. "Are you listening to a single word I'm saying?"

"Yes, I'm listening! I'm not a trained magician, you are."

"That's a good point. Be very careful about using the spell. The angels might refuse to obey you and instead destroy you for your impertinence. Finicky beasts, angels."

"What I mean is if you and Ibrahim Pasha use the same system of magic, that means he's not stronger than you. You're evenly matched. So why don't you fight him yourself?"

Sinister laughter filled the tent. Taddeo and Myrddin stared openmouthed as Ibrahim Pasha entered, followed by his giant retainers carrying nets, catch poles, and boar spears.

"Why not indeed?" the Grand Vizier said.

"*Wwwwoof,*" Myrddin said, playing innocent.

The men slowly advanced upon Taddeo. They hemmed him in.

"Not him, you idiots," Ibrahim said. "The dog!" He smiled. "Myrddin Wyllt, I presume."

Taddeo realized the entire thing—being shown the library, the distraction of the war council—had all been a setup to get Myrddin to reveal himself. They'd been duped.

The Grand Vizier had suspected Myrddin being Leo all along and had contrived this simple trap. Did nothing escape the man's notice?

"Crap," Myrddin said. He bared his teeth and growled at the retainers. They retreated a step.

"The great *Sihirbaz*. It is truly an honor to meet you, Myrddin. Or shall I call you by your other name? The name of legend?"

"I'm known by many names."

"But the most famous by far is Merlin the Spellbinder."

Myrddin shrugged. "If you say so. That was long ago."

"I am something of an admirer of yours. I've been searching for you. And now is the time."

"It doesn't *have* to be the time."

"Oh, but it does." The Grand Vizier's dark eyes gleamed with fierce light. "We must settle our affairs once and for all. A magical duel. A contest of sorcery both light and dark. The magic of Asia versus the magic of Old. We shall each invoke the might of the angels until there be civil war in Heaven. We shall recite the names of Allah until the stars tremble in their sockets. The final battle, your vast power against mine, and let the winner take the world!"

"No, thanks," Myrddin said and disappeared in a flash of light.

"*Bok*," Ibrahim said. *Crap.*

For a while, no one said anything.

Ibrahim muttered, "He'll be back. I'm *sure* he'll be back."

"So," Taddeo ventured, "you know, about being flayed alive and fed to ants..."

The Grand Vizier started as if surprised to see Taddeo still standing there. "*You.* As for you, you are quite blameless, my son. I admit my ruse was a test for you as well as Merlin, and you passed. I heard you tell the wizard to fight his own battles."

"Right," Taddeo breathed. "Good."

"He was trying to place a wedge between us, and he failed."

He nodded with vigor. "That's exactly what happened."

"Next time, the man will not escape me so easily. I will be better prepared. Now let us resume our business. Shall we play our game?"

Outside the pavilion, a column of cavalry cantered past with their lances and feathered turbans. Behind them trudged another company of dirty men carrying pickaxes, shovels, and lanterns.

"Workers," Ibrahim explained. "Digging graves for your Austrian friends."

Taddeo nodded. Of course they were.

Except they weren't.

Lanterns, he thought. *They have lanterns.*

The question was, how could he get this information to Marie?

After the game, he'd be permitted use of his mirror, but he had a feeling the Grand Vizier had figured out his code and understood everything he told her.

"You seem distracted," Ibrahim noted as they approached their table.

Taddeo tapped his forehead. "Strategy."

"Today, I think you shall play White. My beloved Ottomans are yours. Since you will soon be in the service of the Sultan, this too is appropriate."

As they set up their pieces, the man added, "We're only here because of this game, you know. My greatest wish is to return the army to Istanbul."

"Pardon my saying, but that doesn't sound like you, Excellency."

"You think me disingenuous? You can ask the Sultan. He would likely have you sodomized with a golden spear and thrown into boiling lead for your impertinence, but before ordering such just punishment, he would tell you what I am saying now. Vienna is not important to take this year. We came for Hungary. Allah, the Firm, the Steadfast, has willed that the infidels cower behind their walls, and now all Hungary is ours. So why stay here and suffer cold and hunger? It's time to go home and fight another day. We are playing a long game."

"Then why don't you?"

"And release you? No, first, I must defeat you. We have two more games. And if you win today, we must stay another five days as Allah wills it."

"All I have to do is lose, and we'll leave."

"And become a valued member of the Sultan's slave-family, where you have seen from my example how far a man can rise on his merits. Where else in the world can a sailor's son, a slave, rise to become the highest counselor to an Empire and make history? We are a nation of opportunity."

"A nation of *slaves*," Taddeo noted.

"A nation of many peoples, customs, languages, and gods. All of them slaves to the State, which dispenses security and justice. Even the Sultan is a slave to his empire. A slave to an ideal. Just as you are a slave to science, no? Your father's approval? And love for a domineering woman, hmm? You shall have them all in my service."

"I don't see how my father would approve of me serving his enemies."

"His business partner," Ibrahim corrected. "That is, when we're not fighting. I imagine he would approve of service to the Sultan as much as he would to the Holy Roman Emperor."

"Well," Taddeo said. The man had a point. "That was complicated."

"It always is." The Grand Vizier removed a letter from his pocket.

"My agents intercepted this correspondence just yesterday. From Gregorio. That is his seal?"

Taddeo felt his center of gravity plummet from his chest to his feet. "It is."

"It's for you. Read it. I found it quite revealing."

Taddeo opened the letter with trembling hands and read:

Dear Son, I have become privy to the most astounding Tales of Adventure concerning You and Prospero. I understand if You are fighting for the Empire against France and its Allies then either a Woman or Money must be involved, in either of which Case I applaud your Judgment and for finding your own Way in the World, honoring your Heritage by becoming your own Man on your own Terms. Though your Mother worries, I would understand that You wish to remain distant from Home for longer than the appointed Time, and have enrolled your Brother into the Family Business, affording you a handsome Allowance for You to continue to pursue such Adventures abroad. For all of these Endeavors, including your recent Marriage, I give you my Blessing. However, We are not pleased with the outrageous Expenses incurred buying Provisions for the Spanish, notably a great deal of Wine. Never buy Goods from an Army on the March. I shall have to deduct the Expense from your Allowance. Your Father, Gregorio.

Then he breathed again.

"I believe this releases you from any familial obligations concerning your future," Ibrahim said. "Certainly, you would agree with that interpretation."

Taddeo felt lightheaded. He read the letter again, which both praised and banished him. "I would."

"I will tell you something. I will never eclipse the Sultan, but you will eclipse your father. Of this I am certain. Now. Enough talk. Shall we have a cup of *kahve* and resume our contest?"

Taddeo started the game with an unconventional flank attack. His opening promised sharp play, and the game rapidly evolved into a bloody melee that swirled around the center of the board,

Ottomans and Hungarians savaging each other like beasts before withdrawing, circling, and pouncing again. Taddeo had a difficult time staying focused, distracted as he was by thoughts of Myrddin's visit, his father's blessing, and Ibrahim's offer of a career in the service of the Ottoman Empire. He grabbed at the first good move he saw instead of first checking to make sure there wasn't an even better one. He only thought four moves ahead.

At last, he found himself facing the prospect of victory in just a few moves.

WHITE TO PLAY AND WIN IN THREE MOVES.

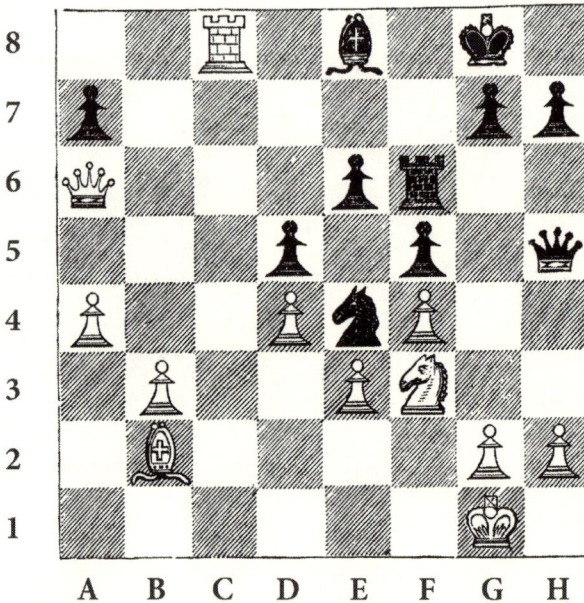

Taddeo realized he could win and buy another five days for Vienna. Or he could simply let the Grand Vizier win and take his offer of a bright future living with Marie in the Ottoman capital.

"The Sultan sustains the *Ehl-i Hiref*, the Community of the Talented," Ibrahim tempted. "The artistic societies number in the hundreds. Painters, goldsmiths, book binders, and other craftsmen. I could see you becoming its chief administrator as your first assignment at court."

Taddeo's hand hesitated over the board. Then he made up his mind.

He moved his Queen A6-C6, threatening the Black Bishop at E8, which couldn't respond, seeing as it was pinned by the White Rook at C8.

Ibrahim moved his Rook F6-F8 to protect his Bishop.

Taddeo moved his Bishop B2-A3 and threatened the Black Rook at F8.

The Grand Vizier moved his Pawn H7-H6 to open some room for his King to escape. Taddeo moved the White Queen C6-E6, which placed the Black King in check.

"I resign," Ibrahim said with a sigh. "You have won again. Well played."

Both men stared at the board. They felt drained.

In the end, Taddeo couldn't betray Marie. He knew she would have wanted him to win.

"May I tell my wife the news?"

"Of course. Again, I shall honor my word."

He transmitted:

MY LOVE I WON FIVE DAYS RESPITE STOP.

Moments later, the reply came:

MY HERO TADDEO I LOVE YOU STOP WE ARE REJOICING STOP.

He sent back:

I AM SAD YOU ARE MINE END.

Ibrahim, who'd observed the exchange, frowned. "What was that?"

Taddeo reddened. "I know it's silly. But I *am* glad she's my wife."

The Grand Vizier shot him a strange look. "Of course you are. Some women find it comforting to hear the obvious repeated."

Come on, Marie, he thought. *Please don't get me flayed alive and fed to ants.*

After several tense moments, she responded:

ME TOO MY SWEET STOP GOOD NIGHT END.

Taddeo looked up at Vienna, which appeared more like a pile of burned-out ruins than a city with each passing day. Marie had been smart enough to play along. He loved her more than ever.

He hoped she'd gotten the message.

Chapter XVI

SKIRMISHES

arie raced out of St. Stephen's as a round hit it. Stone fragments showered onto the steps. Men huddled under the awnings of the buildings across the street. A team of horses bolted past in terror, dragging a fiery wagon trailing smoke and sparks. A gun discharged on the city wall in a cloud of gunpowder. Round shot whistled into the Turkish camp.

"I'm coming across!"

"Wait!"

The sky darkened. Fire arrows hissed to the ground. Marie heard them clatter off walls and rooftops. A man toppled from the wall with a scream.

"Now, Colonel!"

Marie put her head down and ran. A cannonball plowed into the street at her feet. She jumped over it and kept going.

"What is this building?" she gasped at the men.

"A tavern," said a bearded ruffian.

"I'm looking for Count Nicholas von Salm."

"I saw him at the commissary this morning."

She dodged arrows and cannon shot all the way there, where Marcus Beck, the commissary general, told her he'd gone to St. Stephen's.

With a groan, she went back the way she came.

She found the tavern emptied and ablaze. Drunkards staggered down the street waving swords and wine jugs. Prospero pumped water onto the blaze from a length of hose connected to a curious iron device shaped like a human heart in turn connected to a cistern mounted on top of *The Prometheus.*

"I call it 'Prospero's Steam Pump,'" he told her. "Steam condenses on one side, sucking water in, while on the other side it is under pressure, forcing the water out."

Marie coughed on the thick black smoke. "Brilliant."

"War makes the best laboratory, no? To paraphrase Plato, necessity is the spark of great invention. Plus in war, there are no pesky qualms about ethics."

"Have you seen Myrddin? He hasn't come back from the Turkish camp."

Prospero sniffed and turned away to focus on the flames. "I know where he is *not.*"

"Where?"

"He is not here revolutionizing European fire safety, as I am!"

Once the man got like this, she knew, there was no dealing with him. She reentered the church and climbed the stairs to find the *Feldherr* sitting on the floor of the tower's observation room with his Bible, his lips moving as he read.

"Count Nicholas! What are you doing here?"

The hero of Pavia looked at her over his book. "Are you kidding? The city is burning to the ground. This is the safest place. The Sultan will never get me here." He turned and shouted out the nearest window, "NEVER! DO YOU HEAR THAT, YOU PRICK?"

"*Feldherr,*" she said. "We have a problem."

"I'm in no mood for problems. For days, the Duke has kept me tied up in constant council. I should also point I came up here for a little alone time."

Marie pressed on, explaining the chess games Taddeo had been playing against the Grand Vizier. The old man stared at her as if she were a lunatic, his mouth hanging open.

"Balderdash," he interrupted. "There is no respite. Who would believe such a thing? Your hapless husband is being played. The only reason the heathen haven't stormed the walls is because their cavalry won't fight without their horses, and their infantry only outnumber us two or three to one. They have no siege guns. It is all quite obvious."

"So they *are* up to something."

"Of *course* they're up to *something*. Did your husband say anything important in his messages, or is this all a waste of my time?"

"That's what I wanted to talk to you about. His last message was, 'I am sad you are mine.'"

The old count's eyes widened. "*Mein Gott*, woman, that is a real problem!"

"I agree—"

"But you were only just married!"

Marie pursed her lips. "I think he intended a different meaning, *Feldherr*. Something of strategic value he couldn't say openly in front of the Turks."

Nicholas slapped his forehead. "*Ach*. They are digging tunnels and intend to mine our gates. Of course!"

Right now, hundreds of Turkish laborers excavated the earth, removed it in wheelbarrows, and propped up the tunnels with lumber. They prepared barrels of gunpowder to explode once they burrowed as far as the city walls.

She nodded. "I was thinking the same thing. So what do we do about it?"

"We must engage them with counter mining. Obviously."

"But how do we know where their tunnels are? They're, well, underground."

The Count returned to his Bible. "*I* don't know. Ask your friend the mad scientist. Pick a direction and start digging." He glanced up at her. "Go, woman!"

Marie raced back down the stairs on aching legs. Prospero coiled his hose in front of the burning tavern. The cistern on the back of the steam wagon was missing. Drifting gray smoke blanketed the street like a fog.

"The rogues confiscated my water," the scientist complained. "Said the tavern was a lost cause, and they needed the water for *drinking*. So much for revolutionizing fire safety. Some people simply cannot perceive the greater good!"

"Prospero—"

"I had it in principle, anyway. I shall count that as a win."

"I need your help—"

"As Plato once said—"

Count Ruprecht galloped onto the scene on his charger. He waved his hat.

"Milady Dubois! And how are you this glorious day?"

Marie and Prospero ducked under an awning as the sky darkened with another rain of arrows. Ruprecht didn't even flinch as the shafts hissed around him.

He looked up at the sky. "Frightful weather we're having, what?"

"Count Ruprecht, I need your help."

The boy's eyes bulged. "And I am eternally at your service, milady!"

"Go and gather my regiment. Anyone who is sober and able to work."

Ruprecht pulled his hat lower over his eyes and set his jaw. "Has the hour come at last? Will the Turk storm the city?" He drew his sword. "By God, the Sultan will pay a bloody price for it!"

"I have learned their engineers are mining our gates."

The young count grinned. "I shall instruct the men to bring shovels."

"There isn't a moment to lose. Ride, Count!"

"Huzzah!" He spurred his mount into a gallop that splattered clods of mud onto Prospero's already sooty doublet.

Prospero brushed himself in silent rage. "Did you ever wonder why people place so much value on the most ridiculous things? Why is killing people so exciting?" His expression became wistful. "Why do the bards not write odes to sanitation? Why are there no songs about astronomy? Why does no one tell their children the story of Ptolemy's Stone?"

"Prospero, I need your help."

He crossed his arms. "*My* help? What can *I* do? Build something constructive no one wants? All I do is try to create things that make people's lives better. For what do you need *me*?"

"We need you to save Vienna."

"Just remember, '*I teslim*.'"

"Prospero, you are a great man," she coaxed, "and I need you to apply your brilliant intellect as a great scientist and Imperial officer to save the city—as only you can do."

"Okay, now I am getting more interested."

Another man screamed on the wall. The Janissaries had occupied the ruins of the suburbs, and their crack shots were picking off the defenders one by one.

"Two questions. First, how do we know which gate is being mined?"

"That is simple enough. We must assume they are mining all of them and make preparations accordingly. The most probable targets are the Scottish Gate and Kärnthner Gate."

"How do you know that?"

"Were you not paying attention all those hours up there in the tower?" He sighed. "Of course not, you were too busy worrying for our poor Taddeo, who is under constant threat of being forced to live a life of power and luxury in one of the greatest nations on the earth. Most of our strength is concentrated in the western forts facing the Turkish line, so they will hit us from the north, the south, or both where we are weakest, *capisce*?"

Her face turned bright scarlet. "Got it."

"Do not be embarrassed."

"I'm not embarrassed. I'm angry."

"Just the same. As a precaution, you should place lumber against the gates so that if they do go boom, they will fall outward instead of inward. What is your second question?"

Marie steeled herself for more abuse. "How will we know if the Turks are getting close so we can start counter mining? We can't dig a tunnel at every gate."

"Do you really need a genius for these questions? Do not answer that; clearly, you do. First, you will need to post guards in the cellar of every building near the walls."

Marie nodded. "We can do that."

"Next, you must confiscate the drums from the boys who are continually making an infernal racket with them and put them in the cellars as well. Put peas on the drums. When the Turks get close, their labors will send vibrations through the earth. If the pea moves, send for Martin Luther so he can say a prayer for us."

And after that, they'd dig. Dig for their lives. Dig until they found the Turkish tunnel, killed the miners, and set fire to the pit-props to make it collapse.

"Thank you, Prospero," Marie said. "You've been a big help."

"Is that it? I could build a seismograph to find the tunnels for you. We set off some powder in a cellar to release energy through the earth, measure the reflected and refracted waves returning, and look for anomalies—"

She perked up at this. "How long would that take you?"

"With proper resources, I could have a working prototype ready in—ah, *merda*."

"Oh. Sorry, Prospero. We don't have time for anything fancy."

"The Magus can do anything but refuses to help a single soul, while all I want to do is help the entire human race but I am not allowed!" He stormed off in a huff.

"You *were* helpful!" she called after him. "Ah, to hell with it." She went to make the necessary preparations.

In a cellar next to the foundation of the Scottish Gate, the pea trembled along the taut surface of the drum. Marie arrived to find the place bright with lanterns and loud with babbling Landsknechte. With their weapons and broad, hulking shoulders, the giants packed the cramped space, sucking out all the air and replacing it with body odor.

They quieted as she put her ear against the damp wall. She smelled ancient dust and stone.

The Turks were coming. She could feel them. Tiny vibrations in the earth.

Marie stepped back and beckoned the regiment's resident

artist—a prolific man whose specialty was drawing pornographic graffiti on ruins, notably boobs and genitalia—and pointed at a spot. He grinned and drew a portrait of the Sultan. An oafish smiley face wearing a turban.

"From now on, no one says a word," she warned them. "We'll dig in shifts straight toward the Turkish lines. If you're not on a shift, get out and wait your turn."

The Landsknechte piled their gear and weapons, stripped off their shirts, and spit in their hands. The men attacked the drawing of the Sultan with pickaxes and hammers and broke a hole in the wall. Viennese workers carted away the pieces.

Marie needed more support. The Turks likely had multiple tunnels going, and she couldn't be everywhere at once. Someone needed to ensure John von Greissenegg, who commanded the city militia, posted men in all the cellars near the walls. The gates needed to be propped with supports as Prospero had instructed. Count Palatine Philip was useless, sitting in council day after day eating his *palatschinken* and slowly digesting all the good advice he was getting.

She needed Count Nicholas. Vienna needed the hero of Pavia now more than ever.

In St. Stephen's tower, he gripped the parapet and laughed down at the Turkish guns as their balls banged and broke against the stout walls.

"IS THAT THE BEST YOU CAN DO, *SCHWEINHUND*?"

"*Feldherr*," she said. "The Turks are mining the Scottish Gate."

The old veteran fixed a baleful eye on her. "*Ja, ja.* And?"

"And we need your help."

"The Sultan has been trying to kill me all day. Every gun out there is firing at me now." He cupped his hands around his mouth and called out: "AND I AM STILL HERE. HA, HA!"

Marie pressed on, explaining what she needed.

Count Nicholas nodded. "Obviously. Let's go."

As long as he's on our side, Marie thought, *we can't lose. The men*

311

believe in him. The commanders respect and listen to him. He has fifty years of hard warfare in his head. He's our hero.

Outside, on the steps, a cannonball broke against the walls of the church over their heads. Salm groaned and slumped against her.

"Count Nicholas!"

He held his side. "Damn." A dark stain spread across his shredded doublet. "I should have worn my armor today."

She dragged him back into the church and summoned the surgeons.

"Damn it all!" Nicholas raged. "The sneaky bastard finally got me."

"Don't die, Count Nicholas. We need you."

He gripped her wrist. "I won't give the Sultan the satisfaction. But it's up to you now, girl. The other commanders are all idiots. You have learned your lessons well. Use what you know."

Count Ruprecht arrived at the gallop, flung himself from his horse, and raced up the steps.

"My God, Count!" he cried. "Just look at you!"

"*Ja, ja.*"

"Are you slain?"

Nicholas grit his teeth. "I'm wounded. Obviously."

The young count bent his knee. "Count Nicholas, I swear by the sword I trust with my very life that your death shall be avenged."

"Stop talking to me as if I'm dead!"

"When I cut off the Sultan's head, I shall cry, 'For the memory of Salm!'"

The surgeons arrived at last and hauled the groaning old man onto a stretcher.

"Thank God you've arrived," Nicholas said. "Get me the hell out of here."

As she watched him go, Marie never felt so alone. Taddeo was a captive, Prospero was pouting, Myrddin had disappeared after sneaking into the Ottoman camp, and Count Nicholas had been wounded. Even Martin Luther had flown the coop, taking God with him.

Ignoring Ruprecht's entreaties, she returned to the cellar near the Scottish Gate and found her Landsknechte flirting with the water bearer, a buxom blonde who giggled at the attention. They stiffened at the sight of their commander. She grabbed the nearest shovel and pushed it into moist soil alive with bugs and worms. The Landsknechte returned to work.

Shifts came and went, carpenters arrived to place the pit-props that kept the earth from falling in on their heads, water bearers brought buckets to relieve their thirst, laborers moved the piles of dirt. Marie worked without cease. There was nothing else for her to do but keep trying.

After some days, a heavy hand landed on her shoulder.

"Rest, Colonel," the mercenary said. "We can do this. We won't let you down."

She nodded dumbly and staggered out of the tunnel, surprised by how long it had grown. It took her minutes to reach the surface, where she blinked in gray light. She saw no fires burning, but ashes fluttered through the air like snow. It was like the end of the world.

Nearby, Prospero sat astride *The Prometheus*. The front of the carriage had been fitted with a metal scoop to push the massive piles of dirt toward the walls, where it was used to reinforce the earthworks.

"So this is what your fate had in store for us," he grumbled over the chug of the steam engine. "Reduced to menial labor with ashes in our hair." He shrugged. "*Così sia*."

"Has Myrddin come back?"

"Why would he? The man has a natural aversion to doing anything useful."

"What about Count Nicholas?"

"I saved him from the butchery of the surgeons," Prospero said. "He will recover."

"Thank you, Prospero."

"It is our great pleasure," he muttered. "He had them bring him back to the church tower, where even now he heckles the Sultan. He also issued orders. Everything you wanted has been done. The city is on guard against all subterranean threats."

Marie nodded and blew a sigh. "Good."

"Speaking of which, we should return to the tower ourselves."

"Why?"

"*Bella*, it is the fifth day. Taddeo is playing his last game. For his freedom."

"Taddeo!" She'd lost track of the days underground. She broke into a run.

Halfway up the street, the mercenaries called her back.

They'd found the Turkish tunnel.

Marie looked up at the church tower.

Prospero patted her on the shoulder. "Go and slaughter some Turks. It will make you feel better. I will attend to Taddeo and give you a complete account."

She buckled her cuirass as she entered the basement. The men cracked their knuckles and tensed for action. No one said a word. The crowd parted as she passed among the warriors.

At the end of the tunnel, she stood facing the dirt wall. Little tremors in the soil sent waves of dirt crumbs cascading down its face. The air smelled like minerals. She took off her hat, put her ear against the wall, and listened.

Muffled voices spoke in another language. Turkish. She heard the clank of tools. A hammer pounded at lumber, which she guessed was a miner putting a pit-prop into place. Someone said something and laughed. Another voice chimed in. More laughter.

Marie drew her sword and inserted it into the dirt. When she no longer felt resistance, she withdrew it. She stood less than a foot from the Turkish tunnel.

"*Bella!*" Prospero shouted from the main room. "I have conceived a solution to your Turkish problem. I will build a giant furnace and bellows, and we will smoke them out!"

Marie froze as a mercenary clamped his hand over the scientist's mouth.

Aaargh, she thought. Even in her head, she kept her voice down.

The Turks stopped talking.

She put her ear against the dirt again but heard nothing. Someone was there, she knew, standing with his own ear against the wall.

"*Salut,*" she said and heard a gasp.

Stepping back, she thrust her sword deep into the soil and felt a shock vibrate up her arm. A man howled. The blade came back red.

"Kill them all, my beauties!" she screamed.

"HERE WE COME." The mercenaries flung their bodies against the wall and crashed through in a blinding cloud of dirt.

A large crowd of Turks gaped at them.

"*Bok,*" one said as the Germans tore into them with their two-handers.

The Turks fought savagely with pickaxes and shovels. The narrow tunnel filled with grunting, struggling men who hacked blindly at each other and fell screaming underfoot. Marie thrust, pushed, and thrust again. Hundreds of Landsknechte poured into the tunnel behind her. She had to move forward or die. She discharged one of her pistols with a blinding flash that lit up a dozen snarling faces.

Prospero, swept along in the melee, appeared at her side.

"*I teslim!*" he screamed. "*I teslim!*"

With the singular exception of the scientist, no quarter was asked, and none given.

The two masses of men pushed against each other face to face. Crushed by hot writhing bodies, Marie fought for air. She couldn't move her arms; her legs left the ground. She headbutted the man in front of her. Sparks danced in front of her eyes. Dropping her sword, she reached to her hip, wriggled free her second pistol, and worked it under the miner's chin. The gun fired with a deafening crash.

Then something gave. The Turks lost heart. They tried to flee but had nowhere to go, packed into the tunnel like rats. They hacked and climbed over each other each other in a blind panic while the *Landsknecht* flood surged against them. The Germans chopped them down and trampled their bodies into the bloody mud.

Marie yanked Prospero out of the press, and together they stood against the wall gasping for breath while the mercenaries ran past howling with bloodlust.

"Please do not shoot a gun in here again," the scientist panted. He tapped a wood barrel at his feet. "Gunpowder. Ba-da boom."

"We'll take it with us before we fire the supports."

"And I will go to the tower to check up on Taddeo."

"I'm coming with you. I have to know what's happening to him."

"Milady, where are you?" Ruprecht called. "Milady?" He appeared before them and paused to look around the Turkish tunnel. "Oh, very moody."

"Count Ruprecht, did you need me for something?"

"Yes! We have a problem, milady. Er, a rather *big* problem."

Outside Vienna, Taddeo and the Grand Vizier sat in cushioned chairs and sipped *kahve* while servants brought the pieces and board and the cannon boomed all around them. Taddeo looked at the distant church tower and wondered if Marie looked back at him.

Ibrahim Pasha set up the Ottomans. It was his turn to play White.

"And now begins our final contest," he said.

"It has been an honor to play against you. I've quite enjoyed it."

The man offered an enigmatic smile. "As have I."

If Taddeo won this last game, he'd earn his freedom. The Turks would go home to Istanbul, and he'd go home to Marie.

The Grand Vizier opened with a King's Pawn Game, which turned into the King's Gambit.

"Where did you get your democratic ideas, Taddeo?" Ibrahim said as they sipped their *kahve*. "Your views do not exactly fit with Venetian republicanism."

Taddeo moved his Knight. "It all started with me thinking about Good. The idea of our Creator guiding our every action is too problematic to take seriously. Perhaps the Creator made the world to run on its own and is merely passively observing Man's progress. If we discount the idea of the Creator providing a moral system, a simplistic view of Good is that pleasure is good and suffering is bad. That is well for individuals, but what is the role of a society in which individuals work together toward the Common Good? I concluded the greatest good is achieved when happiness is maximized for the greatest number of people."

"That is an interesting idea. But most people live no better than animals. Why should we care about their happiness?"

Taddeo warmed to the conversation. The Grand Vizier had so far demonstrated himself as an honorable adversary and a generous host. He was obviously a highly intelligent man. Maybe Taddeo could convince him of some of his ideas. Perhaps they could change the world together into one without war, poverty, and ignorance.

"If wealth and power make a man noble and poverty like a beast," he explained, "then all men would become noble if wealth were expanded and shared equally."

Ibrahim moved his Bishop to pin Taddeo's Knight. The man's play had improved. He no longer hunched over the board stroking his carefully trimmed beard with his ringed fingers. His play was rapid and confident as he developed a simple, elegant, and unstoppable attack from the center.

For the first time, Taddeo considered the possibility he might have to play for a draw.

"Ah, but where would we find this fabulous wealth? If everyone had everything he wanted, who would provide the labor? What would there be to buy with it?"

"The answer to all of these questions can be found in science, Excellency. Scientific progress can increase wealth, production, leisure, education. There would be plenty for everyone. Machines would automate most forms of labor. We would all work together for the common good."

"There would certainly be no need for a Sultan," Ibrahim mused.

"In time, the people would rule themselves in a simple democracy." Realizing he tread on thin ice talking about the security of the Ottoman emperor, he added quickly, "But it would take generations for this to happen. In time, the State would simply wither away on its own."

"I admit I find your views quite intriguing. But you are forgetting one thing."

"What's that?"

"Human nature. Life is competition, my young friend. The strong have always ruled the weak. So it always has been, so it always shall be. It is the natural order of things. Allah, the Giver of Life, saw fit to make it so."

"But everyone would have everything they needed. There would be no more competition."

"Everyone would feel they had a right to everything no matter how much there was to go around. Everyone would fight everyone, and there would be nothing. The State, therefore, is essential. People submit to its authority in exchange for protection from anarchy. That is why your *fulmen* idea will not do for us. No king in his right mind would ever invest in such a thing. Kings are better off investing in pageantry, patronage, war, and religion, all of which unify the people and build loyalty to and enhance the legitimacy of the State. People do not matter. Only the State, which lives forever to serve the nation, is ultimately of any real importance. No, as Vizier of Science, you will build better arms, bombs, gunpowder manufacturing, and siege guns to keep our perfect State strong and help it expand."

"You want me to…" He shut his eyes, unable to believe the words. "Design and build weapons that kill large numbers of people. This is what the Vizier of Science does?"

The idea made him sick.

"Welcome to the real world, which is exactly as it should be," Ibrahim said with a smile.

"Perhaps you are right," Taddeo said, growing hot. "But if that's true, then the soldiers on both sides of this war are fighting the wrong enemy. Even with all their differences, they have more in common with each other than the kings who lead them. The real enemies are classes, not nations. It would be better if the soldiers in both of the armies here joined forces and fought the monarchies that exploited them instead of each other."

Ibrahim threw him a sharp glance. "That, my friend, is the most dangerous idea in the world. You are indeed a very dangerous young man, Taddeo. I am starting to believe destroying the Empire from within was your goal all along."

Taddeo sagged. "I just want to make people's lives better."

"I see you are upset with me. You feel I was not honest with you about the position I offered. I concede the point. But you have not been entirely honest with me as well. For example, I learned just before our game that the Viennese destroyed our mining operations at the Scottish Gate. You doing, I believe. You betrayed your parole and sent Marie Dubois a message."

"Um," Taddeo said with an audible gulp. "I'm sorry?"

Ibrahim laughed. "Why would I be angry? We have been playing a game, Taddeo. That is all. But it was my game, and I play a long game. Win a few, lose a few, as long as you win in the end." He dropped his Queen next to Taddeo's King. "Checkmate, my young friend."

The Kärnthner Gate exploded in the distance with a resounding crash. Taddeo stood and watched in horror as the gate and part of the adjacent wall collapsed in a massive cloud of dust.

The Grand Vizier added, "It is said, 'He who laughs last, laughs best.'"

Thousands of Azabs raced howling toward the breach.

And behind, marching wave after wave under their proud flags, came the unstoppable Janissaries.

~ Chapter XVII ~

ARMAGEDDON

A company of Spaniards arrived first at the gap. They locked shields and drew their swords as one. The air whistled moments before a Turkish salvo landed in their midst. Bodies and weapons cartwheeled through the air.

Aside from a few dazed survivors, there was no one to stop the Turkish tide.

Sensing victory, the Azabs rushed headlong with wailing cries.

And then hesitated at the sight of the bizarre monster that now appeared in the breach.

The Prometheus chugged into the massive dust cloud piloted by Prospero, who turned green at the sight of the screaming horde. Black smoke billowed from the exhaust pipe. The steam wagon lurched and banged over the rubble of the wall.

There was no escape. There was nowhere to go. The Turks were everywhere.

Prospero, however, wasn't trying to escape.

"*Basta!*"

He flung himself from the carriage to land in a dramatic tumble. *The Prometheus* ground on toward the Azabs. His head ringing, Prospero sat up and watched its progress.

He wiped a tear from his eye. "*Arrivederci, amore mio.*"

The steam wagon plunged into the horde.

The barrels of Turkish gunpowder ignited.

WHUMP

The earth jolted as if God slammed his hand against the ground.

WHUMP-BUMP

The Prometheus collapsed inward before bursting in a blinding flash and massive fireball. Hundreds of Azabs spun and crumpled in heaps.

"Occam's Razor," the scientist swore, astounded by the unspeakable horror of it.

The horror of losing such a magnificent invention, that is. Not to mention Taddeo's masterpiece. The boy would be devastated.

Two miles away, Taddeo pumped his fist at the sight. "*Per la vittoria!*"

Ibrahim snorted. "The game has only just begun. Watch and learn."

The explosion bought the defenders valuable time. Columns of shouting mercenaries raced through the streets of Vienna and converged on the breach. Marie arrived first and found Martin Luther picking his way among the dead and dying, alternately administering last rites and shaking his fist at the Turks.

"Prospero!" Marie spread her arms to hug him. "That was one of the most selfless and heroic acts I've ever seen." She resisted adding a patronizing, *I knew you had it in you.*

He huffed past. "Cannot talk! I have to go change into my kaftan."

Her companies deployed into a hedgehog bristling with pikes and muskets aimed at the onrushing army. Cannon mounted on the rooftops hurled shells into the horde. Marie's heart sank at the sight of her enemies. Maybe Prospero had the right idea; nothing could stop this attack.

The very ground trembled at their advance. They filled the horizon. Thousands upon thousands of shrieking devils in the shape of men wearing turbans and rags. The Azab roar washed over the mercenaries. The Landsknechte gripped their pikes and set their faces toward the enemy, but each man looked inward. Men who'd never known fear confronted it for the first time. Many pondered the reward of Heaven and the punishments of Hell. Some bargained with God; promises were made, deals struck.

Look at all of them, they told themselves. *They're endless. So many, and we're so few. I just want to be left alone. I was doing just fine without them. Just let me be.*

The line wilted as the mercenaries shifted here, took a step back there, sought refuge behind the backs of comrades.

They would have fled, if only there were some place to go.

A crystal note pierced their gloom. At the rear of the formation, Marie sang her death song, but it quickly changed into something else. Some recognized in its sad and lonely notes the age-old story of the woman who dies of homesickness in her own bed because her home resides in the heart of her husband who has gone off to fight in the Crusades.

Across the line, men burst into tears. No speeches about defending their faith, dying for the Emperor, or even the prospect of a bonus had the power to stir them now, but this did. It reminded them of the only things worth fighting for—their families, their homes, the sweethearts they left behind to suffer in quiet yearning.

The song changed again. The note lilted and soared. The roar of the Azabs faded before its strength. The Landsknechte blinked, struck by visions of a Valkyrie riding the sky. A beautiful armored woman on a winged warhorse plunging through the ether to succor the dead and dying. Some saw her wearing the face of loved ones; some saw Marie. If they died today, she would get them home. She would deliver them all safe to Paradise.

The song, which had started as a death song and became a love song, ended as a song of life. As the Azabs closed, it rose to a fever pitch of fury.

The line held, stiffened, became iron.

"Your war is just," Martin Luther shouted in his cranky German while holding a cross over his head, "and God is with us."

The Ottoman tide, just moments ago a seething mass of men and steel, came into focus as thousands of individual snarling faces.

Marie's song reached its crescendo.

The line parted to clear a narrow path through the formation.

"HERE SHE COMES!" the Landsknechte roared.

Marie sprang forward.

While the men around her had looked inward, so had she. She'd remembered the hungry times of her youth and pondered the Fate that had brought her together with Myrddin and set her on the journey of her life. She passed mercenaries who performed last-minute armor checks, flexed their shoulders, dirtied their hands for a better grip on their pikes. Every head turned as she raced past; the hopeful bearded faces became a blur as she built up speed. She saw the dragon skull on her standard and felt the plumes and foxtail bobbing on her wide-brimmed hat. She thought of the men who'd taught her hands to war during the dream time, her *sensei* who'd told her that the Way of the Warrior was found in accepting that she had already died.

She no longer did. Now she wanted to live. She wanted to fight for her life. A warrior accepted he was dead but also said yes to everything life offered.

The words of the wizard who'd raised her came to her:

You will find your own way. You must come to understand the one thing that is most important to you, and fight for it. That is how you will learn to fight for yourself.

With an aching heart, she thought of Taddeo.

I'm coming for you, baby, she vowed.

All of her life, all her memories, had led to this. Had led to him. The only thing that mattered. The only thing truly worth fighting for. The hungry times were over.

And fight she would. It was what she was born to do.

I'm coming for you, baby, and nothing is going to stop me.

Marie leaped high into the air and landed with a crunch on a turbaned face. Around her, the mass of Azabs struck the pikes with a resounding *crack* followed by screams, shouts, and the ring of steel. The arquebusiers volleyed, dropping scores of men in withering fire. Then everything melted away as she became a killing machine.

She thrust, parried, chopped, feinted, retreated, lunged. The Azabs crowded around, big brutes with bearded faces, and fell away howling. Bodies landed at her feet. Her buckler warped as she slammed it into another snarling face. She lopped off a hand at the wrist. Another body splashed into the bloody mud. The dead and dying piled around her. She stayed in constant motion, always shifting, never hesitating. She struck down a score of the enemy, then another, but more kept coming, and now she heard the music of the mehters and the steady tramp of the Janissaries growing ever closer.

"Allah! Allah! Allah!" the Janissaries roared.

The Azabs closed in with their scimitars.

"*La!*" she said, her blade flashing.

Marie wheeled, ready to strike, and saw Count Ruprecht grinning back at her. Leo bounded past to lunge snarling at the nearest Muslim.

"Thought you'd steal all the fun, did you, milady?" He skewered an Azab. "Glad you saved a few for me!"

"There's plenty for everyone."

He laughed. "What a rousing fracas!"

Marie saved her breath. She spared a glance over her shoulder and was surprised to find she'd fought some fifty paces into the body of Turks. Back at the gap in the wall, the line held. Reinforcements rushed into the area as the Azabs hurled themselves at the unbreakable Landsknechte. Guns crashed with puffs of smoke that collected in a drifting fog. Cannon on the rooftops raked the Azabs with deadly effect. The air smelled like powder and blood.

The Azabs lost their nerve. Men drifted away from the assault. The rest soon followed, streaming back to the Ottoman camp.

The Landsknechte let out a ragged cheer.

"Leaving so soon?" Ruprecht thrust his sword into a fleeing man's back. "For Salm!"

The Janissaries broke into a run. "*VUR HA!*"

The Ottoman war cry, which meant: *KILL THEM ALL!*

"Time to go," Marie said. "Now!"

"But the party's only just—" He turned and paled. "Blast it, let's go."

They ran, the Janissaries hot on their heels in their blue coats.

"Get down!" she screamed just before they reached the Landsknechte.

They dove to the dirt as the Janissaries halted, leveled their muskets, and fired with mechanical precision. Marie heard the thunderous crash and saw the mangled smoking bodies drop in front of her. The Janissary front rank reloaded as another came forward, presented, and fired, blasting fresh holes in the ranks of the Europeans. The air hummed with shot. Across the line, men screamed and fell. The Landsknechte hedgehog was coming apart.

The Janissaries continued their inexorable advance, almost haughty in their indifference. These slave-soldiers were the best in the world, and they knew it. They'd never been beaten. They'd conquered Hungary, Rhodes, Egypt, Arabia, and Persia. They'd slaughtered millions. Now they'd come to conquer Europe. They would roll over Vienna and leave nothing behind but a memory that itself would be erased by time.

In moments, they'd charge and finish it.

A hand reached to help her up. She raised her chin and saw the Magus's wizened, bearded face. "Myrddin!"

"Has anyone ever told you that you look like a wizard?" Count Ruprecht asked him.

"Now listen here, sonny. I *am*—"

His eyes widened. "Sir, your staff is glowing!"

Myrddin started to respond but shook his head instead in a gesture of impatient dismissal.

Martin Luther waved his cross at the glow, trying to extinguish it. "What vile sorcery is this, thou worshipper of Satan?"

"We don't have time for theology, Martin!" Marie said. "Let the man work!"

"Thank you, Marie," the wizard said. "Stand back, children." He raised the oak staff with its sleeping faces high over his head. "AVALON!"

And slammed it against the ground before them. A deep tremor rippled outward from the strike. In a flash of light, four giant knights appeared mounted on powerful warhorses. Their flesh looked dead and waxy, their eyes vacant and glassy. They wore Roman armor of leather and chain mail and carried heavy shields.

Marie heard them speak in her head.

Merlin! said the bearded giant wearing an iron crown. *My old friend.*

King Arthur, Sir Lancelot, Sir Gawain, Sir Galahad, it's good to see you again.

Why did you deliver us from the Tree? King Arthur said.

To fight for the weak.

Count me in! Sir Lancelot said and noticed Marie for the first time. *Oh, hello.*

I want to go back, Sir Galahad said. *To the Dream.*

We were dead, you know, King Arthur pointed out. *And quite happy about it.*

Um, Myrddin said. *I thought I was rescuing you. I thought...*

What were you expecting? the king asked.

I thought you would be a little grateful. I only recently even remembered who you were and how to bring you back.

We were in Avalon, Merlin. Why would we want to return to this world of war and death? We couldn't understand why you left us. Why you decided to wake.

Was I happy? Myrddin stroked his beard. *I don't remember.*

You said you had work to do here. Have you done it?

It was a good question for which the Magus had no clear answer.

Sir Galahad: *Can we go back now?*

We'll help first, Sir Lancelot said, winking at Marie. *Since we're here.*

All right, old friend? King Arthur said.

My enemies are there, Myrddin answered. *Now, I can't tell you what to do because—*

Sir Galahad: *Aye, aye, we know—*

King Arthur: *You swore an oath not to harm any man.*

Sir Gawain: *He never had a problem with us doing it for him, though, did he?*

Sir Galahad: *Ha!*

Sir Lancelot: *Christ on a Cross. Let's just go kill those fellows so we can go home.*

King Arthur: *We'll do as you ask, Merlin. Just promise you'll send us back.*

Merlin: *You have my word as a magus.*

The knights rolled their eyes at each other to show what they thought of their old friend's word as a magus, and drew their broadswords as one.

King Arthur raised his sword to salute the Turks.

Albion!

The four ghost knights spurred their mounts. The giant horses shrieked like demons and snorted bursts of steam before lunging into a fast gallop.

"Magnificent," Marie breathed. She turned to the Magus. "What important work did you come back to do, Myrddin?"

"I didn't have any special work to do."

"Then why did you come back?"

The wizard frowned and said, "I was lonely."

ALBION!

King Arthur and his knights crashed into the Janissaries, cut down their nearest opponents, and rode on. The broadswords rose and fell. Each blow was a killing blow. Blood and brains splashed across their heavy blades.

Marie shrieked loud enough to make the Magus flinch.

"Hey, now," he scolded, but she was already gone.

It was time for the Janissaries to learn a lesson in fear.

Time for the killing.

Marie raced after the knights with Leo and a whooping Count Ruprecht at her heels. The Landsknechte charged with a primal roar and plunged into the ranks of the Janissaries.

Marie leaped high in the air, sword flashing—

"An interesting move," Ibrahim observed. He stroked his pointed beard. "We have entered the middle game, and Myrddin Wyllt has revealed himself at last."

Taddeo watched Marie and the knights chop their way deep into the Janissary host. Blue-coated bodies flew through the air in a spray of blood. "It's over, Excellency. You've lost."

"We have yet to play the endgame, my friend. An endgame in which I will destroy the Viennese and then Myrddin Wyllt. All according to my plan."

"If you stop this now, I'll come with you. I'll build your bombs. I'll build you weapons that will conquer the world."

Ibrahim spared him a quick amused glance. "But I already own you, boy. Soon, you will be a vizier of the Ottoman Empire. Try to act like one."

The Grand Vizier raised his hands and stroked the air as if playing an invisible harp. He spoke the charm of creation.

Taddeo felt the presence of the thing before he saw it. The heart-pounding terror of a lucid nightmare in which one wants to run in blind fright but has forgotten how.

A cloud of fat black flies swirled before the Ottoman wizard. The air buzzed with invisible mosquitoes, hissed with the voices of snakes, fluttered with the vibrations of thousands of tiny wings. The cloud thickened as the creature formed.

The monster stood more than ten feet tall. A giant muscled apparition. Its head was made of black flies, its torso a pulsing horde of locusts, its arms and legs a thick tangle of serpents. Seething piles of scorpions formed its feet.

"*Master*," the creature said in a deep booming voice Taddeo felt deep in his chest.

"Behold the Ifrit, the most powerful of the infernal Jinn," Ibrahim said.

"*What is thy bidding, O Master?*" the Ifrit intoned with meaty lips shaped by a pair of writhing snakes. Desert sands drooled from its gaping maw.

The Grand Vizier swept his hand across the battlefield. "Kill my enemies! Kill them all and destroy their city. Every stone. Every timber. Every living thing."

The crude face morphed into a terrifying grin. The snakes writhed in ecstasy. The clouds of bats that formed its hands crumpled into leathery fists. Scarab beetles raced excitedly about the thing's pulsing body.

"I obey."

The Ifrit shrieked as it burst into blue fire. The apparition turned and faced Vienna.

"What about Marie?" Taddeo cried.

"Your wife is dangerous. Too dangerous to bring with us to Istanbul."

"What will happen to her?"

"The Ifrit will destroy her body and consume her soul."

"No!"

"She would only have caused more trouble for you. You'll thank me for it later."

Taddeo watched the Ifrit flow laughing across the ground toward the Europeans.

He'd finally seen the Grand Vizier's true colors. The man's eternal pain fed a deep and abiding well of bitterness in his soul. His father had been murdered at sea, and he in turn had been enslaved by the murderers. The Pasha wanted to conquer the world so he could watch it burn. Make everyone a slave to the new father he'd come to love, a strong father who would never die and never erred—the State with its cold iron fist. Taddeo understood now that the man held no special love for the Turkish nation and its empire. Ibrahim saw it only as a vessel for a perfect instrument he used to bend millions to his will.

A bright shaft of light shot toward the sky from Vienna.

The Magus.

The sky turned gray and rumbled as massive storm clouds formed over the city.

Not storm clouds, Taddeo realized. Smoke. Rolling mountains of it.

The dragon roared as it fell from the cauldron, smoke billowing from its snout. The Magus had summoned a spirit of Old Europe, one of the greatest children of the Old Ones. Even at a distance, Taddeo quaked at the sight of its fierce face, black scales, and massive wingspan that scattered the clouds around it.

"Now the real battle has joined," Ibrahim said. "Arabia versus Europe, and let the winner take all." He sounded giddy. He'd finally gotten the great magical contest he craved.

The Ifrit stopped in its tracks and expanded. It grew to a massive height and rose in the air on a noxious wind.

Claws splayed, the dragon struck it like a meteor while the armies hacked at each other in blind bloodlust, oblivious to the cosmic battle going on above them.

The monsters tore at each other snarling. Taddeo watched in breathless anxiety. The spirits merged in a raging storm of smoke. Lightning flashed within the tempest, followed by deafening claps of thunder.

Fight hard, dragon, Taddeo prayed.

Next to him, Ibrahim grit his teeth. "Come on, Ifrit. You can do it."

The clouds began to implode. Sucked inward to some vacuum. The dragon howled.

The Ifrit was *eating*.

It ate the lightning. The thunder. The clouds. Parts of the sky itself.

The dragon reeled from the contest with a flap of mighty wings. A jet of liquid fire poured from its throat and enveloped the Jinn.

The Ifrit ate that too, laughing its belching laugh.

The dragon retreated further, receding. It had lost, and they were doomed.

The boy now knew what he had to do.

He had to speak the words of power Myrddin had taught him in the Pasha's tent.

If he did, he could fight Ibrahim and defeat him.

Or...

Ibrahim would destroy him.

The angels would destroy him.

He would destroy himself because he had no idea what he was doing.

Taddeo remembered his father telling him the greatest men asked for forgiveness, not permission. They took risks and fought for what they wanted.

His father lived according to his own advice. Gregorio himself was such a great man, Taddeo knew. Perhaps, in the letter he'd sent, he was recognizing the same in his son. It was true Taddeo had chosen to give up his birthright by refusing to enter the family business, but Gregorio had given something even more precious, which was his father's hard-earned respect.

If Gregorio represented the life that might have been, Prospero represented the life he thought he wanted. To be a *homo universale*, a great man like Michelangelo. A man who lived free and existed to create. A man who could change the world with his mind. Prospero played fast and loose with his principles and methods, but he essentially lived as the great man he so desperately wanted to be. He may have been a bit of a coward who avoided causes like the plague, but he owed the world his survival, if only so his labors could make it a better place.

Taddeo thought of all the great men who inspired him— Archimedes, Leonardo da Vinci, Ptolemy, Gutenberg, Michelangelo, and all the rest—and cringed at the thought of even one of them dying before he'd made his mark. How many other heroes of science, art, and literature might have been, but were struck down by war, pestilence, and accident? He couldn't help but wonder what the world would have become if they'd all survived.

Taddeo had a great mind; he knew this without hubris. Did he not also owe humanity a debt of service? He could go to Istanbul and produce inventions that could be used for war but could also make people's lives better. Flying machines, automated road builders, foodstuffs that lasted longer on the march, medicines to cure the plagues that followed armies everywhere. The Grand Vizier would have his wars, but in the end, Taddeo might still win. If there was one thing he'd learned from the man, it was how to play a long game.

But if Prospero presented a vision of a life Taddeo craved as a scientist, Marie offered a life worth living as a man. Inspired by his love for her, he'd conquered his shyness, fought hard for what he wanted, learned to live in the moment, and collected the courage to reject his birthright and live his own life his own way. He'd gained a woman who loved him for who and what he was, with whom he shared a mutual fascination and attraction, and who surprised him with her boldness and different perspective. She made him happy. Happier than he'd ever dreamed. The truth was there really was no point of changing a world without Marie Dubois in it.

Taddeo now saw everything he'd gained—his freedom and the one great love of his life—about to be destroyed by the man standing in front of him. A brilliant but bitterly ruthless and ambitious monster he'd grown to respect and even love a little.

In the end, the choice was easy to make.

Because there really was no choice.

It was time to listen again to his father and risk everything.

He raised his arms to the heavens and cried:

> *O servants of God,*
> *Whose breath spells life and death,*
> *I summon thy power of Creation!*

Taddeo felt a vast unseen Presence.

Since the first forms of life appeared on the planet, it had absorbed the events of the world and its billion stories of life and death.

It was older even than that. Older than old. Older than time itself.

It was everywhere.

It focused its all-seeing eye on *him*.

The Presence permeated him, sniffed his atoms, inspected every firing neuron. Taddeo wilted under its sight. He sensed the being could obliterate him with a mere thought.

He heard it speak: *What dost thou desire of Me, O Man?*

Stop them, he broadcasted with his mind. *Make the killing stop. Make them go home.*

Nothing happened. The Presence evaporated as quickly as it had come, leaving an aching emptiness in Taddeo's soul.

He fell to his knees gasping.

Ibrahim shook his head. "You know nothing of magic. You have meddled with powerful forces you cannot hope to understand. You're lucky to be alive."

"I had to try."

"I admire your courage, but you have failed. See how the Ifrit obeys me still? And when it is done with Vienna, we shall deal with your insolence."

"I wish you wouldn't," Taddeo said.

He watched in horror as the Ifrit swept over the embroiled Landsknechte and Janissaries. Snarling face to face, they still hacked at each other furiously in an orgy of mutual slaughter.

It's over, Taddeo thought. *We've lost, and the Pasha will own the world.*

The Landsknechte began to giggle.

The Janissaries, with their white turbans and blue coats and angry faces and swords dripping with blood, were *hilarious*.

The mercenaries quaked with great peals of laughter. Some fell to the bloody ground howling while others hugged their ribs. Tears streamed down red cheeks.

The Janissaries backed away in horror. This infernal laughter made them want to scream. The laughter of devils. It gripped their souls and squeezed. They reeled in blind panic.

Then they did something they'd never done before. They ran.

The Janissaries threw down their guns and swords, stampeded

back to their camp, and struck their tents while the Sultan watched in stupefaction on his golden throne.

Ibrahim wheeled. "You! What? How?"

Taddeo knew. It was simple, really. Evil always had the edge against good, but love was always stronger than hate.

The man fumed. "Have I ever told you the Ottoman punishment for slaves who disobey their masters?"

"Um. You give them extra work?"

"WE FLAY THEM ALIVE AND FEED THEM TO THE BLOODY ANTS!" the Grand Vizier screamed with clenched fists.

"Unless I flay you first," Marie said. "Starting with your ass."

She was a fearsome sight. Splattered in dirt and gore. Her hat pulled down low over her eyes. Her sword stained with Turkish blood.

She was the most beautiful thing Taddeo had ever seen.

Ibrahim shrugged. "All right then. Well played. I concede the game. You have won."

Marie spat on the ground. "It's not over, Ibrahim Pargali Pasha. You have plagued us with monsters, tried to have me murdered, vexed the man I love as a father, and threatened the man I love as a husband. Now is the time to settle our scores. A trial by combat. Your skill versus mine, and let God issue justice as he sees fit. Draw your sword, pig-dog. I have come for vengeance, and I shall have my satisfaction—along with a piece of that turban as a trophy."

"No, thanks," he said and disappeared in a burst of black smoke.

"*Merde,*" Marie said.

"I'm glad you didn't kill him," Taddeo told her.

"Why?"

"He was one hell of a chess player."

They laughed and ran toward each other.

The Ifrit materialized between them as a pulsing mass of wet, foul-smelling black frogs.

"*Pray, what is thy bidding, O Master?*" the Jinn croaked. A torrent of squirming eels gushed from its grinning maw to land with a wet plop on the ground.

"Um, Myrddin?" Taddeo said.

"Command me, or I shall claim thy soul."

"Myrddin! Help! How do I make it stop?"

The wizard appeared. "Ye Gods! Didn't I tell you to be careful?"

He instructed the Ifrit to return to the netherworld. The mass of frogs splashed to the ground and hopped burping away in all directions.

"Thank you for rescuing me," Taddeo grinned at Marie.

"Thank you," she grinned back. "For everything."

"You're welcome," Myrddin grumbled.

Taddeo and Marie kissed while the Landsknechte shook the sky with wild cheering. Count Ruprecht huzzaed and tossed his hat. Leo caught it in his jaws and ran away with it.

"So where do you want to go next, my husband?" Marie asked. "I'm thinking Venice."

"What about our mercenary regiment?"

"It's not much of a regiment anymore. Most of them are dead."

"Gattinara offered me a post at court if we survived the siege."

"And me a spot in his personal guard. It's not for us, my husband. No more chancellors for us. No more grand viziers and their games. Just us, making our own way."

"Just us, my wife," he said, loving the sound of that.

"With the victory bonus that Gattinara owes me, we'll have enough money to start our own laboratory. We'll bring *fulmen* to the people."

"We'll change the world."

"We'll make history."

"Just the two of us."

"Just the two of us," she agreed.

His heart filled to bursting. "I love you, my wife. I'm so glad we found each other."

"I love you, my husband. I'm so happy I have you."

As long as they had each other, they'd never want for anything ever again.

They kissed.

Church bells rang across Vienna, celebrating the salvation of the city.

They kissed.

They kissed.

They kissed.

The New World

～ The Last Word ～

Prospero, the world's greatest scientist, and Myrddin Wyllt, its greatest wizard, strolled across the smoking battlefield strewn with corpses and discarded equipment. They crossed a trench filled with brackish water and broken weapons. Crows swarmed among the fallen. Scavengers stripped the dead. Horses pulled wagons piled with the dead toward a massive bonfire. It was a nightmarish scene, enough to make any man reflect with a heavy heart on the frailty of life and the horror of his mortality.

But not Prospero. He was sulking, not reflecting.

He had been virtually banished.

Not from Austria, no. Not even from the Empire. From Europe itself, on a fool's errand.

The Archduke Ferdinand himself had arrived at Vienna in the nick of time to congratulate its brave garrison for holding fast against the Ottoman flood and saving his capital.

Prospero and the Magus had been singled out for special distinction as Heroes of the Empire. Finally, the scientist had gained the glory he deserved. At last, he'd eclipsed his great brother. It was true Michelangelo painted the Sistine Chapel and carved David, but did he ever play a part in saving Europe? Ha!

Prospero absorbed the Archduke's praise with a vacant smile and imagined people accosting his divine brother on the street to ask him if he was truly related to the man who'd saved Christendom from the Turk.

His reputation, scrubbed clean at last and elevated to new heights, assured him of a brilliant future of lucrative scientific projects.

Then the Archduke had to go and ruin everything.

"While it is your noble sacrifice and acumen in war which I hold in such high esteem, the Empire seeks further service from you esteemed scholars," said this droll noble and heir to the Habsburg dynasty.

"Whatever you require, we shall provide it!" Prospero said grandly. Already, he was being tasked with a great project that would shake the world.

"Ah. Good. Failing in alchemy, Mercurino Gattinara, my brother's grand chancellor, now seeks His Majesty, Charles V, to delay Heaven and rule forever on this throne. As such, it is our pleasure that you find the land of Bimini spoken of by the Arawak tribes, the land of the Macrobians mentioned in the writings of Herodotus, to obtain the Water of Life. Find its source, procure a significant quantity, and return it to Valladolid so that Charles may bathe in it. Or drink it. Whatever is most efficacious."

"Immortality is overrated," Myrddin said, who knew something about it.

"Be that as it may," Ferdinand said, "we would wish it for my brother. Prospero Buonarroti, Myrddin Wyllt, we charge you with finding the Fountain of Youth."

Prospero paled. It could be anywhere, even if it existed. "The world is a big place, my lord duke. Where would we even begin?"

"The legends tell us it is in New Spain."

For the first time, Myrddin observed, the scientist had been caught at a loss for words.

"Would our apprentices be required to attend us?" the Magus asked.

"Of course. It is for the good of the realm."

Myrddin nodded with satisfaction, and not just because the Archduke's quest had reduced Prospero to the brink of tears. It sounded like a dangerous and ultimately fruitless journey into the unknown, filled with violence and hardship. Just the kind of thing the youngsters would enjoy.

It would give him an excuse to stick around Marie Dubois a while longer and keep an eye on her. He knew it wasn't very wizardly to love her as if she were his own daughter, but even wizards could indulge their human side sometimes.

There was something else too. It had been fun to do real magic again. Magic that made a difference. Magic that made things better.

Of course, there was no way to really make things better. Not in any truly real or lasting way. But he appreciated the illusion.

For Prospero, it was an offer he couldn't refuse.

"The Archduke called me a patriot," he now muttered, half to the wizard and half to himself. "I am beginning to understand that a patriot is a man who does suicidal things that benefit others without compensation."

He paused and wondered if there might be a bright side to this.

For all his genius, he couldn't think of a single one.

"*Così sia*," he said with a sigh. Next to him, Myrddin lit his pipe. He gripped his staff onto which the sleeping faces of Arthur, Lancelot, Gawain, and Galahad had been returned. In time, he would deliver them back to Avalon as he'd sworn.

"I wish I had my hookah," the scientist said.

The wizard produced a second pipe from his sleeve, gave it to Prospero, and lit it. The two men toked in peace. They watched the sun travel across the sky.

"Is it true you can see the future, Magus?"

"It's been said that I can."

"That is not an answer."

Myrddin shrugged and said nothing.

"Do we ever get past the Rebirth? Grow up and stand on our own two feet?"

"I wouldn't say you ever grow up," the wizard answered.

"Will we ever surpass the Romans? That is all I want to know."

"The Age of Rebirth will lead to the Age of Reason in which science will be prized above religion and superstition. Revolutions will slowly transform the face of Europe into democratic states in which the monarchies have little political power. Technological advances will bring about the Industrial Revolution, which will reduce the craftsman in favor of the factory, and dramatically increase wealth and goods. This wealth will be concentrated in the hands of a new ruling class called the capitalists, leading to mass poverty. In the aftermath of great wars involving machines and men, people will demand that governments act to support a minimum standard of living for themselves, resulting in the rise of the welfare state. In the twentieth century, even after its horrific wars, Europe will be more peaceful and united than it has ever been. Technology will continue to progress, connecting the peoples of the world into a single global village. Men will prolong life, create it, travel from one continent to another in a single day. Scientists will understand how the universe was created. Men will go to the moon and explore the planets. The number of the men on the earth will number in the billions. But all man's science and technology will eventually lead to his doom. Overpopulation, environmental depletion, changing the weather itself, and, ultimately, wars fought over water will lead mankind to the brink of extinction in the twenty-first century."

"So everything ends," Prospero said.

"Yes. Everything ends."

"What a marvelous journey it will be. I wish I could see it."

They smoked for a while longer. At last, the scientist put his pipe away. He'd found the bright side to all this.

"I suppose we'd better get a start on our journey. We will go by land to Venice and catch a boat there for Spain. I wish I still had my *Prometheus*!"

The wizard said, "You changed your mind then? You really want to go through with it?"

"The New World is filled with mystery. Who knows what marvels we shall discover?"

"Well," Myrddin said. "I suppose it could be fun. I've never been there. And the youngsters will complain, but secretly they'll love it."

"I want to see everything you described, right to the end." Prospero's eyes gleamed. "I just need to find this Fountain of Youth first."

Immortality, he thought. Why not? Anything was possible with science.

"Or magic," the wizard said, reading his mind.

Prospero marched back toward Vienna. He had to tell Taddeo of their quest, gather provisions, map their route.

He said over his shoulder, "Not that I look forward to sharing such a quest with the likes of you. I am becoming convinced I shall never be rid of you."

"Um. Prospero?"

The scientist turned with an irritated frown. "Yes?"

"Observe carefully."

The wizard held up a lead musket ball. Then he swept his hand over it.

"*A la kazam, a la kazoo!*"

Revealing a gold ball.

"*Presto,*" Myrddin said.

"You," Prospero sputtered. "You could do it this whole time!" He let out a convulsive sigh. "Sometimes, I really hate you."

Myrddin barked his harsh wheezing laugh. He put his hands behind his back and shook his sleeve, dropping the lead ball to the ground.

POSTSCRIPT
FATE OF HISTORICAL
DRAMATIS PERSONAE

Charles V: The Holy Roman Emperor and King of Spain continued the difficult task of governing his large and fractious empire while fighting the French and Ottomans. In 1542, he even personally led a joint Ango-Spanish invasion of northern France. By the last war in 1551, during which he no longer fought his old rival Francis but instead his son, Henry II, he'd had enough. In 1556, after thirty-four years of rule, he abdicated the throne, giving Philip II, his son, Spain and its colonies, and Ferdinand, his brother, the Habsburg lands. He lived in peace at a monastery until he died at the age of fifty-eight.

Ferdinand: After the Ottomans failed to take Vienna in 1532, the Archduke of Austria made peace with Suleiman, putting the western part of Hungary under Habsburg control while the eastern part, ruled by Zápolya, remained an Ottoman vassal. In 1538, Ferdinand signed a treaty with the childless Zápolya, naming the Archduke as his successor, but in 1540, just before he died, the Hungarian had a son. Ferdinand invaded to press his claims, but Suleiman thrashed him so soundly that the Holy Roman Empire was forced to pay tribute to the Ottomans for the next five years. He succeeded Charles V as ruler of the Habsburg lands and Holy Roman Emperor after his brother's abdication. His motto was, "Let justice be done, though the world perish." He died in Vienna in 1564.

Francis I: The King of France continued to loathe his rival Charles V and covet Italy for the rest of his life, engaging Spain in inconclusive wars in 1535 and 1542. The Franco-Ottoman alliance he forged endured for many years. In 1534, he sent Jacques Cartier to explore the St. Lawrence River; in 1541, he sent Jean Francois de la Roque de Roberval to settle Canada. He died on his son's birthday in 1547. His last words were to complain about the burden of the crown, which he'd once regarded as a divine gift.

Ibrahim Pargali Pasha: While leading Suleiman's army against the Persian Empire in 1532, the Grand Vizier's hubris got the better of him, leading to a big mistake. He called himself *Serasker Sultan*, which angered the actual Sultan, Suleiman. Ibrahim also ran afoul of someone even more cunning than he, the Sultana Roxelana. Ibrahim supported Mustafa, Suleiman's first son, as heir to the throne. If Mustafa became Sultan, however, he would follow tradition and kill the other princes, including her children. As a result, she is alleged to have sown doubts about Ibrahim's loyalty; years later, she did the same to Mustafa, ensuring her own son's ascension to the throne. Because Suleiman had sworn an oath not to kill his friend Ibrahim, he had to get a *fetvâ*, a special sanction by an Islamic leader allowing him to renounce it. This was granted in return for building a mosque in Istanbul. In 1536, the Grand Vizier was executed for treason. For the rest of his life, Suleiman regretted killing his friend.

Mercurino Gattinara: The Grand Chancellor died the following year in 1530. His ambitious vision of a worldwide Catholic empire would never be realized.

Nicholas von Salm: The count died of his wounds sustained during the siege of Vienna the following year, having reached the ripe old age of seventy.

Philibert de Châlon: The Prince of Orange led the Empire's principal army in Italy until dying during the siege of Florence in 1530, just before the war ended.

Suleiman the Magnificent: Suleiman marched against Vienna again in 1532 but, again harassed by bad weather and delayed by the siege of a smaller town, failed to even reach the Austrian capital. In 1541, he returned to defeat the Austrians, forcing the Holy Roman Emperor Charles V and the Archduke Ferdinand to renounce their claim to Hungary and pay tribute for the territory they still controlled. In 1533, he launched a war against Persia, captured Baghdad, and proclaimed himself Caliph. His navy defeated Spain's, securing control of the Eastern Mediterranean. The nations of North Africa east of Morocco joined the Empire, leading to a plague on Spanish shipping by the Barbary Pirates. In 1565, he suffered a major defeat when his forces tried to take Malta from the Knights of Malta. Suleiman, the greatest and longest-reigning of the Ottoman emperors, died the following year during a campaign in Hungary.